T0278646

holly HORROR™

The Longest Night

holly HORROR ™

the Longest Night

Michelle Jabès Corpora

Penguin Workshop

PENGUIN WORKSHOP
An imprint of Penguin Random House LLC, New York

First published in the United States of America by Penguin Workshop,
an imprint of Penguin Random House LLC, New York, 2024

Holly Horror™ and related trademarks © 2024 Those Characters
From Cleveland, LLC. Used under license by Penguin Young Readers.

Inspired by the characters of Holly Hobbie

PENGUIN is a registered trademark and PENGUIN WORKSHOP is a trademark of
Penguin Books Ltd, and the W colophon is a registered trademark of
Penguin Random House LLC.

Visit us online at penguinrandomhouse.com.

Library of Congress Cataloging-in-Publication Data is available.

Printed in the United States of America

ISBN 9780593523117

1st Printing

LSCC

To my daughters, G & E:
You are my past,
my present,
and my future.
I love you.

I have endeavoured in this Ghostly little book to raise the Ghost of an Idea which shall not put my readers out of humour with themselves, with each other, with the season, or with me. May it haunt their houses pleasantly, and no one wish to lay it.

—Charles Dickens, *A Christmas Carol*

1

"**E**vie? Are you there?"

Evie Archer blinked. The voice on the phone was muted and distant, as if someone were calling to her while she was lying at the bottom of a swimming pool. It was peaceful down there, in the daydreaming. Quiet. There were no thoughts, no painful memories. There was nothing at all. And that was just fine.

She didn't want to return to the surface, but she knew she had to.

Evie rubbed her eyes, dragging herself back into the present moment. She was sitting in the wicker fan-back chair in her bedroom, with Schrödinger purring in her lap. Around her, Hobbie House groaned and creaked like it always did when the cold New England wind blew over the Berkshires. She pulled her patchwork quilt more tightly around her shoulders and readjusted the phone against her cheek. "Yeah, Tina, I'm here," she replied. "Sorry, I just spaced out for a minute."

"You need sleep," Tina said with a sigh.

"You sound like my mother," Evie said wryly. She had only known Tina Sànchez for about two months—they'd met on Evie's first night in Ravenglass—but she already felt closer to the police chief's daughter than she had to almost any of her friends back in New York. After all, she'd shared things with Tina that she'd never told anyone else. And Tina was there for her when . . . Evie grimaced, wishing she was back at the bottom of that pool.

"It's late," Tina went on. "C'mon. We can go over this stuff again tomorrow."

Evie clenched her fist until her fingernails bit into her palm. Schrödinger shifted and the purring stopped, as if he could sense the tension suddenly pouring off her in waves. "No, no," she said. "I want to do it now."

"Evie, you've got to stop blaming yourself for—"

"Please, Tina. Now."

It had been two weeks since that ill-fated homecoming night. Two weeks since Evie had fallen into the land of shadows, since she and her brother, Stan, had emerged from the gold mines unscathed. Two weeks since Desmond had gone in and never come out.

Sleep and peaceful daydreams weren't going to bring him back. She had to focus. Concentrate. Remember. No matter how much it hurt.

There had been a great deal of confusion the day after homecoming—at first, no one was even sure that Desmond had gone into the mines at all. Friends at the dance had heard him say he was heading there, but no one had actually *seen* him go in. People held out hope that he'd taken a fall in the woods, that his phone had run out of batteries, that he would come limping home the next day, feeling sheepish. Search parties had scoured the woods up on the mountain and the mine tunnels for two days straight, and if it hadn't been for Mom putting her foot down, Evie would have joined them. Then, at the end of the second day, they'd found a boutonniere. A cream white lily, wound with a still-fresh spray of baby's breath. It had been lying near the mouth of a mine shaft, hundreds of feet deep.

The news article in the *Pittsfield Post* described Chief of Police Victor Sànchez presenting the boutonniere to the victim's parents and getting confirmation that the item did indeed belong to their son, Desmond King. There hadn't been any further details, but Evie had imagined the scene in her head dozens of times. Chief Sànchez walking toward them, his face a mask of sorrow. Mr. King seeing the flower in the chief's hand and falling to his knees. Mrs. King clutching a framed photograph of Desmond in her arms and crying out—*No, not him, not my baby . . .*

The nightmares she'd had when she'd first moved to Western Mass—the ones of Holly Hobbie, the Lost Girl of Ravenglass— stopped the day she faced down the darkness in the mines. But these new horrors, they didn't come to her in dreams. They came in every waking moment she had to live with the knowledge that Desmond—beautiful, wonderful Desmond—might be dead because of her.

The only thing she'd had to hold on to those past two weeks was the packet of papers she'd found underneath a loose board in her bedroom closet. Papers that Holly told Evie to find when they met down in the Shadow Land. She'd been calling it that since she got back home, capitalizing it in her mind, giving a name to the place that was nowhere and everywhere at once. *You can find my notes*, Holly had said, *now that I remember where I left them. About Sarah. About . . . everything. Maybe you can finish what I started.* Evie knew now that her cousin Holly had been investigating the nineteenth-century disappearance of Sarah Flower, known by locals as the Patchwork Girl, right before she herself went missing from Hobbie House. With a shiver, Evie remembered something else Holly had said right before letting her go.

Sarah and I, we're not the only ones down here.

Whatever else lived in that terrible place might have taken Desmond. And Evie was convinced that the answer to finding him lay somewhere within Holly's notes about Sarah Flower, and the history of Ravenglass.

"Okay, okay," Tina said. "We'll go through it. But quickly—I have school in the morning." She paused. "Speaking of school . . . When, um, when do you think you'll come back?"

Now it was Evie's turn to sigh. The thought of walking through the halls of Ravenglass High, and the stares and whispers that would inevitably follow, filled her with a special kind of dread. She glanced out the window, where she could still see the muddy tire tracks and footprints left behind by TV crews, news reporters, and social media influencers looking to get a peek at the infamous Ravenglass "Horror House," which had reemerged into the limelight after forty years' slumber. It was already a good story when people realized that Evie had vanished on the anniversary of Holly Hobbie's disappearance from the house in 1982. When they found out that Desmond had been Evie's date to the dance and was now missing himself—the story only got juicier.

There'd been good reason for Evie holing up at home for the first few days, but it had been a week since the last reporter had come sniffing around, so her excuses for skipping school had started to lose their potency.

Still . . .

"I'm not sure," Evie murmured. "Soon, I guess." She didn't give Tina time to press her further. "Anyway, let me get over to the closet." She stood up, lifting the big orange cat off her lap and placing him on the bed. Schrödinger grumbled, stretched, and gave her one last, sustained glare before sauntering out of the room. *Off to go mole hunting*, Evie guessed. Grasping the old brass doorknob, she opened the closet and adjusted her bedside lamp to illuminate the papers taped on the inside of the door. There were photographs, handwritten letters, and papers of all kinds—old and yellowed and faded with age. Evie was sure they'd have been in even worse shape had Holly not stored them in a cool, dark place all those years ago. Each of the items, in one way or another, had something to do with Sarah Flower and her family, who'd lived in Hobbie House when it was first built in the mid-1800s. It was everything that was left of the little girl. *Except this*, Evie thought, touching the gold locket at her throat. It had been Sarah's, and then Holly's. Now it was hers.

"So," she began, her fingers on the locket, "in 1851, Sarah Elizabeth Flower is born to parents William and Mary Flower. Mrs. Flower dies in childbirth, leaving Mr. Flower to raise Sarah on his own. He's a well-respected man in the community, so when Wallace Brand comes to town looking to mine for gold, he hires Mr. Flower to be his foreman. Things seem to be going fine until Mr. Flower's sudden death some years later. They find his body in the cellar of Hobbie House, and Sarah is blamed. She goes missing around the same time, and neither appear in any records after that. Work in the mines tapers off at that point as well. The house and land lay vacant for years, then it changed hands several times, but it was rarely lived in for long—until the Hobbies bought and renovated the place sometime in the 1970s. Does that sound right so far?" A moment of silence passed. Evie pressed the phone closer to her ear. "Tina?"

"No, that's right," Tina said. "I just . . . Look, Evie, I believe you, okay? When you told me about Holly, and this shadow place, and everything else—I believed you then, and I believe you now. I'm just not sure this is a healthy way to process what happened to Desmond. Maybe there are answers to be found in these old papers, and you know my little writer's heart can't resist a good story. But I think you also have to open yourself up to the possibility that Desmond is . . . well, that he's—"

"You know what," Evie blurted, cutting her off. "Maybe you're right. Maybe we should call it a night."

Another beat. "Yeah," Tina whispered.

Silence filled the line between them.

"Hey, so . . . is everything okay with you?" Evie asked after a moment. She realized what a selfish friend she'd been over the past couple of weeks, since they'd first met. Sure, Tina had been much more interested in poking her nose into Evie's business than talking about herself, but Evie hadn't done much to counter that. Other than knowing her dad as the police chief, Evie knew next to nothing about Tina's life. Recently she'd found out that Tina had an older brother in college—Carlos—and a younger brother named Danny who was in second grade at Ravenglass Elementary, but that was it.

"Oh, me?" Tina said, sounding a little surprised. "I mean, sure. My tito and tati are flying in from Puerto Rico tomorrow, and Mom has been cleaning the house for six days straight, so there's that."

"That's nice."

"I guess."

Evie quirked an eyebrow at Tina's sarcastic tone. "Don't you get along with your grandparents?"

"They're staying until New Year's," Tina said flatly. "People complain about having to spend time with their families for a week. Imagine what it's like to have them around for two *months*!"

Evie got the feeling that there was more to it than that, but decided not to question her further. It was late, and clearly there were things neither of them wanted to talk about. "I get it," she said instead. "Talk to you tomorrow, then?"

"Tomorrow," Tina agreed, sounding relieved. "Night-night, Farmgirl."

"Night, Tina."

Evie ended the call and tossed her phone on the bed. She sat down next to it and rewrapped herself in the patchwork quilt like a burrito. It was after midnight, and although Evie felt tired, she knew she wouldn't be able to sleep. She decided to go to the attic.

When she first moved into Hobbie House, everything about it seemed sinister. A Pandora's box of chaos that once opened, couldn't be closed again. Back in New York, Evie thought things couldn't get any worse than they were after her parents got divorced, but when the gift of a rent-free house turned out to be a curse, she soon found out how wrong she really was. But ever since the events of homecoming night, the house felt different. Warmer. No longer her adversary, it had shared its secrets with her, and she had done the same. They understood each other, Evie and the house. She feared it no longer. It was what lay beyond the walls of Hobbie House that frightened her now.

Which was why Evie found herself pulling down the stepladder to the attic in the middle of the night, while her mother and brother were fast asleep in their beds. Just a month ago, going up to the attic—even during the day—terrified her. But for the past two weeks, she had gone up there almost every night, taking an electric candle along to light her way. It was comforting, somehow. But that wasn't the only reason. She went to the attic on the off chance that someone would be waiting there to meet her.

At the top of the ladder, she set down the electric candle and reached for the little pull chain, turning on the single bare bulb that hung from the rafters. That done, she climbed up, dragging the patchwork quilt with her.

The attic didn't look quite as old and forgotten as it had when they'd first arrived. Mom and her broom had eventually made their way up there to sweep away the dust and dead spiders, and replace them with neat piles of clearly labeled storage boxes full of holiday bric-a-brac and old souvenirs. Still, she hadn't removed most of the Hobbies' old things they'd left behind, including Holly's steamer trunk. Evie opened it up, smelling the cloud of rose-scented air that wafted up from within. She ran her fingers along Holly's things—the old dolls, the dress with pearl buttons, the stained white scarf with lace along the edges. The blue bonnet, the thing that had started it all, lay on top, its blue ribbons curled up into itself like a sleeping cat. Evie thought it had belonged to Holly when she first found it, but her sense of it being a lot older than forty years had been correct. Like the locket, it had once belonged to Sarah Flower. All three of them, Sarah, Holly, and now Evie herself, were connected—not only by the house, but by something else, too.

Whatever it was, it wasn't finished yet.

With shaking fingers, Evie did the same thing she'd been doing almost every night since Desmond had disappeared. She pulled the bonnet onto her head, tying the ribbons under her chin in a bow. Then, wrapped in her quilt, she turned to the white full-length mirror and stared at her reflection, praying that someone else's face might be looking back at her.

"Where are you, Holly?" Evie whispered. "Why won't you talk to me?"

She stared into the mirror. Underneath the bonnet, her long, copper-colored hair was lank and unwashed. There were dark circles under her eyes, making the spray of freckles across her face look muddled. The awful red rash on her right cheek, which had been a constant reminder of what had happened homecoming day, had finally faded, leaving nothing but a dry area where it had once been. Sometimes it still felt like it was there, though—the pain hovering over her skin like a ghost.

"First, you won't leave me alone," she went on. "You take over my life, you haunt my dreams, you make me feel like I'm losing my mind—and now? Now that everything is so messed up, *now that I need you*, you just . . ." Her voice had risen to an angry, ragged rasp. Her eyes were stinging, her nose starting to run. She sniffed and wiped her face with her forearm. She glared back at herself in the mirror, pressing one hand against the cool glass, hating both what she saw and what she didn't see.

"Talk to me!" she cried.

But just like every other night, there was no answer.

Meanwhile...

Jack Míng Chen lay on his belly on the living room floor, watching his favorite TV show. He was wearing his favorite footed pajamas, the blue ones with teeth along the hood that made him look like a shark. They'd been a gift for his seventh birthday the year before, and they were almost too small now. But Jack was going to wear them for as long as he could. His best friend Danny had the same pair, and whenever Danny came over for a sleep-over, they'd both wear the pajamas and slither around on the hardwood floors, pretending to be on the hunt.

"Five more minutes, Jack!" his mom called from the kitchen. "Then it's toothbrushing and bedtime, okay?"

"Okaaay . . . ," Jack moaned. Five minutes was not enough time to finish his favorite episode, but usually when his mom said "five minutes," she really meant fifteen, so he wasn't too worried. What was worse was the racket his parents were making, running the sink, clattering forks and dishes, trying to soothe his mewling baby sister, and worst of all—*talking.*

"Elena Sànchez told me this morning at the bus stop that Victor called off the search for that boy from RHS—the Kings' son?" his mother was saying.

"Not surprising," his dad replied as the baby whined and bur-bled. "It's been a couple weeks, hasn't it? They probably only kept it going this long for the parents' sake."

Jack's mom tutted. "It's just *awful.* I've always said those mines are dangerous. I've told Victor, more than once, that they should have that place sealed off with concrete. Maybe now they will."

The mines up on the mountain were forbidden territory for

both Jack and Danny, but that didn't stop the boys from riding their bikes up there as often as they could. Edgewood's wooded paths made it easy to get through the neighborhood and reach the mountain road unseen. They liked playing at being explorers near the ominous black mouth of the mine entrance, pretending to find gold buried in the dirt. They'd make up stories about the ghosts that lived down there, and often imagined going inside and finding a skeleton—dry flesh hanging in rags from its bones, a treasure map gripped in its cold, dead hand. They were too scared to actually go inside, but they'd dare each other to see who could get closer, until one of them poked the toe of their sneaker past the threshold. Then they'd leap onto their bikes, whooping, and pedal like crazy all the way home.

Jack imagined that high schooler lying somewhere in the darkness, in the silence, decaying just a little bit more each day. *I guess there really will be a skeleton down there now*, he thought with a shiver. To drown out those unwelcome thoughts, he turned up the volume on the TV, stuck one of the shark head's felt teeth into his mouth, and focused on the show.

It was a show about four kids who had to solve mysteries with the help of someone named "the Puzzlemaster," who sent them clues through coded messages they found all around town. Jack had already seen every episode, twice, but he didn't care that he already knew all the answers to the puzzles. For instance, in the part he was watching, he knew that three of the kids would find a hidden message inside a book at the school library, but wouldn't be able to figure out what it meant until the fourth kid arrived and told them, because of something she had learned in history class.

Jack watched eagerly, sucking on the shark tooth, as one boy pulled the book off the shelf and looked amazed as it magically opened to one special page—

A flash of movement from the window startled him. Jack dropped the sodden fabric from his mouth and looked up. It was almost as if a shadow had walked past, shutting off the moonlight just for a moment. But there was nothing there. Jack thought maybe it was the neighbor's cat out on the prowl again. It often liked to lurk in the Chens' backyard, killing birds. Jack remembered just a few weeks ago, when he'd found the dead finch out on the patio. Its small, soft body torn, its yellow feathers sticky with blood. No matter how much his mom sprayed the patio with cleanser, the stain left behind just wouldn't wash away.

Shrugging, Jack watched his parents take the baby up to bed, and estimated he had at least another ten minutes before they came for him. He refocused on the show. The three kids were crowded around the book, perplexed by the puzzle inside it.

"Maybe it has something to do with the page numbers?" one kid guessed.

Wrong, Jack thought.

"What if we're supposed to read every other word?" said another.

Wrong again, Jack thought. It made him feel smug, knowing more than those dumb kids. If the Puzzlemaster had chosen him instead, he'd have been able to figure out the clues on the first try. That was a fact.

"Come on, you guys!" the first kid cried. "We've got to solve this before time runs out! Ticktock!"

Now the door to the library opens, and the last kid comes in, Jack thought. He stared at the door in the background, waiting.

The door swung open, slowly. A beat passed. The three kids in the foreground continued to study the book.

Jack cocked his head and scooched closer to the TV. Was it frozen? No, the three kids were moving. Breathing. Why wasn't the fourth kid coming through the door like she was supposed to?

But there *was* something coming through the door. Something dark, like a shadow. It crept into the brightness of the scene, along the carpeted floor, the walls, the bookshelves lining the background. The three kids didn't seem to notice it at all.

But Jack noticed. "This isn't right," he muttered to himself. "This isn't how it's supposed to happen . . ." He picked up the remote control from the floor and pushed the stop button, but the show kept playing. He smashed the power button with his thumb, but the TV stayed on.

On the screen, the shadow was coming closer, rolling over the shoulders of the kids, over their fingers touching the book, and then the book itself. They just stared silently, still perplexed by the puzzle, still living in the moment as if nothing was wrong.

"Mommy . . . ?" Jack said. He tried to shout, but his voice was as soft as feathers. He tried to sit up, tried to move away from the screen, but found that he couldn't. Like the kids in the show, all he could do was remain just as he was. Looking, and breathing.

"Almost time for bed, Jack!" his mother called from upstairs.

Jack whimpered. But she was too far away to hear him.

And then the darkness reached the screen, and Jack felt relief that it could not pass through that barrier, that somehow the logic of the world would keep it inside.

But in the moment it took for Jack to take his next breath, the black thing had reached through the screen, pressed past it like a hand through water, and reached out toward him.

Before he could loose a scream, it filled his eyes and his mouth with a great, dark silence.

A moment later, the show continued. Jack lay on the floor, just as if nothing had happened. He stared at the TV with dark, unblinking eyes, his slippered feet kicking back and forth in a clockwork motion.

Tick.

Tock.

Tick.

Tock.

On the show, a happy, smiling girl entered the scene, bringing answers to a puzzle yet unsolved.

2

Evie sat on a squashy green couch in her aunt Martha's second-floor apartment, a steaming mug of cinnamon tea warming her hands. Outside the front window, white flurries whirled over Main Street, making Ravenglass look as quaint and lovely as a town in a snow globe. Thanksgiving was still three weeks away, but the businesses and restaurants were already gearing up for the holiday season, and the streets were busy with tourists from all over who'd come to enjoy a little slice of Americana.

Evie watched them walk by—cheeks pink with the cold, arms heavy with shopping bags—and wondered what it must feel like to be so carefree.

"Gingersnap?" Aunt Martha said, offering a plate of spice-scented cookies.

"No, thanks," Evie replied, and sipped her tea.

Aunt Martha's shoulders sagged. She set the plate on the coffee table and lowered herself into an armchair. She wore smoke-gray leggings and a medallion-print tunic in shades of blue. Her long silver hair was loose, and she gathered it into a ponytail before reaching for her own mug of tea and a cookie. "So," she said, taking a small bite of a gingersnap. "How's your mom doing? I haven't talked to her in a few days."

Evie shrugged. "She's all right, I guess. She's been trying to be home earlier in the evenings, but with the holidays coming up, the inn has been busier than ever." Mom's job at the Blue River Inn seemed to be growing in responsibilities by the day—she'd only worked there for a month or so, but she'd already made herself indispensable. Normally, Mom's workaholic ways irritated Evie, but things had been better between them lately. Not perfect, but better. Evie knew she wasn't staying at work to avoid being home anymore, she was just *busy*. And that was okay. Evie wanted to be alone, anyway.

Aunt Martha nodded, chewing. "And Stan? How's his ankle?"

"Healing," Evie replied. "Dr. Rockwell says because of the kind of fracture it is, he'll have to be non–weight bearing for four more weeks. So he's annoyed, of course. But at least now he's gotten used to the crutch."

"Well," Aunt Martha said, tucking her bare feet under her. "It could have been a lot worse."

Evie thought about how close she and Stan had come to not getting out of the mines at all. How close they had come to dying down there in the darkness. "Yeah," she said softly. "It could have." She tried to ignore the unspoken words, the ones that hung in the air between them.

You could have ended up like Desmond.

She took another long swallow of her tea, hoping it would dispel the chill from her body.

It didn't.

Aunt Martha finished her cookie, and was toying with the heavy silver chains she wore around her neck while watching the passersby outside the window. "I just love this time of year, don't you?" she said with a smile.

"I didn't realize you were a big Christmas person."

"Oh, I'm not," Aunt Martha said. "People forget that before Christmas even existed, this time of year was special because of the winter solstice."

"The solstice," Evie mused. "Isn't that the shortest day of the year?"

"Yes," Aunt Martha said. "And the longest night."

Evie drained the rest of her cup and set it down on the table. "It doesn't sound like much fun to me."

"I guess it's not very fun," Aunt Martha admitted. "But it is very meaningful. People have been celebrating the solstice since time immemorial. Gathering together at a time of great darkness to celebrate the return of the light." She glanced back at Evie, set down her own mug, and sighed. "Sweetheart, I know you love your old aunt Martha, but I'm no dummy. You didn't just come over here to visit and reject my gingersnaps. What do you need?"

Evie shifted uncomfortably. "I need . . ." She hesitated. "I need you to read my cards again."

Aunt Martha sat back in her chair, surprised. "Your cards? But I thought you didn't—"

"You were right, that first time," Evie broke in. "About

everything. The reading you did, the Celtic Cross, it brought me back home when I was down there in the dark. Remember?"

Aunt Martha's nostrils flared. "Yes," she said. "I remember."

Evie hadn't told her aunt everything that had happened, how the symbols from the tarot cards had given her the strength to fight back against the shadows, or how she'd heard Martha's prayer in her head and followed her voice out of the maze of tunnels to safety. But she'd told her enough to make her understand that something uncanny had happened in the mines. That somehow, her missing cousin Holly Hobbie had brought her down there, and that Evie had made peace with her.

"You want to ask about Desmond," Aunt Martha said, and shook her head. "Evie, I don't think this is a good—"

"*I need to do something!*" Evie broke in, nearly upsetting her tea. It came out louder than she'd intended. Shaky. Desperate. She set the mug down on the table and sat back into the couch, folding her arms around herself. "Sorry," she whispered. "I just . . . I was able to see things before, but now I can't. It's like I'm listening but I can't hear anything. I need help. Please."

Aunt Martha regarded her for a long moment. "All right," she finally said. "As long as you understand that there are limitations to the answers the cards can provide. I'm thrilled that you see value in the tarot now, as I do, but they're supposed to be used as a guide, not an instruction manual."

"I understand," Evie said. She'd say whatever Aunt Martha needed to hear to give her a reading. She didn't know where else to turn.

"Come into the reading room, then." Aunt Martha stood and

led Evie next door. The heavy purple curtains blocked the sunlight, casting the room in deep shadow. Aunt Martha flitted about, lighting a lamp and a few candles, and turning on the calming, ethereal music she favored for her readings. Usually, the room smelled like sandalwood, but that day it had a distinctly different smell. It was earthy and sweet, and reminded her of winter.

"Frankincense and myrrh," Aunt Martha said as if reading her thoughts. "A healing scent, don't you think? Something to keep your spirit warm on those long, cold nights." She plucked her usual Rider-Waite tarot deck from one of the shelves along the wall and settled into the overstuffed chair in the middle of the room, her silver chains tinkling softly as she moved. Evie squeezed past the low, tapestry-covered table and sat in the chair across from her. "I want you to take some slow, cleansing breaths, Evie," Aunt Martha said, shuffling the cards. "Clear your mind. Focus on your breath going in and out."

Evie did. It was hard to clear her mind, as cluttered as it was, but this was important. She listened to her breath and allowed herself to be pulled down into that deep, quiet place at the bottom of the swimming pool.

"Good." Aunt Martha handed Evie the deck. "Now concentrate on your question as you shuffle the cards. When you're satisfied, hand them back to me. We'll just do a simple three-card draw this time. Past, present, and future."

Evie nodded, closed her eyes, and mixed the cards. They were cool and smooth against her fingers. She thought of Desmond. His face, his eyes—the way the sunlight shone against his deep brown skin. She thought of the way he smiled when he asked her to homecoming with a hand-sewn message, and the way his lips felt against hers as they kissed for the first time in the pouring rain. *Please tell me where he is*, she thought. *I have to know what's happened to him. How do I find him? What do I have to do to get him back?*

She opened her eyes and handed the cards back to her aunt. Martha took them reverently and, after a single, silent moment, laid the top three cards down on the table between them.

Aunt Martha pointed to them one by one.

"The past . . ."

The Three of Cups. Three women dancing in a circle, each raising a golden goblet in her hand.

"The present . . ."

The Hanged Man. A man dangling upside down by one ankle from a tree branch, his arms behind his back, a golden halo around his head.

"And the future."

The last one made Evie gasp. It showed a man and woman chained to an altar, where a great horned monster perched, looming over them both.

The Devil.

Evie forced back the wave of fear that threatened to overcome her and concentrated on the cards. *You can't run away this time*, she told herself. *It's too important. You have to face it, whatever it is.*

The meaning of the first card, the Three of Cups, was so clear that it made a shiver roll down her spine. *Three girls*, Evie thought. *Me, Holly, and Sarah.*

"Playmate, come out and play with me, and bring your dollies three . . ."

The eerie song floated back to her, unbidden, and Evie suppressed a whimper rising from her throat. She knew that Holly and Sarah weren't dangerous now, that Evie had helped bring Holly back to herself—but that didn't erase the terror Evie had felt when she'd first encountered them.

The other two cards—her present and future—were more difficult to understand. *That makes sense*, Evie thought. *If I understood what's happening now, and what's coming, I probably wouldn't be here at all.*

Aunt Martha was studying the cards, too, leaning close to the table, her long, slender fingers pressed thoughtfully to her lips. Finally, she sat back in her chair as if she'd reached a conclusion. "This . . . situation that you're asking about. In the Three of Cups, the cards are saying that it came to be through a sisterhood of sorts. These three women are bound together—through friendship, family, or unseen connections. I realize that losing Desmond was a tragedy, but this card suggests that his loss wasn't the only result of what happened. There was good there, too. You shouldn't forget that."

Evie thought of Holly, still trapped in a shadow of the past. Was she better off now that Evie had destroyed the darkness in her mind and given her back her humanity? She wasn't so sure.

"In the present, we have the Hanged Man," Aunt Martha went on. "This card suggests a trial, or a sacrifice."

Evie sighed. "He looks pretty stuck. Just like I am right now."

Aunt Martha cocked her head. "Perhaps that's how you feel, but that's not what this card is telling you. The Hanged Man isn't in that position by accident, or as some kind of punishment. He's there because he took a leap of faith. You see the ring of light around his head? That indicates enlightenment. His act of faith doesn't just bring resolution, it also allows him to see the world from a new perspective, and to know when it's the right moment to act. He's there because he chose to jump, Evie. And he trusts that he'll end up exactly where he's meant to be."

Evie nodded, feeling a lump rise in her throat. "And the last one?"

Aunt Martha tented her fingers and glanced down at the Devil card in Evie's future. "Do you see how the man and woman are chained? This card often represents a sense of entrapment. You're in a situation where it seems like there's no way out. But like the Moon card—remember that one?—this is also a card of illusion. Because if you look closely, those chains around the woman's neck are loose. She could take them off anytime, if she wanted to. The Devil wants you to lose hope, but if you push fear aside, you'll see that the path home lies right before you."

Thinking the reading was done, Evie sat back, frustrated. Not with Aunt Martha, but with herself, for thinking the tarot could actually give her a straight answer. Sure, the reading gave her a lot to think about, but nothing to go on, no way forward. She rubbed the heels of her hands into her eyes, trying to ward off the growing sense of panic in her belly.

"One more thing," Aunt Martha said.

Evie looked up, hopeful.

"The Devil card," Aunt Martha continued. "What I said is true, but it also has another meaning that might be significant."

"What is it?" Evie asked.

"The Devil also represents our dark side—our shadow selves.

The parts of us we don't want to reveal to others, but that live inside us nonetheless. Those are chains that can never be broken. Our shadows follow us wherever we go. But they'll only hurt us if we let them."

Evie froze, and a cold chill crept up her spine.

Our shadows follow us wherever we go.

Aunt Martha was staring at her, concern plain on her face. "Are you all right?" she asked.

"Yeah," Evie said. "It's just . . . a lot to take in."

"Which is why I didn't think this was a good idea," Aunt Martha said with a grimace. "You only just recognized your psychic skills, not to mention you're going through a serious trauma. I don't want to overwhelm you at a delicate time like this."

Evie shook her head. She'd barely given a second thought to the fact that after years of believing she was hallucinating, of hiding all the things she saw and heard from other people, she finally had confirmation that, like her aunt, she had some psychic—or more specifically, spirit channeling—abilities.

"Yes, well, a lot of good my 'powers' are doing me now," Evie muttered. "I finally figure out I have them, and they stop working."

Aunt Martha reached out to touch Evie's hand. "You need to be patient with yourself, sweetheart. All those traumatic experiences you just had? Those kinds of things can create a psychic block. It's like . . . your spirit putting up a protective wall to shield itself from more damage."

"Well, how do I get rid of it?" Evie asked.

"It's different for everyone," Aunt Martha said with a shrug. "For some people a special person or object can trigger the return of extrasensory perception. For others, it's just time. Time to heal. Your mind put up that wall for a reason."

Evie clenched her fists. "I don't *have* time," she retorted. "I have to find him!"

Aunt Martha licked her lips and sat back in her chair. "Evie," she said slowly. "I know you don't want to hear this, but you have to realize that Desmond probably isn't coming—"

"He's coming back," Evie interrupted. "He's out there, okay? I can *feel him*." She put a hand over her heart, where the pain had been ever since the morning she'd found out he was gone. "I was right about Holly, and I'm right about this. You believe me, don't you?"

Aunt Martha looked at her, Evie's anguish mirrored in her eyes. "I believe that you feel him," she said. "You felt Holly, too. Saw her. Touched her. But she's not coming back, Evie. And Desmond might not be either."

Evie stared back at her, silent, until a sob broke free of her throat. Then Aunt Martha was at her side, holding her as she cried.

"I'm so sorry for everything you've been through," Aunt Martha whispered as she stroked her hair. "It's too much. Too much for anyone. But it's over now, okay? You're safe."

Evie pulled back. "It's not over," she said, her voice shaky. "That's what I'm trying to tell you. That's why I'm here. Whatever happened down there—*it's still happening*."

Aunt Martha gave her a searching look. "If that's true," she said, reaching back to pick up the Hanged Man from the table. "Then you need to remember to have faith."

Evie took the card and ran her finger across the man's serene face, surrounded by light. "But what if I don't have the strength to jump?"

Aunt Martha smiled. "You will."

When Evie reached the road to Hobbie House, she saw an unfamiliar green sedan parked in the grass nearby. The engine was off and the windows dark, so she couldn't tell if anyone was inside. Pulling her coat tighter around her face, she sped up hoping to make it to the narrow lane as quickly as possible. Her boots crunched on the frozen ground as she went, her heart beating a little faster with each step.

But before she could reach the driveway, both car doors swung open and two men stepped out. "Miss Archer!" the driver called, motioning her to stop. He had slicked-back hair and a forgettable face. "My name is Tim Crane; I'm a reporter from the *Pittsfield Post*. If I could have just a *moment* of your time—"

"No," Evie said, shaking her head. "Please, go away." *I thought I'd seen the last of these people*, she thought, and she tried to walk past the reporter.

He stepped in front of her, blocking her way. "Now, Miss Archer, that's no way to be. I thought you and your family would appreciate us waiting until all the hubbub died down before coming to speak to you. We just want to know what really happened down there in the mines—"

"I told the police everything they wanted to know," Evie said. "There's nothing more to say. Now, please—"

"Are you sure about that, Miss Archer?" the reporter said. "You've been made out to be quite the hero in this thing—rescuing your brother like you did—but what about your connection to the missing boy, Desmond King? I have witnesses on record saying that not only were you Mr. King's homecoming date that night, but you were also exhibiting some strange behavior before leaving the school."

The other man, taller and bearded, raised a camera to his eye and started snapping pictures. Evie raised a hand to block her face from the lens.

"Isn't it true that you violently attacked another student at a local restaurant just days before the events in the mine?"

Click click click. Clickclickclickclick.

"Do you have a history of mental illness, Miss Archer?"

Evie tried to turn away and go back up the street, but the two reporters followed her every move. "Leave me alone!" she said.

The second man lowered his camera and glanced at his partner. "Tim, maybe we should go," he said.

"No," Crane said harshly. "We drove all this way for a story. We're going to get one." He turned back to Evie. "If you don't tell us your side of this, then we'll be forced to use what we've got. And believe me, you wouldn't like the sound of it."

Evie wanted to punch this man in his stupid, boring face, but she knew that doing so would only make things worse. All she needed was a photograph of her assaulting a reporter printed in the local newspaper.

"Well? Are you going to tell us the truth, Miss Archer?"

At that moment, another car turned onto the street. It wasn't her mom's little silver car, but a big black SUV bearing New York plates. It sped up, screeching to a stop in the middle of the road right in front of them.

Crane nearly jumped out of his skin at the car's rapid approach, and the photographer fumbled with his equipment as he tried to get out of the way. Evie just stood there in shock as a barrel-chested, dark-haired man in a black T-shirt jumped out of the driver's seat and stormed toward the reporters like a thunderhead.

"Hey, what's your problem, buddy?" the reporter shouted. "You nearly killed us! I oughta—"

The dark-haired man took a fistful of the reporter's shirt and shoved him to the ground. "Who the hell do you think you are, harassing her like that?" the man growled, dangerous. "You want me to call the police, or should I take care of this problem my-self?" He advanced on the reporter, fists clenched at his sides.

Crane scrambled to his feet, rumpled and filthy, cowed by the man's threats. "We don't want any trouble, okay, buddy?" he said, his hands raised in surrender. "Just wanted to ask the young lady a couple questions. Didn't mean her any harm. We'll go, all right? We're going. See?" He nudged the cameraman toward the green sedan, and they both hurried back to the car. Within a minute, they'd gunned the engine, spun the wheels in the gravel, and taken off back down the road.

Evie and the dark-haired man watched them go. Once they'd disappeared around the bend, the man wiped his workman's hands on his gray utility pants and glanced up at her. He cleared his throat, awkwardness settling between them like a fog. "Hey there, chickadee," he said.

Evie looked back at him, a swirl of emotions twisting through her heart. "Hi, Dad," she said.

3

The road to Hobbie House never seemed so long.

Evie sat in the passenger seat of her father's plush SUV, hugging her shoulder bag to her chest like a life raft. Even though the car was a rental, it already smelled like him—a mixture of metal and fire, forever burned into his skin after years of work in front of a furnace. His black T-shirt bore the name of his studio, Vitrum, along with a line drawing of his famous Ocean vase, the one that mimicked a blue wave cresting. Prog rock spilled on low volume from the radio, and Dad tapped his fingers on the steering wheel in time with the music. "Well, I don't see that guy coming around here again, do you?" he said, a note of amusement in his voice.

"You'll be lucky if *that guy* doesn't press charges," Evie said. She froze the moment the words left her lips. *Did I really say that?* She could count the number of times she'd talked back to her father on one hand. He'd never raised a hand to her, nor even his voice, really. But he was intimidating in a quiet, brooding way that always kept her at arm's length. And yet here she was, talking back. She waited for a response, wondering if that burst of anger she'd seen earlier would return.

But all Dad did was smirk. "A man like that is too weak to admit he's been pushed around by a guy on the street. He won't tell a soul, and he'll swear his little friend to secrecy. We won't hear from them again." He said those last words with such conviction that it annoyed her.

"I didn't need rescuing, you know," she muttered. "I would have been fine without you."

Dad must have heard the undercurrent flowing beneath those words. *I've been fine without you.* But if he noticed, it didn't seem to affect him. "I'm sure you would have," he replied mildly. "It was that reporter I was worried about. When I drove up, it looked to me like you were about to knock out his teeth."

Evie blinked. That was *exactly* what she'd been thinking when he drove up.

She grumbled under her breath. Her father's easy, casual manner irritated her. How dare he roll into town this way, right after her life had turned into some kind of haunted dumpster fire, and act like everything was fine? Like this was just a normal visit, and not him making an obligatory appearance after it was all over and done? Who did he think he was? That's what he had shouted at Tim Crane, but he really should have been asking himself that question.

She glanced over at him. He looked the same. Robby Archer: great artist, mediocre dad. His clothes, his music, his ever-shifting moods, his messy black hair shot with gray, they were all completely, exactly the same.

Evie glanced at her own reflection in the side-view mirror. She looked older, somehow. And haggard. She swallowed.

It's me who's changed.

Dad pulled up to the house and parked next to the little silver car. Mom must have heard them coming, because she was through the kitchen door before Evie even got out of the SUV. Her caramel-colored hair was pulled into a loose ponytail, and she was dressed in a soft maroon sweater and cream leggings. She watched them approach, and Evie couldn't help but admire her mother's control as she saw her ex-husband for the first time in months. Her face was as passive as a glacier.

"Robby," she said, by way of a greeting. "You could have told me you'd be arriving today."

"Yeah, sorry," Dad replied, shrugging. "I managed to finish things up at the studio a couple days early, so I decided to hit the road after rush hour this morning. Slipped my mind, I guess." He chewed his lip. "Turns out my timing was good, though—I ran off some reporters who were hassling Evie at the bottom of the lane."

Mom's eyes widened. "*More* reporters?" she said, flustered. "I thought we were done with all that. Where were they from? I'm going to call and complain . . ." She pulled out her phone.

"I dunno," Dad said.

"It was the *Pittsfield Post*, Mom," Evie broke in.

"Look, I scared them off," Dad said. "I wouldn't worry too much about it."

"Well, sure, *you* wouldn't," Mom muttered, glaring at the screen as she typed. "You weren't here when they mobbed the house. You weren't here when it all—when everything was . . ." Her passive expression began to crumble.

Dad looked at her and sighed. "I'm here now," he said quietly.

Mom raised the phone to her ear as it started to ring. She met his eyes, nodded once, and said, "Come inside. Just wipe your feet on the mat."

Evie followed her mother into the yellow light of the kitchen, grateful to get out of the cold, and set her bag down on the counter near the door. Dad lumbered in behind her, his gaze drinking in Mom's tasteful décor. Almost immediately after they'd moved into Hobbie House, she'd transformed the place from a dusty wreck to a warm, lovely home. She'd saved some of the original pieces—the butter churn in the corner, the framed needlepoint on the wall, the hardwood table and chairs—and added modern details of her own. Watching Dad's face as he looked around, Evie realized that although Mom wasn't exactly an artist, she did have a flair for sprucing things up and making them beautiful.

"Looks nice in here," Dad said, standing awkwardly by the door.

Mom glanced at him, the phone pressed against her shoulder as she stuffed folders and other brochures into her messenger bag. "Thanks," she said, and then spent the next minute leaving an angry message on the *Pittsfield Post*'s voicemail.

Evie was hanging up her coat when she heard someone thumping slowly down the stairs. "Dad?"

She turned to see Stan emerge from the hallway, leaning on his crutch, his foot encased in a plastic boot. He was still wearing his old black hoodie, and looked skinny and about as haggard as Evie did. He'd lost a little weight since the incident in the mines and wasn't sleeping well, which worried both Evie and

Mom in equal measure. Evie felt like the air was sucked out of the room as the three of them stood there, waiting to see what Stan would do.

"Dad!" Stan cried, and hobbled his way across the room. In an instant, Dad had stepped forward and wrapped Evie's brother in his arms.

"Hey, big guy," Dad said, his voice thick. "How's the ankle, huh? You all right?"

"I'm fine," Stan said. When Dad released him, Evie noticed Stan adjust to stand up straighter. "It's no big deal."

Dad grinned and ruffled Stan's dark brown hair. "That's my guy," he said. "You'll be back out on the trails with your friends before you know it! Did you figure out how to use the bicycle pump on your tires?"

"Yeah," Stan replied. "Thirty psi on the gauge, right?"

"Right."

"Whoa, whoa, whoa," Mom broke in. "That fracture *is* kind of a big deal. Bike riding is a month away, at least. If the fracture doesn't heal correctly, we could be looking at surgery, and—"

Dad took a step back. "I know. I'm just trying to cheer him up a little."

"Encouraging him to do something reckless isn't helpful, Robby."

Dad grimaced. "Lynne, will you please—"

Evie glanced from her bickering parents to Stan, who was staring at them with tired, sad eyes. Mom saw it, too. She stopped midsentence and waved a hand toward Robby. "It's fine. Forget it. I've just . . . We've been through a lot, okay?" She nodded at the ground and picked up her bag. "I've got to spend a couple hours at work, and then I'll be home for dinner."

She started to make her way toward the door, but Dad stopped her. "I'm . . . I'm not staying here, Lynne. I got a room at the Blue River Inn. I thought it would be better if I gave you guys some space."

You've given us all the space in the world, Evie thought.

"Oh." Mom blinked. "Yes, that is better."

A beat passed. Stan looked as if he'd tasted something bitter.

"That's where I work, you know," Mom added. "The Blue River Inn."

"Ah," Dad said. "Well, if it's anything like this house, I'm sure I'll be quite comfortable."

Mom swallowed, saying nothing.

"How about I stick around with the kids while you're gone, and then I can head over to the inn once you get back. I won't impose on you for dinner. I'm sure I can pick something up in town."

"Sounds fine," Mom said, slipping on her coat.

"Good," Dad replied.

"Well, see you all later," Mom said. She had the courtesy to give Evie an apologetic look before disappearing out the door.

Evie walked over to the refrigerator and pulled out some grape juice. She took a long drink right out of the bottle, put it back, and suddenly felt completely exhausted. "I'm going to lie down on the couch for a while," she said dully.

"Sure, honey," Dad said. "Take a break. Stan and I will have a snack and catch up, right?"

Stan nodded. He glanced at Evie uneasily, with a look that unmistakably said *you better not screw this up for me.*

Evie blinked at him in surprise. Stan had been angry ever since they'd left New York, and she just naturally assumed it was for the same reasons she'd been angry. He hated leaving his friends and his life, hated this new place, and hated what the divorce had done to their family. But as crazy as it was, she never considered that maybe it was more than that. *Maybe he hated leaving Dad.*

Her head hurt. Pushing the thoughts away, she lurched down the hall into the living room and collapsed onto the couch. She pulled a crocheted throw over herself and was asleep in an instant.

Evie woke to fading light and the sounds of button mashing. She sat up, rubbed her eyes, and squinted at Stan, who was on the floor in his video game chair, playing something on the Xbox. He was wearing headphones, so he only noticed her when she waved.

"Where's Dad?" she mouthed.

He shrugged, and then pointed one finger up.

Taking a shower, maybe. Evie yawned, heaved herself free from the siren song of the couch, and made her way upstairs. At the landing, she saw that the bathroom door was open and the light was off. "Huh," she said, and glanced into Stan's bedroom. Empty. It was only when she walked past her own bedroom that she saw her father standing in front of her closet. The door was open, with her latest project hanging from it—a bouffant-style cocktail dress in emerald green, with an irregular pattern of black rhinestones sewn along the neckline. She'd never worked with rhinestones before, and had been spending a little time each night affixing more. Her father was examining it, his head tilted to the side, a serious look on his face.

"What are you doing?" Evie exclaimed in irritation. "This is my room, you can't just come in here." She glanced nervously at the closet door—luckily, the dress covered up nearly all the papers about Sarah Flower that she'd taped there. She could feel a flush rising to her cheeks.

"The door was open," Dad replied as if that made up for anything. He hadn't taken his eyes off the dress. "You made this?"

Evie huffed. "I— Well, yeah," she stammered. Why was it so difficult to be properly mad at him?

"Stan said you'd been doing a lot of dressmaking these past couple months." He turned his attention to some of the other items hanging inside the closet. He pulled out a shirt that she'd upcycled with antique buttons. "Are these the ones that Stan found for you?" he asked, touching a green glass one with his finger.

"Yes . . . ," she said. Stan had given her an old jar of buttons just after they'd moved in to Hobbie House. "How do you know about that?"

Dad hung the shirt back in place and shrugged. "He keeps in touch over text." He said it as a matter of fact—with no hint of resentment, hurt feelings, or anything else. Evie thought about the texts from him she'd ignored those first few weeks and felt her jaw clench.

No, she thought. *Don't you dare feel guilty. He was the one who left. He was the one who gave up on this family. Not you. He's the one who's in your room right now, poking his nose where it doesn't belong!*

"Dad, I'd prefer if you didn't—" she started to say, walking forward.

"What's this one?" And before she could stop him, he'd pulled out the patchwork dress.

The dress that had come to her in a dream, that had consumed her mind and body for weeks, made from hundred-year-old fabric and hundred-year-old memories, ripped apart and put back together again. The dress she had worn to a dance, and down to the bottom of a nightmare.

Evie wanted to shout at him to put it back, but the way he was looking at it made her pause. It was no casual glance, but a studied, intense appraisal. She waited.

"These are good, Evie," Dad said. He ran a hand down the blousy fabric. The white ditsy, the brown gingham, the blue paisley. "Especially this one. There's something different about it. Can't really put my finger on what, though." He carefully hung the dress back in its place.

Out of the soup of emotions that roiled inside her, a small bubble of pleasure rose to the surface. "Thanks," she said, and then stepped forward to gently close the closet door.

Finally taking the hint, Dad made a move to leave. "Your mom texted to say she's on her way home. Guess I'll head back to the inn for the night."

"Okay."

Dad paused in the doorway, then turned around to face her. "Evie," he said slowly, meeting her eyes. "Are you, um . . . are you okay?"

Evie was impressed. Dad's usual way of dealing with emotional turmoil within the family was to pretend it wasn't there. And yet here he was, addressing it directly. Although, considering the seriousness of this particular turmoil—avoiding it would be nearly impossible. After all, that was the very reason he'd come to visit in the first place. After it was all over, Mom had filled him in on Evie's increasingly strange behavior since they arrived in Ravenglass in October, culminating in her miraculously rescuing Stan from an abandoned gold mine. It was a bizarre story that left her parents—and pretty much everyone else—with a lot of unanswered questions. Fortunately, Chief Sànchez had given up trying to understand how Evie had gotten down into the mines, considering the entrance had been cordoned off by the police. She'd claimed a temporary memory loss, and he'd eventually, grudgingly, accepted that was the best he was going to get out of her.

"We just want to know what happened that night," the chief had said.

You wouldn't believe me if I told you, she'd thought.

Only Tina knew the whole truth. Aunt Martha knew some of it, her mom even less. Burdening people with the knowledge about Holly and the Shadow Land seemed unnecessary. And telling her dad was out of the question. She didn't need to give him any more reason to think she was unstable. *I won't let him make me doubt myself again, not after everything I've been through.* Mom hadn't been the only one signing off on the traumatic visits to Dr. Mears all those years ago. Just like always, Dad had gone along with the path of least resistance and allowed it all to happen, to keep happening, until everything fell apart.

"Yeah," she said. "I'm fine."

"Okay," Dad said slowly. "If you're fine, then why aren't you back in school?"

Evie clenched her teeth. So it was a trap. *Why did you have to come here?* she thought angrily. *Mom and Stan and I finally start to get settled into something resembling a normal life, and now you decide to show up.*

She didn't say any of that. Instead, she replied, "I've just been waiting until things calm down a bit before going back. You saw those reporters—there's been a lot of unwanted attention."

Dad nodded. It was a good excuse, and she knew it. "That's true," he said. "But you can't wait forever. You've got to go back sometime, Evie. Get it over with. Rip off the Band-Aid. It's not going to get any easier."

"Mm-hmm," she said, looking at the floor.

"Well, all right, then." Dad slapped his hand against the door frame, as if announcing the end of his "big talk." He looked relieved. "I'm off. Maybe I'll see you tomorrow? I'll text your mom to see what the plans are."

Evie should have felt relieved, too. He hadn't pressed her for more information, hadn't demanded better answers, or seen through her lies. He was leaving. It was exactly what she wanted.

Then why did she feel so awful inside?

"Maybe you will," she said hollowly.

He gave her doorway one last pat before thumping down the stairs, saying a quick good night to Stan, and heading out the kitchen door.

Evie sat on the edge of her bed, listening to the sound of his SUV turning around in the drive and staring at her closet door.

Later on, at dinner, Mom dropped the bombshell.

"Your father and I spoke on the phone a little while ago, and we both agreed that it's time for you to go back to school, Evie," she said. "Tomorrow."

"What?" Evie exclaimed, flabbergasted.

"Look, I know your dad and I don't agree on much these days, but we agree on this. Being home isn't doing you any good. It's time to move on with your life and get yourself back to normal."

"You're assuming she was ever normal in the first place . . . ," Stan mumbled.

"Stan!" Mom said pointedly. She turned back to Evie with an exhausted sigh. "Tomorrow's Monday. New week, fresh start— you'll be able to catch up on work before Thanksgiving and the Christmas holidays come along. It'll be good for you. Okay?"

Losing her appetite, Evie set her fork down on the half-eaten plate of spaghetti and salad. She knew it was hopeless to fight them, but that didn't make the prospect of a return to Ravenglass High any less dreadful. "Fine," she said.

Mom put a hand over hers and squeezed. "I know it's hard, honey," she said softly. "But I also know how strong you are. You'll get through this, I promise."

Evie nodded. Mom's behavior toward her had shifted dramatically since they'd come back from the mine, and Evie was grateful. But even with the improvement in their relationship, Evie knew she couldn't tell her mom that she believed Desmond was still alive, that something down in the dark had taken him . . .

Back to normal, Evie thought. *Is such a thing even possible?*

Evie lay in bed late that night, trying unsuccessfully to fall asleep. This always happened when she took a nap late in the day, and usually there was nothing to be done about it but stay up and read until exhaustion finally took over.

She'd gotten through about twenty pages of her current book when the sound of a bird call outside caught her attention. It had been quiet aside from the roar of the ancient heater coming on and the wind rushing through the bare branches of the trees. Then, a singular song. Something familiar.

"Whip-poor-will?"

Frowning, Evie put down her book and rose from the bed, padding to the window in bare feet. The yard was dark, a crescent moon barely illuminating the field and the cold forest beyond. Everything was still, except for something under the old apple tree. Something darker than the night, something moving.

A slender thing. A figure in a long black dress.

Then another sound floated up to her. A deep, scraping noise. *Scrrrch. Scrrrch. Scrrrch.*

"Holly," Evie breathed. Without another word, she ran from the room, down the stairs, and out the kitchen door. The cold took her breath away, cutting like glass straight through her thin nightgown. The frozen grass crunched against her bare feet as she ran.

The figure was nowhere to be seen.

"No," Evie moaned. "Holly! Where are you?" she shouted, not even caring if she woke her mother and brother in the process. "Come back! Please!"

And then she noticed something strange about the tree. She walked closer, squinting in the gloom, until she could see that words had been freshly carved into the thick bark of the trunk. Evie traced her fingers around each letter and read:

FIND HIM

FIND ME

"What . . . ?" Evie whispered. She shook her head. "No, that can't be it. How am I supposed to find Desmond without you? What am I supposed to do?" She pressed her hands against the tree in desperation. "I can't do this by myself, I can't—" Suddenly she felt something wet and pulled away. She stared at the tree as liquid oozed out of the carved letters like sap. But it wasn't sap.

It was blood. It dripped down the tree trunk, masking the message in a flood of gore.

Evie looked at her hands and saw that they, too, were covered in smears of blood. "Holly," she cried, stepping back from the tree. "What is this . . . why are you doing this?" She tripped over an exposed root and began to fall—

And woke up in bed, the book lying open against her chest.

She sat up, her heart beating wildly. *It couldn't have been a dream*, she thought. *It felt so real! I was outside, I felt the cold . . .*

But when she looked at her hands, they were clean. And when she got up to look out the window, no shadow stood under the old apple tree.

She got back into bed, waking Schrödinger, who'd been curled up at her feet, as she did so. He padded over to her and pushed his face against her hand, purring. She picked him up and he didn't put up a fight. Something about his soft, warm body made her feel more rooted. More certain that she was really awake. That this time, it was real.

"What was that all about, Schrö?" she whispered. "What's Holly trying to tell me?"

Find him, find me.

Wasn't that exactly what she'd been trying to do all along?

Outside, a sound broke through the stillness, and Evie felt her world shift sickeningly on its axis.

"Whip-poor-will?"

Meanwhile...

"Well, that was a waste of an afternoon."

Tim Crane coasted along the winding road leaving Ravenglass, angry and longing for a cheeseburger. The photographer sat on the passenger side, half listening while he reviewed pictures on his camera.

"We won't get back to Pittsfield until nightfall," Crane went on, "and when we do, we'll have nothing to show for it. Who does that guy think he is, anyway? Putting his hands on me like that?"

"The girl's dad, I think," the photographer muttered, still scrolling through photos.

Crane huffed. "I oughta take him to court. I was just *trying* to do my job, and this meathead thinks he can put his hands on me. The nerve."

"Mm."

Crane flipped on the headlights. Night fell fast up in the mountains, and the sun was already sinking behind the horizon. "All the other guys have put a lid on this story, but they're not *local*, see? They don't know how far down the story goes. They don't know all the dark doings that have gone on in that house. All that Patchwork Girl, urban legend stuff, the Hobbie girl going missing in the eighties, and now this. I'm telling you, Mark, there's something about that place. Something . . . off, you know? Not just the house, either, but the whole damn town. And I'm going to figure out what it is. Maybe not today, but I'm not letting this go just because some loudmouth dirtbag pushes me around." After a moment, Crane turned to look at his partner, who was still studying the tiny display window on the back of his DSLR camera. "Hey! Are you even listening to me, man?"

Mark sighed. He'd been working with Crane for more than a year, and he'd realized early on that it was best to tune out his partner's constant rants and stick to monosyllabic responses. Crane rarely noticed, anyway. He didn't need anyone to talk *to*, just a body to talk *at*. Really, a cantaloupe on a tripod would have done just as well. But there were moments, like that one, when Crane was so fired up that he needed real conversational engagement to be satisfied. "Sure, I'm listening," Mark said, glancing up. "Just checking to see if I got any decent shots of the Archer girl. Were you serious about printing the story without her statement? All we've got are some nothing quotes from the chief of police and a whole lot of probably unprovable, inflammatory accusations from the mayor's daughter. I doubt the boss would give it the green light—"

"You just worry about the pictures and let me worry about the boss," Crane broke in.

"No problem," Mark muttered.

As Crane launched into another tirade—this time about the *Post*'s editor in chief and his lack of "journalistic courage"—Mark mentally turned down his partner's volume and focused his attention back to the camera. He'd taken a burst of photos while the girl was trying to get past them, hoping to get a clear shot. He found one where she was looking at the camera, her body half turned away, her long reddish hair blowing in the wind. It was good—dramatic. Mark was about to take note of the photo number when he noticed a dark blur in the wooded background. He squinted and zoomed in, trying to see what it was. An animal? Or something on the lens, perhaps?

"Hey, did you see that?" Crane was asking.

Mark looked up. There was a thick forest on one side of the mountain road, and a beautiful, panoramic view of the Berkshires on the other. "See what?" he asked.

"I could have sworn I saw a guy standing in the trees at the edge of the road, just where we took that last turn."

Mark shook his head. "I didn't see anything. Who'd be out walking around here, anyway? Hikers? Not at this time of year."

"Guess not," Crane muttered. "My ex-wife liked to hike, did you know that? I never understood it. Walking around in the woods all day, looking at birds or whatever. Seems like a gigantic waste of time—"

Mark rolled his eyes, turning his attention back to the pictures once again. Regardless of what the dark smudge was, it would have to be edited out of the photo, and that took time. Maybe he'd be lucky, and one of the next shots wouldn't have it. He advanced to the next image, which was almost identical to the previous one. In that one, the dark blur was even larger.

"What is that . . . ?"

He advanced to the next shot, and again, the girl looked almost the same. Although, did she look a little frightened in this one? The thing was even larger in that shot, and looked as if it had reached the edge of the forest. It looked less like a blur and more like someone's shadow. But it had been cloudy out, and none of the three of them would have cast a shadow like that one.

Mark began to feel something cold and heavy settle in his belly. His hands shaking, he advanced to the next picture, and the next, and like a digital flipbook, the images on the screen moved forward in a stutter step. The girl's face seemed to contort more with each frame, until it had twisted into a mask of horror. And the thing, the shadow, it came closer and closer until Mark thought he could see something within the darkness. A face with wide eyes and an open mouth ready to scream.

It was only when he felt it reach through the back of the camera toward him that Mark realized the face was merely a reflection of his own.

Mark screamed, and Crane jumped midsentence, swerving the green sedan into the opposite lane. "What the hell, Mark?" Crane shouted, steering back to the right as the car just barely navigated another hairpin turn. He glanced over at the photographer. "You almost made me crash the car!"

Mark said nothing. He was still looking down at his camera.

"Mark? Mark! What the hell is wrong with you?" Crane was starting to feel a little squirrelly. The photographer was acting like he couldn't even hear him shouting. "Answer me, damn it! What made you scream like that?"

For a moment, Mark didn't move, and then he slowly looked up at Crane. He blinked at him with colorless, black eyes, and a face that seemed suddenly too long, too gray. He raised one finger to his lips and smiled. His mouth was too wide, with teeth that glinted strangely within.

"*Shh,*" Mark said.

Now it was Crane's turn to scream. The mountain road curved sharply to the right, but the green sedan kept heading straight on. Crane hit the brakes, but it was too late—the car careered off the road and slammed into a tree. The sound of it was so loud that it echoed off the mountainside. A flutter of birds burst up from the surrounding forest, startled into flight. When the car hit, the reporter's body was ejected through the broken windshield and thrown free of the car, landing ten feet away on the soft forest floor.

For a few minutes, the only sounds were the birds, asking questions, and the hisses and clanks of the ruined green sedan. Then another noise—a deep, harsh gurgling—joined them. It was the sound of Tim Crane dying.

He lay there in the leaf mold, the ground drinking up his blood, trying to speak. To curse. To scream for help. But he couldn't do any of that. His chest had been crushed in the impact. For once in his life, aside from the little wet sounds, he was as quiet as a mouse.

He couldn't move his head, only his eyes. So, when Mark pushed the door open and stepped out of the wrecked sedan, Crane was watching. He watched as Mark walked right by him, not even giving him a second glance. By the time Mark reached the mountain road and started to make his way back to Raven-glass, Crane had stopped watching anything at all.

As the sun set under the mountains, and the birds nestled into sleep, the forest forgot all about the car and the man, and swallowed everything up into stillness.

4

With each step Evie took toward Ravenglass High, she could feel the resistance increase, like a long, invisible cord pulling her back toward home. The last time she'd stepped foot in that building, she'd been a girl possessed. Even now, homecoming night felt like a half-remembered dream—vivid, frightening, and impossible. If dozens of fire and rescue personnel hadn't seen her come out of that mine, she might have believed that it had never happened at all.

But it did happen. And returning to school would surely bring all those memories surging back.

As she turned onto the campus road, she saw clusters of students making their way toward the building on foot, and getting out of their cars in the parking lot nearby. The sound of their familiar chatter made her stomach churn, and she immediately regretted the cup of coffee she'd gulped down with a bagel that morning.

She stopped, hesitating. The resistance was so strong she

nearly turned back. No one had seen her yet. There was still time to change her mind.

But finally, she took another step toward the campus. Then another. Until she had joined the flow of students and it was too late to run home. Her father was right about one thing. There was no way out of it. Today, tomorrow, or next month, going back would be painful. She might as well get it over with. She'd already mentally prepared herself for all the uncomfortable situations she was likely to encounter, and frankly, it couldn't possibly be as bad as what she'd already been through.

What doesn't kill you . . .

She had nearly reached the school's front courtyard when she saw students ahead of her move around something blocking the sidewalk. It was only when she reached it herself that she saw what it was. A pile of fresh and wilted flower bouquets, prayer candles, and photographs encased in plastic and tied to the chain-link fence.

Evie stopped dead. Another student walked straight into her from behind, muttering under his breath before shouldering past her toward the school. Evie didn't bother apologizing, transfixed by the scene at her feet.

It was a memorial. For Desmond.

Someone had used Styrofoam cups to write out Desmond's uniform number—19—in the fence, and others had tied handwritten messages there, the words faded by weather but still readable.

MISS YOU, BRO

RHS ISN'T THE SAME WITHOUT ITS MVP

LONG LIVE THE KING

By far the worst of it were the pictures. Desmond in his football uniform. Desmond posing with the rest of the homecoming court. Desmond laughing in the hallway with his friends. In one photo, he wore the same light pink T-shirt he'd had on when Evie first met him. She stared at that beautiful, contagious smile, and suddenly the possibility that she would never see it again overwhelmed her. She took a great, gasping breath of freezing air and squeezed her eyes shut, blocking out the sight of so many faces, all of them his.

But even then, the sweet smell of dying flowers remained, reminding her again of everything that came before.

Suddenly, Evie felt a strange, crawling sensation, like she was being watched.

She opened her eyes and turned to see a small boy in a red coat standing nearby. He looked a few years younger than Stan, maybe seven or eight. He was probably on his way to the elementary school, which was on the same campus as RHS. It was pretty early for him to be here, but then again, some parents had to drop their kids off before school to make it to work on time. In one hand, the boy held a black plastic lunch box labeled with bright green letters. JACK.

He was staring at her, his eyes piercing behind a black fringe.

Evie fidgeted under his gaze. "What?" she asked.

Jack didn't move, didn't even blink. He was pale and had dark circles under his eyes, as if he hadn't slept in days.

Then the boy looked away, west, toward the mountains. "It's getting dark," he said. "Isn't it?" He looked back at her.

Evie glanced around. A blanket of clouds covered the sky, bathing the entire town in a dull, gray light. It wasn't bright out, but it was early morning—certainly not getting dark. Kids were weird. Sometimes they liked to say things just to see how other people would react. "I guess," she said.

Just then, the high-school warning bell rang. If Evie didn't hurry up, she'd be late for her first class.

"Ticktock," Jack said, his eyes still on her.

Without another word, Evie turned away and rushed up the stairs to the front doors with the other stragglers. She took one last look back at the sidewalk and saw that Jack hadn't moved. In his coat, he was a bright red spot in a sea of gray, one last autumn leaf clinging to a bare winter tree. He was looking up toward the mountains again, like he was waiting for something to happen.

Evie could have sworn that a hush fell over the main hallway the moment she entered it. Like a pall thrown over the students walking to their classes and loitering at their lockers, all the sound in the building seemed to be muted and filled with an undercurrent of whispers. The crowd parted before her as she went, giving her a wide berth. It felt as if she had a scarlet letter pinned to her chest.

Before, Evie would have just walked straight to class without even stopping at her locker. Stoop-shouldered, eyes on the ground, as if the weight of their curiosity and disapproval was too heavy to bear. But she refused to be that person anymore. She'd gone through hell and come back a very different version of herself. She didn't need their approval. And if they were going to go ahead and get out of her way, that was just fine.

Taking a deep breath, Evie held her head high, stopped at her locker, quickly collected her things for first period, and slammed it shut again. That done, she turned and came face-to-face with her least favorite person in Ravenglass.

Kimber Sullivan's eyes widened with shock when she registered Evie's face. The mayor's daughter looked terrible. Her blond hair was lank and dull, and her makeup so poorly applied that it only served to exaggerate the haunted look in her eyes. A pair of jeans and an unflattering black sweater had replaced her usually fashionable outfits.

Looks like I'm not the only one who's changed, Evie thought.

The last time Evie had seen Kimber was on homecoming night. She'd accosted Evie while Holly had been possessing her, compelling her to experience the kind of evening Holly had missed out on forty years before. When Kimber had gotten in her way, Holly had shown herself to the girl in all her horrifying, skull-faced glory. At least, that's what Evie thought had happened, from Kimber's reaction. Evie hadn't seen her since, though Tina had said that the girl was "in a bad way."

She's not wrong, Evie thought.

"You . . . ," Kimber said, her lip trembling.

Evie hugged her books a little tighter but didn't allow the anxiety to show on her face. *Be like Mom*, she thought. *Be a glacier!* "Hello, Kimber," she said coolly.

"Why are you here?" Kimber asked. Her voice was dry, as if it hadn't been used in a while.

"I don't know, it's a school day?" Evie said with a shrug. "I had to come back sometime," she added, echoing her father's words.

"You . . . you're . . . ," Kimber stammered. *A freak? A monster?*

"Going to be late for class? Yes, I am, if I don't get over there right now—"

She had started to shoulder past the girl when Kimber grabbed her arm with a surprisingly powerful grip. *"What did you do to me?"* she hissed, her blotchy, twisted face close to Evie's.

Evie looked her straight in the eyes. "I showed you what it's like to be scared and alone," she said in a low voice. "Now live with it. I did."

With that, she pushed past Kimber and continued down the hallway, entering the Family Consumer Science classroom with only seconds to spare.

Kimber didn't follow.

When Evie caught sight of the familiar long tables, each crowned with white Singer sewing machines, she felt herself relax a little.

"Well, well, well," Ms. Jackson said, rising from her desk. "Miss Archer, welcome back. I was wondering when you would rejoin us." Ms. Jackson's salt-and-pepper braids flowed down her back, and she wore a burgundy jumpsuit over a white cotton top.

"Hey," Evie replied with a smile. FCS was her favorite class, and had been a refuge for her since moving to Ravenglass. She was actually looking forward to working in Ms. Jackson's classroom again, designing, cutting, and sewing at all hours. "Did I miss much?"

"Nothing you can't catch up on in a day or two," Ms. Jackson said with a wink. She knew Evie was the best seamstress in the school, and encouraged her in the craft more than anyone had before. "I've got most of the classes working on costumes for the winter show. They're doing *A Christmas Carol*."

"Oh, cool," Evie said, nodding. She'd seen various versions of Dickens's Christmas tale growing up in New York, once in an off-off-Broadway production, and a couple of movie versions. Her dad had made her watch *Scrooged* when she was in elementary school—which scared her half to death. Right after that, Mom had put on *The Muppet Christmas Carol* to try to erase the damage.

"Yes, very cool," Ms. Jackson agreed. "Opening night is December twenty-second, so we don't have a lot of time to waste—" She craned to look over Evie's shoulder at the rest of the class. "All right, everyone, enough chitchat! Take your seats, please. Morning announcements are about to begin—we'll get started as soon as it's done." Turning back to Evie, she said, "Find a seat and I'll set you up with a project in a few minutes."

Evie nodded and moved into the room. She went to her regular table and stopped for a moment, her eyes resting on the empty seat next to hers.

Desmond's seat.

She could almost feel his warm, bright energy still hanging in the air above it. She sat down and breathed into the emptiness his absence left behind.

"Good morning, Miners!" the announcements bellowed over the PA system. "It's a great day at Ravenglass High! With Thanksgiving break quickly approaching, we have a lot to be thankful for, and a lot to do before everyone gobbles up their turkey dinners . . ." Evie half listened to the drone of the announcer, her mind adrift with a dozen unformed thoughts, until the mention of Desmond's name pulled her violently back into focus.

". . . and the loss of Ravenglass's beloved homecoming king, who was a dear friend to so many of us, is a tragedy that we have only begun to process. To start healing as a community, the King family has invited anyone who would like to pay their respects to attend a celebration of life for Desmond at Ravenglass Congregational Church this Saturday morning at ten a.m. Refreshments will follow the service at Birdie's Diner until noon."

Evie gasped. Grief bloomed in her heart, taking up so much space that there was no room left for anything else. She couldn't speak, couldn't breathe, couldn't think of anything other than the impossibility of Desmond's death.

It can't be true. It can't!

How could they have confirmed Desmond's death without a body? Was the evidence they'd found inside the mine really enough? How could everyone just give up on him?

She wanted to run out of there, but the eyes of every other student in class rooted her to the spot, like a pinned butterfly. So instead, she just put her face in her hands and waited for it to be over.

A minute later, the announcements concluded, and Ms. Jackson gave everyone else in class their marching orders. The teacher's words, the chatter of students, the hum of sewing machines—all of it flowed over her like something distant and incomprehensible, while she sat deep below, trapped in her sorrow.

"Miss Archer . . ." A gentle word, followed by a soft touch on her shoulder.

Evie looked up, sniffing. "Yeah," she said, glancing up at Ms. Jackson. "Sorry."

"No apologies necessary. This has been . . . hard . . . on all of us." Evie could see tears stilled in her teacher's eyes. Ms. Jackson gave her a quick, pained smile. "But it helps to keep your hands busy. Yes?"

Evie nodded.

"Good. Because I have a very special project for you, young lady. One I think only you can handle. Are you familiar with the story of *A Christmas Carol*?"

"Sure, I've seen it a few times." Even if her childhood memories of it might be hazy, the tale of Ebenezer Scrooge and his bah-humbug ways was so well known, it might as well be part of the universal consciousness.

"Well, I'd like you to design and build the costumes for the three ghosts. The Ghost of Christmas Past, the Ghost of Christmas Present, and the Ghost of Christmas Yet to Come. What do you think?"

"Sounds like fun," Evie replied. "Fun" seemed like an alien concept at the moment, but Evie deeply appreciated her teacher's efforts to distract her.

"Great!" Ms. Jackson said, her brown eyes sparkling. She handed Evie a thin paperback book, yellowed with age. CHARLES DICKENS'S A CHRISTMAS CAROL. THE COMPLETE TEXT. "For inspiration," she explained.

"Thanks," Evie said, flipping through the pages. There were some black-line illustrations throughout that looked like they'd been drawn long ago.

"Oh, and remember: The part with the Ghost of Christmas

Yet to Come is the most climactic scene in the whole show, so that costume's *really* got to be good. You can make him look scary, can't you?"

Evie stopped at a page near the end of the book, which had an illustration of Scrooge kneeling on the ground, his hands pressed to his face much like Evie's had been just moments before. Standing before him was a faceless, black hooded figure, pointing down to the ground where Scrooge's grave lay.

Evie swallowed, suddenly cold.

"Yeah," she said. "I think I can do that."

5

By the time lunch rolled around, Evie was so exhausted with the sheer effort of holding herself together that she couldn't imagine facing everyone in the cafeteria. She needed a minute to breathe.

Moving against the flow of people, Evie slipped out a side door and into the courtyard beside the cafeteria—a concrete patio dotted with small trees, bushes, and wooden benches, where students could eat outdoors when the weather was nice. That day, it was cold and deserted.

Perfect.

Evie settled into the corner of a bench, buttoned her coat all the way to the top, and pulled the salami sandwich and chips she'd brought out of her backpack. But before she could take a single bite, she caught a group of students watching her through the window. She could see their faces close to the glass, their mouths saying things she couldn't hear. She suddenly felt like an animal in a zoo.

Stowing the food back into her bag, she stood up and walked toward the sports fields by the side of the school. She'd lost her appetite. Hoping it would help, she plugged in her earbuds and turned on her favorite music, a mixture of indie rock and classic eighties pop. She walked aimlessly, not really caring where she ended up as long as it was away from everyone else.

But being alone was easier said than done. Everywhere she went, unwelcome companions followed. Memories of the football stadium, the grassy field where she'd collapsed during the homecoming game, and the path where she and Desmond once walked on their way up the mountain road. They followed her as surely as Holly had all those weeks ago, invisible tormentors that only she could see.

Determined to get away from everything familiar, Evie cut across the parking lot behind the school and ducked under a rail fence into a thin copse of trees. She turned the volume up on her music and sang along to "When Doves Cry," hoping the sound would drown out the memories flooding into her brain.

The trees gave way to a narrow, twisty road she'd never seen before. Ravenglass had all kinds of little back streets that were artifacts from an earlier time. Some of them had street signs, others had names only the oldest locals remembered. This seemed to be the latter. Evie was wandering across it, humming to herself, when something dark rushed toward her from the corner of her eye. Then she heard it: the deep, animal rumble of an engine as a figure on a black motorcycle approached at high speed, hurtling straight toward her.

Evie backstepped and tripped over a rock, the sound of her own cry muted by the music still blasting in her ears as she toppled back into the grass. At the same instant, the rider saw her, hit the brakes, and swerved, missing her by inches. She watched in horror as the bike slid out from underneath him and he went barrel rolling across the asphalt until he finally came to a stop. The motorcycle slid only about half as far, landing in the soft grass at the side of the road.

For a moment, everything was still.

Prince was still crooning about what it sounds like when doves cry. Evie yanked the buds from her ears and clambered to her feet. She touched her body with her hands, reassuring herself that she was actually unhurt. Miraculously, she was. But what about the rider?

"Oh no," she whispered, and ran over to the prone figure, who was still face down on the ground. "Oh my god, are you okay?" She kneeled at the man's side. He wasn't wearing any protective gear, not even a helmet. He could have internal injuries, a broken neck, or worse . . . She pulled out her phone with trembling hands. "I'm calling nine-one-one," she said, fumbling with the screen.

"Don't," a husky, muffled voice said.

Evie looked down. The man groaned, pushing himself up to his elbows with effort. He was wearing faded jeans, black boots, and a distressed leather jacket with a triangular Union Jack patch on the shoulder. She was shocked to see he wasn't a man at all— but a boy about her age. More than that, she'd seen him before in school. He looked up at her with deeply set eyes that were half hidden by a lock of chin-length, wavy black hair. He regarded her with a look of tightly controlled irritation.

"Don't bother with an ambulance. I'm fine," he said, brushing dirt from his face. His voice had an unusual lilt to it—one that seemed oddly familiar. British, maybe?

"But—you're bleeding," Evie said, gesturing to the gash across his cheek. All along the left side of his face, his copper skin was raw with scrapes and scratches, and there were bits of gravel still embedded inside the deepest cuts. She reached out instinctively to brush it away, but the boy pulled back.

"I said I'm fine," he snapped.

"Okay, okay," Evie said, sitting back. "I was just trying to help."

"Well," the boy said, getting to his feet, "maybe next time you'll look where you're going before you wander into the middle of the road. That'd be right helpful."

Evie scoffed, standing up right after him. "How was I to know some maniac was going to rocket down a back road on a motorcycle? Are you even old enough to ride that thing?"

The boy had walked over to where the motorcycle lay in the grass and lifted it as gently as if it were a newborn lamb. "You're all right, luv," he muttered to it, ignoring Evie completely. He was of average height and build, although his broad shoulders and slim waist made him look larger than he really was. After he'd inspected the bike from stem to stern, his square hands carefully checking every inch of its body, he looked up at her. "Not that it's your business, but I am old enough to ride—just. And this is not a *thing*, this is a Triumph Bonneville SE in Phantom Black." He set the bike on its kickstand and gave it a pat. "Lucky Bonnie got off with only a nick."

Evie's jaw tightened. "You know, last time I checked, a decent human being would care more about running down a girl in the street than a scratch on his bike, but whatever."

The boy stood and looked at her as if he was going to say something, but didn't. Blood dripped from his cheek onto the collar of his jacket. He used the back of his hand to wipe it away.

"Why aren't you wearing a helmet, anyway?" Evie added. "Are you trying to get yourself killed?"

The boy gave her a long look—his expression serious instead of flippant for the first time. Then he cleared his throat. "As much as I'm enjoying this conversation," he said, the casual tone returning, "don't you have somewhere to be? No offense, but you don't seem like the school-skipping type."

Evie felt the heat of anger rush up to the freckles on her cheeks, and she shook her head. "Unbelievable . . . ," she muttered, and turned to go. She was walking back into the copse of trees when she heard him call out.

"Wait—" he said, coming toward her. "Is this yours?" She turned to see him holding Sarah Flower's gold locket. It swung lazily from the gold chain clutched between his fingers. Evie's hand instantly went to her throat. It must have slipped off when she fell.

"Yes," she said, annoyed that he'd interrupted her attempt to storm away.

"Hey, um," he muttered when he reached her. He ran his fingers through his hair and looked as if whatever words he was trying to say were stuck in his throat. "I, um—I may have been a bit harsh there, so . . . anyway, I'm glad you're all right. Here." He pushed the locket toward her.

"Was that an apology?" Evie asked wryly.

"Close enough, innit?" he said, shrugging.

She snorted and reached out to take the necklace. But the moment the boy placed the locket in her palm, the world around her stutter-stepped, becoming crooked and strange. The color drained from everything—the sky, the trees—until it was all sepia-toned, like a coffee stain. The boy had vanished—or rather, most of him had. She could almost see him out of the corner of her eye. But when she tried to look directly at him, it was like he wasn't there at all.

Evie's heart began to race. *It's happening again . . .*

She felt a weight in her hand, but it wasn't the locket—that was back on her neck somehow. It was something else, small and cold, with pointed edges that dug into her palm like spider's legs.

Then, a sudden blast of noise—like a gunshot.

She gasped and dropped whatever was in her hand to the ground.

It lay there in the dry grass. Not a spider, but an old-fashioned silver pin. It was shaped like a sprig of leaves, bursting with berries made from pearls.

She stared at it, confused, and suddenly noticed a dark smudge across the pin, coloring one cluster of the berries red.

Her hands were sticky. Why were they sticky?

Evie held them up in front of her. She knew what she would see, but that didn't take away from the horror of it. The horror of all that blood.

It was on her hands, her clothes—had she been wearing a dress before? She thought perhaps the pin had stabbed her, but a tiny wound could never bleed that much. And somewhere in the back of her mind, she knew that the blood wasn't hers.

What have I done?

The thought entered her mind, and she couldn't tell if that was hers, either.

What have I done?

Then, from somewhere, or maybe everywhere, a voice called out to her. *"Evie!"* it cried. *"Look for the truth, Evie!"* It was Holly's voice.

Evie scanned the landscape, desperate. Every tree, every distant signpost, looked like a dark figure in a black bonnet. But none of them were. "Holly!" Evie shouted. "Where are you?" The coffee-colored world was starting to break down. It stutter-stepped back and forth into light and color, though Evie willed it to remain. "No!" she shouted. "Wait!"

"The truth will set you free." The words seemed to drift along the air and blow the world back into its normal state.

Evie gasped as she found herself once again standing in front of the boy, both of them still holding on to the locket. He dropped the chain abruptly, no longer the same cocksure rider he'd been just a moment before.

"What—?" Evie said, breathless.

The boy shook his head, a look of consternation on his face. "Who are you?" he muttered. He studied her until recognition dawned. "Wait a minute. You . . . you're Evie Archer. You're the girl who lives in that house."

Evie nodded, too excited to be hurt by the growing apprehension on the boy's face. A dozen half-formed thoughts filled her mind: *What just happened? Was it something to do with the locket?* She needed to understand.

"I've got to go," he said, taking a few steps back toward the road.

"Hold on!" she said.

The boy looked back at her, but only for a second. And in that second, before he pulled the bravado back over his face like a shroud, she saw something else there.

Fear.

Evie was about to say something when the warning bell rang. She only had five minutes to get back inside and to her class on time.

"Better hurry," the boy said, before walking briskly back to the road.

Evie shook her head, dumbfounded. She had questions for him, lots of them, but she got the feeling getting answers wouldn't be easy. There was a wall around him, Evie could feel it as surely as if it were built with brick and mortar. She knew because she had one just like it.

In a moment, the boy had nimbly mounted his motorcycle, gunned the engine, and ridden off and away. She watched him go, realizing that after everything that had happened, she didn't even know his name.

"Well, hey there, Freckles," Tina said when she saw Evie before next period in the hall. "I heard you were back today. You could have given me a heads-up, you know." Tina wore a hooded crop top over black sweatpants and a pair of cherry-red Chuck Taylor high-tops. Her curly hair, once a faded shade of seafoam, was freshly dyed a deep alpine green. She shifted the backpack slung over her shoulder and gave Evie a critical look as they walked to their next classes. "What happened? Did you roll down a hill or something?"

"Something," Evie muttered, picking a twig out of her hair. "I was walking around the back of the school and nearly got flattened by some guy on a motorcycle."

"Some guy?" Tina asked, instantly curious.

"Yeah. He must be a student here; I've seen him around. Dark, shaggy hair, vaguely British accent, looks like he could be Indian or Pakistani . . ."

"Great cheekbones? Pouty lips?" Tina asked.

"Well, I don't know about all that. Mostly what I noticed was his attitude."

"Sounds like Sai Rockwell. Dr. Rockwell's son."

Evie snapped her fingers. "Of course! That's why his accent sounded so familiar. It's British, but sort of faded. Like he's been here a while. It's exactly what his dad sounds like." She even remembered Dr. Rockwell mentioning that he had a son—a senior at RHS.

Nagasai.

Evie had met Dr. Rockwell when her mom had rushed her to his office after being exposed to a toxic flower called "tread softly." Given her not-great experiences with medical practitioners in the past, Evie had been surprised by how much she liked the brash, outspoken doctor. He'd joked around and put her at ease. "His dad is nice, though," Evie added. "Sai kind of seems like a jerk."

Tina shrugged. "Hard to say. Nobody knows him very well. He's in and out of here like a shadow. Sometimes he'll be in class, other times, he won't show up for days at a stretch."

"Huh," Evie mused. After a moment, she bumped shoulders

with her friend. "Listen, I'm sorry I didn't tell you I was coming to school today. My parents gave me the ultimatum late last night, and I was so freaked out that I just didn't think about it."

Tina waved the apology away. "Hold on a minute, did you say *parents*? Like plural?"

Evie nodded. "My dad's in town. To do his fatherly duty and make sure we're all okay, or whatever."

"So, are you?" Tina asked.

"Am I what?"

"Are you okay? Or are you 'whatever'?"

Evie exhaled as the news about Desmond and his memorial came rushing back. "I honestly have no idea."

As if Tina could read her mind, she said, "I'm so sorry, E. I really—"

"It's not over," Evie broke in. "I'm not giving up on him. Not yet."

Tina nodded. "Okay. We'll keep trying."

Whether Tina really believed there was a chance of saving Desmond, Evie didn't know. But the fact that Tina would even entertain the idea that he was trapped in some dark shadow world underground . . . that was a big step forward.

"I can come and hang after school if you want," Tina said brightly. "Be like a buffer between you and stress. I'm very distracting, you know." She fluttered her eyelashes.

Evie managed a small smile. "You certainly are," she said. "Yes, I would love that." Tina had arrived at her classroom door and was about to make her way inside when Evie stopped her. "Hey, you're not coming over just to avoid going home, are you?" She remembered what Tina had said about her grandparents' visit, and how uncomfortable she was having them at the house for so long.

Tina scoffed and shook her head. "Of course not," she said. "I'll see you after school."

"See you," Evie said, thoughtful. She'd lied to a lot of people since she'd moved to Ravenglass. To her mother, her aunt, her brother—and to Tina, too. She'd lied about what she was going through, telling everyone that she was just fine. She'd tried to stop doing that since coming back from the mine, but some habits were hard to break. One side effect of lying about her own level of wellness for so many years was that she could recognize, almost instantly, when someone else was doing it, too.

So Evie knew, without a doubt, that Tina was lying through her teeth. She wasn't okay. But at least at that moment, she'd rather focus on Evie's problems than her own. Knowing this made Evie feel a little better about monopolizing Tina's time, but only a little. *I'm going to find out exactly what's going on with her*, Evie promised herself.

The rest of the school day went by without incident, although Evie had a difficult time focusing on much of anything. Every time she tried to pay attention to what her teacher was saying, her eyes would drift to the classroom windows, outside, to the tree line. She'd think about the vision of blood and the silver pin, and Holly's voice, begging her to keep looking for the truth. Her fingers would find the locket, refastened around her neck, and she'd hold her breath and wait for something to happen. After all, the vision had come when she'd touched the locket, so wouldn't it make sense that it was some kind of psychic trigger, like Aunt Martha had talked about?

But nothing happened. No vision. No voices. Nothing.

She wanted to feel invigorated by the vision—it was a step forward, wasn't it? But like the dream of the message on the tree, it seemed to provide more questions than answers. And the fact that it had happened in the presence of someone like Sai Rockwell only infuriated her further. Did his father know he was skipping school, zooming around town without a helmet, and nearly running over girls in the street? Not exactly ideal behavior.

Then again, Dr. Rockwell wasn't like any doctor she'd ever met. Not just because he was honest and warm, but because there was something about him, something strangely familiar.

It was then that she realized exactly what it was. He had a wall around him, too. Built from those strange Rorschach paintings she'd seen around his office. He'd hinted at a past that he hadn't wanted to talk about, when he'd been a psychiatrist in Oxford instead of a general practitioner in a small Massachusetts town. What was it that he'd said about his old life?

"Sometimes it's better to burn it all down and start over. Sometimes we need to go where our memories cannot follow. Although they do anyway, don't they?"

She knew that feeling all too well.

Dr. Rockwell had his secrets, which meant they were probably Sai's secrets, too.

Maybe the doctor and his son aren't so different after all.

Meanwhile...

The old man wiped his hands with a dirty rag, for all the good it would do. Decades of grease had seeped into his pores— unwashable—and he wondered if at this point, more engine oil ran through his veins than blood. He'd opened Murphy's Auto Body in Ravenglass nearly thirty years back, and after all this time, he was still pretty much the only mechanic in town. That was good, but it also meant that the slow days were few and far between.

His wife couldn't do much about the condition of his hands, but she insisted on keeping his brown coveralls spick-and-span. And damned if that woman didn't do it, despite all the muck he got into each day. He was all bones and leather, but Ginny still kept him looking sharp in those coveralls. She was a good old girl, that was for certain, and had put up with all his nonsense for more years than he'd ever expected her to. He touched the name patch on his chest, the one she'd hand sewn for him in fire-engine red. Lucky for her, his name only had three letters to worry about: R-O-Y.

It had become a habit of his, touching that patch every once in a while. Just as a little reminder of Ginny. She used to come in every day at lunch so that they could eat a meal together, but she wasn't going out much lately, what with the cold weather making her arthritis flare up. So, Roy had gotten in the habit of meeting Howard down at Birdie's for a sandwich and coffee during his lunch break. Howard did the books for a used-car dealership down the way, and probably hadn't seen a day of hard manual labor in his life, but he was good company. They'd talk about cars, mostly—but sometimes Howard had a funny story about the old days, or Roy would have a tale to tell from his shift volunteering at the Ravenglass Fire Department. Roy knew that his days at the RFD were numbered—he had a hard time just walking around in his bunker gear, no less fighting fires wearing it. But he wasn't ready to quit. Not yet.

He glanced over at the clock on the far wall of the garage. Only 7:00 p.m., and already as dark as a thief's pocket. Technically the shop was closed, but one of his regulars had brought in his Caddy that morning with an engine light on, and Roy had been too busy with oil changes to take a look. He didn't want to head home without having a crack at it first. He picked up the phone and gave Ginny a call. She usually didn't mind him coming home late—but he liked to let her know nonetheless.

"Oh, I'm just workin' on that crochet for the Kings, hon," Ginny said when he asked what she'd gotten up to that day. "I feel so bad about their boy. Gotta do somethin' with my hands. I'll be at it all night, so you just take your time and be careful." After setting the old plastic wall telephone back in its cradle, Roy pulled the Caddy into the garage, turned up the volume on his radio, and got to work.

Everything checked out under the hood. Roy had a hunch that maybe something had gone awry in the undercarriage, so he kicked his creeper over to the car so he could scoot under and take a peek. On the oldies radio station, Brenda Lee was singing "A Good Man Is Hard to Find."

Roy hummed along as he slid beneath the Caddy and began meticulously checking each piece of the puzzle, one by one. His breath billowed out in clouds as he worked—even with the little propane heater running, the shop got real cold at night.

After five minutes, Roy was no closer to diagnosing the problem. Spark plugs were fine, the catalytic converter checked out, and there weren't any vacuum leaks, either. It was a real thinker, this one.

The radio started playing "Sleep Walk" by Betsy Brye. Boy, that one brought him back. He savored the last weeks before Thanksgiving, when the stations still played regular music. After that, it was wall-to-wall Christmas tunes until the new year. Ginny loved every minute, of course, but Roy could take it or leave it. There were only so many times he could hear Bing Crosby dreaming of a white Christmas before it was enough already.

Suddenly the song disappeared into a mess of static. Roy's brows furrowed. He'd never known his old radio to lose reception—it'd been working like a horse for going on thirty years. Would be a shame if the thing went on the fritz now . . .

Fortunately, the song reemerged a few seconds later, clear once again. He was about to get back to work when he suddenly saw someone standing at the foot of the Caddy.

The sight of the two feet gave him a start, and he banged his head against the underside of the car. "Ah!" he grunted in pain. Rubbing his head, he turned to look again at the person standing there. From his vantage point beneath the car, all he could see was the bottom of the man's tan-colored slacks and a pair of patent-leather shoes.

"We close at six," Roy called out, annoyed. "Come back tomorrow."

The shoes didn't move, and no one spoke.

"I said we're closed!"

After a moment, Roy sighed. It wasn't this guy's fault that he'd hit his head. No point taking out his anger on a stranger. "What, you break down on the road or somethin'?" he said, a little more kindly. "Call Triple-A."

Still, nothing.

Roy squeezed his eyes in frustration. All he wanted was a quiet evening with his music and his Caddy problem. But it looked like he wasn't going to get it. "Oh, all right. I'm comin'." With effort, he rolled out from under the car and hauled himself to his feet. "So," he began, brushing at the grit on his coveralls, "what seems to be the prob—"

But when he looked up to see who was waiting for him, no one was there.

"The hell?" Roy muttered. He walked to the back of the car, peered into the gloomy corners of the shop, and then stepped out into the frosty evening, his boots crunching on the light coating of snow on the ground. The world was silent, the road empty of cars and lit only by the occasional streetlight. *Strange*, he thought, walking back into the shop. *Guy must have given up and left, but he sure did it quick.*

It didn't even occur to him that there had been no footprints left behind in the snow.

Roy's head was throbbing where he'd bumped it. He gave it another rub, and his fingers came away stained with blood. "Damn." Ginny would definitely make a fuss—probably call Doc Rockwell to come check him out in the morning. She always worried too much.

He was making his way back to the creeper to continue his work when he saw something reflected in the Caddy's side-view mirror. He leaned down, squinting, and felt the blood drain from his face. It looked like someone was standing behind the car, right where the shoes had been. But the figure had no features—no clothes, no face. It was like darkness in the shape of a man.

"Hey!" Roy shouted, and he spun to see the back of the car. Again, no one was there. But when he glanced at the mirror a second time, the figure was back—closer now. It looked as if the thing was standing right behind him.

The pain in Roy's head was making him dizzy. His eyes locked on the mirror. The thing seemed close enough to be breathing down his neck.

He moaned, softly. Fear had robbed him of words. The radio was still playing, though "Sleep Walk" was almost done.

The last thing Roy saw were the words engraved at the bottom of the side-view mirror:

OBJECTS IN MIRROR MAY BE CLOSER THAN THEY APPEAR.

6

aturday was beautiful. Bright morning sunshine had burned through the thick cloud cover and driven back the biting wind, leaving behind a serene, unseasonably warm day. Evie walked with her mom toward the church, dressed in a handmade black wrap dress and gray wool coat. The sun should have been a welcome respite after weeks of gloomy weather, but instead it felt cruel. In movies, it was always raining at funerals. That dark, somber dreariness would have felt right that day. A warm, pleasant breeze didn't. The fact that the world didn't reflect her sorrow was like a slap in the face.

Ravenglass Congregational was a pretty little white church with a sage-green roof and a single steeple that tilted a little bit to the left. It probably hadn't been renovated in fifty years or more, but a paint job here and there had kept the place looking prim, if a little worn around the edges. The arched stained-glass window in the front of the building featured Tiffany-style white lilies on a sky-blue backdrop. Evie felt sick as she looked at them, remembering the sweet vanilla smell of Desmond's boutonniere on homecoming night.

Don't go there, she told herself. *He's not gone, no matter what they say . . .* But her nerves were already frayed.

A large crowd had gathered in front of the church, and the parking lot was packed with cars. It seemed like half the town had turned out for Desmond's "celebration of life." She saw the entire Sullivan family, Mom's boss from the inn, Ms. Jackson and some other teachers from RHS, and Dr. Rockwell, too. But from what she could tell, Sai wasn't with him.

Evie scanned the crowd for Tina, and finally found her standing with Chief Sànchez and the rest of her family, including what looked like her grandparents. Tina was wearing an ill-fitting black dress, and looked like she wanted to crawl out of her skin.

Evie turned to her mother and said, "I'm going to go talk to Tina. I'll find you when it's time to go in."

"Sure," her mom said. "I need to text Stan, anyway, just to make sure he didn't burn the house down making breakfast." Her brother had decided to stay home and make eggs and toast for Dad, who was heading over to Hobbie House before meeting them at Birdie's for the reception. "Are you sure you're okay?" Mom asked before Evie stepped away. There was worry in her eyes.

"No," Evie said, forcing herself to be truthful. "But what do you expect?"

Mom nodded and squeezed her hand.

Evie wound her way through the throng to Tina's side. "Hi," she said.

Tina turned to see her, and her posture immediately relaxed.

"Hi," she replied, and then seemed to brace herself for what came next. "So . . . how're you doing?"

Everyone seems to be asking me that, she thought. But instead of feeling exposed and burying her feelings deeper where they couldn't be seen, Evie tried to see it in a positive light. *I guess there are a lot of people who care about me.*

Out of the corner of her eye, she saw a huge photograph of Desmond in his football uniform set on an easel near the church door. She did her best not to look at it. "Terrible," she said. "You?"

Tina shook her head. "Tati convinced my mom to make me wear this dress they brought from PR. Apparently none of my other clothes are 'appropriate.'"

Evie lifted an eyebrow. "I did wonder about that," she said, eying the dress. "Did you find out anything more about why this ceremony is even happening? I mean, it's only been a few weeks, and they never found a . . ." She couldn't get herself to say *body*.

"My dad said that because of the physical evidence found inside the mine and its proximity to the mine shaft, the authorities concluded that Desmond must have fallen inside and that a body would never be recovered. That gave them grounds for presumption of death. And I think . . ." Tina glanced over at the church door, where Desmond's parents stood greeting mourners as they arrived. "I think they wanted to give Mr. and Mrs. King some closure."

As more people filed inside, Evie realized that if she wanted a seat, she'd have to hurry. "Thanks for letting me know," she said to Tina. "I'll find you later, okay?" Her friend nodded, and reluctantly turned back to her family, tugging at the hem of her dress.

Evie found her mom in the line of people, her anxiety growing the nearer they came to the door. There were so many people, she thought maybe she could get by unnoticed, but as soon as they got close, a big group moved inside, leaving Evie standing right in front of Mr. and Mrs. King.

Mr. King saw her first. He looked like he had aged ten years. His black suit was pressed, but the rest of him was wrinkled and worn. Even so, his resemblance to Desmond still sent Evie reeling. She wanted to run away, back to the car, back home, anywhere but here—but forced herself to remain. Mr. King locked eyes with her for a moment before looking away, shaking his head. Just then, she remembered how much she reminded Mr. King of Holly, the girl he used to love.

I guess now we both know what it's like to be a painful reminder of someone you've lost.

Mrs. King was wearing a simple black sheath dress and jacket, with a fascinator hat and netting pulled over the top half of her face. She looked the picture of decorum—that is, until she caught sight of Evie.

The forced smile on Mrs. King's face transformed to fury in an instant. "How dare you come here!" she whispered. "Today of all days? *Haven't you done enough?*"

"Mrs. King, I—" Evie stammered. "I just wanted to say—"

"I told you to stay away from him, but you just wouldn't *listen*," Mrs. King went on, quiet but full of rage. All around them, the remaining crowd filed into the church, murmuring, trying not to pry and failing. "You just had to get your claws into him—and now look! Look what's happened!"

Evie was paralyzed with horror and humiliation. Next to her, Mom was similarly frozen, her eyes flicking nervously from Evie to Mrs. King and back. "I'm so sorry," Evie said. "I never meant to—"

"Oh, I'm sure you didn't mean to," Mrs. King interrupted, her face contorted with anguish. "You're just an innocent victim, too, isn't that right?"

"Gloria . . . ," Mr. King said, putting a hand on her shoulder. "Let's go inside."

But Mrs. King wasn't finished. "If it weren't for you, he'd still be here!" she said, the last words devolving into a sob. "I'd still have my baby!"

Evie couldn't breathe. The accusation had sucked all the air out of her lungs. She felt her mother's arm around her shoulders, but still she couldn't move. Mr. King was bustling his sobbing wife into the care of an aunt and cousin waiting just inside, who surrounded her like a protective wall. He came back outside a moment later, an apologetic expression on his face.

"She's just . . . distraught," he explained to Evie and her mother. "Of course you're both welcome to come inside and pay your respects."

Mom nodded, but Evie could barely meet his eyes. She knew that Desmond had made the choice to go into the mine, and that she had nothing to do with what had happened to him there. So why did it still feel like it was all her fault?

Her pain was nothing compared with what Desmond's mother was going through. Whether or not Evie deserved her anger seemed almost irrelevant. In the end, Mrs. King was right. If Evie had never met her son, had never fallen in love with him and told him the truth about everything, they wouldn't be mourning him. Maybe losing him wasn't her fault, but Evie wasn't innocent, either.

Most of the church pews were already filled by the time Evie and her mom got inside, so they took a seat in the back corner. Sunlight poured through the windows on both sides, illuminating the dark cherrywood of the rafters and pews. The spiced, earthy smell of the place reminded Evie of Aunt Martha's reading room. *Frankincense and myrrh*, she remembered. Folding her trembling hands in her lap, Evie stared out the window into the mountains, and waited.

Within minutes, the minister appeared—a stocky, middle-aged man in a black robe and an embroidered white stole draped around his neck. The chatter among the assembly quieted immediately as he took his place behind the pulpit. "Grace and peace to you," the minister said in a deep, bell-like voice. "My name is Reverend Walker, and I'd like to welcome you to Ravenglass Congregational this morning. I know not all of you are parishioners here, but please know that these doors are always open to those in need of guidance, wisdom, and fellowship." He paused, and Evie could feel the tension in the room heighten as they prepared for his next words. "We gather here today on a solemn occasion. An occasion that no man of faith, no teacher, no coach, no friend or family member ever wants to imagine: the loss of a young person, standing at the edge of a very bright future. But today we do not simply mourn that loss; we join together to celebrate the life of someone dearly cherished by this community. One of Ravenglass's beloved sons, Desmond J. King."

Evie gasped, a little sob she immediately stifled. A woman nearby began to cry. In the pew in front of her, a line of boys she recognized from the RHS football team shifted in their seats, sniffling, their heads bowed. Outside, the sun shone, and what had been a welcome warmth quickly became stifling. Evie tried to breathe, but there was no oxygen in the room.

"And now," the minister continued, "please turn to hymn number eighty-one and join me in singing, 'How Great Thou Art.'" Evie took up a hymnal from the pew in front of her and did her best to sing along, but her voice barely rose above a whisper. After that, she clenched her teeth through three readings, recited by tearful cousins and friends, and braced herself when the minister cleared his throat and began again.

"From a young age," he said, "Desmond always wanted to help people—to cure whatever ailed them. I still remember the day, nearly ten years ago, when young Desmond happened upon another child who'd fallen down just outside after services and gotten a nasty cut on her knee. In a flash, he'd taken off his white jacket and pressed it to the wound until the girl's parents came to her rescue. Now, I'd bet Mrs. King wasn't too happy about the state of his church clothes, but that was Desmond all over. Always putting others before himself."

Evie tried to stop the memories from coming, but they flowed over her, unbidden. Desmond's hand, warm and smooth, holding hers like a prince in a fairy-tale ballroom.

Holding it above your heart will help stop the bleeding.

She put one hand over her mouth. *It's not true*, she thought. *He's still out there, I know he is.*

"As the years passed and Desmond grew into a young man,

everyone knew that he was destined for great things. To follow in his father's footsteps and be a leader in this beautiful community that he called home."

A beautiful prison is still a prison.

She remembered the pink sunlight on his face as they walked the mountain road, and the lopsided grin as he confessed that he wanted to move away from Ravenglass and become a nurse. Would that dream ever happen now? Or would the truth about what Desmond really wanted die with him?

No! Desmond isn't dead!

A silent battle raged within her, neither side ready to give in.

And then, someone whispered in her ear. So soft that it raised gooseflesh all along her neck.

"He's still here," it said.

Evie startled. Behind her sat the little boy in the red jacket she'd seen at school, sandwiched between his parents. He'd leaned forward in the pew, his face still ghostly pale, and watched her with eyes ringed with dark circles. "Shh, Jack. Be quiet," his mother muttered, pulling him back into his seat. "Sorry," she mouthed at Evie.

Evie turned back around, her heart hammering. The heat inside the church was unbearable now. The reverend's voice droned on, becoming incomprehensible as sound began roaring in her ears. She needed air or she was going to pass out. And that wasn't the kind of attention she wanted.

Lurching to her feet, Evie stepped out of the pew and hurried to the side door. "Evie!" her mother whispered after her. "Where are you going?"

Evie shook her head and didn't answer. There were probably

dozens of eyes following her every move, but she didn't care. She opened the door and slipped through, closing it quietly behind her.

A cool blast of air hit her as she stepped outside, and she felt better almost immediately. She leaned against the metal handrail, the dizziness fading with every breath. When she'd regained her bearings, she looked around and saw that she was standing on a short flight of stairs that led to the church cemetery.

Curious, Evie made her way down to walk among the stones. She wasn't ready to go back and face the rest of the service—not yet. She'd give herself five minutes and then return to her seat. Mom would understand.

The cemetery was small, protected from the encroaching vines and wild shrubbery by an old wrought-iron fence. She'd only ever been to historic cemeteries in the city—like the one at Trinity Church in Manhattan, where Alexander Hamilton was buried. That felt like being in a museum. This . . . this was different. It felt private. Personal. Despite the fact that there were nearly two hundred people sitting a few yards away from her inside the building, out in the graveyard the silence was complete.

Most of the headstones were at least seventy years old. She passed granite markers from the 1930s and '40s, whole and unbroken, but as Evie progressed farther into the cemetery, the graves got even older. The oldest ones were near the back fence, made of crumbling limestone and dated in the 1850s. *That would have been around Sarah Flower's time*, Evie thought with interest. She bent to study the graves more closely, her shoes sinking into the soft, loamy ground.

A cherub atop a small stone marked the grave of Anne Miller, who had died at the age of four. "Hush!" the epitaph read. "Angels hover near." Nearby, a pair of clasped hands were carved at the bottom of a faded grave for Samuel Taylor: "A true husband and loving father." Some of them had become unreadable, the words and memories of those who lay below worn away to nothing.

She stopped at a group of stones that all looked similar in shape and style. One had a broken chain at the top, another a pillar, similarly broken. A third had a sickle engraved among a sheaf of wheat, its blade curved around their stalks. "Here lies George Brown." "Ellis Williams." "Asa Davis." The names were familiar somehow, though she couldn't put her finger on why. Strangely, they all seemed to be men who had died in the same year: 1857. There were dozens of reasons why this could be—after all, Evie knew from her research that a cholera epidemic killed people worldwide throughout the 1850s—but it still struck her as odd. She brushed her fingertips along the words of Henry Anderson's grave, which read:

WE SHALL SLEEP, BUT NOT FOREVER,

THERE WILL BE A GLORIOUS DAWN.

WE SHALL MEET TO PART NO NEVER,

ON THE RESURRECTION MORN.

However, it was the last two gravestones Evie found that really left an impression on her. They were all simple limestone, with a spray of blossoms at the top of each. One was larger than the other, and read:

MARY AND WILLIAM FLOWER

DEVOTED WIFE AND MOTHER,

SHE HAS GONE TO HER HOME ABOVE

RELIEVED FROM THE TRIALS OF LIFE.

HE TOILED FOR HIS TOWN AND GOD,

HIS TRIALS ARE ENDED,

HIS REST IS WON.

The smaller grave had only a single flower—a rose with a broken stem. The engravings weren't as deep or carefully carved, as if they had been made in a hurry.

SARAH FLOWER, it read.

WE PART TO MEET AGAIN

BORN MAY 1, 1850, DIED DECEMBER 23, 1857

Evie realized that the grave must be a cenotaph because Sarah's body had never been found. The idea of an empty grave filled her with sadness. How could there ever be closure?

Empty, just like Holly's grave.

She swallowed. *And just like Desmond's will be.*

On the edge of a sudden wintry breeze rode the bittersweet scent of dying flowers. Evie shivered and rose to her feet, suddenly wishing she were back in the stifling press of bodies instead of standing out in the cold, alone.

The snap of a twig sent her whirling to see a figure about ten yards away, retreating toward the church. He had his back to her, but she'd recognize that leather jacket anywhere.

"Sai?" she said into the silence.

He stopped midstep but didn't turn around.

"What are you doing here?" she asked.

Sai faced her then, thumbs looped in his pockets. "Dad said I had to come," he said. "But he didn't say I had to go inside. I'm just messing about till it's over."

Evie threaded her way through the gravestones to meet him. "Did you know Desmond?" she asked.

He shrugged. "Knew *of* him, more like. Who didn't? The king and all. Seemed like a decent bloke."

Evie nodded. "He was."

Sai's eyes flicked to hers. Evie hadn't realized how dark they were—like deep pools. "I'm sorry," he said softly.

He must have known that she and Desmond had been to homecoming together, if not from school gossip, then certainly from the news. But he didn't ask her any questions, press her for details, or offer a pitying glance. He left it at those two words—*I'm sorry*. She appreciated that.

"How's Bonnie?" she asked, eager to change the subject.

Sai blinked.

"Bonnie? Your beloved motorcycle?" she went on. "Is she still traumatized from nearly being hit by a teenaged girl?"

A slow smile crept across his face, and he scoffed. "She's fine. Nothing a little buff won't sort out." He rubbed the back of his head. "You're all right, then?" he asked quietly.

Evie nodded. "I've had worse."

Sai chuckled. "Yeah," he said. "Tell you what: I'd rather be out riding than stuck here. Perfect day for it."

"I guess it is," Evie said, taking in the bright blue sky. She sighed, guilt tugging at her. She'd started to relax a little, talking to him. *You want relief from the pain, but you don't deserve it*, she thought. *Not yet. Not until you bring him home.* "I should get back in there," she said, the tightness returning to her chest. "Are you coming?"

"Nah, I'm good out here," Sai replied. "Maybe I'll go meet the neighbors, as it were." He gestured at the gravestones.

Evie started to walk past him toward the stairs, but hesitated. Something told her there was more to Sai's reluctance to attend the service than he let on. "Why won't you go inside?" she asked. "You said you didn't know Desmond, so . . ."

Sai offered her a tight smile. "Rather not talk about it, if that's all right with you."

There was that wall again. Of course, if he didn't want to tell her, that was his business. "Sure," she said. "Well, see you later, then."

"Later," he agreed.

As she walked past him, something underfoot—a protruding tree root perhaps—tripped her up. She started to fall, toppling right into Sai.

"Whoa there," he said as she caught herself against his chest. He reached out to steady her, his strong hand gripping her forearm. "If you keep falling down every time you see me," he said, chuckling, "I'll have to start wearing a hazard sign." She was embarrassed, but only for an instant. Because in the next moment, the world froze and went dim, like someone had thrown a blanket over the sun.

Evie's heart quickened.

Another vision.

She looked at Sai, but he was faded and blurry, though she

could still feel his soft leather jacket against her hand. Somewhere underneath, she felt his heart beating fast, just like hers.

She turned away from him, scanning the cemetery. "Holly?" she shouted. Her voice sounded strange and muted, like she was deep underground. "Are you there?"

Something flashed at the edge of the graveyard, just beyond the wrought-iron fence. There and gone, like frames flipping by in an old film reel. But the more she focused on that spot, the more that something seemed to materialize. The slender, dark shape of a girl in a black dress and bonnet.

Evie's breath caught in her throat. The girl's ginger hair tumbled down over her shoulders, cobwebs strung through it like a garland, as if she'd just come through some deep, dark place. Evie noticed for the first time that her left eye was green, but the right one—the one that had once been the gaping hole of a skull—was deep violet, the color of an old bruise. She stared back at Evie, her narrow, sharp face like a hollowed-out version of Evie's own.

Just like me.

"Holly!" A thousand questions spun through Evie's mind: *Where has she been all this time? Why am I seeing her now? What has she been trying to tell me?* Evie tried to run toward her, but it was like moving through water. "How do I find him?" she cried. "Please help me."

Holly shook her head. When she spoke, her voice was like a whisper in the wind, soft and labored. *"You've found him,"* she said. *"Look with him, look deeply, and have patience."* She pointed down toward Sarah Flower's grave.

"Found him?" Evie said, confused. "No, I haven't. What do you mean?"

She wanted to ask more but was distracted by something pulling at her ankle. At first, she thought she'd gotten tangled up in the tree root that had tripped her. She tried to pull her foot away, but the thing only held her tighter. She looked down and gasped.

It was a hand, reaching out from beneath the earth, and it was trying to pull her down with it.

7

E vie reeled in horror as the hand wrenched at her ankle, dragging her down with terrifying strength. She fell, and her
hands scrabbled on the mossy ground for something to hold
on to. Her nails scraped across the edge of a flat stone plaque, and
she tried to grip it with her fingertips. But the hand would not let
go, its fingers digging painfully into her skin. She searched for
Holly, but the specter of her cousin had vanished.

Desperate, Evie turned to look for Sai. She could see him a
little better this time. He still stood in the same spot, unmoving
and blurry. "Help me!" she cried, but her voice was swallowed up
by the sepia-toned world.

With all her might, Evie wrenched her leg away, until finally
the grip on her ankle faltered. She clambered back to her feet—
but managed only a couple of steps back toward Sai before another hand grabbed her, and another. Two, three, four of them
sprouted from the graves like unholy blooms. Flesh peeled like old
wallpaper off some of them—others were only bone. They grabbed

at her feet, her legs, the hem of her long dress. Caught, Evie felt herself falling again toward the cold earth, which she half expected to open up and swallow her.

No, no . . .

And then there were other hands on her shoulders, pulling her away. But these were different—warm and whole. They dragged her to her feet and straight out of the world.

Evie gasped as she found herself back in the bright morning, under a winter-blue sky. The warm hands released her, and she whirled to see Sai standing there, his lips parted in shock, his eyes wide.

It took a moment before Evie recovered enough to speak. "You . . . you saw it, didn't you?" she stammered. "You were there. You pulled me out . . ."

Sai shook his head. His copper skin was as pale as milk. "I don't know what you're talking about," he said. He took a step back.

"No, you're lying," Evie said, insistent.

"You've found him," Holly had said. Evie thought she was talking about finding Desmond, but what if she meant someone else? *"Look with him."*

"I don't know what you're on about," Sai said, his voice trembling with fear and anger. "But you'd better leave me alone." He turned and started walking away.

"Sai!" Evie called. "Please, wait!"

But he didn't stop. She watched until he turned onto one of the side roads off Main Street and disappeared.

Evie sighed. Her whole body was shaking, and she suddenly felt terribly weak. She made her way over to a wooden bench at the edge of the graveyard and sank down into it. It seemed like more than a coincidence—running into Sai twice in less than a week's time. *Why do I need him?* she wondered. *What's he got to do with all this?*

Her ankle was throbbing. Pulling her dress aside, she looked at it and saw four small bruises forming there. They were deep purple, and the exact shape and size of fingerprints. Fear lanced her body.

It's not possible . . .

The visions weren't real. They were just happening in her mind. They couldn't really hurt her.

Could they?

Inside the church, music swelled loud enough for Evie to hear from outside.

"'Amazing grace,'" the mourners sang, "'how sweet the sound, that saved a wretch like me! I once was lost, but now am found, was blind but now I see.'"

It took Evie another ten minutes to calm down enough that she could return to the service. Her hands wouldn't stop trembling, and she couldn't shake the feeling of the cold hand still clamped around her ankle. She pulled out her phone and stared at herself in the camera view, working to arrange her face in a way that looked somber, not horror-struck. Finally, she slipped quietly back inside the church and into her pew. A dozen heads turned to follow her. Evie caught Kimber glaring, her tearstained face a picture of unmasked hate.

As Evie settled in next to her, Mom reached out to pat her leg, a balled-up tissue pressed in one hand. Closing her eyes against the emotion roiling between the walls of the church, Evie clasped her hands and prayed that Holly was finally leading her in the right direction.

Afterward, Evie and her mother drove the short distance to Birdie's for the reception. The diner was already packed by the time they got there—the oldies radio station barely audible over the chatter, the air spiced with sesame oil, garlic, and gochujang. The huge posterboard of Desmond had been brought inside, and it presided over everything at the front of the restaurant. Many of the mourners were there—most of the football team, Kimber and the rest of the Sullivans, Desmond's family. Evie swallowed, feeling hot and stifled. She didn't want to be there, but she really needed to talk to Tina about what had just happened in the graveyard.

"Hey," Mom said, loud enough to be heard over the din. "There's Stan and your father in the corner booth."

Your father. Evie remembered when she was a little girl, it was always *"There's Daddy!"* Then later, it became *"go tell your dad"* this and *"your dad said"* that. But ever since the divorce, it had been *"your father."* So formal. So distant. She hadn't heard her mom say it much since they'd moved to Ravenglass, but there it was again. Evie craned her neck to see Stan sipping at a glass of Korean strawberry milk and Dad tapping at the table, a mug of coffee and a plate of soboro pastry in front of him. Unlike everyone else in the diner, who were in church clothes, Stan and Dad wore nearly matching black tops and jeans. When Dad caught sight of them, he raised two fingers in greeting. "You go," Evie told her mom. "I'll be right there."

Mom nodded and made her way over to the booth. Evie pushed through the crowd of people, past the counter where Birdie—resplendent in her bright yellow apron—shouted commands at her platoon of waitresses as dishes of steaming food appeared on the pass.

Scanning the restaurant for Tina, she slipped by the line of diners seated at the counter on old-fashioned metal stools, two of which were the same old men she'd seen eating there before. One thin and leathery in brown coveralls, the other round and rosy like a teapot. "You wouldn't believe these new coupes we've just got in, Roy," the round man was saying eagerly. "Sleek little numbers, with TVs on the dash bigger'n the one I got at home! You love to see it, but good luck fixin' those babies. Seems like you got to be some kinda computer genius to sort them out."

The thin man, Roy, said nothing. He simply stared blankly into the cup of coffee that a waitress had just filled. His friend didn't seem to notice, though, he just kept prattling on about cars. Jostled by the crowd, Evie accidentally bumped into Roy as she passed by. A little hot coffee glugged over the edge of the mug onto the man's hand, but he didn't flinch.

"Oh!" Evie said quickly. "I'm so sorry!"

Roy turned slowly, and Evie saw that his face was pale and slack, his eyes sunken. He looked at her, expressionless, despite the angry burn rising on the back of his hand. When he spoke, he hardly moved his lips at all. And despite the softness of his voice, she heard every word loud and clear.

"You should watch where you're going, little girl."

Evie felt a chill down her spine, and she nodded, wordless. Next to Roy, the round man was still going on and on. Evie suddenly felt desperate to be away from them, and moved toward the other side of the diner. She found Tina tucked into her usual booth.

"Where's your family?" Evie asked as she slid into the seat beside her. She was anxious to forget about her unpleasant encounter with the old man.

"Tati was tired, so they went home," Tina said with obvious relief. She tilted her glass of strawberry milk toward Evie. "I'm drinking my feelings. Want some? You probably need it even more than I do."

"You're not wrong," Evie admitted, taking a sip. "So listen," she went on, lowering her voice. "I saw Holly. Twice this week. The visions are back, and I think she's trying to tell me how to find Desmond."

"Really?" Tina replied, a touch of doubt in her voice. "Are you sure?"

Evie scoffed. She wanted enthusiasm—not hesitation. "Of course I'm not *sure*," she said, a hot flush rising on her cheeks. "I'm not sure of anything! But I *saw* her, okay? I saw Holly!"

Tina sat back in her seat. "Okay, fine," she said, raising her hands in surrender. "You saw her."

Evie sighed, the anger waning as quickly as it had come. "I'm sorry, I didn't mean to snap at you. You're, like, the only person I can talk to about this stuff. The last thing I want to do is push you away. I just . . ." She gestured at everything around her. "This . . . has been a lot. I think maybe I haven't been handling it as well as

I thought. I have to believe that he's still alive. But all this has been making it so hard."

Tina's face softened. "Yeah, I know. So what did Holly tell you?"

"She told me to find someone. At first, I thought she meant Desmond, but now I think she wanted me to find Sai Rockwell."

"Sai?" Tina looked confused. "Why him?"

"I have no idea," Evie admitted. "But both times I had the visions, Sai was there. And what's more, I think that he saw them, too."

"No way. He must be freaked."

"He is," Evie said. "But he won't admit it. He doesn't even want to talk to me. But if he's connected to this somehow, I have to find out more about him."

Tina's eyes flicked over Evie's shoulder. "Well, *he* might be able to help," she said.

Evie turned to see Dr. Rockwell come through the door of the diner in a short black peacoat. He looked around, nodding at the people who greeted him in turn. At first glance, Evie never would have guessed that Dr. Rockwell and Sai were father and son. The doctor was very fair, his brown hair almost fully turned to gray—totally unlike Sai with his wavy black locks and warm copper skin. But as she looked at him, Evie began to see similarities between the two. Their long, slender bodies and high cheekbones. The deep-set, intense eyes. She wondered what their relationship was like. She wondered what secrets they were keeping, and how she might root them out.

"I have an idea," Evie said after a moment.

"You're going to be sneaky, aren't you?" Tina asked.

"I'm going to be a little sneaky."

Tina smiled. "You'll text me later?"

"Of course."

"This is why I keep you around, you know," Tina said, swirling her straw in her glass. "For the entertainment value."

"I know," Evie said, smiling back. The expression felt alien on her face—it had been many days since she'd last smiled. Thank goodness for Tina. Her sense of humor had been Evie's saving grace since she'd arrived in Ravenglass. She hoped one day she could return the favor.

Evie made her way over to the doctor, who had moved to the counter and was waiting for Birdie to notice him. "Doctor Rockwell!" Evie called.

The doctor turned toward her voice and brightened when their eyes met. "Well, well, well," he said. "All healed up, are you?"

Evie touched her face where the rash had once been. "Yes," she said. "It was gone within a few days."

"Good, good," Dr. Rockwell said, shoving his hands into his coat pockets. "It's lovely to see you again, Miss Archer—though I wish it were on a less somber occasion. I understand you and Mister King were friends?"

"Yes," Evie replied. "We'd only known each other for a few weeks, but we had gotten . . . close."

Dr. Rockwell shook his head. "You've had a terrible shock, I'm sure."

Evie's ears perked up at that. *Now's your chance*, she thought. "Actually," she began, "now that you mention it, it has been really hard these past two weeks." She swallowed, hardly believing what she was about to say. "I was wondering if maybe I could come and, um, talk to you about it. I remember you telling me you used to be a therapist, right? Back in England?"

Dr. Rockwell blinked several times, clearly taken aback by her request. "I'm, ah, flattered," he stammered. "But as you say, I 'used to be' a psychiatrist. No longer. I can't treat you, Evie. But I do know a very nice woman two towns over—"

"I don't want a very nice woman," Evie insisted. "I want you."

Dr. Rockwell shook his head in puzzlement. "Me? But why?"

"You're the only doctor who's ever been honest with me," Evie said. "You're the only one I trust." And though she was making the request as a means to an end, that part, at least, was the truth.

Dr. Rockwell looked at her for a moment, troubled. "I couldn't very well do it at the office," he said. "I wouldn't want to set a precedent for—"

"I could come to your house," Evie broke in. It was incredibly forward of her, but the proposal was the key to her success. "Please," she added. "It's not easy for me to ask for help."

He rubbed his temple with two fingers, closed his eyes, and sighed. "If I allow this," he said, "and that is a big *if*, I'll have to get your parents' consent first. It would be unofficial therapy, off the books."

Evie's jaw tightened. She'd hoped to keep her parents out of this, but it looked like getting them involved was the only way. Surely they'd agree—after all, they'd been trying to get her into therapy again for ages. "Of course," she said. "They're sitting right over there." She pointed to the corner booth.

Dr. Rockwell looked and sighed again. "Right. Well, let's go talk to them."

Evie led the way through the crowd until they were standing

in front of the booth where Mom and Dad were gritting their teeth through small talk while Stan played a game on his phone. Both of them looked relieved when Evie and the doctor appeared.

"Doctor Rockwell, what a pleasant surprise!" Mom said, standing up.

"Isn't it just," Dr. Rockwell replied with a small, charming smile. "And please," he added, leaning in, "call me Peter."

Mom blushed, actually *blushed*, and said, "Oh—all right." After a long, awkward moment, she blurted, "Oh! Where are my manners? This is my son, Stan, and my, uh—" She faltered, and then pressed on. "My ex-husband, Robby."

Dad reached out a thick, muscled hand, all the while giving Dr. Rockwell a none-too-subtle once-over. "Pleasure to meet you," Dad said, shaking the doctor's hand firmly.

To Dr. Rockwell's credit, he didn't even flinch. "The pleasure's all mine," he replied. If he noticed the tension in the air, he had the grace not to respond to it. Clearing his throat, he began. "So, your daughter Evie here has come to me with an interesting proposal that I really must discuss with you."

Mom's and Dad's eyes met for an instant, confused and curious. Evie laced her fingers together nervously.

"Back in Oxford I had a private practice—not as a GP but as a psychiatrist. Evie discovered this when I treated her last month, and now she's asked if she could come speak to me at my home about some of the experiences she's had of late. I told her that she could just as easily see a practicing therapist, but . . . well, she was really quite insistent that it be me. I realize this is highly irregular, and I completely understand if you don't—"

"We're fine with it," Mom broke in.

Dr. Rockwell froze, his eyes flicking back and forth from Mom to Dad. "Are—are you certain?"

Dad looked at Mom. "Yes, are we?" he asked pointedly.

Mom gave him a warning look. "If Evie wants to talk to him," she said in her sweet-but-dangerous tone, "then I think that's wonderful, and that we should let her do what she thinks is best for her mental health."

Evie could see the muscles in her father's jaw working hard to keep his mouth shut. "Fine," he said. "If my daughter wants to talk to you, then I guess that's what she'll do."

"Well, all right then," Dr. Rockwell said with a shrug. "If you think it will help, she can start one afternoon next week. I'm usually free on Tuesdays."

Mom was ecstatic. "Perfect," she said. "Thank you so much, Doctor—I mean, Peter. It means a lot to me that you'd take the time out of your busy schedule for my Evie." Looking at her, Evie felt a stab of guilt for creating this whole ruse just to get closer to Sai. *Mom is still worried about me*, she thought, and wished it wasn't so.

Evie noticed her father looking at her, but when she met his eyes, he looked away. She could tell he was upset, but she couldn't really understand why. After all, she was finally doing what they'd wanted her to do—willingly!

Whatever. Evie didn't care. What mattered was that her plan had worked.

"Mom, can we go now?" Stan said, tired of his game. "My foot hurts."

"Sure, honey," Mom replied, pulling Stan's crutch from under the table.

"Remember to keep that elevated, all right?" Dr. Rockwell said. "And do your exercises!" He turned to Mom. "I'll be in touch about the appointment for Evie."

"Great," Mom said. "Thanks again."

Dr. Rockwell gave Evie a tight smile before melting back into the crowd. Mom handed Evie her credit card. "Can you pay the bill so I can help your brother outside?" she asked.

"I can take care of it," Dad retorted.

"It's fine," Mom said. "I don't need you to pay."

Dad sighed heavily and followed Mom and Stan toward the door. Card in hand, Evie made her way to the counter and handed it and the bill to Birdie.

Birdie took them, looked at the bill, and then back at Evie. "You didn't eat," she said accusingly.

"Oh, yeah. I'm sorry, Birdie. I guess I didn't have much of an appetite today."

Birdie frowned. "If you're sad, you should eat. If you don't eat, then you're angry on top of sad, and then where does that leave you?"

Evie opened and closed her mouth. "I . . . I don't know."

"Nowhere good!" Birdie exclaimed. Turning around, she pulled a soboro pastry out from under a glass dome and stuck it into a brown paper bag. "Free of charge," she said, handing it over.

Evie took the bag, which smelled like cake and peanut butter. "Thanks," she said.

The ghost of a smile crossed Birdie's serious, pink-cheeked face, and then she turned to shout more commands into the steaming kitchen.

"How's Mama Bird?" Evie asked. The chair where Birdie's elderly mother always sat was empty. "I haven't seen her in a little while."

"Sick," Birdie said with a worried expression. "Happened over-night, a few days ago. Hasn't been herself since."

"That's awful," Evie replied. "I hope she feels better soon."

Birdie's eyes crinkled. "You're a good girl," she said, patting Evie's hand. "A little stupid, but very good."

Evie smirked. "Bye, Birdie," she said. She started toward the door and caught the same old man staring at her from his stool at the counter. His friend had gone, and his coffee sat untouched. She thought he would turn away once he saw her looking back at him, but he didn't. He simply sat, unblinking, his eyes oddly flat.

Why did she get the sense that other eyes were on her, too? She scanned the crowd, searching, and caught glimpses of people turned her way—but whenever she tried to focus on them, the crowd shifted and changed. Across the room, Desmond's smiling face loomed, frozen.

I have to get out of here.

She rushed out the door and didn't look back.

Meanwhile...

As soon as Gloria King and her husband arrived back from Birdie's—their car laden with flower wreaths and sympathy bouquets—the family dog was at their feet, whining to go out. They'd remained at the diner until every guest had gone home, then helped Birdie and her staff clean up the mess left behind. Meaning that Rocky had missed his midafternoon walk and wasn't shy about letting them know how he felt about that.

"Okay, Rocky, okay," Mrs. King said, setting down her parcels on the dining room table.

Mr. King came in after her, silent and empty-handed. He tossed his keys into the silver dish on the counter, then made his way to the family room and sat in the rose-colored easy chair without even taking off his shoes.

"I'll take him," Mrs. King said unnecessarily, as it was clear that Mr. King didn't intend to. She reached for the red harness and leash hanging on a hook by the door.

Mr. King said nothing.

Mrs. King fastened the harness around the dog's body while Rocky licked her cheek. He was a black dog with white paws and a white blaze over his face—a mishmash of boxer, beagle, German shepherd, and American pit bull that the Kings affectionately called their "super mutt." Desmond had seen a post about him on the local Humane Society's social media page when he was twelve years old and had begged his parents to adopt him.

"I'll do my homework every night without you asking, *and* take out the trash," she remembered him saying. "He's been there for over a year, Mom. Nobody wants him. But *I want him*. Please?"

Gloria had struggled with the decision. She hadn't grown up with dogs. She thought they were too much work, and the Kings already had their hands full. But her son's pleading face had done her in. He never asked for much, so when he did, she had a hell of a time saying no.

To his credit, Desmond had done most of Rocky's caretaking over the years. He had fed him, walked him, picked up his poop from the yard. Sure, Mrs. King had taken over some of those responsibilities here and there once Desmond was on varsity and had practice every day after school, but it wasn't until two weeks ago—until he disappeared—that Rocky had become her full-time job.

She was amazed at how much Desmond's absence affected the dog. At first, he wouldn't leave Desmond's room. He'd sit at the foot of the bed, curled in a tight black ball, and would cry piteously if anyone tried to get him out. He didn't eat for three days. After a week, he started acting a little more normally, but anyone could see that Rocky was in mourning just as much as they were.

She had never really loved the dog like she did after that.

In the mudroom, Mrs. King quickly swapped her black dress flats for sneakers, and her wool coat for a puffer jacket. She'd change clothes after she came back from the walk.

Rocky made a beeline out the front door as soon as she opened it. She followed him into the front yard, almost as relieved to be outside as he was. Their house was beautiful—spacious and tastefully decorated—but without Desmond in it, it felt like a tomb. Too empty, too quiet. James had taken to sitting in front of the TV for hours at a time, and every morning there was a little less whiskey in the bottle on the bar. They were in the same house, but he felt untouchable, drifting away from her on the tide, and she didn't have the energy to try to reach him. She was using every ounce of it to keep from drowning in her own despair.

A blanket of early evening clouds had covered up the sky, dropping the temperature at least ten degrees. Mrs. King zipped her puffer coat up to her chin, shrugging against the cold. She and Rocky had gotten into the habit of going up the mountain road to the quarry and back—about a thirty-minute walk. The road was steep and treacherous with loose gravel and stones, which forced her to concentrate on her footing and had her panting within minutes. She liked that. Anything to stop her from thinking.

That day, though, the thoughts still came.

Thoughts of her beautiful boy, rotting in the dark.

She gritted her teeth against a moan that came, unbidden, from deep in her belly. The face of Evie Archer—or was it Holly Hobbie?—rose up in her mind. The fruits of that family tree were poison. She knew this. She'd known it since high school, since she'd had to rebuild James from the wreckage that Holly had left behind. And now, another one just like her had come into the life they'd built and destroyed it. She centered all her pain and anger on that wide-eyed face, and it gave her the strength to keep going. James was broken, and someone needed to be there to keep the household and the quarry running. It wasn't just her family at stake—the whole town depended on them. So if she needed to fuel her fire with rage, if she needed someone to blame to stop from falling apart, then she was going to damn well blame Evie Archer and not think twice about it.

Mrs. King walked briskly up the mountain road behind Rocky

and hardly even broke a sweat. When they reached the top, they turned back toward home. They were halfway down the mountain again when Rocky stopped and sniffed the air, hackles raised.

"C'mon, boy," Mrs. King muttered. "Let's go. It's getting dark." It was only four o'clock, but the cloud cover that had returned that afternoon made it seem like dusk. She tugged on the leash, but Rocky didn't budge. He just stood there, staring into the woods. Then he started to whine, straining against his lead. Mrs. King studied the place where he was looking but saw nothing. Probably just a squirrel or a rabbit, camouflaged against the forest floor. Rocky could never resist a rabbit. "Let's go," Mrs. King repeated, irritation creeping into her voice. The day had finally caught up to her. She was exhausted. All she wanted to do was crawl into bed.

Then, before she even realized what was happening, Rocky turned around and squirmed out of his harness. "Hey!" Mrs. King said in alarm. She lunged for him, but the dog slipped away and took off like a bullet into the woods.

"Rocky!" Mrs. King screamed. In a panic, she left the road and followed him into the trees, desperately trying to keep the dog in sight. She ran, slipped, fell against the rocky ground, and rose up again, ignoring her stinging hands and the dry leaves stuck in her hair. She kept running. "Rocky!" She saw his black form darting into a gathering of trees and followed close behind.

I've already lost Desmond, she thought. *I'll be damned if I'll lose his dog, too.*

She reached the trees thirty seconds later and leaned down to catch her breath. "Come here, boy," she wheezed. "You want a treat? Come get a treat." She saw Rocky ahead, facing the opposite direction and whining. She squinted into the fading light, trying again to see what he was looking at.

A shadow near one of the trees moved.

She stared at it for a few seconds. The blood drained from her face.

"Desmond?" she whispered.

As if in a dream, Mrs. King stumbled toward the shadow, one hand reaching out to it. "Desmond? Is that you?"

The shadow fled, and Rocky chased it deeper into the woods. Crying now, hysterical, Mrs. King followed. Branches whipped at her face as she went, and she nearly fell at least two more times, tripped up by the underbrush. Finally, she found herself in the very last place she wanted to be.

Standing before the mouth of the gold mine.

She scanned the area, blinking, trying to get her bearings. How had she ended up here? She must have gotten turned around somewhere, because she should have passed the mine much earlier on her walk. Rocky was sitting motionless in front of it, his whines replaced by a deep, low growling. Mrs. King fell to her knees, wrapping her arms tightly around him before he could run away. "Oh, you stupid dog," she cried into his short black fur. After a moment, she clipped the harness back around him and cinched it tight. She looked everywhere for the shadow she'd seen, but it had vanished into thin air.

She gazed through tears at the yawning hole of the mine. Bits of yellow crime scene tape flapped in the breeze, the sole evidence of everything that had happened there. Other than that, it was wide open, and black as pitch.

Mrs. King's rage returned. Where were the wooden boards she'd demanded be nailed to the opening, closing it forever, preventing anyone else from going down there again? She'd watched them hammer them into the old beams, she'd bought the nails herself. How could they all be gone?

If some neighborhood kids did this, I'm going to make them wish they'd never been born . . .

Not only that, but just for a moment, some random cruelty had made her believe that Desmond was back. Some trick of the light, or of her shattered mind.

Suddenly, her anger at Evie and the kids and the dog blossomed into anger at everything in the whole world, a world that had seen fit to murder something perfect for no good reason at all, and not even leave her a body to bury.

Mrs. King had always kept it together; was always in control. But right then, no one was watching. She was alone on the mountain. So she stared down into that darkness, that place that had swallowed up her boy, and she screamed all her pain down into it.

"Give him back!" she wailed. "Give him back to me, damn you!"

Rocky's growls changed to frightened barks. The sound pulled Mrs. King out of herself and back into focus. Her screams must have spooked the dog. She quieted down and started to pet him. "It's okay, Rocks," she said, soothing. "I'm sorry, I'm sorry."

Get ahold of yourself, Gloria.

But Rocky didn't settle. He just kept barking, each one getting a little higher pitched. He started to back away from the mouth of the mine. Sniffing and wiping her nose on her sleeve, Mrs. King got to her feet. "What is it, boy?" she whispered. "Is there something down there?"

She took one step toward the opening. Two.

The darkness inside was total, like a solid form that could be touched.

A subterranean breeze carried a scent to her from within. Not a smell she'd expect, like the mineral tang of stone or the smell of still water.

It was the smell of lilies.

She took another step, and her foot crossed the line of shadow cast by the overhanging cliffside.

Something within wrapped around her ankle like a snake. With a small, startled scream, Mrs. King was pulled inside, cutting off the sound abruptly.

There one moment—the next, gone.

Rocky barked once more, backing away, and then ran full tilt back down the mountain, his red leash trailing after him.

8

Two stone lions guarded the entrance to the Rockwells' house in Edgewood, a small, careworn Cape Cod the color of ash. Evie stopped to look at the lions as she walked up the path to the front door, peering at their featureless, lichen-covered faces. From the look of them, Evie thought they probably predated the current owners. They might have been quite formidable once, but now they just looked sad, frozen forever in a toothless snarl. A white Land Rover was parked in the driveway, and nearby, nestled behind a cluster of hedges, was a separate garage. Evie could hear rattles and clanks coming from that direction, and the sound of music. She didn't recognize the song, but it sounded British and angry.

She smiled with satisfaction. Sai was home. As it was a Tuesday afternoon, she'd assumed he would be, but there was always the chance he'd be out somewhere, which would have been a real pain. Sure, she could have chased him around the school or hunted him in town, but cornering him at home just seemed a whole lot easier. Now all he had to do was stay put until her session with Dr. Rockwell was finished. Not only that, but she was betting that the conversation with Sai's dad might prove fruitful as well. Holly said she needed him, but to get Sai on her side, she needed to understand his connection to this. Failure wasn't an option.

Evie knocked on the door. It opened a few moments later to reveal Dr. Rockwell standing there in a rust-colored sweater, jeans, and brown leather loafers softened with age. "Come in, Evie," Dr. Rockwell said. "I've just put the kettle on. You okay with builders?"

Evie was taken aback both by the doctor's casual dress and by the question. "What's builders?"

"Just what we English call a strong cup of tea," he replied, leading her through a cramped hallway into the kitchen. "One you can stand a spoon in, as they say." The house was clean and comfortably untidy, but clearly lacked what Evie's mom would describe as a "feminine touch."

"Sure, I love pretty much any kind of tea," Evie answered, taking everything in.

"Milk and sugar?"

"Yes, please."

After pouring the tea and handing Evie a bone china mug decorated with blue flowers, he led her into a small study. There was an armchair and a couch—just as there had been in the office of Dr. Mears, her old psychiatrist—but that was where the similarity ended. Unlike the stately, plush Manhattan office, this room was warm and welcoming in its disarray. The couch and chair took up the center of the room, along with a low coffee table. By the window, an aging laptop computer sat on a wooden desk, surrounded by piles of books and mugs sprouting ballpoint pens. Framed pictures covered the walls: an oil painting of the Bridge of Sighs, an old map of Oxfordshire printed in yellows and greens, and a few more of Dr. Rockwell's strange Rorschach paintings in bright watercolors. There was also a small print of Alice from her adventures in Wonderland. The young heroine was pulling aside heavy drapes to reveal the little door hidden behind them, a key in her hand. Evie knew the scene well. Alice finds the door to the Queen's Garden, but she's too large to fit through it. She goes through one transformation after another—nearly drowning in her own tears—before she finally gets where she wants to go.

"You like Alice?" Evie asked, delighted and a bit surprised. Dr. Rockwell was a middle-aged man; what interest could he possibly have in a children's story? Sure, it was her favorite book, but she always worried people would think it was childish to still love it as she did.

"Oh, yes," Dr. Rockwell replied. "He lived in Oxford most of his life, you know—Lewis Carroll. Or rather, Charles Dodgson. Complicated man. Brilliant, though. I like that drawing most of all. When I was a psychiatrist, I used it to remind my patients that in order to reach our destination, we must often change in ways we don't think possible. Like Alice, we must be elastic with our sense of self, enough to allow room for the idea of being—not someone else—but a version of us we never even knew was there." His eyes lingered upon the drawing, wistful, before turning to her and gesturing toward the couch. "Shall we begin?"

But Evie was looking at another picture on the wall, smaller than the rest. It was a photograph of a woman with wavy black hair just past her shoulders, bright copper skin, and eyes like dark pools. She was sitting on a bench in a beautiful, sunny garden, and she was laughing—an open-mouthed, unabashed laugh. She was touching something on top of her head, a crooked daisy-chain crown. Her other hand was around the waist of a young boy straddling her knee, a boy with skin and hair just like hers. He looked four, maybe five years old. The woman was looking at whoever was holding the camera, but the boy—the boy only had eyes for her.

Dr. Rockwell noticed Evie staring at the picture, and his face darkened.

"Is that—?" Evie began.

Dr. Rockwell cleared his throat and set his teacup down on the table before taking a seat in the armchair. "Yes, that's Nagasai and Mrs. Rockwell," he said, his voice strained. "Chandravathi."

There was an awkward pause as the unasked question hung in the air between them. *Why isn't she here?*

"She died," Dr. Rockwell said, the words falling from his lips like two stones. "Three years ago. There was an accident in the car, with a lorry."

Evie's hand instinctively went to her mouth. "Oh," she breathed. "I'm so sorry." Her mind whirled as certain things—the family's immigration to the middle of nowhere in Massachusetts, Sai's un-willingness to enter the church—suddenly made a lot of sense. Those walls that the doctor and Sai had built up, they were pro-tecting *this*. She felt awful for bringing it up, and didn't know what else to say.

"It's all right," Dr. Rockwell said, waving her concern away. He was still looking at the picture, his eyes distant. "She died instantly—that's what they said. Knowing that she didn't suffer gave me a lot of peace." He nodded, winding his long fingers into a tangle in his lap. "But Sai was with her. In the car. His heart stopped for two minutes before they brought him back. And even then, we weren't sure . . ." His voice trailed off, and Evie could see him reliving those memories. She couldn't imagine what that must have been like, to be alone and reeling from a devastating loss, but unable to mourn because of the fear of losing another.

Then, something else occurred to her. Maybe, just maybe, that was the key to Sai's connection with Evie.

Dr. Rockwell sniffed, and then shook himself and glanced back at her with a rueful smile. "You see? This is what you get from a washed-up therapist. You listening to me instead of the other way round."

"I don't mind," Evie said, snapping back to attention. She cupped her tea in both hands. "It makes you seem like a real person, instead of some kind of robot."

"Your old doctor must have been a real winner, eh?" Dr. Rockwell said, leaning back to grab a small notebook and a ballpoint pen from the cup on the desk. "Well, no robots here, Miss Archer. Only supremely flawed and very real, flesh-and-blood men."

Evie chuckled. "You seem like a really good therapist," she said. "Why did you stop?"

Dr. Rockwell tapped the cover of the notebook with his pen, a tragic smile creasing his long, craggy face. "'Physician,'" he said solemnly, "'Heal thyself.'" Then he looked up at her. "Now, enough about me. Let's talk about you."

Evie was amazed at how quickly the hour passed. She talked to Dr. Rockwell about a lot of things—Desmond, moving away from New York, the divorce. She managed to avoid mentioning anything . . . supernatural . . . with relative ease. Turned out, she had plenty of problems not including her ability to communicate with shadows. Although she hadn't intended to treat her time with Dr. Rockwell as a real therapy session, it ended up being one anyway.

"You're far from the only one dealing with grief around here," Dr. Rockwell said as they were wrapping up. "Just remember: Everyone grieves differently." He slapped his thighs with both hands. "So. Again next week?"

Evie nodded. "I'd like that." She was surprised to find she meant it.

He walked her to the door, and moments later she was outside again, flanked by the faceless lions. She turned her coat collar up against the chill and listened. The same punk rock still spilled from the open garage. Taking a deep breath, she wound her way around the hedge toward the music.

Sai was sitting on the concrete floor of the garage in front of the Bonneville, dressed in a burgundy hoodie and ripped jeans. His wavy black hair was tucked behind his ears, and the remnants of the scrapes and cuts on his face were hidden behind a couple of days' worth of dark stubble. The motorcycle was raised a few inches off the ground on a black metal stand, sleek as a panther. Unlike the house, the garage was utterly tidy—every tool hung neatly on hooks along its walls, and the various plastic bottles of oils and fluids stood with military precision along the back of the wooden worktable. With the music masking her footsteps, Sai didn't even notice her arrival. Evie watched him for a moment, his hands glistening with grease as he gently rubbed at the machinery inside the back tire with a soft yellow towel. He looked totally at peace, and she felt a pang of guilt for what she was about to do.

"Hi," she said.

Sai started at the sound of her voice and jerked his head in her direction. When he saw who it was, his brows furrowed. "Evie," he said, a note of nervousness in his voice. "What are you doing here?"

Evie felt her cheeks get hot. She wasn't in the habit of being where she wasn't wanted, but this was too important. "I started seeing Dr. Rockwell for therapy, and this was my first day. I heard the music and figured you were here, so I thought I'd come say hello."

Sai scoffed. "Dad doesn't do therapy anymore."

Evie shrugged. "He's doing it for me."

"Huh," Sai muttered, and then went back to the business of his motorcycle, picking up a spray bottle and carefully misting the machinery he'd just wiped down. He seemed to be making a deliberate effort not to look at her.

Sai clearly wanted to be left alone—he'd made that abundantly clear back in the cemetery—but Evie couldn't just abandon the plan after it had worked so beautifully. But the discomfort of standing there, watching him, was almost unbearable.

Evie bit her lip. "What, um . . . what are you doing there?" she ventured.

He stopped misting and wiping, but said nothing.

"Sai?"

Finally, he looked at her. His lips were pressed into a thin line. "What do you want from me?" he said, barely loud enough to be heard over the music.

Evie laced her fingers together and looked at them. "I just . . . want to talk."

When she looked back at Sai, he was staring at her with obvious exasperation. He shook his head. "I'm cleaning the chain," he finally said. "I try to fix her up after every couple rides. The country roads can throw up a lot of grit. Are you satisfied now?"

Evie watched silently as Sai went back to his work. She waited about thirty seconds and said, "How old is she? Your Bonnie."

He sighed. Deep and weary. But then: "She's a 2011 model. Classic. But I've only had her a couple years. Got her for a song. Half of what she was worth."

Evie could sense he was loosening up. A little. "She's a really nice bike," she said, her voice urging him to continue.

He did. "After I got her, I did some bodywork, got new tires, and replaced the old handlebars with clip-ons to give her more of that café racer feel," he went on. "I finally got the exhaust wraps on a few months ago. Makes her a little noisy, but I like the sound, so I don't mind."

It was the most Evie had ever heard him say. She could see his body slowly relaxing as he spoke about something he loved. "I've never ridden one before," she said, thoughtful. "Why do you like it so much?"

Sai stopped what he was doing and sat back, considering. Apparently, she'd hit him with a legitimately interesting question. "Lots of reasons, I guess," he finally said, gazing past her to the road beyond. "But mostly, I love the speed. Rocketing down the back roads, taking the curves, the bike reacting to every movement of your body. It's this . . . breathless, insane freedom. You're alone, and the world is rolling off your back, and nothing can reach you. Nothing." His eyes flicked to hers and then away, as if he hadn't meant to be so honest.

"That sounds nice," Evie said quietly. "Being unreachable. You're not supposed to be able to run away from your problems, but—"

"But with a fast bike, you can try," Sai finished, with an almost imperceptible grin.

Evie blushed again, but this time for a different reason.

Stop messing around and get to the point, she told herself.

But before she could broach the subject, Sai got up and walked over to her. He smelled like kerosene, sharp and intoxicating. "Want a ride home?"

"What?" she said, taken by surprise.

"Getting late now, it'd be a treacherous walk. Anyway, you said you've never ridden. No time like the present. Just give me a second to set up and you can ride on the back."

"But—"

A moment later, a motorcycle helmet was tossed her way. She caught it in both arms and stared at the thing, dumbstruck. *Why is he doing this?* "Are you trying to scare me off, or something?"

Sai was shedding his hoodie and pulling on the ubiquitous leather jacket. "What if I am? Is it going to work?" he said.

She considered that. "No."

He sighed and shook his head. Again, there was that little smile. "Well, guess I'll give you a ride, anyway." After adding extra foot pegs to the back of the bike, he led Bonnie off her stand and rolled her to the entrance of the garage. "Get on, then."

Evie regarded the heavy black helmet with unease. "Don't you need one?" she asked, remembering his bare head when she first saw him.

"My skull is harder than yours," he said, and tilted his head toward the seat behind him.

Evie sighed, exasperated. "Fine, fine," she said, and fitted the helmet over her head. It wasn't heavy, but looking through the visor made the world look even darker. Then she ungracefully mounted the bike, scooching herself up close to Sai and setting her feet on the pegs.

A moment later, the motorcycle roared to life. It hummed underneath her like a wild thing, eager and hungry.

"Don't go too fast, okay?" Evie shouted over the engine, her stomach fluttery with excitement.

"Hold on," Sai replied.

Evie hesitated, half wondering if touching Sai would cause her to have another vision. But when she wrapped her arms around his waist, nothing happened. She relaxed, but only for an instant. Because then the bike was moving, rolling smoothly down the drive and onto the road. And then, with a throaty rumble, they were flying.

Evie gasped, and reflexively squeezed herself against Sai's body as they sped past houses, straight out of Edgewood, until there were only thick woods on either side. She felt his broad chest underneath the thin leather jacket, and under that, the thrumming of his heart. She didn't know where he was going, but it certainly wasn't the most direct route to Hobbie House. He sped down winding roads, cresting hills, and Evie's belly filled with butterflies every time they rocketed down the other side. Without slowing down, they raced around hairpin turns, Evie's body moving with his as the bike leaned sideways, caressing the edge of the road. On her right, the trees opened up to reveal a vista of naked forest spread out just below, the crooked finger of the Blue River snaking through it. Beyond that, dark mountains loomed.

Evie took it all in, suddenly consumed by the breathless joy of simply being alive.

As they reached the straightaway up to Hobbie House, Sai put on one final blast of speed before rolling to a stop at the base of her driveway. He flipped the kickstand, leaned the bike onto it, and dismounted with ease. His face was flushed and radiant, his black hair windswept. "There you are, then," he said, giving Bonnie a satisfied pat.

Evie's legs were jelly when she stepped off the bike, her body feeling like it was still moving at eighty miles per hour. She stumbled like a drunk, and Sai steadied her, laughing. "I told you not to go too fast!" she said, pulling off the motorcycle helmet.

"I didn't," Sai retorted. "I went just fast enough."

She tried to be mad at him, but a giggle escaped her lips, betraying her.

What are you doing? A voice inside Evie's head snapped her out of her adrenaline haze and back to reality. *You're supposed to be figuring out how to use this guy to find Desmond, but instead, you're flirting with him!*

Shame washed over her like a cold shower. She needed to focus. She'd wasted too much time already.

"Thanks for the ride," she said, handing the helmet back to

him. "Hey, um . . . before you go, I've been meaning to ask you something. When we were in the graveyard, there was a moment . . ." She faltered. Where did she even begin?

Sai's radiance faded the moment she said the word *graveyard*.

"You saw something, didn't you?" Evie said, moving closer to him.

Sai shook his head. "No," he said roughly.

"Yes, you did. You saw the same thing I did," Evie shot back. "A girl in a bonnet and a long dress—and those hands, those horrible dead hands grabbing onto me and dragging me down. I know you saw them because you pulled me out of it. You knew what was happening. You saw it the first time, too, when we met on the road. The gunshot, and the blood—"

"Stop it," Sai said, a little louder now. His nostrils flared. "You know, for a second there, I really thought you were interested in *me*. Guess I was wrong." He started to turn back to the bike.

"Wait!" Evie pleaded. "Look, I'm sorry. I'm really not trying to deceive you. It's just that . . . here's the thing . . ." She struggled to put any of it into words.

Just tell him. You've got nothing to lose!

"Desmond is alive," she blurted.

Evie registered the incredulous look on Sai's face. *No turning back now.* She kept going. "Almost no one believes it except for me," she said. "I'm the only one who can find him, and for some reason, you're the only one who can help me do it." She paused for breath, and was grateful that Sai was still listening. "The night that Desmond got lost," she continued. "I found something. This . . . place. I know it sounds crazy, but I swear it's the truth."

She told him everything. About Holly's attempts to pull her

down into the darkness, Sarah Flower and the legend of the Patchwork Girl, and how she went down into the gold mines to rescue Stan. The whole time, Sai stayed silent, his face expressionless.

"While I was down there, in the Shadow Land," Evie went on, "I could have sworn I heard Desmond's voice calling me. Right before I left, Holly warned me that something else lived down there. I got the feeling that she and Sarah were afraid of it—that maybe it was the thing that kept them there in the first place. I think—" She took a deep breath. "I think that thing, whatever it is, took Desmond. He didn't fall down a mine shaft. Something has him. And it's up to me to get him back."

She fell silent. The whole story had probably taken only ten minutes to tell, but it felt like hours had passed while she'd spilled her guts out there on the street. Evie gripped her hands into fists, waiting to see what Sai would say.

He scoffed. "This is mad," he said, pointing at her. "You're mad."

Just a month ago, Evie would have agreed with him. But things had changed. "Maybe I am," she replied. "But I'm telling the truth, and you know it. *You saw it, too.*"

Sai grimaced and looked at the ground. "Even if I believed you," he said, "what does all this have to do with me?"

"I didn't understand it at first," she admitted. "But I think I do now. After I got out of the mine, I couldn't communicate with Holly anymore. I tried, because I thought she'd know how to get Desmond back, but the connection was gone. Nothing but little whispers of her in my dreams. Until the day I met you."

"But I didn't *do* anything," Sai argued.

"You died, Sai," Evie said. "In that car accident."

Sai stiffened. "How did you—?"

"Your dad told me," Evie said, apologetic. "It just came out in conversation. I'm sorry—normally I would never dream of invading someone's privacy this way, but I'm desperate. You had a near-death experience, right? What if that means you're somehow more in tune with the Shadow Land where Holly lives? It's like, on the border between life and death, so in a way, you've already been there. You have a connection to it. Maybe when I touched you . . . you broke through whatever is separating Holly and me, and closed the circuit. Like some kind of, I don't know, psychic conduit."

Sai began to pace back and forth across the road, running his fingers through his hair. "I don't want this, okay?" he said to her. "Whatever *this* is? I don't want it."

"I know," Evie said softly. "Believe me, I didn't want it either. But we can't change what we are. The more we push it away, the more we fight, the more it hurts instead of helps us. That's something I had to learn, too." She sighed. "All I know is, Holly said I need you. There's a reason you came into my life when you did."

"I shouldn't even be here," Sai was muttering to himself. "I shouldn't . . ."

Evie turned to him, her head cocked. "What do you mean? Does your dad need you home or something?"

"Not what I meant." Sai wasn't looking at her.

Evie suddenly realized they'd just been talking about Sai's near-death experience and paled. "What do you mean, you shouldn't be here?" she asked again.

"Forget it," Sai said, waving her words away.

"No, I'm not going to forget it," Evie shot back. "You can't just say something like that and expect me to—"

"Because it should have been me!" he said, his face alight with pain. "It should have been me who died, not her. Okay? Not her." His voice was sharp, searing. "So don't tell me that I'm here for a reason, that I'm the way I am for a reason, because there isn't one. Don't tell me that me being here without her is going to help you, or anyone else, because that's a lie. There's no reason for anything, and the sooner you figure that out, the better."

Evie stood frozen, shocked into silence by Sai's sudden outburst. She remembered the photo of that little boy sitting on his mother's lap, looking up at her with devotion in his eyes, and it filled her with heartbreak.

Sai started to turn back toward his bike again, but then reconsidered. "You know what? You're right," he said softly. "I did see something in that graveyard. And I'd be lying if I said it was the first time I've seen something that wasn't there. But it's not *real*, Evie. Okay? I'm just . . . broken. And I guess you are, too. So please just stop acting like it means something and let it go."

"But Sai, it *is* real," Evie said, recalling the bruises on her ankle. "Maybe not in the way we're used to, but it *exists*—it can hurt us. Hurt others. I doubted it, too, but I was wrong. Whatever took Desmond . . . it's out there. What if it takes someone else? What if it doesn't stop?"

Sai rubbed a hand across his face and wouldn't meet her eyes. "I'm sorry," he whispered, and walked away.

Evie watched him go, the rumble of the motorcycle more subdued somehow, as if Bonnie could sense her owner's agitation.

She carried her failure like a stone up the narrow lane to Hobbie House, devastated by how it had all gone so terribly wrong. She'd moved too quickly. She'd said too much. It had been foolish of her to think that Sai would just open up and trust her, especially after she weaseled her way into his space and then ambushed him with wild tales of shadow worlds and psychic connections. Maybe it would have gone better if she'd spent weeks getting to know him before bringing it all up, but she didn't have that kind of time. Not that it mattered now—she'd completely alienated him.

She'd misjudged Sai, she realized. She'd thought he was hard, unflappable, insensitive. But that was just the wall that surrounded his true self. Beyond that wall, hidden where no one else could see, Sai kept his fear and his pain. And in her eagerness for his help, Evie had blundered right into his most private place. No wonder he'd pushed her away. After all, he hadn't invited her in.

Evie wished she could take it all back and try again, but it was too late for that. Worst of all, she realized that the person she'd hurt, the complicated person hidden behind that wall, was someone uncomfortably familiar. Someone just like her.

9

vie sat in the FCS classroom one evening later that week with a few other students who were also working on costumes for *A Christmas Carol*. Christmas music played softly on Ms. Jackson's Bluetooth speaker, which they'd all joked about because it wasn't even Thanksgiving yet. While the others sewed costumes for Tiny Tim and family, Evie pored over her notes and sketches. It was a welcome distraction from the total lack of progress she'd made since the confrontation with Sai. There had been no more clues, no visions. Nothing.

She'd spent some time creating a sketch of the silver-and-pearl pin she'd held in the vision, and trying to figure out what kind of plant it was. At first, she thought it was holly—which would have made sense—but since the pearls were originally white, not red, she concluded that it was actually mistletoe. The two, which were both closely associated with the winter holidays, did look similar. But what did a sprig of mistletoe have to do with anything? People kissed under it at Christmastime—what of it? It seemed so frivolous, Evie had no idea why it would appear in one of Holly's cryptic messages.

After that, instead of wallowing, she'd decided to try to clear her head by forgetting about it all for a while and focusing on the play. She'd spent days reading Ms. Jackson's tattered copy of Dickens's book, pulling out all the relevant details about the three ghosts that visited Ebenezer Scrooge.

Ghost of Christmas Past

- "Like a child . . . Wore a tunic of the purest white; and round its waist was bound a lustrous belt"—Gold foil lamé? Check storage room
- "It held a branch of fresh green holly in its hand" Can ask Fiona at inn for fresh cuttings
- "Its dress trimmed with summer flowers" Best to use silk for these—ask Ms. Jackson to order
- "From the crown of its head there sprung a bright clear jet of light" Small battery pack with LCD light, maybe attached to back of dress?

The freshman they'd cast for Christmas Past fit the role perfectly. Grace Bailey was tiny, with a button nose, warm brown skin, and a feathery halo of raven hair. Evie had taken her measurements earlier in the week and had already finished a sketch of her costume: a cloud-light blouson dress with uneven edges dotted with tiny white silk flowers. That one was pretty easy, as was the costume for Christmas Present, played by the quarterback on the RHS football team, Colin Flanagan.

Ghost of Christmas Present

- "Clothed in one simple green robe, or mantle, bordered with white fur" Heavy velvet (hunter green) with ivory shag (faux)
- "On its head it wore no other covering than a holly wreath, set here and there with shining icicles" Ask Fiona re: holly—maybe some wire and quartz for icicles
- "Girded round its middle was an antique scabbard; but no sword was in it" Stage manager might have a prop for this

Colin was known for his antics on the field and for his flaming red hair, which he had been growing out for the show. By the time Evie took his measurements earlier that week, he had a fuzzy red beard growing in as well. He'd been solemn while she stretched the measuring tape around his chest and down his arms—not at all the bombastic boy she'd seen playing with Desmond at the football game in October. In fact, he barely said a word the entire time. Did he blame her for what had happened to Desmond, too?

The sketch for his costume was nearly finished. For both ghosts, it was the accessories that really made them pop.

The last one, though—that costume had been giving her serious grief.

Ghost of Christmas Yet to Come

- "Shrouded in a deep black garment, which concealed its head, its face, its form, and left nothing visible save one outstretched hand"
- ???

She stared at the note and then back at the blank sheet of paper in front of her. She wanted to do right by Daniel Santos, the hulking Brazilian junior who'd been cast in the part and had apparently stolen the show in the last RHS performance. But unlike Past and Present, there were almost no details whatsoever in the book about Christmas Yet to Come. A black hooded robe? It was just too simple. Boring, even. No, she needed something more.

Evie closed her eyes, blocking out the sounds of other students moving around her, talking about the show, and the rhythmic *whum-whum-whum* of the sewing machines. In the darkness, she cleared her thoughts of everything except the idea of this dreaded spirit, coming in the night with tidings of a future without hope or love.

From the depths of her mind, an image rose. Evie didn't recognize it at first, but after a moment, after her mind brushed the cobwebs from her memory, she realized it was from a dream. A dream she must have had more than once, but that she'd forgotten the moment she woke. Like the illustration in *A Christmas Carol*, the figure she saw wore a black hooded robe. But this figure was bigger than a man, and the hole where its face should have been was as black as midnight. The hem of the robe was torn to shreds, and they twisted and curled upon themselves like writhing snakes. Hollow-eyed faces with yawning mouths formed within its folds, as if souls trapped inside the thing's body were pressing against it to get out.

Evie opened her eyes with a gasp. Her hands were freezing. She rubbed them together for warmth until the chill that had come over her faded. That done, she picked up her pencil and did her best to replicate the image she'd imagined, writing small notes to herself in the margins.

- Build wire extension to add height? Maybe something to mount onto Daniel's shoulders
- Drape with heavy black linen—distress with sandpaper— use wood glue to stiffen fabric and shape folds into hands and faces
- Maybe black netting to obscure features behind the hood?

She finished ten minutes later and sat back to admire her work.

Ms. Jackson came to peer over her shoulder. "Oh, Evie," she breathed, "that is fantastic. I get the heebie-jeebies just looking at it."

"Yeah," Evie agreed. She looked at the faceless, ghastly thing on the page, and suddenly had the urge to destroy it. To crumple it up into a ball and throw it away—or better yet, burn it.

She shook the thought away. *You're being stupid. It's perfect— Ms. Jackson said as much.* Still, Evie's eyes kept being drawn back to it, like it was some forbidden thing she'd unwittingly brought into existence, like a creature who only came to life once you'd spoken its name.

"Oh goodness!" Ms. Jackson exclaimed a little while later. "Sorry, guys—I totally lost track of time!" Evie looked up from her work and peered at the clock. 8:03 p.m. "You all had better get on the road. Pack it up, everyone!"

Evie gently rolled up the kraft paper she'd been using to cut out patterns for the Christmas Past dress and carefully stowed everything in her cubby. She yawned. The intense concentration had given her a headache. It was definitely time for bed.

"Got any big Thanksgiving plans?" Ms. Jackson asked as Evie slipped into her coat.

Evie shook her head. "Not really, just dinner with the family here in town," she said. She left out the part about how incredibly awkward it was going to be. First of all, her father had decided to stay in Ravenglass until Christmas, surprising literally everyone. He said things back at the studio were running smoothly without him, and that his room at the inn was the perfect place to work on his new line of glass décor. Plus, he'd added, it was a chance to spend more time with his family. Stan had been thrilled—Evie and her mom, not so much. But there was nothing to be done. He was staying, and that was that.

To make matters worse, Mom had found out that Dr. Rockwell and Sai would be alone on Thanksgiving and—Mom being who she was—had invited them to join the Archers for dinner. Evie figured that Sai probably just wouldn't show up, but if he did . . .

The whole night promised to serve up a big, steaming bowl of cringe.

At least Aunt Martha would be there. She would surely help break up the tension. Evie hadn't seen her since she'd done Evie's tarot reading—the one with three cards.

Past, present, and future.

Evie froze, looking down at the sketches in her hand.

"Well, that sounds nice," Ms. Jackson said. "Hurry home safe now. Good work today!"

"Thanks," Evie mumbled, still staring at the sketches of the three ghosts. After a moment, she slipped the drawings inside her notebook and shoved them into her backpack. Ms. Jackson switched off the lights, and they all trooped outside and went their separate ways.

Normally Evie took a shortcut through the woods, but since it was dark out, she decided to walk down Main Street most of the way home. It was Friday night, so there was plenty of foot traffic in town—couples having fancy dinners at All That Glitters, shoppers picking up last-minute items at Ravenglass General, and tourists studying the holiday displays that had popped up in many of the shop windows. The town was twinkling with light and movement, but Evie barely noticed any of it. She was still shaken from the memory of the tarot reading and its eerie similarity to what she was working on for the school play. It couldn't just be some kind of weird coincidence, could it?

Coincidence or not, it was a reminder of what she'd been avoiding since her failure with Sai. Sure, she'd told herself she was "clearing her head," but was she really? Or was burying herself in schoolwork, costume design, and mindless social media scrolling all just an attempt to keep herself from thinking about Desmond? He'd been gone for so long now. And it had been days since she'd gotten any kind of sign from Holly. Part of her wondered if Holly's silence was because she didn't have Sai to help her, but another smaller, very quiet part also wondered if maybe everyone had been right all along.

Maybe Desmond wasn't coming back.

During her session, Dr. Rockwell had explained the stages of grief. "You don't necessarily go through them one at a time," he'd said, and Evie certainly felt like she was playing through denial, anger, and bargaining all at once. "But they always end the same way."

Acceptance.

Evie felt a wave of sorrow begin to bloom in her chest. She didn't want to believe it, but what if he really was gone?

"Need a ride?"

Evie was jerked from her thoughts by a voice so close that it sounded as if it were perched on her shoulder. She turned to see a man in an old pickup truck driving on the road next to her, his passenger-side window rolled down. When she looked closer, she realized it was the old man she had bumped into at Birdie's Diner. The mechanic named Roy.

"Um, no thanks," Evie said, instinctively giving him a little smile before increasing her speed down the sidewalk.

"Shouldn't be out walking alone this late at night," Roy said, keeping pace with her. "It's not safe." The truck rumbled, a low warning.

"I'll be fine, thank you," Evie said, her voice starting to shake when she noticed just how alone she was. The foot traffic had vanished behind her, and on this section of road, the streetlights were few and far between. She hadn't been paying attention to her surroundings—hadn't even noticed the man roll up behind her. A sheen of cold sweat formed on her brow. *Stupid, stupid, stupid . . .*

She ducked into a narrow delivery lane between two buildings, hoping to lose him in the twists and turns of the back alleys. Evie knew dozens of ways to get home, even in the dark, so getting lost wouldn't be a problem. She risked a glance over her shoulder and saw that he'd stopped the truck at the mouth of the lane, revving his engine. He was staring after her into the night, his eyes shining strangely in the darkness of the cab.

Evie hurried around corners, dodging garbage cans, trying not to think of the muck she nearly slipped in, or the crawling sensation on the back of her neck. She had to keep moving. Her vision narrowed to a singular focus, like a hunted animal. She tried to stop the fears from rising up, but couldn't. *What if he's following me?* she thought. *What if he knows who I am because of all those news stories, and he wants to grab me?* Or worse still, what if he was just one of those people who prowled small towns, searching for young girls out on their own . . .

This lane leads out to Bluebell Road, she remembered as she saw the opening ahead, bathed in yellow light. *The police station is only a couple blocks away. If I can just get there before he—*

Evie ran onto the sidewalk, took a sharp left turn, and crashed straight into someone standing there. She stumbled and cried out, scrabbling back from the grasp of whoever it was she'd run into. A streetlight shone overhead, blindingly bright after the murk of the alleyway. Evie blinked rapidly, willing her eyes to adjust. Was it Roy? Had he driven around the block more quickly than she could run and blocked her way?

But the person standing just beyond the streetlight's reach was tall and broad, nothing like the wiry, grizzled old man she'd seen at the diner. The points of his shoes were perched on the edge of the light—patent-leather dress shoes smeared with mud. Evie blinked again, floaters dancing in her eyes as more details of the man slowly emerged, like a ship being raised from the bottom of the sea.

A champagne-colored suit, torn and filthy.

A gold pocket watch hanging from a chain, its cracked glass glinting in the reflected light.

A once-beautiful face, the deep brown skin turned a sickly shade of gray.

And the smell of earth and stone and rot, from somewhere deep underground.

Evie's whisper was a baby's breath, pulled from her lips on the night wind.

"Desmond?"

He looked at her with eyes that were too large, too black.

Evie's heart thundered in her chest. She couldn't swallow, couldn't breathe, and dared not look away for fear that he would vanish like a daydream. A sickening mix of joy and shock and horror churned through her body, making her dizzy. "Desmond . . . ," she said again, high and thin and laced with hysteria. "What . . . what's happened to you?"

But as soon as she asked the question, she knew he wouldn't be able to answer it. Because as the final details of his body came into focus, Evie saw that—like in a nightmare she'd once had, what seemed like an eternity ago—Desmond's lips were sewn shut.

10

The seconds passed like hours as Evie stood, paralyzed in that pool of light. Desmond stared at her, unblinking, his lips quivering behind the cruel black thread that bound them together. She felt hot tears pricking her eyes as she looked at him, but dared not make a sound. It was so quiet, she could have sworn she could hear the ticking of the pocket watch that hung from Desmond's silk vest.

Tick.

Tock.

Tick.

Tock.

Her mind spun. Before she even knew what she was doing, she started to reach for him, to touch the gray flesh of his hand just to see if he was real. *Please, don't let him be like Holly*, she thought. She'd never even considered that she might see him this way, that she might be tortured with a vision of Desmond reduced to a hollow specter.

Tick.

Tock.

Desmond's black eyes flicked down as her fingers touched his skin. It was as cold as death. He flinched and moved away, shaking his head. "Please," Evie begged, quietly, desperately. "Come with me. Whatever's happened to you, we can fix it. I can help you—"

But Desmond was holding a finger to his lips, his hand shaking violently. It looked as if every movement caused him pain. He pointed over her shoulder, to a distant corner of Bluebell Road, and she turned to look. At first, she couldn't see anything. But then, something moved across the glass storefront of a laundromat, something black that blotted out the reflected streetlight. Then it moved across the windows of the apartment building next door, flowing thick and bog-like across the glass, leaving them dark as pitch.

"What is it?" Evie exclaimed. All the hairs on the back of her neck were standing on end, and she felt electrically charged with fear. "Desmond, what is that?"

Evie watched as he raised both hands in an odd gesture. He made two L-shapes, like finger guns, and pointed them toward the woods, moving them up and down with trembling hands.

She shook her head in confusion. What was he doing?

Tick.

Tock.

And then it dawned on her. She'd seen that gesture before— during Desmond's football practices and the homecoming game. It was one of the signals the coach gave the players when he wanted them to execute a specific movement during a play. And she knew exactly what this one meant.

Run.

"No," she begged, watching the dark thing advancing out of the corner of her eye. "I can't leave you. How will I find you? How do I save you?"

Desmond's face was creased with agony as he shook his head and kept making the gesture, faster and faster.

Run run run.

Hyperventilating, Evie stumbled away from him on wooden legs, across Bluebell Road and onto the asphalt trailhead leading into the woods. When she risked a look back at the place where she'd been standing, Desmond was gone.

Despite the streetlights still shining on them, every single window and storefront on the street was like a void, a black hole reflecting nothing. Like dozens of little mouths just waiting to swallow her up.

Evie turned to the woods and ran.

Somewhere above the treetops a new moon hid in shadow, leaving only starlight to illuminate her path. Evie wasn't as familiar with this branch of the trail—she usually picked up the one near the high school—so when she reached a fork, she had no idea which way to go. She stopped, panting, peering into the murk first on the left, then the right.

One would lead her back to the path she knew; the other might take her deeper into the woods, farther from rescue. But they both looked the same. There was no telling which was which.

She was still standing there when a sound broke the soft quietude of the forest. A harsh, grating, scraping noise. It was coming from behind her. She whirled around, adrenaline flooding her once more. Roy was standing near the trailhead, silhouetted by the ambient glow of the streetlights. He gripped a tire iron in one hand, and it was dragging along the ground behind him as he shuffled forward.

"*Evieee,*" he called. Ice slipped down her spine at the sound of his voice, guttural and singsong at the same time. She wondered how he knew her name. "*Come out, come out, wherever you are. I told you it isn't safe to be out here alone.*"

Evie's instinct was to stay completely still, but she knew she had to get out of there. Whatever had happened to Roy, he was still an old man. Unless he'd acquired some supernatural powers, she should still be able to outrun him.

"*Evieee,*" he called again, a little closer now. "*I know you're broken, Evie. But I love broken things. I take them apart and put them back together again, and when I do, they're even better than they were before . . .*"

Evie stared down the two paths and willed herself to pick one. *Left. Go left*, a voice in her head said. Without a moment's hesitation, she tore down the left-hand path without looking back.

For a minute or so, she thought she could still hear the dragging sound over the pounding of her feet and her ragged breath. A couple of times, she could have sworn she heard him calling her name. But soon after that, the sounds began to fade into the distance. When she recognized first a memorial bench, and then a broken tree half blocking the trail, she knew she was on the right track. But she didn't stop. Not when she reached the clearing, or the road to her house, or even the narrow lane. Only when she slammed into the kitchen of Hobbie House, scaring the daylights out of Stan, did she finally stop running.

Stan was sitting at the kitchen table drinking hot chocolate and watching Netflix on his iPad. He stared at her with round eyes as she collapsed onto the floor and started to cry.

Evie spent the next hour racking her brain, trying to decide what to do. After swearing Stan to secrecy about her outburst, she went upstairs and immediately texted Tina to explain what had happened.

Tina sent a shocked emoji, followed by

> 💀 You're sure this actually happened?
> it wasn't one of your vision things?

> it happened. i touched him. i touched desmond.
> he was real. i don't know what's happened to
> him, but it wasn't just a dream.

> and this old guy attacked you?

> yeah, but there was something
> wrong with him.

> clearly.

> no, not normal wrong. weird wrong.

well, you should go talk to my dad at the station. he'll know what to do. weird or not, you can't just say nothing after someone tries to assault you on the street.

Evie hesitated. She felt uncomfortable about the idea of involving the police. She'd only recently gotten herself out of the public eye—the last thing she needed was another scandal. But then again, Tina was right, she couldn't just say nothing. What if Roy attacked someone else? She'd be partly to blame for staying quiet.

okay, i'll talk to him in the morning. i hope you're right about this.

lol, your life will get a lot easier when you just accept that i'm right about everything 💀

Early Saturday morning, Evie sat in a patrol car outside Murphy's Auto Body with Chief Sànchez. The car was parked in the small lot next to a blue Toyota with a crumpled fender and the same old truck that she'd seen Roy driving the night before. Evie shivered and wrapped her arms around herself. After a sleepless night, she'd gone to the station in person, telling her mother she was going to Tina's. She'd asked to speak to the chief in private and had told him a slightly altered version of the events of the night before.

She left out the part about the old man's eyes, and of course, about seeing Desmond. To his credit, Chief Sànchez listened without interrupting, and offered her some coffee in a little paper cup. When she was done, he was quiet a minute. "That's quite a serious accusation," he finally said. "I hope you realize that, Miss Archer."

Evie felt sick. "I know," she said. "I'm just telling you what happened."

The chief nodded. "Well, what do you say we go over to the shop, and I'll talk to Roy myself? When I'm done, I'll drive you home. Does that sound all right?"

She swallowed. "But what if he sees me?" she asked.

"You'll be safe, trust me. Okay?"

"Yeah," she murmured. What other choice did she have?

It was only a five-minute drive to the auto shop. Evie had never ridden in a police car before, and she distracted herself by studying the various gadgets mounted to the dashboard. "Stay here," the chief commanded before getting out of the car.

Evie nodded wordlessly and watched the chief walk up to the garage. Warm, buzzy light spilled out from inside, and the chief stopped at the open door, nodding in greeting to someone inside. A conversation began. Evie wished she could hear what they were saying. The chief was doing a lot of nodding and gesturing toward town, but one thing he wasn't doing was making an arrest. Then, after what seemed like only a few minutes, Chief Sànchez was walking back to the car. He opened the door and ducked into the driver's seat next to Evie.

She clasped her hands together in her lap, anxious to hear what he was going to say.

Chief Sànchez laid his hands on the steering wheel and sucked his teeth. "I spoke to Roy," he began. "He says he did see you walking by yourself when he was on his way home from the shop last night. But he didn't stop, and he certainly didn't chase you into the woods. He says he drove straight home to his wife, and was in bed by nine-thirty. Now, I know that's only his word, but, Miss Archer . . ." Here he paused, taking a deep breath before saying, "I'm inclined to believe him."

Evie started to protest, but the chief raised a hand to stop her. "Now, this doesn't mean I'm not taking your report seriously. We've got our share of creeps just like any other town, and things have certainly been hopping around here lately, so it's not outside the realm of possibility that there's a dangerous individual on the loose. I'll tell my officers to keep an eye out during their patrols. All I'm saying is, I don't think the person you saw was Mr. Murphy. That man's been a fixture in this town for decades. I know him. He's a volunteer firefighter. He's in his seventies, for goodness' sake. I just . . . I can't see it, Evie."

Evie shook her head. It was going wrong. All wrong.

"Look, I'm not saying you didn't see Roy in his truck—we know you did. And I did tell Roy that because we can't confirm his whereabouts at the time of the allegation, my officers will be keeping an eye on him. But you admitted it yourself, it was dark in the woods. Whoever you saw, whoever was following you—I just don't think it was Roy Murphy."

At that moment, Roy himself walked out of the garage and stood there in his brown coveralls, his hands stuffed in his pockets. As the chief started the car and pulled away, Roy raised one hand in a half-hearted wave. His eyes looked normal. He seemed exhausted and confused—just a harmless old man.

None of it made sense.

If that's Roy Murphy, Evie wondered, *what was the thing I saw last night?*

Evie was quiet as Chief Sànchez drove her back to Hobbie House. She could hardly blame him for reacting the way he did—after all, Evie was the source of still-unsolved strangeness in town, and not the most reliable witness. Besides, after seeing Roy Murphy in the light of day, she had to agree that he wasn't the same man she'd seen the night before. He had been . . . *possessed* by something, something akin to what had happened to Desmond, but that could come and go at will. It almost reminded her of the strange boy in the red coat. He'd acted so oddly that day on the street, and in the church, too. Could they be connected?

The car radio squawked to life, breaking Evie out of her thoughts. *"Calling all units,"* it said. *"Code Two at the Blue River Inn."*

The chief picked up the radio. "Go ahead."

"Owner reports suspicious behavior by a guest. Please respond."

"Copy," the chief replied. "I'll head over now. Tell Hassan to meet me there."

"Confirmed. Oh, and one more thing."

"Go ahead."

"The chief over in Pittsfield called again. She's asking if we've had any updates about the missing photographer."

The chief sighed. "Tell her if I have anything to report," he said, an edge of irritation in his voice, "she'll be the first to know."

"Copy that. Thank you, Chief."

Chief Sànchez set the radio back in its holster and shook his head. "When it rains, it pours . . . ," he muttered.

Pittsfield . . . , Evie thought. *Weren't those two newspaper guys who harassed me from Pittsfield?* "Someone's missing?" she asked, trying not to sound overly interested.

"This reporter from Pittsfield wrapped his car around a tree a little while back, on the road out of town," the chief replied. "Apparently he had a passenger with him. A photographer named Mark Woodland. But Mr. Woodland wasn't at the scene and has yet to be located."

Evie's brows furrowed. "That's strange," she said.

Chief Sànchez turned onto the road to Hobbie House. "Sure is," he agreed.

"What happened to the driver?" she asked, remembering the aggressive, bullying reporter her father had nearly beaten to a pulp.

"Dead on arrival," the chief replied.

"Oh," Evie said, her voice hollow.

Chief Sànchez pulled up to the bottom of the narrow lane and stopped the car. "Normally I'd speak to your parents about what's happened here, but I really need to get to the inn. Can I trust you to give them a full report, Evie?"

Evie swallowed. "Of course," she lied. "Thank you."

"Good, good," he said. "I've got my hands full lately as it is. Seems like everyone's lost their minds in this town all of a sudden. Something in the air." Evie got out of the car and slammed the door shut. The chief rolled down the window and pointed a finger at her. "And, Evie?" he said.

"Yes?"

"No more walking alone at night. Got it?"

Evie nodded. "Yes, sir."

"Good girl."

Evie watched him drive away, and as soon as he'd turned the corner, she pulled out her phone to text Tina.

> something is going on in town, and it's bigger than desmond. much bigger.

11

PUMPKIN KISSES AND HARVEST WISHES.
SWEATER WEATHER IS BETTER WEATHER.
GRATEFUL. THANKFUL. BLESSED.

Evie closed her eyes and prayed for the serenity to accept the things she could not change. She could forgive her mother many things—her obsessive desire to clean every inch of the house before guests came over, her anxiety about silverware placement, even her bizarre belief that one must use only cranberry-colored napkins at a Thanksgiving dinner. But she couldn't forgive her love of corny seasonal signage. It was, quite simply, a bridge too far.

"Mom, can I please move this?" she said, pointing to the PUMPKIN KISSES sign taking up valuable counter space.

"Just leave it, honey," her mom said, momentarily ceasing her ministrations over the green bean casserole. "There's plenty of space on the table for the potatoes."

"Fine," Evie huffed, lugging the steaming bowl of mashed potatoes over to the kitchen table, which had been set for seven. What she wanted to do was throw the sign in the garbage, or onto a funeral pyre of every sentimental knickknack her mother had ever purchased, but instead she just nudged it over a few inches. With malice. "Where's Stan?" she asked. "Why isn't he helping?"

"*Stan!*" Mom shouted. "*Get off the iPad and come help your sister!*"

Evie peeked into the living room, where Dad and Aunt Martha sat in front of a roaring fire, drinking from tumblers of mulled wine, engaged in a lively conversation. Schrödinger was there, too, his front paws up on the coffee table, sniffing the cheese board with interest. Mom would have shooed him off, but Aunt Martha offered him a slice of Manchego instead.

Evie was always amazed at how well Aunt Martha got along with Dad. Then again, they were both unconventional people, used to taking the road less traveled. Aunt Martha laughed at something Dad said, and he smiled that wolf smile of his and drained the rest of his glass. Evie grumbled, turning back to the chaos of the kitchen. It was definitely better that Aunt Martha was here to smooth things over so that they could all enjoy the evening. But somehow, Evie almost preferred the tension to this friendly, party atmosphere. Maybe it was wrong of her to feel this way, but she didn't want her father to feel welcome here. She wanted him gone.

I thought you were mad at him for giving you too much space, a little voice said. *For not caring enough. For not being there*. Evie gritted her teeth at the annoying part of her brain reminding her of her hypocrisy. *Shut up, will you?* she told it.

Stan came thumping down the stairs a moment later, crutch in hand. He made his way over to the table and snatched a dinner roll from the breadbasket.

"Hey!" Mom exclaimed, batting at him with an oven mitt. "You're supposed to help with the food, dummy, not eat it."

"When are we eating?" Stan asked around a huge bite of bread. "I'm starving."

Mom looked at the German cuckoo clock on the wall and grimaced. "Soon, I hope," she replied. "We're just waiting for the Rockwells. Hopefully it will all still be hot by the time they arrive."

As if on cue, headlights shone through the kitchen window, and Evie glanced over to see a white Land Rover pulling into the driveway. "They're here," she said, her chest tightening with anxiety. She still hadn't spoken to Sai since their argument on the street. She'd gone back to his house for another session with Dr. Rockwell, but Sai hadn't been there. It was a particularly painful kind of rejection—because it wasn't just Evie he was rejecting. He'd turned his back on the part of himself that they shared, too.

Evie steeled herself as she heard two car doors slam and footsteps on the gravel. *Just do like Mom does*, she told herself. *Smile and get through it.*

"Lynne, hello! Hello, everyone!" Dr. Rockwell said as he came through the door, lusty and festive. "Sorry we're late. We got a bit . . ." He glanced behind him. "Held up." He handed Mom a serving dish covered with tinfoil. "I brought a pudding— plum pudding, to be exact. Hopefully it's not rubbish."

Mom took the plate, her eyes round with pleasure. "Plum pudding! I've never had it. How perfect!"

Dr. Rockwell shrugged off the compliment. "We don't normally do Thanksgiving at our house, so I wasn't sure what to bring. Not like us Brits to celebrate you Americans getting away from us." He winked charmingly.

Mom laughed too loudly, and Evie flushed with embarrassment. *Are they flirting with each other?* she wondered with horror. *Could this night get any worse?*

It could. A moment later, Sai came through the door dressed in loafers, black jeans, and a white button-down shirt that looked like it was worn exactly once a year. He stood as stiff as his starched collar, emanating a message that no one else seemed to notice but Evie received as clear as day.

I don't want to be here.

Mom welcomed him inside, and his mouth twitched into the impression of a smile before he scanned the room. His gaze lit on the kitschy signs on the counter; the kitchen table, color-coordinated and laden with aromatic dishes; Dad and Aunt Martha, entering from the living room with empty tumblers in hand; and finally, Evie.

She expected him to be cold. She expected his jaw to clench right before he turned away and ignored her completely. She probably would have deserved it, too. Still, even after everything that had happened, Evie had to suppress the urge to grab him by the shoulders and beg him to help her.

"You can't force him to do the right thing," Tina had told her at school before the holiday break. "Did you ever consider that maybe your psychic ability is misfiring? I mean, you're super stressed, I can't imagine you sleep much, and you're still pretty new to this whole supernatural scene. These experiences you've been having could just be expressions of your inner turmoil or something. Maybe if you chill out for literally one entire second, your vision will become clear again."

Tina's argument seemed reasonable, but chilling out—even for literally one second—felt more impossible with each day that passed. No matter what else was going on, her mind never strayed very far from that night with Desmond and Not–Roy Murphy. Because ever since, Evie couldn't shake the feeling that time was running out.

Still, she'd promised herself not to bring it up with Sai at Thanksgiving. Maybe if she just acted normal during dinner, he'd eventually open up to her again. Probably not, but what other choice did she have?

So Evie stood up straight and prepared to greet Sai as if nothing totally crazy had ever happened between them. Sai looked at her, a slight grimace crossing his face. His eyes took in the caramel-brown shift dress she was wearing, the one with the white satin piping around the collar and hemline. Suddenly self-conscious, she touched her hair, which she'd twisted into a braided chignon and secured with a pearl-studded hairpin. When he met her gaze, she found herself blushing. He swallowed visibly.

"Hi," he said.

Evie blinked. "Hi."

When his grimace quirked into a small, hesitant smile, Evie felt the flutter of something coming back to life inside her.

Hope.

And maybe—though she'd deny it vehemently—something else, too.

Mom clapped her hands, snapping them out of the moment. "All right, everyone—food's getting cold," she said. "Let's eat!"

The food was delicious, but Evie could hardly wait for the meal to be over. Mom had ordered her to sit across from Sai at the table, and all throughout dinner, Evie caught him stealing glances at her. He had something to say, that was certain, but they'd have to wait until they were alone to talk.

Everything seemed to be going off without a hitch, much to Evie's surprise. Dad spent most of the evening talking to Aunt Martha and Stan, leaving Mom and Dr. Rockwell to have their own conversation. It wasn't until there was a lull in Dad's stories about the wayward interns back at his studio that things started to go awry.

"So, how is it going," Mom was saying, "you know, with Evie?"

Dr. Rockwell cleared his throat, suddenly aware of listening ears around him. "Quite well. Although I'm afraid I'm going to have to put things on pause for a bit," Dr. Rockwell replied quietly. "Things have picked up considerably at the clinic lately, and I've had to work extra hours. But you should be very proud. Evie is quite a remarkable young woman."

Dad was looking at him over the rim of his wineglass. "Yes," he said. His tone was friendly on the surface, but Evie could feel the edge beneath. "You've gotten cozy with my family pretty quick, haven't you?"

A chill fell over the room. Aunt Martha set down her fork with a clatter, and Stan shifted uncomfortably in his seat.

"I'm sure I don't know what you mean," Dr. Rockwell said, his voice even.

"Don't be silly," Dad countered. "You're a professional mind reader—you know exactly what I mean."

Dr. Rockwell cleared his throat. "Robby, please don't get the wrong idea. I—"

"No, I get it," Dad broke in. Evie felt her stomach twist, and she wondered just how many glasses of wine her father had emptied. "You're single, still somewhat new to the area, just like Lynne. You see a good thing, you want to reach out and take it. I get it. I really do."

"Robby!" Mom protested, looking mortified.

"I'm not reaching out and taking *anything*," Dr. Rockwell said, the color rising in his face. "If your son breaks his ankle and comes to my clinic, I will fix it. If your ex-wife chooses to invite me to dinner, I will attend. And if your daughter wants to talk to me about how these past few years have affected her, I will listen." His voice became quiet, laced with contempt. "What you should be asking yourself, Robby, is why isn't she talking to *you*?"

Dad's nostrils flared.

Evie stared at him. *Please don't do anything stupid*, she thought, her pulse racing.

But then Aunt Martha put one bejeweled hand on Dad's forearm, and he deflated. Without another word, he pushed his chair back from the table, stood, and plodded into the living room. Stan followed him, and then, after a pained grimace toward Mom, Aunt Martha went after him, too.

Dr. Rockwell swallowed and pushed his own glass of wine away. "I'm so sorry, Lynne," he said, hardly able to meet Mom's eyes. "That was incredibly unprofessional—I don't know what came over me. This is your home, your holiday, and I've—"

"You've done nothing wrong," Mom muttered, shooting daggers toward the living room. "I should have known that Robby wouldn't be able to get through the night without putting his foot in his mouth." Weary, she turned to Evie. "Honey, would you help me clear the table? Honey?"

Evie felt sick. The tension, the raised voices—all while sitting together at the dinner table. It brought the memory of that night flooding back. The night years ago, that ill-fated dinner in New York, the very last one before the separation and the divorce. The night that she'd always believed had broken her family once and for all.

"I have to go," she murmured, and fled up to her room. No one tried to stop her.

Evie was sitting cross-legged on her bed when there was a knock on her bedroom door. "Come in," she said, figuring it was her mother coming to check on her and mourn the untimely death of her perfect evening.

The door creaked open slowly, and Evie was surprised to see Sai standing at the threshold. "Can I hide in here, too?" he asked.

Evie exhaled into a laugh. "Sure," she said, relieved. "Is it pretty bad down there?"

Sai shrugged. "I dunno. Your aunt must be a magician, because she's brilliant at the art of misdirection. She's telling some pretty wild stories, which your little brother seems to enjoy. But you could still cut the tension in the room with a knife."

"I bet," Evie replied, looking down at her lap.

Sai focused on the item lying there. "What's that?" he asked.

Evie held up the blue bonnet she'd brought down from the attic. "This belonged to my cousin Holly," she said. "And before that to Sarah Flower, the Patchwork Girl. I told you about them, remember?" She fingered the delicate lace that edged the bonnet, worn to gossamer by time. "After what happened to me, I never thought I'd want to see her again. But now . . ." She paused. "Now I just wish she'd talk to me. In a weird way, she helped me move past all that fear and anger I was holding on to—about my parents and the divorce and everything. The fighting at the dinner table just reminded me of it. When I came back from the mines, I thought I was done with those feelings. With the fear. But it was only the beginning of something else, something *worse*, and I don't know what to do." Evie bit her lip. She hadn't meant to say so much. It just all came out in a rush.

Sai was watching her, thoughtful. He closed the door softly behind him and went to sit in the wicker fan-back chair by the window. He leaned over, elbows on knees, and laced his sinewy brown fingers together, studying them. After a long moment, he spoke.

"I saw her, you know."

Evie's brow furrowed. "Saw who?"

"My mother."

"What do you mean you saw her?"

Sai swallowed and began. "Dad honored Indian tradition by arranging to have Mum cremated within twenty-four hours of the accident. He tried his best—but I don't know that it mattered all that much. None of my grandparents on either side of the family ever really approved of the marriage. But Dad still tried to make everyone happy and give her a proper send-off. I was in the hospital, not even conscious yet, so obviously I couldn't be there. But once I got discharged a month later, Dad organized a memorial service for her at this Unitarian church we used to go to. He invited all their friends from medical school, colleagues, and that. Mum was a cardiologist, so they had a lot of the same friends. I was just sitting there in the pew, listening to people talk about her, and I felt . . . numb. It just didn't feel real. None of it did." Sai's voice began to tremble. He paused and took a deep breath before continuing. "Everyone was singing this song. Something about 'love will guide us through the dark night,' and they were so damn *earnest*. And then I wasn't numb anymore, I was *angry*. I didn't have a song of peace in my heart, and I never would. Nothing about what happened to her made any sense. Nothing would ever be all right again."

Evie looked down. "I can understand that," she said.

"I was thinking all these thoughts," Sai continued, "and everybody else was just singing. And then, there was this movement from the side door near the front of the church, and I thought someone had come in late. But when I looked . . . it was her."

Evie's eyes widened.

Sai's voice had lowered to a whisper. "At first, I thought, *Oh good, Mum made it*, but then I realized what an insane thing that was. She couldn't be there. She was dead. *It was her bloody funeral.* I kept looking, waiting for someone else to see her, but no one did. They were too busy reading from the hymnals, singing along. I just stared at her. I couldn't move. She was all dressed in white, the way you do at Indian funerals, and she looked the same as she always did. She was watching me, and she looked so . . ." It was getting difficult for him to talk. "She looked so *sad*." He shook his head. "The song ended, and I must have glanced away for a moment, because when I looked back, she was gone." He paused. "I've never told anyone about it. Never."

"That's why you didn't want to go inside the church, isn't it?" Evie asked.

Sai nodded. "I didn't want to believe that seeing her meant anything. It was easier, after the accident, to believe that nothing had meaning. That it's all just chaos. Random, stupid, pointless chaos." He locked eyes with Evie. "And then I met you."

When he looked at her, Evie felt that energy pouring from him again, but this time the message wasn't hostile. It was deep, magnetic. Subconsciously, she leaned forward, closer to him.

"Every time I touched you, I saw these . . . visions," he said. "Impossible visions. And then suddenly you'd just appear everywhere I went, insisting that we'd both seen the same thing and that you needed me. And it flew in the face of everything I'd been telling myself all these years. And I didn't want to deal with that. I didn't want to deal with you."

"But . . . you're here, dealing with it now," Evie said, confused. "What changed your mind?"

Sai licked his lips. "Ever since you told me all that mad

stuff—about Desmond and all the rest—I haven't been able to get it out of my head. It's like I can feel something happening. Like a shadow falling across me, even though there's no one there. It won't stop. No matter what I do, it, won't stop."

Evie nodded. "I know. I feel it, too."

"And Dad keeps talking about how patients are coming in with unexplained weakness and exhaustion . . . Some of them are even saying they're sleepwalking. Waking up in places without knowing how they got there. It's connected, isn't it?"

"I don't know for sure, but I think so," Evie replied.

Sai scoffed. "You know, I didn't even want to come tonight. Dad had to badger me for half an hour before I agreed. I hadn't really changed my mind about any of this. Until I saw you." He looked at her, and she could see herself reflected in his dark eyes.

Evie felt her face redden. "I'm glad you did," she said quietly.

He stood and walked around the room, stopping to look at the old photo of Holly and the dried rose on her dresser. "Maybe it's this place, too," he murmured. "As soon as I walked in, I got this . . . welcoming feeling. Like something really wanted me to be here."

"Are you sure that wasn't just my mom?" Evie said with a chuckle. "If you haven't noticed, she's pretty extra."

But Sai wasn't listening anymore. He'd made his way over to the window and was staring out into the front yard, toward the old apple tree.

"Sai?" Evie said. "What is it?"

Sai didn't reply. His face was strangely frozen, passive. And then his lips started to move.

"The harbinger comes before, and the shadow follows soon after," he whispered.

A chill ran along Evie's spine. "What?" she said.

"The harbinger comes before, and the shadow follows soon after," Sai repeated, his eyes on the tree, unblinking.

Evie stood up from the bed and went to him. "What is that? What are you saying?"

"Theharbingercomesbeforeandtheshadowfollowssoonafter." The words were blurring into one another now, like they were being pressed out of Sai's body, over and over again. She saw that he was gripping the window frame so tightly that his knuckles had turned white. *"Theharbinger—"*

"Sai!" Evie shook him by the shoulder, her fear spiking into panic.

As soon as she touched him, he gasped and stumbled away from the window, his face pale and shiny with perspiration. He turned to her, eyes wild. "What—" he stammered between ragged breaths. "What the hell was that?"

"I'm not sure," Evie said, her mind whirling. *The harbinger . . .* She thought about how Desmond had appeared to her that night in town, right before the creeping darkness came. Perhaps because the book was so fresh in her mind, it brought forth thoughts of Jacob Marley, arriving on Scrooge's doorstep with a rattle of chains and a dire portent.

"I am here tonight to warn you, that you have yet a chance and hope of escaping my fate."

She thought, too, of Desmond's frantic gestures, telling her to run.

"You will be haunted by Three Spirits."

"It was like someone speaking through my mouth," Sai was saying. "I could feel her, smell her . . . like flowers . . ."

Evie glanced at the bed, where the blue bonnet lay across her patchwork quilt.

"I think she's trying to help," Evie said. "Now that we're together, somehow she's strong enough to get through to us."

"Who is?"

Evie swallowed. "The Lost Girl of Ravenglass," she replied. "Holly Hobbie."

Meanwhile . . .

Ding-dong!

"'Here We Come A-Wassailing,' everyone," Fiona Hawthorn whispered as the carolers arranged themselves in a half circle on the brick walkway. The house was a white Cape Cod, small and neat, decorated with multicolored twinkling lights. Little plastic candy canes lined the walkway up to the door, and a large Christmas tree glowed behind the gauzy curtains in the front window. Up and down the street, other houses competed for attention— some bearing dripping icicle lights, some with illuminated reindeer grazing on the lawn, and others that simply had a single electric candle lit in every window.

Kimber Sullivan adjusted the Santa hat on her head and pasted on a smile. When a harried-looking mother opened the door with a toddler balanced on her hip, she and the others launched into song.

"Here we come a-wassailing among the leaves so green;
Here we come a-wand'ring so fair to be seen.
Love and joy come to you, and to you your wassail too;
And God bless you and send you a Happy New Year, and
God send you a Happy New Year . . ."

When it was done, the woman thanked them, grasped the round-eyed little boy's hand to make him wave goodbye, and shut the door.

Kimber let the smile fall from her face. "Dad, how many more times do we have to do this?" she asked.

"Until we're done," Mayor Sullivan muttered in reply. Like all the carolers, he wore a Santa hat and matching red scarf. "Now stop complaining. Even if your mother wasn't too sick to come out, it's about time you started carrying your weight again. I've had just about enough of your theatrics." At that, he turned to Fiona. "Where to next, councilwoman?" he asked brightly.

Kimber gritted her teeth as she and the four others followed in their wake. What she wanted to do, more than anything, was scream.

Since homecoming night, her life had been a living hell.

She'd been hidden away in her house for a week, not allowed to see or speak to anyone. They'd taken her phone away and put a password on the Wi-Fi. Then she'd been carted to some expensive shrink three towns over—because God forbid anyone in Ravenglass found out—to discuss her problem. And she'd been forbidden, on threat of permanent deletion of all her social media accounts, from ever talking to a single soul about what had happened that night.

Not that it mattered. Because she'd said plenty just after it happened. Right there on the floor of the RHS hallway, seconds after she'd run out of the gymnasium. She'd been hysterical, inconsolable no matter what her friends said or did. She just kept repeating the same thing, over and over again.

She's a monster.

When she finally went back to school, she did her best to "be normal" like her parents wanted. And she managed it, at least for a few days. But then, in the still moments—while she listened to class lectures, or sat in the cafeteria, or stood at the mirror in the girls' bathroom—she'd see her again.

That face.

That horrible face.

With the flesh peeled and rotten on one side, exposing bone and gristle and grinning white teeth.

Then that voice, the one she'd heard in her nightmares every night since, saying, *"Get out of my way."*

Within a week, Kimber had stopped spending an hour every morning choosing the perfect outfit and doing her makeup and hair. She had just put on whatever she could find that was still clean and walked out the door. All of her friends noticed, of course, but none of them were brave enough to say a word. She almost hated them more for that.

Cowards.

But it wasn't their fault Kimber's life was ruined. No, there was only one person to blame.

Evie Archer.

Everything had been fine before she'd showed up in town. She and Desmond surely would have gotten back together had Evie not put a spell on him and taken him away. Kimber knew that Desmond had been interested in Evie only because she was different, like a shiny new toy, and that he would have tired of her if he'd been given the chance. Kimber had always known she was meant to be with Desmond. In middle school she'd even practiced signing her name—*Kimberly King. KK.* Her life—their life together—was going to be perfect.

Now he was dead, along with Kimber's future. In a little over a month, her perfect world had turned upside down, and every time she tried to sort through the wreckage to see what was left, all she found was rage.

"Pretty cold out here, huh?" Colin Flanagan had slowed down to walk next to her.

He'd been trying to sidle up to Kimber ever since Desmond had disappeared, as if he wanted to reserve his spot in line to be her next boyfriend. It disgusted her. Kimber didn't bother to respond.

Undeterred, Colin tried again. "You know, that Archer girl is on the costume crew for the winter play. She had to measure me for my ghost costume and barely said two words the whole time. Creep. I bet she was eyeing me for her next victim, you know? Like a . . . a black widow or something. But I'd never fall for that. I've only got eyes for one person, and it definitely isn't her."

Kimber could feel his gaze boring into the side of her head, as if what he'd just said was, in some distant universe, subtle and clever. "Don't talk to me about her," she snarled.

Colin raised both hands in a defensive posture. "Okay, okay," he said quickly. "Sorry." He was silent for a moment, obviously trying to think of something safe to talk about. "So, how'd you get roped into caroling duty? I didn't have much of a choice, myself. Coach thought it would be good for one of us to go, since . . ." He trailed off.

Kimber knew exactly what Colin was about to say.

"Since Desmond won't be doing it anymore."

She winced, but decided to throw the idiot a bone. "My mom's sick," Kimber replied dully. "Since last week. She's tired all the time, hardly even gets out of bed. She says it's something going around, but Dad thinks it's just PMS." She chuckled. "Mom didn't like that very much. Anyway, since she couldn't come, it was up to me to put on a pretty face and walk all over town singing 'Jingle Bells' to a bunch of soccer moms and old people."

"It couldn't have been that hard," Colin said, looking at her meaningfully.

"Hard?" Kimber asked, confused.

"To put on a pretty face." He winked at her, and grinned.

Kimber sighed, cursed her sore feet, and kept walking.

"This is the Kims' place," Fiona said as they stopped in front of a periwinkle-blue house with a neatly manicured lawn. The woman managed the Blue River Inn *and* still found time to be a member of the town council—quite a busybody. She probably knew the zodiac signs of every person in Ravenglass. "They're business owners," she continued. "So we should definitely stop here. Someone's home—there's a light on."

Mr. Sullivan nodded. "It will probably be the mother—as I recall, Birdie works most weeknights."

"Okay, carolers," Fiona announced, turning to the group. "We've got a very elderly lady here, so let's do 'Silent Night.' Nice and sweet, all right, crew?"

The carolers made agreeable noises and arranged themselves in front of the doorstep in a half circle. Fiona went up to use the doorknocker.

Knock. Knock. Knock.

Then she stepped back and joined the others.

A minute passed. Kimber started to think the old lady must have fallen asleep, and that they were standing there, freezing their butts off, for nothing.

Then the door opened. Mrs. Kim—or Mama Bird, as people called her—stood there in a floral nightgown, her wide feet bare against the hardwood floor. A sickly looking yellow light spilled out of the house, setting her in silhouette against it. She wore plastic eyeglasses, so thick that Kimber couldn't even see her eyes beneath them. The lenses shone in the reflected light like two gold coins.

Fiona turned to the group and began mouthing words and waving her hands in time. "One, and two, and three, and—"

"Silent night," they sang, nice and sweet, "holy night, all is calm, all is bright . . ."

Kimber sang along with them, the bell-like tones of her soprano voice rising above the others. Back when they were dating, Desmond used to say her singing was almost as beautiful as her face. The memory brought a lump to her throat, and her voice quavered. Angrily, she drove the feelings deep down, suffocating them in the pit of her stomach.

"Sleep in heavenly peace," they sang. "Sleep in heavenly peace."

As they finished the first verse, Kimber began to notice something strange. Despite their fairly impressive performance, Mrs. Kim hadn't moved a muscle. She wasn't smiling, she didn't have her hands clasped together as many people did as they listened to the carolers. She was just standing there, stock-still, her hand resting on the doorknob.

What's wrong with this lady? Kimber thought with irritation. She rolled her eyes. Here they were, doing their civic duty, and she couldn't even bring herself to *smile*?

"Silent night," the carolers went on, "holy night . . ."

Kimber noticed that Fiona was suddenly singing off-key. She was always the one who kept pitch for the group, so that came as a surprise. Then her father joined her. And then Colin. By the time they'd finished the second verse, the song didn't sound nice and sweet anymore. It was discordant, jarring. Kimber tried to sing louder to compensate, but that only made it worse. The song lurched on.

"Sleep in heavenly peace," they sang tunelessly. "Sleep in heavenly peace."

Finally, around the middle of the third verse, Kimber couldn't stand it any longer. Her feet ached, she was cold, she was tired, and now everyone was acting stupid. "What is wrong with you?" she muttered to Colin.

But Colin kept singing. When she looked at him, his face was slack, his eyes hooded in darkness. He was just staring at Mrs. Kim, his voice harsh and dissonant.

"Colin!" Kimber said, louder now. A squirming grub of panic crawled into her gut. *What the hell is going on?*

She ran over to her father, but it was just the same with him.

"Silent night," they droned on, relentless.

"Stop it!" Kimber shouted. She ran to each of them in turn, shaking them by the shoulders, slapping them across the face, but it did no good.

"Holy night . . ."

Feeling that now-familiar sense of unreality coming over her, Kimber turned to Mrs. Kim in her doorway. She looked otherworldly now, lit from behind by that terrible, sulfurous glow.

"All is calm, all is bright . . ."

Mrs. Kim's eyeglasses no longer shone like golden coins. They were flooded with an impenetrable blackness that filled Kimber with a horror so deep, so new, that it dug down into her, found everything that she'd buried there, and pulled it all right out into the open. Raw and naked and full of pain.

"Sleep in heavenly peace, sleep in heavenly peace."

Finally, Kimber did what she'd been wanting to do all night. She screamed.

12

It was two weeks later when the air started to smell like snow. Autumn peacoats gave way to puffy winter jackets, Christmas music played in every shop, and there was a pervasive sense of anticipation as the holiday season got into full swing.

Unlike most everyone else in Ravenglass, Evie didn't exactly feel anticipation.

It was more like dread.

Wherever she went, whether it was to school, to Birdie's, or even just walking down the street, she couldn't shake the feeling that people were watching her. Staring at her when she walked past them in hallways, or when she turned her back after paying for a hot cocoa at the general store.

On the outside, the town seemed bright and jolly, bursting with festive cheer.

But Evie sensed something sinister in it all, lurking just under the surface. Something that made the songs she used to love sound ominous and strange.

The feeling began after Thanksgiving and had only gotten stronger since. Evie, Tina, and Sai had gathered at Birdie's that weekend to discuss what to do next, but the planning took longer than Evie had hoped. After she and Tina had fully briefed Sai about the whole Holly and Sarah saga, he had thrown himself headlong into the investigation alongside them. She'd assumed once she'd convinced Sai to help, everything else would just sort of fall into place.

It didn't.

In fact, Evie felt nearly as lost as before.

They'd carefully recorded everything that had happened since Desmond's disappearance. The details of every vision, every piece of information they'd learned from Dr. Rockwell, Chief Sànchez, and anyone else they could think of. Evie had even invited Sai back to her house one Sunday when her mother was at work and stood in the middle of the kitchen holding his hand.

Nothing happened.

Which turned it into possibly one of the most awkward moments of her life. Made even more so by Stan spying on them from the hallway and laughing. It was hopeless, trying to salvage the morning after that. They'd tried touching the locket again, even tried returning to the road behind the school and the church to re-create the situations when the other visions had occurred.

No such luck. Holly stayed quiet.

It had been Tina's idea to visit the library.

She'd been poring over the Sarah Flower papers, and realized that Holly must have obtained most of them at the Ravenglass Library Museum and Archives. "Maybe she missed something," Tina had reasoned.

Evie was inclined to agree. After all, Holly had told her to "finish what I started." So they'd been making visits ever since, trying to understand the link between what had happened to Desmond and a little girl who lived more than a hundred years ago.

Evie was walking down Main Street, on her way there for the third time that week, when she saw Tina, Mrs. Sànchez, and Tina's grandmother turn the corner and start walking in her direction. She stopped just in front of the Ravenglass General and waved them down. Tina's stormy expression brightened at the sight of her.

"Oh! Hello, Evie," Mrs. Sànchez said as they approached. Tina's mother shared the same dark, curly hair and light brown skin as her daughter, but otherwise, the two were completely different. While Tina was wearing her usual beanie and leather jacket over an anime T-shirt combo, Mrs. Sànchez was dressed conservatively, in a pair of navy slacks and an ivory wool coat. Evie had met her only once or twice before and wasn't sure how the woman felt about her friendship with Tina. After all, if Tina was the first to know nearly everything that went on in Ravenglass, surely her mother knew it all, too. And Evie's reputation varied widely in town, depending on who you talked to. To some she was just the new girl, but to others, she carried the stain of the Horror House. "Merry Christmas," Mrs. Sànchez added as they stopped in front of the General. "How's your family? Doing well, I hope?"

"Yes, thank you for asking," Evie said politely.

"This is my mother, Tati Ortega," Mrs. Sànchez said, indicating the elderly woman next to her. Tati was a tiny, wizened woman with tightly curled white hair and cherry-red lipstick. "Mamá, this is Evie Archer, one of Tina's friends from school."

"Very nice to meet you, Mrs. Ortega," Evie said.

Tati inspected Evie with unsettling speed and precision. "Mmhm!" she grunted, then plucked a crumpled paper from her handbag and began consulting it with total concentration.

Evie glanced at her friend. Tina rolled her eyes.

"You're *sure* this place will have the gandules?" Tati asked. "Already we are missing the recao for the sofrito. What kind of Christmas dinner would it be without arroz con gandules?"

Mrs. Sànchez sighed patiently. "The sofrito will be *fine*, Mamá. I know cilantro isn't what you usually use, but you are the only one who will notice the difference. And yes, Tony always puts some cans of gandules aside for me at this time of year."

Tati grumbled, crossing items off her list with acute vigor. "First you tell me I don't need to hand grate the plantains for the pasteles—oh, I should use a *food processor*—and now you say no one notices my sofrito." She shook her head. "Whatever happened to *tradition*?"

"That's not what I—" Mrs. Sànchez started to say.

"Mom, can I go with Evie?" Tina broke in. "We were going to do some more research at the library for that school project I mentioned."

"Sure, honey," her mother said, distracted by Tati's deep examination of the contents of the store window. "Just be home by five thirty."

"What?" Tati said, frowning. "I thought the girl was coming home with us to help with the cooking?"

"Ay, Mamá, déjala sola," Mrs. Sànchez said soothingly. "She'll be home later on."

Tati sucked her teeth, then turned to open the door to the

General. A little silver bell tinkled. Flustered, Mrs. Sànchez followed her inside.

"You see what I mean?" Tina exclaimed as they walked side by side.

Evie shrugged. "Yeah, I mean your grandma seems pretty intense. But isn't it kind of nice to have her there, making a bunch of delicious food and all?"

Tina scoffed. "You don't understand," she muttered.

"Maybe not," Evie agreed. "I didn't really get to spend much time with any of my grandparents. I never met my one grandfather, and my grandmother died when I was young. Dad's folks live out in California somewhere and don't visit much."

Tina fell silent.

Evie wondered if she'd said the wrong thing. "I don't mean to suggest you shouldn't get upset at your grandma," she said, trying to backtrack. "I totally understand that things can be hard at home during the holidays. You should have seen my house during Thanksgiving."

"Preach," Tina agreed, a grin piercing her gloom. "And also: same. Tati spent the entirety of that evening complaining about turkey dryness and my choice of hair color, clothing, and . . . well, basically all the choices. Carlos gets to be the prince, riding home on a stallion made of scholarships, and Danny is still cute, so he gets away with everything. But me? I'm just not *quite* right." She chuckled humorlessly. "Like pasteles in a food processor."

Evie bumped her with her shoulder. "You've got to work on your self-talk," she said. "You're more like . . . pasteles with creative spices added. Pasteles with pizzazz."

Tina scoffed. "Tati hates pizzazz."

"Maybe," Evie said, shrugging. "Maybe not. Anyway, I like your pizzazz. It perfectly offsets my simple, provincial charm."

Tina stopped and put a hand to her chest in mock emotion. "Are you, Evie Archer, being witty? I . . . I'm so proud. The student has become the teacher."

Evie laughed, pleased to have cheered Tina and, at least momentarily, cheered herself as well. But they were getting close to the library now, reminding her of where they were going and why. Reality settled back onto Evie like a heavy burden.

She took a deep breath. *Okay, time to focus.*

"So, the plan for today," she said. "I think we should spend the afternoon going through that box from the 1850s again, piece by piece."

Tina looked unconvinced. "But we went over it already, twice. There's nothing more to learn there, Evie. Holly already copied all the significant pieces forty years ago. They're in your backpack."

"I know," Evie said with a sigh. The truth was, she didn't know what else to do. After some brainstorming, they'd hypothesized that Desmond was somehow being used as a carrier for a dark spirit—akin to Holly herself—to spread its influence throughout the town. Sai's vision about a "harbinger" fit with that theory, as well as Evie's memory of Holly saying that she and Sarah weren't "alone down here" in the Shadow Land. But the identity of that spirit—and its connection to Sarah Flower—still remained a mystery.

"Maybe Sai will have an idea," Tina suggested. "He hasn't been staring at this stuff for as long as we have."

"Maybe," Evie agreed.

The Ravenglass Library Museum and Archives was a redbrick

colonial building with a white columned portico at the front. The columns had been decorated with garland and red ribbon, and a holiday wreath hung on the polished wooden door. A librarian in a Christmas scarf sat at a desk in the lobby and nodded at them as they entered. Evie smiled and nodded back, but there was something about the woman's unblinking gaze that unsettled her. She could almost feel the librarian's eyes on her back, like a physical touch, as they passed by her desk on the way to the stacks.

You're being paranoid, Evie scolded herself. But she shivered all the same.

Sai stood at a table covered in piles of old books and folios, staring thoughtfully at a map spread open in front of him.

"Anything?" Evie said by way of greeting.

Sai wagged his head back and forth in an uncertain motion. "I found this map of Ravenglass from the late 1850s that shows which town structures existed back then. Which is interesting, I guess, but probably not important."

"We'll see about that," Evie said, her curiosity piqued. She dropped her bag on a chair and went over to peer at the map. The old document lay on a sheet of onionskin paper, but other than some water damage and crease marks, it was in remarkably good condition. Evie leaned close, studying the hand-drawn roads, the familiar curve of the Blue River, and the sketches of important landmarks around the border. It was amazing how many things hadn't changed over more than a century's time. Main Street remained the same, with the town hall building and even the building they were standing in marked on the map. Hobbie House was there, too. But another small structure, high up on the mountain near the mines, intrigued her. "What's this?"

"That's the old King place," Tina said. "The log cabin where the first Mr. King settled before he founded the quarry. Apparently, it's been there forever."

"Where'd you get this map?" Evie asked Sai. "I thought I'd scoured the entire collection, but I've never seen it before."

Sai looked smug. "I said 'pretty-pretty please' to the lady at the desk, and she let me into a back room that's closed for renovations. They stopped work until the new year, so she didn't think it would do any harm, as long as we put everything back where we found it."

"'Pretty please,' eh?" Evie said with a smirk.

"Book ladies and English accents, luv," Sai said with a wink. "Works every time."

"Right," Evie said a little too brightly. Sai watched as she unfurled the scarf from her neck and discarded it on her chair, his eyes on her neck like a caress. She swallowed, suddenly feeling too warm.

Tina was glancing back and forth between them, an exasperated look on her face. "Come on, Farmgirl," she said, yanking Evie by the arm. "Let's check out the new room Motorhead over here flirted his way into."

Embarrassed, Evie followed Tina into a dusty room that looked prepped for a new paint job. White tarps covered the bookshelves and display cases, and assorted ladders and paint cans were gathered into one corner of the room, waiting for their owners to return. Tina ducked under one of the tarps on a bookshelf and disappeared. "Hmm," she said, her voice muffled. "More folios. We got maps, *Birds of North America*, *A Visual History of Western Massachusetts* . . ."

As she rattled through more titles, Evie lifted the tarps from some of the displays and peered underneath. One had a first edition copy of *Moby-Dick* and photos of Herman Melville and Mount Greylock, the tallest peak in Massachusetts. The display described a theory that the mountain was actually the inspiration for Melville's white whale. Another was about the mystery of Burnt Hill, an unexplained stone circle in nearby Heath. Nothing particularly helpful there. What she uncovered in the third display, however, made her heart leap into her throat.

"Tina . . . ," she called. "Look."

Tina ran over as Evie whipped the tarp free of the display, sending a cloud of dust motes into the afternoon light spilling in from the window.

"Jackpot," Tina whispered.

The display was titled THE RAVENGLASS GOLD RUSH! It contained nearly a dozen items from the 1850s—well-preserved daguerreotypes, handwritten papers, a canvas miner's cap with an oil lamp mounted to the brim, a shallow pan, and a small pickax with a rusty head. Sai ambled in and peered over their shoulders. "Would you look at that . . . ," he said wonderingly.

"Check out the date!" Evie exclaimed, pointing to a small card indicating the source of the artifacts.

THE RLMA WOULD LIKE TO THANK THE LATE FLORENCE JONES AND THE JONES FAMILY FOR BEQUEATHING THESE ARTIFACTS TO THE TOWN OF RAVENGLASS AFTER THEY WERE FOUND AMONG HER ESTATE IN 1987, it read.

"If these items were found in 1987," Evie continued, her voice rising in excitement, "that means Holly never had access to them.

She disappeared five years before that. This could be what she needed us to find to complete her work!"

"Okay," Sai said, his eyes scanning the artifacts. "If that's true, then what part of this display tells us something we don't already know?"

Silence fell as the three of them examined every inch of the display case. "This just talks about Wallace Brand," Tina mumbled. "How he came over after the California gold rush, found gold flake in the river, started the mine, blah, blah, blah . . . Nothing new here."

"This section is about the decline of mining in favor of lumber by the 1860s," Sai added. "And this paper here is just another list of workmen, like the one Holly included in her research. Asa Davis, Joseph White, George Brown, Henry Anderson . . ."

Evie shook her head and kept looking. There had to be *something* here. She was sure of it. Her gaze slid across a picture of a group of people standing in front of the newly built entrance to the gold mine. They were all serious-faced men in black trousers and rough white shirts, the whites of their eyes bright against dirt-stained faces. Two men stood front and center of the group—in the leadership positions. One was a rangy, weather-beaten man with thinning, light-colored hair and muttonchops. His clothing wasn't much different from what the other men wore—but of a finer quality, and he wore neither a jacket nor a tie. His jaw was set sternly, but Evie could see the hint of a twinkle in his eye. She liked him immediately.

The other man stood in stark contrast to his partner. He was tall and broad chested, but of a paler complexion, and his hair shone glossy and black. He wore a three-piece suit—trousers, jacket, and vest—complete with a satin puff tie. His gleaming, catlike eyes seemed to bore straight into Evie as she studied the image.

Evie's hands began sliding slowly down the surface of the glass with a low, moaning squeal. Her palms had begun to sweat.

Tina noticed her looking at the picture and consulted the label underneath. "'The Ravenglass miners with Foreman William Flower and Mr. Wallace Brand, 1857,'" she recited. "Wow, so that's Sarah's father!" Tina said, pointing to the fair man. "This must have been taken pretty close to the time he was killed."

But Evie didn't answer. She was staring at a single, tiny detail, probably not much larger than the head of a pin. The pocket watch hanging from Wallace Brand's vest. It was clearly an expensive piece, and yet it had a crack right down the middle of its face.

Just like the one Desmond had been wearing that fateful night when Evie saw him.

Slowly, Evie began to pull all the pieces together in her mind, weaving something that felt close to the truth.

"It's Brand," she said, looking at Tina and Sai in wonder. "He's the third spirit. He's the one doing all this."

Tina looked bewildered. "Wallace Brand? But it can't be him. He's a local hero. He's, like, the most important man in Ravenglass history!"

"Maybe history got it wrong," Evie murmured. She told them about Desmond's pocket watch. "When I saw him, he was struggling against something, as if he were under a spell. I wanted to save him, but he could hardly move, like even the effort of warning me off took every ounce of strength he had." Her voice faltered on the last two words, and she felt Tina's hand move gently over hers. Evie took a deep breath. "I think . . . I think that watch is serving as some kind of talisman, something to keep Desmond in Wallace Brand's thrall and to carry some part of his spirit out into the world. And it seems like it's spreading. Like a virus."

"'The harbinger comes before, and the shadow follows soon after,'" Sai intoned, his face pale.

"Right," Evie said. She reached inside her shirt and lifted out the locket that belonged to Holly and Sarah before her. "Kind of like how this necklace connected me to Holly and allowed me to find her in the Shadow Land after Stan disappeared."

"Okay, I'm liking this so far," Tina said, starting to pace. "But how could Wallace Brand have turned into this shadow demon you're describing? There's no record of him being killed, or disappearing into the mine, or anything like that. He just left town when the gold mining dried up."

Evie shot her an inquiring glance. "Did he?" she asked. "Or are we just assuming he did because there aren't any records of him after 1857?"

Tina stopped pacing and stood for a moment, arms akimbo. "Good point. And if the records missed that, what else are they missing?"

"Exactly." Evie turned back to the display. Something else was bugging her, something *she'd* missed. "Sai, where's that paper with the list of workmen?"

"Here," Sai replied, pointing. "George Brown, Tom Sullivan, Ellis Williams . . ."

Evie stared at the names for a whole minute before it hit her. "Now I remember why the names on those old gravestones at the church sounded so familiar!" she exclaimed. "I'd seen them on

Holly's list of workmen from the mine. They were all young men who died in the same year—1857. The same year this photo was taken, and when everything about gold mines and Wallace Brand stopped. I thought they'd all died of cholera or some terrible disease, but what if it was something else?"

"If they were all mine workers," Sai reasoned, "then maybe it was some kind of mining accident. It's a dangerous job and was even more so back then." They all glanced over at the display case, where the canvas miner cap and its mounted oil lamp looked like a poor defense against the darkness of a mine.

"That makes sense," Tina agreed. "But a disaster of that magnitude would definitely show up in the records. Unless . . ."

"Unless what?" Evie asked.

Tina's face darkened. "Unless this hole goes even deeper than we thought."

The three of them put everything back where they had found it and returned to their table in the main room of the library. Sai leaned back in his wooden chair with his arms crossed over his chest. "Let's say this Brand bloke really is our bad guy," he began, "and something awful really did happen to those miners. Where does that leave us? What are we supposed to do to stop him? And what does all this have to do with the girl, Sarah Flower?"

"This has always been about getting Desmond back," Evie said. "If Brand is using him to get control of everyone in town, we need to cut that connection. Maybe then everyone will go back to normal." She sighed. "But you're right, Sai. We're still no closer to figuring out how. I mean, I snuck into that mine half a dozen times when Desmond first disappeared, and there was nothing there."

"If Holly wanted us to investigate Sarah Flower," Tina said, "then there must be a reason—an answer we haven't found yet. If Sarah's dad was the foreman, that means he worked with Brand on the regular and knew everything that went on in that mine. He died the same year all this happened. They blamed Sarah for his death, and she disappeared around the same time. Maybe the key to getting into the Shadow Land to rescue Desmond is figuring out the truth of what really happened to Sarah and her father."

Sai nodded. "All right then. So where to next?"

Evie suddenly remembered the vision she'd had the first time she'd met Sai—the pin in her hand, the blood, and the faint smell of vegetation in the air. A deep, earthy smell. At first, she associated it with the mine, but there was another underground place she hadn't considered. A chill rippled down her spine as she realized what she had to do, and a familiar, haunting melody filled her mind.

Playmate, come out and play with me,
and bring your dollies three.
Climb up my apple tree,
look down my rain barrel,
slide down my cellar door . . .

"We go back to Hobbie House," she whispered. "Down to the root cellar. That's where they found Mr. Flower's body. Where this whole horrible thing started."

And where, Evie wondered grimly, was it going to end?

13

Evie stood in the kitchen at Hobbie House, staring at the vintage draft blocker in front of the cellar door. The eight featureless cats seemed to be staring back at her with their pinprick eyes, asking, "Do you really want to go down there?"

The truth was, Evie had been in the root cellar several times since homecoming night. She thought that maybe she'd be able to access the Shadow Land the same way she had before, but when she'd shone a light down into the shaft beneath the hidden panel, all she'd seen was dirt.

This time, though—she thought with a mixture of hope and dread—*this time will be different.* Because now she knew in her bones that the cellar was where all the secrets were buried. And because Sai would be there with her.

It was Saturday morning, several days since their discovery in the library. Mom had been working nonstop at the Blue River Inn—apparently Fiona had been out sick for a week—and Dad and Stan were in Pittsfield doing some Christmas shopping, so the house was finally empty.

"You ready?" Tina asked. She, Evie, and Sai were drinking coffee at the kitchen table. A palpable sense of unease pervaded everything, and none of them had said more than two words to one another since Tina and Sai had arrived.

Evie nodded. She got up and poured the rest of her coffee into the sink—it was making her jittery. "I think you should stay up here, Tina," she said, turning around and leaning against the kitchen counter. "Just in case."

"In case what?" Tina asked.

Evie swallowed. "In case something goes wrong, and we need help."

Tina said nothing.

Sai rubbed one hand across his mouth. "Right," he said, standing up and wiping his palms on his jeans. "Come on, then."

Evie started toward the cellar door, and Tina put a hand on her shoulder. "Hey," she said, her voice hoarse. She looked as if she were cycling through a dozen different things she wanted to say, but in the end, all she said was "Be careful."

Giving her friend a tight smile, Evie grasped the knob and pulled the cellar door open with a long, thin creak. A sound like an exhale came from the blackness below as a rush of musty air blew across Evie's face. With it came the bitter, earthy smell of old vegetables. Her heart began to thrum in her throat as dark memories flooded her mind.

Slide down.

Slide down.

Slide down.

She gasped as she felt Sai's warm hand on hers, pulling it away from the doorknob. She hadn't realized how hard she'd been gripping it. Evie looked at him, and his face was oddly calm. "Aren't you scared?" she asked.

Sai shrugged. "Not really." He stared down into the murk. "Guess I've got nothing to lose." He groped along the wall until he felt the switch and turned it on. Three buzzing lightbulbs illuminated the stairwell. Without another word, he began to descend.

Standing there in the doorway, Evie was reminded of summers at the community pool back in New York, where she and her friend Hannah used to go swimming. Evie would stand at the edge, staring down into the deep water, hesitant to take the plunge. Hannah always jumped in first, doing a cannonball that splashed everyone within a ten-foot radius. She did that because once she was in the water, Evie had no choice but to follow. "Jump in," she'd always say. "The water's fine."

Slide down.

Jump in.

Take a leap of faith.

Evie swallowed and took a step down into the cellar, closing the door behind her.

Sai had already reached the bottom and was standing in the middle of the dimly lit room, surveying the cloudy, dust-encrusted jars and rusty tools. "Well?" he asked. "Where is it?"

Evie walked over to the old blue and violet rug and pulled it aside.

Sai kneeled and squinted at the ground beneath. "Nearly invisible, innit?" he said.

"Yeah," Evie said, grabbing a shovel and wedging it in the crack. "I only found it the first time because there was something stuck inside." With a practiced heave, Evie levered the shovel down and pried the secret panel upward. Together, she and Sai lifted it open, revealing the dark pit underneath.

"Cor . . . ," Sai breathed. He threaded his fingers through his thick, wavy hair and gazed down into the abyss.

"What do you think we should do now?" Evie asked.

Sai didn't reply. In the back of the room, the old HVAC unit roared to life like a fire-breathing dragon.

"Sai?" His eyes hadn't left the pit. He was standing stock-still, his lips slightly parted. "Sai, what do we do?"

When he spoke, his voice wasn't just his own. It was twinned with another—familiar and strange. A girlish, childlike voice that had once haunted Evie's dreams. "We find the truth," the voices said together. A second later, Sai reached out and clasped his hand with hers.

Evie cried out as a wave of force passed through her body, as shocking as being plunged into cold water. She tried to pull away from Sai's grip, but he held her fast.

Suddenly Sai gasped as if he'd just come up for air, just as he'd done at Evie's bedroom window. He looked around, wild-eyed. "Bloody hell, what was that?" he said. "It's like something went straight through me."

"Me too," Evie whispered.

Just then, a quiet, childlike humming came from behind them.

187

The melody sounded like a Christmas song. *Deck the halls with boughs of . . .*

The hairs on Evie's neck stood on end. Slowly, she and Sai turned around.

A girl stood in the center of the room, her body in profile as she gazed down at something shiny on the floor. A little piece of gold tinsel. She was wearing a long, old-fashioned black dress, and a bonnet that hid her face from view.

Evie took in a ragged breath, speaking the name quietly, so as not to break the spell keeping the apparition standing before them.

"Holly."

Holly Hobbie turned to look at them with a small smile on her face. A face that had once been half rotted away, that had tortured Evie for weeks, and lured her into the depths of her own personal hell. A face that, thanks to Evie, was whole again.

The shadow smiled. *"Hello, Evie,"* she said, in the same voice that had come through Sai's lips just a moment before. *"Peekaboo. You found me."*

Evie shook her head. "You were here the whole time? God, I should have brought Sai down here a week ago. We could have—"

"Did you find out about him?" Holly broke in.

"About Wallace Brand?" Evie asked. "Yes, just a couple days ago. We uncovered new information at the library."

"Then you came at the right time," Holly said. *"You needed to understand before we could talk properly. I told you to be patient."*

"But why?" Evie asked. "Why couldn't you just tell me exactly what's going on in the first place?"

For the second time since they had met in the Shadow Land, Evie saw fear in Holly's eyes. *"Because he has a hold on me,"* she whispered. *"I can't tell you what you need to know. I can't even say his name. You had to figure it out for yourself."* Holly looked at Sai as if seeing him for the first time. Evie blinked, and suddenly the apparition was close to him, studying him like a brand-new toy. Sai flinched but gave no other sign of terror. He just stared back at Holly, speechless with wonder. *"You found him, too. The lost boy."*

Evie swallowed. She knew Holly was on her side now, but her presence still made Evie quake with fear. "Yes," she replied. "Although I think it's more like we found each other."

"I couldn't speak to you directly, you see," Holly explained, brushing her hand like smoke over Sai's face. *"When I let you escape from the Shadow Land, he was very, very angry. I've never seen him so angry. He used his power to stop me from ever talking to you again. But then I found this lost boy, standing on the edge between light and shadow. And I thought about the game Telephone. I could talk to him, and he could talk to you, and then we could all talk together again. Isn't that fun?"*

The childlike quality of Holly's voice made Evie uneasy. It was almost as if the time she'd spent down in the shadow was slowly erasing her humanity again, turning her back into the monster she'd been. Still, if she was there helping Evie, she was still fighting back. "Yes, very fun," Evie replied, playing along. "But if you can't tell me more details, why did you want me to find you here?"

Holly turned toward Evie, her beautiful, haunting face alight with excitement. *"Because,"* she said in a singsong voice. *"We don't need to tell you if we can show you . . ."*

Evie glanced at Sai, puzzled. He seemed to be thinking the same thing. *Who's we?*

Holly was looking at something behind them. *"Come on now, don't be shy,"* she said, holding out her hand.

Evie turned and had to suppress a shriek when she saw a young girl sitting cross-legged on the dusty floor in the corner of the room. She, too, wore a long dress and bonnet, but hers was made of patchwork cloth. Her hair hung in two plaits, as fair and yellow as spun gold. She would have been a sweet thing to behold, had her face not been the fleshless horror of a naked skull. White and staring and grinning with tiny, overlong teeth.

Sai stumbled back. "Wh-what is that?" he stammered. "No . . . no no no . . ."

"It's all right," Evie said, putting a reassuring hand on his arm, despite not feeling reassured herself. "That's . . . that's Sarah Flower. That's the Patchwork Girl."

Sarah seemed to be as nervous as they were. She skittered over to Holly like a kitten, holding the older girl's arm for comfort. *"Hush now,"* Holly scolded. *"They won't hurt you. They're our friends."* Holly kneeled next to Sarah and looked, unafraid, into the bottomless eyes of her skull. *"Now, I want you to show them what happened here a long, long time ago. You remember, don't you?"*

Sarah shook her head vigorously, her shoulders hunched.

"I know it's scary," Holly went on. *"But you have to, Sarah. If we ever want to be free of him, you've got to show them the truth."*

A moment passed, and no one in the room moved. Then Sarah slowly let go of Holly and turned toward them. As she approached, it took all of Evie's willpower not to recoil, to keep the moan of terror from climbing up her throat. The girl was a thing of nightmares, but Evie knew that if she was ever going to find Desmond, she needed to see whatever it was Sarah had to show her. Next to her, Sai was rigid, his eyes never leaving the girl's bone-white face.

When she was close enough, Sarah stopped and reached out to them. The little skeletal hand seemed to glow under the light of the naked bulb hanging above. Evie could feel something radiating from the girl—something powerful and familiar. But it was only after she'd taken Sarah's hand, and felt the tiny bones close around her fingers that she realized what it was.

It was a secret, long kept and ready to emerge from the dark.

As soon as they touched, the room twisted and blurred. Color slid away, leaving behind the coffee-stained world she'd seen many times before. When everything stopped spinning, the root cellar looked different. The shovel and rake leaning against the wall were new and well maintained. Instead of old, dusty items, the wooden shelves held dozens of bright, colorful jars filled with preserved peaches, beets, cucumbers, string beans, and sauerkraut. Baskets on the floor were filled to the brim with apples and potatoes, and in the corner, four cabbages hung limply from a rope, like desiccated heads left out as a warning. The vegetable smell that had been faint before was strong—a heady mix of soil and green things and sugar-sweet flesh.

"Did we . . . travel back in time?" Sai whispered, gazing around in wonder.

"Yes and no," Evie replied. "I think this is just a memory."

She looked around, and nearly jumped out of her skin when she realized a man was kneeling next to her, staring down into the black pit. He was there but not there, as diaphanous as a sun-faded photograph. Despite that, Evie immediately recognized him as one of the two men from the picture at the library. It was Sarah's father, William Flower. He wore gray pants, suspenders, and a rough white shirt, with the sleeves rolled up to his elbows. Next to him on a small wooden table were what looked like the contents of his pack—a flint and steel, a wood-handled knife, and a gun. He seemed deep in thought when the silence was broken by the sound of footsteps coming down the stairs. Evie turned to see another ghostly man descending into the cellar. He appeared piecemeal—first his black laced boots, then the flash of his gold pocket watch, and then his pale face and gleaming, dark eyes. Evie's heart skipped a beat when she saw something familiar pinned to his lapel. A silver sprig of mistletoe, dotted with pearls.

"Hello, Billy," Wallace Brand said. "You wanted to see me?"

Mr. Flower stood and wiped his hands on his trousers before setting them on his hips. "I did," he said. His voice was grave.

Brand seemed to sense the tension in the room and strode over to Mr. Flower, clapping him on the back. "What's gotten you so long in the face, my friend?" he asked. "I know things have been difficult, but it's nothing a good slug of my finest whiskey can't fix."

But Mr. Flower was unmoved, his face like cut stone. "I know what you did, Wall."

The smile fell from Brand's face, darkening like the sky before a storm. "Really now?" he said lightly.

Mr. Flower nodded. "That collapse in the mine was no accident. I know that section where the men were working back to front—it was stable. It should have been fine. What happened wasn't natural. Something took it out." He stopped and took a breath. "I knew some of those boys since they were *children*, do you understand? Children! I promised their mothers and fathers that they'd be safe in that mine, and you made me a liar." He paused again, his face flushed with anger. "They don't even have bodies to bury! Those boys will rot down in that hole forever!"

Evie paled and thought of Desmond.

If it weren't for you, he'd still be here!

"And you figure that's my fault, do you?" Brand said softly. "The deaths of all those boys?"

"You're no fool, Wall," Mr. Flower said. "A bit of well-placed black powder is all it would take to bring the ceiling down on their heads. That's a fact."

Brand chuckled. "Now, that's a mighty fine story you're weaving, Billy boy. So, in your estimation, I'd go through the trouble of killing those hardworking boys why, exactly?"

Mr. Flower's jaw clenched. "You showed up in town and claimed to have found a vein in these hills. You got everybody worked up into a lather about it, saying it's another gold rush right here in Massachusetts. But all this time, the most any of us have found are pebbles and flakes. Those 'hardworking boys' were getting restless. Suspicious, too. I reckon you got worried they'd tell everyone the truth."

"The truth, eh? The *truth*?"

"Yes, the truth!" Mr. Flower shouted. "Every person down to the farmhands gave themselves over to this godforsaken venture. Gave their sons, their fortunes—and for what? For what?" He got close to Brand, his voice lowering to a whisper. "For nothing. Nothing at all. Because the bottom fact is, Wall, the bottom fact is that *there ain't no gold in Ravenglass.* There never was. You know it, and now I know it. It was all just a con. And you had to murder every last one of those poor boys because they'd finally started to figure it out, too."

Evie put a hand over her mouth. Could it be true? But everything in Ravenglass reflected its gold mining history—even more than a hundred years later. Was it possible all of it was built on a lie?

She expected Brand to get angry, to yell and maybe even hit Mr. Flower, but he didn't. He just looked at him, a wide smile spreading across his face. "Well," he murmured. "I couldn't well have them waking snakes, now, could I?"

Mr. Flower shook his head in disgust. "So you admit it," he said. He poked a finger into Brand's chest. "You're going to hell for this, Wall. But I'm not letting you drag me down with you. By the end of the day, everybody's going to know what you did. And if I have to spend the rest of my life atoning for my part in it, so be it."

Brand heaved a heavy sigh. He lifted the pocket watch from where it hung and polished its broken face on his vest. "We made a good team—you and me—didn't we, Billy?" he said. "We collected a great quantity of money, and made a lot of folks happy doing it. You don't think about that, but you should. Folks love giving their money away if it means they get to be part of something important. I'd hate to think you want to take that from them. Yes, I surely would." He gave Mr. Flower's chest a pat. "Made a good team," he muttered, solemn. "Too bad."

There was a flash of movement, and a deafening crack filled the air.

Evie jumped, a small cry of alarm escaping her throat.

At the same moment, Mr. Flower's body jerked back. "Wha-what did you—?" he sputtered. He stumbled and looked down at his shirt, where blood bloomed like a rose.

Brand lowered the Colt revolver that had appeared in his hand and nimbly reholstered it at his side. "Tsk," he said, shaking his head. "You and those boys were such fine workers. But all good things must come to an end, mustn't they?"

"No . . . ," Mr. Flower said. His lips were covered in blood now. "Sarah . . ." He lurched toward the stairs, but made it only a couple of steps before he collapsed and was still.

Brand watched him for a few seconds, and then kicked at Mr. Flower's foot. It flopped limply against the floor. "Suppose that's it then," he mumbled. Turning, Brand picked up Mr. Flower's gun from the small table and then walked back over to the body. He flipped Mr. Flower onto his back, and was carefully placing the revolver into the dead man's hand when a long creak came from upstairs. The sound of the cellar door opening.

"Daddy?" said a small voice.

Evie swallowed, sick with dread.

Brand stood straight up, his eyes darting up the stairs and down to the body again. His lip curled in irritation.

"Daddy?" the voice said again. "Where are you?" A moment later, little feet came thumping down the stairs, and Sarah Flower appeared.

Evie was shocked. It was the first time she had ever seen Sarah's real face. Not a blur in an old picture or the grinning horror of a skull. She wasn't strikingly beautiful, nor was she plain. The most shocking thing about her was how perfectly ordinary she was. Like any little girl one might see in any little town anywhere. Just a young, innocent child in a patchwork dress, who had never wanted any of this. A child who, right in front of Evie's eyes, had her innocence destroyed forever the moment she saw her father lying dead on the floor.

Sarah screamed. In seconds she was on her knees in front of Mr. Flower, holding his face and calling his name. "Daddy," she cried. "Wake up, Daddy, please! Please wake up!" It took nearly an entire minute before she noticed Wallace Brand standing a few feet away, watching. "What happened?" she wailed. "What happened to him?"

"I'm so sorry, Sarah," Brand said soothingly. "I tried to stop him, but it was too late. It was all just too much for him, in the end. Now come away from there. Come with me, and I'll take care of everything . . ."

But Sarah wasn't listening. She was staring at Brand's hand. It was covered in blood. Then, her gaze slid to the gun held loosely in her father's stiff, cooling hand. When she looked back at Wallace Brand, her eyes were shimmering with fathomless sorrow.

"You killed him," she said softly.

Brand's composure flickered, just for an instant. "Now, you know that's not true," he replied. "You're upset, I understand that. Let's go upstairs, calm down, and together we can—"

"He never liked you," Sarah went on, sniffing, smoothing her father's hair away from his face. She was eerily calm. Evie imagined she must be in shock. "He always said that if you came around when he wasn't home, I should go hide in my room and not come to the door."

"I'm sure he said the same thing about all the men in town,"

Brand said gently, taking a step closer to her. "He was just trying to protect his little girl, like any father would." He took another step. "But he and I were friends, Sarah, you must know that. If he were still alive, he'd want me to be the one to take care of you." He pointed to the mistletoe pin on his lapel. "Christmas is coming soon, you know. That's why I'm wearing my Christmas pin. Do you like it? You can have it, and so much more, if you just come with me. You don't have to be alone. You and I, we can—"

"Stay away!" Sarah cried, suddenly standing and making a move toward the stairs. "Don't touch me!"

Brand froze, his jaw clenching. "Where do you think you're going?" he asked.

Sarah's eyes flicked down to her father's body and then back to Brand, but she said nothing. She didn't need to. It was clear to anyone watching what she planned to do. Run into town with blood on her hands, ready to tell the first person she met that Mr. Flower was dead and Wallace Brand had killed him.

"You know," Brand said. All warmth had fled from his voice, leaving it as cold as ice. "You really are a stubborn little rat. Just like your father." He sighed. "Shame to leave this nice big house so empty, but needs must when the devil drives." With lightning-quick movement, he lunged forward to grab Sarah by the wrist and drag her toward him.

Sarah shrieked in terror. Feeling helpless, Evie watched as Brand grabbed the girl by the throat with both hands and started to squeeze. Sarah gagged and pushed at Brand's chest, tearing the mistletoe pin from his lapel. It fell and skittered across the floor. The two moved in a herky-jerky motion around the room as they grappled, locked together in a silent dance of death. Her face purpling, Sarah tore at Brand's arms and fingers, then at his eyes. He cursed as her nails caught the flesh of his cheek, and he stretched his arms out straighter so she could no longer reach him.

Soon, Evie could see the strength going out of Sarah's arms, her blows growing weaker by the second. Brand could see it, too. His tense expression began to relax as he realized his awful deed was nearly done. Whether his grip on Sarah's throat lessened for a moment, or whether it was simply the girl's last-ditch effort at survival, Evie could never be sure. But in the next instant, Sarah's right hand was reaching, scrabbling across the small wooden table where her father's belongings lay and wrapping her fingers around the hilt of his knife.

The blade flashed through the air, just catching the light filtering in from the narrow window. Brand screamed as the knife raked across his face, slicing a deep furrow in one eye. He let go of Sarah as he pressed his hands to the wound, releasing a string of blistering curses as blood seeped from between his fingers. "I'll kill you, you little—" he snarled, stumbling backward, spittle flying from his mouth. "I'll—"

And then he was gone.

One moment he was there, raging, and the next, he'd taken a step back and disappeared into the mine shaft.

Down below, there was a loud crack, and then: silence.

For a moment, Sarah stood frozen in place, staring at the empty space where Brand had been. Then she heaved a strangled breath into her lungs and began to cough. Tears streamed down her face as she bent double, retching, until finally she collapsed to the floor.

Evie saw the light from the window change, fade, vanish, and return in a matter of moments, as if they were watching hours pass in seconds. Throughout it all, Sarah seemed to move around the room, appearing in different positions. Sometimes she had her head on her father's chest, other times she was leaning against the wall, asleep. But when the light faded for the second time, everything slowed once again. Sarah was on her knees in front of the mine shaft, staring at something in her hand, crusted over with dried blood. She looked like an old woman in a child's body.

Evie leaned over to see what she was holding, and stiffened as she realized it was Brand's mistletoe pin. She watched as Sarah's lip curled, and she threw the thing into the hole to join its owner. Then she put her head in her hands, her narrow shoulders shaking with silent tears.

It was perfectly quiet in the cellar. No sound from outside could penetrate the thick walls and earth surrounding that room. So when the sibilant voice came creeping out from the bottom of the black pit, its words were crystal clear.

"*SsssssssSarah . . .*"

The girl's body went rigid.

"*SsssssssSarah . . . ,*" the voice hissed again.

Sarah shook her head violently. She did not want to hear that voice. She wanted, with every fiber of her being, for the impossible thing to stop happening.

Evie watched the girl's expression with growing discomfort. She knew that feeling. She knew it all too well.

"*It hurts, doesn't it, Sarah?*" the voice went on. It was low and wet and dissonant. "*Oh, but it will hurt more when they find you. They'll say you killed your own daddy. Sure, you can tell them that I did it, but then again, you killed me, too. So who's to say what's true and what isn't?*"

"No," Sarah moaned. "I didn't kill you. It was an accident! You're a murderer!"

"But everyone in Ravenglass likes me, Sarah," the voice continued. *"I brought them excitement and adventure! Not you, though. You're strange. Quiet. No one likes you. I hear them talk behind your back. They whisper about you. They think you're a witch."*

"You're not dead—you can't be." Sarah was rocking back and forth, her arms around her knees. "You're talking to me right now. Dead people don't talk."

"Such a strange, sad child. All alone in the world now, with no one to save you. What a tragedy."

"They don't talk about me . . . I didn't mean to . . ." She was mumbling now, incoherent.

"Come to the edge and pull me up, Sarah," the voice said. *"I promise not to hurt you again. I was just afraid, like you are right now. We all can do terrible things when we're afraid. If you pull me up, I'll be all right again, and I can explain everything. Doesn't that sound nice?"*

Sarah stopped rocking and looked at the hole. She blinked, and Evie could see her addled mind considering the offer. *Don't do it, Sarah*, she thought. *Whatever you do, don't get any closer.* Evie knew all too well what happened when you got too close to the pit.

But it was too late for warnings. All of this had already happened a long, long time ago.

Sarah got to her feet. She sniffed and wiped her red-rimmed eyes, her gaze never leaving the mystery of the deep, black hole.

"*Come and take my hand,*" Wallace Brand said, for Evie knew it was his voice calling out. "*And I'll make it all go away. It's no good being alone. You need a friend.*"

Slowly, Sarah walked to the edge of the mine shaft and peered down.

"Get away from there!" Evie shouted. She knew it was futile, but she couldn't help herself.

Sarah blinked and glanced sideways, and Evie could have sworn the girl looked directly at her.

Something reached up from inside the pit. A dirt-blackened hand encrusted with blood.

"*Sarah!*" Evie screamed.

The girl was still squinting in Evie's direction when the filthy, bloody fingers closed around her ankle.

She shrieked in terror and reached out toward Evie.

Instinctively, Evie tried to grab for her hands, but came up with nothing but air. "No!" she cried.

In an instant, Sarah was gone, too.

Evie fell to her knees at the edge of the mine shaft, the full weight of everything she'd seen coming down on her shoulders. She stared down into the void, but the darkness there was impenetrable. The shadow had swallowed Brand and Sarah both, the first chapter in a story Evie was still writing. She looked up at Mr. Flower's corpse cooling in the corner. He'd died for the truth, and it had been buried with him ever since.

Until now.

The truth will set you free.

A strident voice came echoing from above.

"Guys? Everything okay down there?"

Evie felt the room around her jolt. She gasped as the sepia-toned world froze and then shattered around them.

"Wait!" she exclaimed, trying to stop the vision from falling away. "No, not yet! I still have questions!"

Despite her protests, the world returned to normal in the blink of an eye. The rusty tools and moldering jars were back, and Evie felt herself standing on solid ground. Sai stood next to her, looking dazed.

"We're okay," Evie called weakly.

Tina came clumping down the stairs a moment later, looking anxious. "I heard Evie shouting and got worried." She glanced back and forth between their faces. "Well? Did it work?"

Evie put her hands on her knees and hung her head. She was dizzy, disoriented. Coming back from the vision so abruptly felt like hitting a brick wall at high speed. And witnessing a murder—even one that had happened more than a hundred years ago—wasn't an easy thing to bounce back from either. She took a deep breath, trying to get ahold of herself.

When Evie looked up, Sai's expression made it clear that he'd seen the same thing she had and felt similarly about the experience. He walked over to one of the dusty crates and sat down heavily. "It worked all right," he whispered.

"We know what happened to Sarah Flower," Evie said. Quickly gathering her wits about her, she explained what Holly and Sarah had shown them.

Tina took a seat on the bottom stair and set her elbows on her knees. "Wow. So all this time, people thought Sarah was some sort of twisted killer haunting the town, when she was totally innocent all along." She shook her head. "That *sucks*."

"It does indeed suck," Sai managed. His voice was hoarse with controlled emotion. "Which is all well and good for us to know, but again, how does that help us get to Desmond and stop Brand?"

Evie stared down into the mine shaft, fiddling with her locket as she considered Sai's question. She thought of their research in the library, and the visions Holly had shown her. *She wanted me to know what happened . . . but why?* Suddenly, her hand closed around the locket.

"Tina," she said softly. "What do you know about mistletoe?"

Tina blinked. "Mistletoe?"

"Yes, other than the kissing thing."

Looking bewildered, Tina pulled her phone from her back pocket and started typing. After a moment, her eyebrows rose in surprise. "Huh. Well, that's interesting."

"What?" Evie said, perking up. The idea was a long shot, but something about it felt right.

"'Despite its festive reputation,'" Tina began reading, "'mistletoe is actually a parasitic plant that grows mostly on oak and apple trees. When left to grow freely, it can eventually kill the host tree by sending its roots into the trunk of the tree to feed from its sap.'"

Evie felt the blood drain from her face. She thought of two lost girls playing underneath the apple tree while the shadow of a man loomed over them. A man whose influence twisted around each of their lives like a vine, filling their minds with poison.

"There's something else," Tina added. "'Like holly and the other evergreen plants that are part of the Christmas tradition, mistletoe symbolizes *life that does not die.*'"

Evie swallowed, her mind full of shadows and a place pinned between life and death.

We're not the only ones down here.

She shook her head in disbelief. "That's it," Evie said. "First she showed me what I needed, then Sarah showed me where to find it." Holly hadn't been able to say much, but she'd still managed to tell her everything she needed to know.

"Find what?" Sai asked, now just as confused as Tina.

Instead of answering his question, Evie looked around and asked, "Is there a rope down here?"

"Why?" Tina asked, suspicious. "What are you doing?"

"I promise I'll explain," Evie pleaded. "Just help me first. I have to see if I'm right."

The three of them searched the room and opened crates until they unearthed a length of thick rope from a tangle of old equipment. "Tie it off to that," she said, nodding toward a column. "Hold on to it, too, just in case."

Evie threw the loose end of the rope into the mine shaft. "I'll be right back," she said.

Tina and Sai glanced at each other in mild alarm as Evie lowered herself into the pit. She inched down slowly, keeping both feet on the wall of the shaft and taking one step at a time.

"How deep is it?" Sai called.

"I'm not sure," Evie shouted back. Unlike the first time she'd seen the pit, it wasn't a fathomless black hole, but it was still pretty dark. After about ten steps down, she stopped and shone her phone flashlight down below. It looked as if the rope was just long enough to reach the bottom. Beyond that, it looked like the tunnel branched out into other parts of the gold mine. Whether those tunnels were still passable, she didn't know, and she didn't plan to find out. Her arms burning with fatigue, Evie finally felt her feet touch the ground. She let go of the rope. "I made it to the bottom!" she called up to her friends.

"What's down there?" Tina asked.

"Give me a minute . . . ," Evie shouted back.

Ten minutes passed. It was edging toward fifteen before Evie's weight pulled at the rope again. "Hold on, we'll pull you up," Sai said. Adjusting their grips, he and Tina hauled at the rope, dragging her back to the surface.

Within a minute, Evie was pulling herself over the edge and onto the dusty floor. Throwing the rope aside, she coughed, rubbing dirt from her eyes and brushing it off her shirt and pants.

"Well? Did you find something?" Tina asked, unable to contain her curiosity.

Evie nodded and opened her hand. Inside, tarnished but unbroken, was Brand's silver-and-pearl mistletoe pin. "Sarah threw it in the hole after Brand fell, remember?" she told Sai. "It's been down there ever since."

Sai gingerly picked up the pin and dusted it off with his fingers. Several of the pearls were stained a deep, rust red. "But why would Holly want you to find this?" he asked.

Evie thought about the picture in his father's office of Alice standing by the door, the little golden key in her hand.

"Because to get into the shadow," Evie replied, "we need a talisman. A key. I had the locket, and Desmond has the pocket watch, which Brand must be using to control him and bring him back and forth from our world. If we want to get in, we need something tied to Brand's fate. Something to get us past the walls he's put up around the place." They all looked down at the innocent little pin that lay in Sai's hand. A memory of a winter long ago, soaked in blood. "And there's none more powerful than this."

Meanwhile . . .

Martha Hobbie must have read the same paragraph three times over, and still had no idea what it said.

She was sitting on the love seat in her apartment, wrapped in her purple shawl, with a book and a mug of chamomile tea. Her third mug of the evening. It was nearly midnight, and despite how tired her body was, her mind just wouldn't relax. They were deep into the holiday season now, and Ravenglass was aglow with lights and all the trappings of Christmas cheer. A light snow fell outside her window, turning the town into a picture-perfect scene. But despite all that, whenever Martha went out to do her shopping, she couldn't shake the feeling that something was wrong. The smiles of passersby seemed hollow and strange, and there was a coldness in the air that had nothing to do with the wintry weather. She'd tried to brush it off. Her intuition was good, but not perfect. Perhaps what she sensed was merely the melancholy that many people felt that time of year—when the days were short and the nights a little too long. The holidays were not kind to everyone, she knew that much. Sometimes, instead of being an opportunity for people to appreciate their blessings, it was a reminder of what they'd lost, or never had at all.

Martha assured herself that her innate empathy was to blame, nothing more.

Still, she could not sleep.

She'd chosen something dense to read—a book by Carl Jung that she'd found in the used bookstore several years earlier—thinking it would settle her mind. Jung was heady stuff, but as a psychic, Martha felt it was part of her professional duty to deepen her understanding of the human experience. The chapter she was trying to read was about archetypes—universal truths that Jung believed were shared by every human being. Rubbing her eyes, Martha flipped ahead a few pages, hoping something might catch her interest. She stopped at a heading that read "The Shadow."

"Every man," she read, "even the best of us, has a shadow side to his nature. A side containing not only all his human flaws and weaknesses, but also a darkness—an evil magnetism. We often know nothing of this shadow self, and yet it is as much a part of us as our very name. However, if we allow these otherwise harmless creatures within ourselves to amass and wrest control over us, something truly monstrous can emerge—"

Knock. Knock. Knock.

Martha started, spilling a little chamomile into her lap. "Damn it," she muttered, brushing off the liquid before it absorbed into the fabric. She set her mug and book on the coffee table and glanced at the clock. 12:03 a.m. *Who could be calling at this time of night?* she wondered. It wouldn't be the first time someone in a desperate situation had come for a midnight reading, but it still gave her pause. A misguided pizza deliveryman, perhaps? Before she could decide what to do, the raps came again. Staccato, like three periods in an ellipsis.

Knock. Knock. Knock.

Martha stood and made her way through the apartment into her reading room. It was dark save for the yellow glow emanating from the neon sign on her window. PSYCHIC READER, it announced. She'd meant to turn it off for the night. Perhaps that was the problem—someone on the street had seen it lit and assumed she was still open for business. Relaxing a bit, she went to the door and peered through the peephole into the stairwell beyond.

What she saw nearly made her heart stop.

Standing on her doorstep, dressed in a ragged, filthy suit, was Desmond King.

"Oh my god," Martha said, stepping back from the door. Her shaking fingers fumbled with the chain and the deadbolt, and she was so overwhelmed with amazement and relief that she didn't even stop to wonder why, of all people in the world, he had come to her.

She threw the door open, ready to catch him in her arms, ready to retrieve her phone and call for an ambulance, ready to let the world know that a miracle had occurred. Ready for anything except what she got.

His name died on her lips when she saw his face.

The gray skin. The black eyes. The lips sewn so neatly shut. He stood like an omen at the threshold, waiting to come in.

Martha screamed and slammed the door.

She should have locked it, barred it—should have done so many things, really, but she was too frightened. Her mind was reeling with animal terror, unable to comprehend what was happening to her. Backing away, she tripped over her trailing shawl and sprawled backward onto the floor. Something small in her wrist snapped on impact, but the pain barely registered. She thought about her phone in the other room, but hadn't even begun formulating a plan before the three huge picture windows at the front of her reading room all blew open at once.

Frigid wind and snow blasted in, sending the heavy purple

curtains flying, and transforming the reading room into a shaken snow globe. Martha cried out as papers and loose tarot cards went whirling into the maelstrom. The wind lifted her hair and clothes, whipping them against her face, and she fought to see, to breathe.

I have to close the windows! she thought, and started to crawl toward them, cradling her injured wrist against her chest. She got up and closed them, one by one, but the raging storm didn't stop. It was as if, like an uninvited guest, the wind refused to leave the room once it had gained entry. Martha stumbled back from the windows, feeling trapped. With Desmond—or something that looked like him—standing at the door, how could she escape?

She was just turning toward the main room to find her phone and call for help when her gaze stopped on the picture windows once more. One moment, she was seeing the snow-covered buildings of Main Street through the glass, and the next—it was all gone. Vanished. First the window in front of her, then the next, and the next. As if someone were turning out the lights on the entire world, leaving nothing but inky blackness behind.

The only source of light was the canary-yellow neon sign, glowing in the murk.

"What . . . ?" Martha mouthed, squinting through the uncanny snow still flying in her face. It didn't make sense. None of this made sense. She rubbed her eyes and brushed the windblown hair from her face, but the world didn't come back.

A deep sense of dread crept over her, something akin to the paranoia she'd been feeling, but multiplied a thousandfold. Something small blew into the side of her face. She pulled it off and looked at it. A tarot card.

She saw the great beast, perched before darkness, his captives chained below him. The monster. The shadow self.

The Devil.

The neon light buzzed and flickered like an insect, casting the room in and out of darkness.

Our shadows follow us wherever we go.

"Evie," Martha whispered, the word pulled from her lips by the wind. "Oh god . . ." A wave of understanding washed over her as she realized that she should have trusted her instincts, that she should have taken her niece more seriously. There were so many things she wished she'd done.

But when the neon light went out, and the room plunged into shadow, Martha knew it was much too late.

14

The scene began with the peal of an old clock.

The stage was dark, save for a spotlight on the four-poster bed where the senior playing Ebenezer Scrooge cowered in theatrical terror. He wore a simple dressing gown with a long cap, his face made up with wrinkles and gray whiskers to make him look elderly. "The hour itself!" he cried.

Evie watched from the audience as Grace Bailey glided onto the stage, angelic in a white gossamer gown, illuminated by a light shining from the crown of her head. Silk peonies in red, orange, and yellow were hand stitched diagonally from her shoulder down to the bottom of the dress in a cascade of color. On silent feet, Grace moved like a dancer toward the bed.

"Are you the Spirit whose coming was foretold to me?" Scrooge demanded.

"I am!" Grace replied. Her voice rang out with superhuman volume, echoing around the walls of the mostly empty auditorium. "I am the Ghost of Christmas Past!"

Lorraine, the director, had thought to equip Grace and the other Christmas ghosts with special body mics and filter their voices to give them an otherworldly sound. Evie glanced over at her. She was sitting a couple of rows over with some of the crew members, clapping silently, an excited grin spread across her face. She pulled out her phone and typed something rapidly.

Five seconds later, Evie's phone pinged. She pulled it out of her pocket and saw a text message from Lorraine.

that costume is fire, omg!!! great job, you, it said, followed by roughly seventeen fire emojis. Evie had to smile. Despite a third of the cast being out sick for their last dress rehearsal before opening night, Lorraine somehow managed to maintain her sunny disposition.

Evie, on the other hand, felt as if the walls were closing in. With the talisman in their possession, Evie knew she could hardly wait any longer to return to the Shadow Land. Desmond had been suffering for far too long already. She needed to take the mistletoe pin to the gold mine up on the mountain, use it to access the shadow, and rescue Desmond so that Brand couldn't torment him anymore. A thousand other questions had bubbled to the surface of her mind, but considering how difficult it was for Holly to communicate, Evie doubted that she'd get any more answers from her bonneted friend.

You don't need more answers, she told herself. *You know what you need to do. Take that leap of faith.*

Evie swallowed. As she watched the actors move through the scenes, it reminded her of the play they'd been studying in English class since she'd first come to RHS—Shakespeare's *Hamlet*. A lot of the students found it boring. They thought Prince Hamlet was a pretty lousy character because he finds out who murdered his father in act 1, but doesn't manage to avenge him until the end of the play. "What was he waiting for?" the students asked. "Why didn't he just go and kill Claudius right away?"

The teacher had offered a bunch of different theories, but ultimately said that Hamlet was simply behaving in a very human way. "If you knew you had to do something terrible, something truly unthinkable—even if you knew it was the right thing to do—wouldn't you hesitate? Wouldn't you be afraid of what it might do to your soul?"

Sitting in that darkened auditorium, Evie felt a kinship with the maligned prince. *Just because you know what you have to do,* she thought, *doesn't mean doing it is easy.* Her memories of the Shadow Land were still fresh. She was still healing from the trauma of nearly losing her life and being trapped there forever. She wasn't exactly eager to go back.

"Psst."

Evie craned her head to see Tina and Sai crouched in the row behind her. "Is there somewhere we can talk?" Tina asked. Evie looked from one to the other, a little surprised to see them together. As if reading her thoughts, Tina murmured, "I found him lurking out back, so I just dragged him over here."

"Excuse me," Sai said, affronted. "I do not *lurk*, and I was not dragged. I was waiting patiently. Unlike some people." He raised an eyebrow at Tina. She crossed her arms and snorted.

"Yeah, sorry to keep you waiting," Evie whispered, with a glance over at Lorraine. "With all these people out, rehearsal is taking a lot longer than normal. Why don't we go up to the sound booth? No one's in there right now, so it'll be private."

They quietly made their way up to the booth, where the voices from the stage were being piped in so that the sound and light techs could keep track of where they were in the play. They'd made it to the part where Christmas Past and Ebenezer Scrooge were watching a younger version of Scrooge talk with a beautiful girl whom he could have married. It was so compelling that the three of them couldn't help but stand and watch. "I bring only myself into this marriage," the girl said to the younger man. "My love isn't a currency you can buy or sell. Can you live with that?" She shook her head. "I don't think you can. Not anymore. I release you, Ebenezer. For the love of the man you once were, I release you."

The actor playing the elder Scrooge crumpled into a tragic pose. "I loved her," he cried. "I should never have let her go."

As the spotlight over the young couple faded to black, the Ghost of Christmas Past turned to Scrooge and said, "What is done is done, Ebenezer Scrooge. For I am your regrets, your opportunities missed. I am the things forever broken and unfinished. Come away now. There remains more for you to see . . ."

Evie glanced over at Sai. He was watching the scene intently. When he noticed her looking at him, he cleared his throat. "So," he said. "Tonight, then?"

Evie frowned. "Tonight? We can't go tonight."

"Why not?" Sai replied. "How much longer can we wait?"

"He's right, Evie," Tina said. "We have no idea how many people in town are already affected by whatever evil disease Brand is spreading. Haven't you noticed everyone calling out 'sick'?" She used air quotes around the last word.

"I know, I know," Evie said with a sigh. "Well, I can't just

215

disappear tonight without my mom sounding the alarm—she's still pretty paranoid about what happened last time. And tomorrow is opening night for the show after school, and I can't just not show up for that without raising suspicions either. We'll go Saturday morning. It will be safer during the day, anyway, and no one will be looking for us."

"Okay, that works," Tina said, nodding. "My dad has been pretty intense about me being home by curfew, what with all the weirdness going on."

Sai shrugged. "Fine," he said. "Whatever."

Evie could tell that knowing what they knew was taking its toll on them—just like it had on her. They both looked hollow cheeked and bleary eyed, as if neither of them had slept well in days. A pang of guilt struck Evie in the gut. "You don't have to come with me, you know," she said softly. "I can do this alone."

"You can't, though," Sai said. "Ghost Girl said so. Looks like you're stuck with me."

"I'm coming, too," Tina added. "Sorry, not sorry. I haven't come this far with you to Crazy Town to stop now. Besides, if we make it out alive, it'll be the greatest story of my career." She winked.

Evie shook her head. "How can you joke around at a time like this?"

Tina shrugged. "Because it's better than the alternative, I guess." She checked her phone and grimaced. "I'd better get home for dinner. Not that I want to go."

"Wait," Evie said, stopping her before she could leave. "Is everything okay, Tina? I mean . . . ," she scoffed. "I know it's not okay. Nothing is okay. But are you, like, even less okay than usual?"

"It's fine," Tina said with a sigh. "Tati and I had a fight, and I just don't feel like sitting across the table from her right now. Not that I have a choice . . . Seriously, if my grandma did get possessed by an evil spirit, we'd be in real trouble, because I doubt I'd even notice."

"You don't mean that," Evie murmured.

"I don't know. Maybe I don't, maybe I do," Tina said, not meeting her eyes. "Anyway, I've got to go. Try not to do anything you'll regret while I'm gone." Her eyes flicked meaningfully to Sai, who had resumed watching the play. "Bye," she said, waving.

Evie swallowed. "Bye."

After Tina left, neither Evie nor Sai said anything for a few minutes. Onstage below, Scrooge begged the Ghost of Christmas Past to return him to his bedroom. "Leave me!" he shouted. "Take me back! Haunt me no longer!"

The childlike ghost took his hand and slowly began pulling him away from the pain of his old memories, and all the things that could have been.

As the scene changed, Evie glanced at Sai's serious face and took a breath. "Holly didn't say you had to come with me, you know," she said softly. "She only said I needed you to be able to talk to her. And you did that. You don't have to do this, too."

Sai looked at the floor. "You don't want me . . . is that it?"

"No," Evie said quickly. "No, that's not it at all. I just don't want you to get hurt. And I . . . I want you to do it for the right reasons."

Sai snorted. "D'you mean other than saving the town from an evil shadow monster? Is there a better reason than that?"

"I don't want you doing this because you don't care what happens to you," Evie said. "Because of some kind of death wish."

Sai met her gaze and gave a humorless laugh. "I don't know what you're on about," he muttered.

"You made me wear a helmet, but you don't wear one yourself. 'I shouldn't be here.' 'I have nothing to lose.' Isn't that what you said?" She felt a lump rising in her throat. "I need to know that you don't see this as an opportunity for sacrifice, Sai. Maybe you didn't want me to see what you're hiding behind that wall of yours, but I did." She paused, feelings she'd been suppressing for weeks rising to the surface. "Do you know what I saw? Behind that wall?"

Sai straightened, his expression unreadable. He shook his head.

"Something worth saving."

Sai closed his eyes.

"If you want to go with me," Evie went on, her voice unsteady, "then you need to promise you'll do whatever it takes to come back. I can't bear losing another person that I care about. I can't—"

With one fluid motion, Sai stepped toward her, cupped the back of her neck, and pulled her into a kiss.

At first, she was too shocked to do anything but freeze in his embrace. He held her softly, and she knew she could have pulled away, could have put a hand on his chest and stopped him. But in that moment, standing on the edge of being and not being, with slings and arrows waiting in the darkness ahead, Evie felt herself melting into him. Without conscious thought, she laid her fingers on his stubbled cheek and allowed his heat to warm the chill that had settled in her heart.

It was only when their lips parted and their eyes met that the reality of what she'd just done crashed upon her like a wave.

Guilt. Crushing, suffocating guilt.

Desmond was trapped in the darkness, suffering, and here she was, kissing another boy.

As if he had read her mind, Sai stepped back, running both hands through his dark hair. "Sorry," he said automatically. Then, a moment later, he sniffed and said, "Nah, you know what? I'm not sorry. Even if it never happens again, I'm not sorry."

It took several moments before Evie could speak. "Why . . . ?" she murmured. "Why did you kiss me?"

She saw his eyes flick toward the stage, where Ebenezer Scrooge and the Ghost of Christmas Past had returned to Scrooge's bedroom. He looked like a broken man as he watched the light from the ghost's halo fade into the wings. "Because I don't know what's going to happen to us," Sai said, looking back at her. "And I don't want to have any regrets."

There was a tenderness in his voice that Evie had never heard before—totally unlike the cocky, solitary boy she'd met that first day on the street. It was then she knew that she hadn't blundered beyond his wall this time. This time, he'd let her in.

She didn't know what to say.

"I can't believe that with everything else going on, I still have to worry about costumes for this play," she managed, feeling like a coward.

Sai blinked. "Yeah, it's bonkers," he replied, recovering his cool in an instant. "But the show must go on, yeah?"

Evie nodded. "Yeah."

They both stood silent after that, studying their shoes.

Sai hitched his bag up over his shoulder. "Well, see you later then," he said dully.

Inside, Evie was screaming at herself to say something meaningful, to rescue the moment and heal the terrible awkwardness between them. But all she said was "Okay."

Evie collapsed into a metal chair the moment he was gone. She could still feel the ghost of his lips on hers, and she touched them with her fingers. The guilt she'd felt after his kiss had transformed into confusion. Her feelings for Desmond hadn't waned, and yet thoughts of Sai filled her with excitement. It was as if a chamber in her heart that she hadn't even known was there had opened, like a secret room in a house she'd always lived in.

God, I'm a mess, she thought.

Just then, the door opened, and a member of the stage crew rushed into the booth and shouldered past her. "Out of the way, Evie," he said, bending over the computer controlling the sound and lighting. "I'm gonna miss my cue." He clicked a few things on the screen, and once again the toll of a bell resounded through the theater.

The clock struck one. Again.

Onstage, Scrooge recoiled from the sound, clearly wondering what fresh horrors the hour would bring.

Evie apologized to the crew member and retreated, heading back to the auditorium. At the bottom of the stairwell, she stopped as a chill crept down her spine. It was a feeling she'd been having more and more. The feeling of being watched.

But when she turned around, no one was there.

Evie shook her head, moving down the aisle toward her seat while Scrooge's endless nightmare continued. She had no idea what to do about the turmoil in her heart, but none of that was important now. Time was running out, and the darkness was closing in on them all.

Meanwhile . . .

It was Friday, December 22.

The sun was buried behind a thick embankment of clouds as it rose, blurring the line between night and day. Despite the approach of Christmas, the streets weren't crowded with shoppers anymore, leaving much of the snow-covered ground smooth and unbroken. Shops were mostly empty, and the windows in Birdie's Diner stayed dark through breakfast. Many children, for one reason or another, stayed home from school.

Ravenglass was as still and quiet as a painting, and just as beautiful.

But there was an ominous shade to that beauty that went almost unnoticed. A dark pigment that colored every bright, festive thing with a tinge of dread.

There were those who still went about their business that day. Who were seemingly too wrapped up in their own lives to notice the town's strange desolation. They simply went through their activities as usual, not seeing their solitary footsteps being filled in behind them by the softly falling snow, or the flashing eyes that watched from behind heavy curtains.

The hours passed, one by one, and the people blithely returned to their homes, thinking of hot dinners and television shows. They rattled off the day's events to their husbands and wives and children, who stared back at them and said very little in return. But that was all right, because there was so much to think about, so much to do. It was almost Christmas, after all.

And as the sun began to set behind the mountains that evening, not a single one of them realized that something momentous was about to happen. That it was the beginning of the longest night.

15

It was already half past five by the time Evie came out of her bedroom, dressed in black to blend in with the rest of the stage and costume crew. She needed to get to RHS by six to help dress the cast and ensure everything was ready to go by call time at 6:45. She pulled on her coat and boots, strapped on the hip pack that held her phone and all her emergency wardrobe equipment, and was about to make for the kitchen door when a voice stopped her.

"Evie."

She turned to see her dad standing in the hallway by the kitchen. He must have been in the living room and heard her coming down the stairs. "Oh," she said, a little startled. "I didn't know you were here."

"Your brother wasn't feeling very well after school today," he said.

A chill ran down Evie's spine. Had she seen Stan that day? She couldn't remember. "Is he okay?" she asked.

"Oh, yeah," Dad replied with a wave of his hand. "Probably

just overtired. His ankle still bothers him, and ten-year-old boys don't know how to rest."

Evie's felt herself relax, but only a little.

"Anyway," he continued, "your mom asked me to come look after him while she's at work." He narrowed his eyes at her black outfit. "Where are you off to?"

"It's opening night for the school play," Evie replied impatiently. She glanced at the cuckoo clock.

"You're in the school play?" Dad asked.

"I'm not in it, I just made some of the costumes," she answered. "The three ghosts for *A Christmas Carol*."

"Really?" he said, his eyes brightening. "That's cool. It's tonight? Why didn't you tell me?"

Evie shrugged. "I've been busy."

Too busy to care about your brother, she thought. *Are you going to fail to protect him again?* Evie pushed the thought away. She needed to stay focused. If she didn't, it could all fall apart. "Anyway," she said to her father, "I didn't think you'd be interested."

Dad frowned. "Okay," he said quietly. Then he took a deep breath. "Thing is, Evie—we need to talk."

Evie put her hand on the kitchen doorknob. "I can't right now," she said. "I'm already running late."

Dad sighed in frustration. "This is important," he said. "You've been avoiding me ever since I got here, and—"

With those words, Evie felt her anger rise above the fear and impatience. "*I've* been avoiding *you*?" she said, incredulous. "This is literally the first time you've made any real effort to talk to me."

Dad rubbed the back of his head with one hand. "Fine, maybe

we've both been doing it. The point is, I'll be heading back to New York after Christmas, and I don't want to leave without . . . without making things right between us."

Evie scoffed. "You think one little chat will fix everything?"

"No, of course not. I just—"

"You just need to feel better about yourself so you can go back to your studio guilt-free."

Dad flinched. She'd touched a nerve. "That's not true," he said.

"Yes, it is," Evie replied. She'd never spoken to her father this way in her entire life, but now that the dam was broken, she couldn't stop the words from flowing out of her. "You got your forgiveness from Stan, and now you want it from me. Well, I'm sorry to disappoint you."

She watched him bite back a retort. He was actually stopping and thinking about what he wanted to say before it just spilled out of his mouth. Evie could hardly believe it. It was like they'd switched places—with Evie mouthing off and her dad just taking it in and not saying much in return. What was going on?

Dad's eyes drifted about the room, his expression pensive. She saw his gaze land on the glass bluebird on the baker's rack. He picked it up, cradling it in his hand. "I made this for you," he finally said, his voice soft. "When you were little. Do you remember?"

Evie said nothing.

"I was still perfecting the blue glass back then," he said, holding it up to the light. "I got it just right with this one. No wounds, no cracks."

"Too bad you couldn't manage that with me," Evie muttered, almost to herself.

Dad looked up from the bird. "What did you say?"

"You've always hated broken things," Evie said.

Dad blinked, his brows furrowing. "Evie, what are you talking about?"

Images flashed through Evie's mind.

Shattered glass.

Blood from a thousand tiny cuts.

What's wrong with you?

Evie shook her head. *You have to focus. All of this . . . it can wait.* "It doesn't matter now," she said. "I have to go." And without giving him a chance to respond, she walked out the door into the cold, snowy evening.

She arrived backstage to a scene of total chaos. Lorraine stood at the center of it all, directing cast and crew members, looking more flustered than Evie had ever seen her.

"What's going on?" Evie asked.

Lorraine grabbed her by the shoulders, her expression frantic. "Evie! Oh, thank goodness you're here. We lost half the crew and a few more from the ensemble—some called in sick, others I can't even get ahold of. I have no idea what's going on."

Evie broke into a cold sweat. *You waited too long.* "What can I do?"

Lorraine started to pace. "The crew that's here are all doing double duty, and we'll be okay without the missing ensemble members, but no one has seen Colin Flanagan, and we can't do the play without all three of our ghosts. I'm flat out of ideas . . ." She stopped and looked at Evie. "Wait a minute. *You* could do it! You could play the Ghost of Christmas Present! You've even got red hair! Plus, you've been at all the rehearsals—so you probably know his lines, right?"

Evie blanched. "I—I mean, I know *some* of them—" she stammered.

"Good enough," Lorraine said, and almost shoved her toward the dressing rooms. "Hurry up, now—I'll find someone to get you off book while you get in costume and makeup. We go up in half an hour!"

Bewildered, Evie let herself be trundled along, thinking, *Didn't I have a nightmare like this once?*

Thirty minutes later, Evie stood in the wings, wearing the hunter-green velvet robe she'd made with the white fur collar, a bronze metal scabbard cinched at her waist. One of the costume crew had pinned the wreath of silk holly branches to her copper hair, which spilled loose and wild down her back. She bit her painted lips and peered out into the audience. She was surprised to see the seats nearly all filled.

"We've got a full house!" someone behind her whispered, and a wave of excitement rippled through the assembled cast.

Evie squinted at the crowd, trying to make out familiar faces. She thought she caught a glimpse of Aunt Martha, but couldn't be sure. With the number of people in attendance, she expected there to be quite a lot of noise and chatter, but it was oddly hushed. Once people found their seats, most of them simply sat down and waited for the show to start. The only sound in the auditorium was the festive Christmas music being piped in through the speakers.

"Are crowds normally this quiet?" Evie asked Grace Bailey, who was standing nearby dressed in her white gown.

Grace shrugged. "As long as they clap at the end, what does it matter?"

Something felt off, but Evie was too caught up in the moment to give it any more than a passing thought.

"One last thing," Lorraine said, coming up behind her. "The two little kids we had for Ignorance and Want didn't show up, but I managed to get a replacement for the boy last minute. So Ignorance will be there, but you're going to have to improvise since Want will be missing."

"Okay," Evie said helplessly. The whole thing was a mess.

Moments later, the house lights faded to black and the curtain rose.

Evie shivered with a sudden sense of foreboding.

Showtime.

The first few scenes went off without too much difficulty, aside from a couple of missed cues and misplaced props. Scrooge—in his false beard, nightcap, and scarlet dressing gown—was putting on the performance of his life, and Evie was so captivated that she nearly forgot her own scene was coming up.

The curtain lowered, and Evie hurried across the dark stage to her mark on a wooden throne, surrounded by a feast of prop food and drink. Lorraine handed her a torch with an electric flame and said, "Ready?"

"No," Evie replied. Her heart was beating in her throat. She'd done some small roles in plays back in New York, but nothing like this. What if she forgot all her lines?

"Big gestures, project your voice, you'll be fine," Lorraine said, and ran offstage.

A moment later the curtain rose, and a spotlight followed Scrooge as he wandered onto the stage, a look of fright upon his face.

Evie took a deep breath and switched on the torch. It lit her face in an eerie orange glow. "Come in!" she called, her voice echoing through the silence. "Come in and know me better, man!" The stage lights came on in full now, illuminating the full scene. Scrooge stared at her in amazement. "I am the Ghost of Christmas Present!" Evie announced. "Look upon me!"

Once she got going, it was easier than she'd thought. The scene flowed on, with Evie and Scrooge "traveling" across nineteenth-century London by way of movie scenes projected onto a screen behind them. They passed over snow-covered houses and churches, stopped at Bob Cratchit's house, and then went on to fly over a desolate gray landscape of water and stone.

"What place is this?" Scrooge asked.

Evie stared at the empty place, suddenly entranced. It was as if something in the back of her mind was trying to get her attention. She nearly forgot to say her line. "A place where Miners live," she said, "who labor in the bowels of the earth." In her hand, the torchlight dimmed.

Time is running out.

Evie was barely conscious of the scene at Scrooge's nephew's house passing. Then suddenly the stage light above her head went from warm yellow to white.

Scrooge looked upon her in surprise. "You grow old," he remarked. "Are spirits' lives so short?"

"My life upon this globe is very brief," she said, and her voice trembled. "It ends tonight."

Tick. Tock. Tick. Tock.

"Forgive me, but I see something strange protruding from your skirts," Scrooge said, pointing a finger at her. "Is that a foot or a claw?"

Evie turned to see a small shadow crouching behind her. A spotlight flared upon it, and Evie was shocked to see the little boy from the school and church huddled at her feet.

She remembered the black lunch box. *Jack.*

He was dressed in rags, his face as gray as the stone landscape they'd flown over just moments before. He stared at her with black eyes that glistened with malice.

Evie couldn't breathe. Did no one else see this? She glanced around, but the audience was cast in darkness. There was no sound.

Scrooge elbowed her. "It's your line," he whispered.

Evie swallowed. Her throat was bone dry. "This boy," she said roughly, "is Ignorance. Beware him most of all, for on his brow I see that written which is Doom."

The sound of a clock striking filled the auditorium. Each hour seemed to resonate with the beating of her heart.

Ten.

Eleven.

Twelve.

Midnight.

The stage went black.

Evie stood rigid, with held breath. She knew that this was the cue for the third ghost's entrance and she should get offstage, but she was frozen on the spot. The only light came from the torch in her hand, which flickered weakly in the gloom. She squinted, fighting to see something, anything, in the darkness.

A constellation of eyes flashed back at her from below, like the eyes of predators. They all seemed to be focused solely on her.

A whispered sound passed through the auditorium like wind.

"*Evieee . . . ,*" it whispered, with the breath of a hundred voices.

"No . . . ," Evie said. Her legs felt wooden, but she forced herself to stumble into the wings, away from the sound. She nearly ran straight into Daniel Santos, who was coming onstage wearing the massive costume she'd made for him. Built to rest on Daniel's shoulders, the hooded thing towered over her, a masterpiece of black fabric and purple phosphorescent paint. He glowed in the darkness like a phantom, a train of ragged cloth trailing at his feet. He moved silently toward Scrooge. The old man was bathed in a single, weak spotlight, a look of dread spread across his face.

"Are you the Ghost of Christmas Yet to Come?" Scrooge asked, his voice a lonely echo in the silent auditorium. "Are you here to show me shadows of what will happen in the time before us? I fear you more than any spectre I have seen."

Daniel said nothing.

"Lead on, then, Spirit," Scrooge said. "For the night is waning fast . . ."

Evie watched them with growing apprehension, and suddenly felt the need to run away. She thought of poor Hamlet, who paid the ultimate price for his delay. The deaths of everyone he loved—including his own.

Thus conscience doth make cowards of us all . . .

Evie felt the sting of tears in her eyes. She'd been waiting for the perfect moment, but what if she'd waited too long? How many in Ravenglass were already in Brand's thrall?

I'll text Tina and Sai, she thought. *They'll know what to do.* She ran into the wings and rushed past Lorraine.

"Nice job, Evie— Hey! Where are you going? You've still got curtain call!"

"Sorry," Evie murmured over her shoulder. "I have to go—now."

Lorraine scoffed in exasperation, but Evie didn't turn back. Without bothering to change out of her costume, she grabbed her bag and shot out the stage door into the night. Snow fell softly, and the sidewalk was covered with a light dusting. Evie bent to retrieve her phone from her hip pack, but was startled by a figure standing on the road in front of her.

"Aunt Martha?" Evie said with surprise.

Her aunt wore a thick black shawl and silver chains around her neck. Her long gray hair was loose and shining with captured snowflakes. A bouquet of flowers lay in her arms. White lilies.

Evie felt a frisson of anxiety. "What are you doing out here? Weren't you watching the show?"

"I didn't want you to leave without saying goodbye," Aunt Martha said, handing her the flowers. Her voice was thin and strange, and Evie couldn't help but notice the way her eyes flashed.

Evie looked down at the lilies. She knew flowers were a traditional after-show gift, but something about them made her want to throw the bouquet to the ground. "After all," Aunt Martha went on, "this is a very special day."

"Today?" Evie asked. "What's special about today?"

Aunt Martha smiled. Her gray teeth glistened in the street-light. "Did you forget already? It's the solstice. The day the lord of summer and the Holly King clash in ancient battle. Today, the lord of winter's power is at its peak. Light shines only briefly, and is overtaken by the longest night."

The lilies smelled too sweet, and made Evie's head ache. "The winter solstice," she murmured, remembering.

"Oh yes," Aunt Martha replied with obvious pleasure. "The day the dark lord reigns."

Evie felt the blood freeze in her veins. *Oh god*, she thought.

As if reading her mind, Aunt Martha laughed, and the chains around her neck chimed like bells. "You're too late, my girl," she said merrily. "Far too late."

"What are you?" Evie whispered, backing away.

Suddenly, Aunt Martha's body spasmed, and she hunched forward, her long hair spilling over her face. When she raised her head to peer out between the tresses, her eyes almost looked normal for an instant. Fierce and full of pain. A word formed on her thin, trembling lips before the cloud of black rolled over her pupils once again.

Run.

Evie dropped the lilies onto the snow and bolted, her feet slipping and sliding across the wet ground. Behind her, Aunt Martha began to laugh once more, high and discordant. Evie pulled the phone from her hip pack and sent a text to Tina and Sai as she ran.

> Change of plans, we can't wait until tomorrow to go to the mines.

Tina's reply came almost immediately.

> Are you serious?

> Yes, we have to go tonight.

16

DANGER! KEEP OUT!

The sign was nailed to one of the wooden boards covering the entrance to the abandoned gold mine. Evie stared at it as she stood in the dark forest, waiting for Tina and Sai to arrive. Mrs. King had demanded the entrance be sealed after the search for Desmond had been abandoned, so that no one else would ever blunder into the mine. Evie knew her heart had been in the right place, but now the boards only served as a hindrance to their plan to get Desmond back. Evie tried to imagine what Mrs. King might say if she was able to bring her son home safely. *She'll forgive you*, Evie told herself. *She'll forgive you, and everything will be okay.*

She wanted to believe it. But at that moment, forgiveness felt very, very far away.

Setting her phone on a rock, its flashlight trained on the mine opening, Evie gripped one of the boards with her fingers and pulled as hard as she could. It didn't budge. Ribbons of yellow crime scene tape snaked around her ankles, blown wild by the wind. She kicked them off, picked up her phone, and scanned the area around her, searching for a stick to wedge underneath the boards. Something bright red caught her eye. She walked a few paces and brushed off the snow to reveal a red dog harness and leash. *That's not going to help*, she thought, leaving it where it lay. Eventually, she managed to unearth a thick branch short enough for her use. She was carrying it back to the mouth of the mine when she heard the rumble of a motorcycle approaching. A few moments later, the engine died, and two figures came crunching across the forest floor toward her, flashlights bobbing in their hands.

Tina was panting, her green hair tousled and twinkling with snowflakes. "We came as fast as we could—what are you *wearing*?"

Evie had nearly forgotten she was still dressed in the costume and holly crown from the play. Luckily, the long, fur-lined robe was quite thick and had kept her warm on the trek up the mountain. "I didn't have time to change," she explained. "I came straight from the theater."

"What happened? Why the change in plans?" Sai asked. He was wearing his leather jacket, jeans, and boots—the same outfit he'd been wearing when they first met.

"It's worse than we thought," Evie said. "I was at the play, and it felt like . . ." She shook her head, trying to keep panic at bay. "It felt like everyone in the audience had already been infected. Like they were all just puppets . . . little pieces of *him*."

Sai and Tina looked at each other, their faces suddenly grave.

"I think Brand's power is strongest at night," Evie went on.

"He lives in shadow, after all. That must be why we didn't realize just how many people have been affected. They seemed . . . almost normal during the day. And at night, most people are hidden in their houses, out of sight." She swallowed. "I saw my aunt Martha—or at least, what's left of her. She's been infected, too." Saying it out loud made Evie feel sick.

"It can't be everyone," Tina whispered. Evie could see her thoughts churning, thinking of her family, her friends. "It can't be. When I left home, they were all okay. Weren't they?" A sliver of doubt entered her voice.

"My aunt reminded me of something she'd said weeks ago," Evie continued. "It's the winter solstice. The longest night of the year. If there was ever a moment that Brand was going to make his move, it's got to be tonight. We have to stop him before he finishes what he started."

You're too late, my girl. Far too late.

Evie pushed the thought aside. Martha may have been taken by shadow, but she'd still reminded her of the solstice. That proved that her true self was still strong enough—even for an instant—to fight back and try to help.

There's still time, she told herself. *There has to be.*

"Hand that to me," Sai said, gesturing toward the branch. She gave it to him, and Sai began prying the boards off the mine entrance one at a time. Working together, the three of them managed to open a large enough space to crawl through. They stood back, panting, and stared into the void.

"So you're saying all we have to do is walk in there with that pin you found," Tina said, "and we'll just appear somewhere . . . else?"

Evie pulled the mistletoe pin from her hip pack. She'd kept it with her everywhere she went ever since they'd discovered it in the cellar. She licked her lips, remembering her first bewildering experience with the Shadow Land. "I don't know. I think so," she said. "But if we do, there's something you need to know. That place . . . It can mess with your mind. Make you see things that aren't really there. No matter what happens, we have to stick together, okay?"

Tina nodded.

"Let's go," Sai said, throwing the branch to the ground. Their eyes met. Looking at him, Evie was suddenly on the back of his bike again, hurtling headlong into unexplored territory, clinging to the hope that she wouldn't crash along the way.

Evie pinned the silver brooch to the collar of her robe. Then she turned toward the mouth of the mine, her pulse suddenly racing. An animal terror gripped her heart, and for a moment, she thought she might abandon the whole plan and run. Being pulled into the darkness was one thing, choosing to step into it was quite another.

She thought about the Hanged Man—

About Hamlet, and his sea of troubles—

About Hannah back at the community pool—

Jump in, the water's fine.

Just do it, she told herself. *Don't think, just do.* Taking a deep breath, sending a little prayer into the winter sky, Evie ducked under the remaining wooden boards and stepped into the mine.

The stillness inside was a stark contrast to the snowy bluster of the forest. She shone her flashlight around, but it only illuminated a couple of feet in front of her. Rocks, dirt, nothing more. There was a sound, too, one that she felt more than heard. A low hum that seemed to come from deep in the bowels of the earth. It made the narrow tunnel feel as if it were expanding and contracting, like some great beast breathing in and out. In and out.

Two more beams of light joined hers as Tina and Sai entered the mine. "Doesn't look like much," Sai said after a moment. "Isn't it working?"

Evie sucked her teeth. "I don't know." She felt like she was saying that a lot. "When I came down here before, I was just pulled into a dark hole. I didn't go there on purpose. I didn't have a choice."

A moment passed, and then Sai spoke. "Turn off the lights."

"Oh, do we really have to?" Tina said, her voice quavering with fear.

Sai switched off his flashlight first. Then Evie clicked off her phone. The murk encroached on them all, thick as paste. Only Tina's thin beam was left between them and total eclipse.

"Damn it," Tina moaned. Then her light flicked off.

Darkness prevailed.

Evie froze in place. She blinked rapidly, uncertain if her eyes were open or closed. It didn't seem to make a difference either way.

Without the light to keep its form, Evie's body began to feel like it was falling away from her, spreading like ink in water. She reached up to touch her face, just to make sure it was still there.

Time lost meaning. Had seconds passed? A minute? Ten? She had no idea.

Then, literally in the blink of an eye, something appeared in the distance—so bright and out of place that it was nearly blinding.

A small, crooked yellow door.

"There!" she whispered. "That's the way in."

"Bloody hell . . . ," Sai murmured.

Evie crept through the dark, her hands stretched out in front of her, until she reached the little door. It swung open soundlessly at her touch.

Stepping through the doorway, Evie nearly lost her footing as the world moved under her like a funhouse carnival ride. When it righted itself, Evie was in a familiar kitchen, tinted the color of old things. Windows over the counter looked out over a wide hill, crowned with a single apple tree. A wooden table and chairs dominated the room, and in the corner, a butter churn stood beneath a framed needlework sampler.

The year rolls round, and steals away
The breath that first it gave;
What e'er we do, where e'er we be,
We're trav'ling to the grave.

"We're in Hobbie House," Evie said wonderingly. "Well, it wasn't Hobbie House yet, I guess. It was the Flower House." She touched a fragrant spray of black-eyed Susans and forget-me-nots that stood in a glass vase on the kitchen table. They were still fresh. When neither Sai nor Tina commented on their new surroundings, Evie turned to make sure they'd followed her through the door.

She was relieved to see them both standing just over the threshold, but that relief dissipated as soon as she saw their faces. Both wore expressions of dismay and confusion, and their eyes—though not black like those taken by shadow—were oddly distant, as if they were seeing something that Evie couldn't. She hurried to Tina and shook her by the shoulders. "Hey!" she shouted. "Tina, snap out of it! We made it! We're here!"

But Tina only stared. Not at Evie, but through her. She shook her head, muttering so quietly that Evie could barely make out the words. She put her ear to Tina's lips and listened.

"Tati, please," she whispered. "Don't say that. Please. I should have told you. I should have said. No! Oh god. I didn't mean it. I just thought—No, please, don't go . . ."

On and on.

"Tina!" Evie said again, waving a hand in front of her face. No response.

She went to Sai. He wasn't making a sound, but his face was a mask of pain. The bravado was gone, and he suddenly looked very much like that little boy in the photo with his mother. What nightmare had the Shadow Land trapped him in, to make him seem like a child again? If only she could see it, too . . .

Then, Evie remembered their psychic connection. She'd always brought him into her visions, but could it work both ways? Could she enter his mind, too? Gingerly, she reached out and laced her fingers into his.

As soon as she did, the scene around her stutter-stepped, and Evie nearly toppled over as her surroundings shifted to an empty city street with old redbrick buildings. There was something about the architecture and the street signs that didn't look American. *Where are we?* Evie wondered.

An overturned car lay steaming nearby, its body crumpled like an egg against a low stone wall. A woman stood in front of the car, watching them. Blood covered one side of her face, matting her hair, and dripping down onto her gray University of

Oxford sweatshirt. The other side was still intact. Her thick black hair still shining, her copper skin clear and whole.

"Nagasai," the woman said. She tilted her head to the side. "What happened? I can't remember . . . We were driving home, and then I was here."

Evie looked back at Sai. His eyes were locked onto the woman's face. "Mum?" he whispered.

Oh god, Evie thought as the truth dawned on her. *Not this. This is too much.*

"Mum, is that really you?" Sai took a step toward her.

"No, Sai," Evie said, gripping his shoulder. "It's not real. You're not here—you're in the Shadow Land, with me. Try to remember!"

Sai blinked rapidly, as if he were trying to fight back, trying to hear what Evie was saying.

The woman moved toward them, lurching on a twisted leg. "We were in the car together, weren't we?" she said. "But you're all right. You're all right."

Just as Evie thought she'd gotten through to him, Sai refocused on the specter of his mother. "B-but this happened years ago . . . ," he stammered. "How can you be—?"

"You were saying something to me, weren't you?" The specter went on as if she hadn't heard him, looking at the road and the crumpled car. "We were driving, coming up to the intersection, and you wanted me to look at something across the way. A car, maybe. Or a motorcycle."

Sai looked stricken. Tears broke loose and streamed down his face.

"I turned my head to look, and I didn't notice the light

change," the woman went on. "I just kept going. Then another car came, and I swerved and lost control . . ." Her voice trailed off. She turned back to Sai, her one good eye accusing. "I'm dead, aren't I?"

Sai pressed a hand over his mouth, unable to speak.

"If I had stopped at that light, I'd still be alive," she said, her voice turning hard. "I'm dead because of you."

Sai gasped as if the words were a knife in his gut. He hunched forward.

"Don't listen, Sai!" Evie shouted, shaking him. "That's not your mother! It's not!"

"This is your fault!" the specter that was Mrs. Rockwell screamed.

"I'm sorry," Sai moaned. "I'm so sorry, Mum . . . I wish it had been me . . . I wish . . ."

Evie tried to drag him away, but some invisible force grabbed hold of her, pulling her from the scene. She tried to keep hold of Sai, but he wouldn't follow. His hand slipped out of hers, and Evie gasped as the streets of Oxford vanished to a pinprick. Suddenly she was back in the old kitchen at Hobbie House, standing in front of Sai and Tina, each still trapped in their own personal hell. She looked back and forth between them, feeling hopeless.

"You can't help them now," a voice said.

Evie turned to find a girl in a long black dress sitting at the kitchen table, her hands folded neatly in her lap. She regarded Evie with mismatched eyes, one green, and one violet.

"Welcome back, cousin," Holly said sweetly. "Come to play again?"

"Are *you* doing this?" Evie demanded, gesturing toward Tina and Sai. She remembered all too well the terrible visions Holly had given her the first time she'd been brought to the Shadow Land.

Holly's eyes flicked over to the others. "No," she said. "I learned my lesson. He's doing it. He didn't want anyone else to come without his knowing, and so he set these . . . funny little traps. Like those paper toys you stick your fingers in and can't get them out again." She mimed touching her two fingers together. "All I ever showed you were memories—awful ones, but real. Shadows of the past. What he's showing them aren't memories, aren't shadows. They're nightmares. They reflect nothing but darkness."

"How do I get them out?" Evie asked.

Holly shrugged. "You can't."

"What?"

"They've got to find their own way out of the trap. Just like you did. That's why you're here with me, instead of off somewhere else like they are. You already beat the game, so you don't have to play anymore." Holly smiled when she spied the mistletoe pin on Evie's collar. "You were very clever to find that and make your way here, just like I'd hoped you would. Wearing it will help shield you from his sight." When she saw what must have been a desperate look on Evie's face, Holly's expression softened. "I can stay here with your friends, to make sure they're safe. But you have to go. You have to hurry. Double-quick."

My time upon this globe is very brief.

It ends tonight.

"Okay," Evie said. "But where's Desmond? How am I supposed to find him out there?"

Holly shrugged. "I don't know."

"You don't *know*?" Evie exclaimed, exasperated. "This is your world. How could you not know?"

"This house is my world," Holly replied in an injured voice. "Beyond that, I know nothing. We can't play outside our yard. He won't let us."

Evie began to pace. "You must know something. Please. Just try."

Holly was silent for a moment. She swung her legs back and forth like a little girl. "Well . . . in this place, things go where they belong. Me, you, and Sarah belong to this house, so that's where we stay. Is there a place where Desmond belongs?"

Now it was Evie's turn to think. Did Desmond have a connection to a place that existed back in the 1850s? His house hadn't been built yet, and the quarry had been established in the 1950s, a hundred years later. She tried to visualize the old map of Ravenglass that Sai had found in the museum. Town Hall? No. The church?

"I've got it!" she exclaimed. "The old log cabin up on the mountain—it was here in Sarah Flowers's time, wasn't it? Tina said Mr. King lived there when he founded the quarry!"

Holly nodded. "It's as good an idea as any," she said. "You'd better be going. I hope you find him."

Evie stared at her for a long moment. "But . . . aren't you coming with me?"

"Can't," Holly said. "I have to watch over your friends, remember? And Sarah needs me. She's hiding in her room. She's frightened."

"Don't you think *I'm* frightened?" Evie blurted. "Who knows what's waiting for me out there? You think I want to face it alone?"

The last word caught in her throat. "It sounds to me like Sarah isn't the only one hiding." When Holly didn't reply, Evie shook her head, hands on hips. "You know, one thing I've learned these past few weeks is that we can't control what happens to us, but we can control our reaction to it. We could both blame our parents for our unhappiness. You could blame Sarah and Brand for trapping you down in this place. I could blame Dr. Mears for making me doubt what I saw with my own eyes. We could be Lost Girls forever, if we wanted to. It wouldn't feel good, but it would be easy." She scoffed. "But I'm tired of being lost, Holly. I'm tired of running away. I'm ready to face the truth, even if it's hard." She looked around at the house, the place that had held so much sorrow and still somehow remained standing. "I have to believe that all this happened for a reason, that we're connected by something other than pain. Isn't it possible for you to believe that, too?"

Holly wouldn't meet her eyes. She gazed out the window to the apple tree, its branches heavy with fruit. "I'm sorry," she whispered. For the first time, she didn't sound like a little girl.

Evie glanced at the carved oak clock that hung on the wall behind Holly, its brass pendulum swinging slowly back and forth. Even though she knew it couldn't possibly be that late, the clock read three minutes to midnight. *Maybe it's always that time here*, she thought. Still, in the real world, time was passing.

"I'm sorry, too," she said to Holly, and with one last look at Sai and Tina, she opened the kitchen door and walked out into the realm of shadow.

17

Evie had never known a silence so deep.

As she walked through sepia-toned streets both strange and familiar, she felt as if she had walked into a story already told, into the terrible emptiness left behind after the last word was spoken. It was neither warm nor cold, and no birds sang in the trees. There was no wind.

Evie's shoes made almost no sound as she walked along the hard-packed dirt of Main Street. She recognized the shapes of some of the buildings—the General Store, the Town Hall, the building that now contained the Blue River Inn. But they were hollow shells, lifeless behind dull glass windows. Instead of cars, abandoned wooden wagons lined the street, their days of being pulled by horses long past.

It was all she could do to put one foot in front of the other, to keep going despite the urge to turn back. She kept her mind focused on Desmond—the sooner she got to him, the sooner all this would be over.

It wasn't until she reached the edge of town, not far from the road that led up the mountain, that she became aware of the sound. It was a strange, repeating noise —like a soft scraping followed by a dull strike.

Shhh-thump. Shhh-thump.

Evie stopped and listened, her heart racing. The sound was coming from behind her. Not daring to look, she merely increased her pace toward the mountain pass, raising the hem of her velvet robe so she wouldn't get tangled up in it. But when she rounded the corner and the winding dirt road came into view, she saw something standing at the base of it, waiting for her.

It reminded her of the first time she saw Holly, a living shadow lurking in the field behind her school. Like a creature made of darkness alone. But when the thing moved, Evie realized with revulsion that it was no shadow, but a man charred black from head to foot. He was wearing what was left of a pair of black pants and a rough shirt, both items burned almost beyond recognition. A hat with some kind of twisted piece of metal affixed to the brim was soldered to his skull. Where a face should have been was nothing but a ruin of blackened flesh and exposed bone. A hole opened up in that ruin, and without lips or tongue it spoke in a voice as dry as ash.

"You're not supposed to be here."

Evie screamed.

As she stumbled back, adrenaline flooded her body, and she turned to run from the gruesome sight—only to find yet another man coming up behind her, nearly as badly burned as the first. One of his legs was missing underneath the tatters of his pants, and he leaned on a long spade like a crutch as he shuffled toward her, making a slow, tortured sound.

Shhh-thump. Shhh-thump.

He, too, wore a hat, this one still recognizable enough to see that the metal piece was a sort of tiny teapot with a long spout. An oil lamp, Evie realized. She recognized it from the display about the Ravenglass gold rush at the museum.

All at once, Evie knew exactly who these men were.

George Brown. Ellis Williams. Asa Davis.

The dead miners. The young men who perished in Brand's explosion. Whose bodies had burned down deep in the earth, and whose families buried empty boxes in the churchyard.

They're still here, she thought. *They've been here all along. Under Brand's thrall just like Holly used to be.*

Within seconds, other men began to emerge from inside the buildings, each one twisted by fire into inhuman shapes, the hollow eyes of their skulls fixed on her. How many had burned? Evie wondered. Ten? Twenty? Some of them carried tools—spades, pickaxes, chisels, and hammers. The air took on the smell of charred meat and brimstone.

Evie backed away, but she was quickly surrounded. There were just too many.

Desperate, she looked for an opening between them and tried to charge through it. But the men pushed her back with their shovels. The rusty metal snagged her robe, tearing it, and jabbed painfully into her body. She cried out, trying to block the blows with her hands. When she retreated, other men jabbed at her with the blades of their pickaxes. She scuttled to the center, panting wildly. She could not think, could not process anything but the nearness of her own death. Her mind was filled with the memory of those hands in the graveyard, cold and impossibly strong, pulling her down, and she could not stop herself from imagining them pinning her wrists to the ground and snaking around her throat.

"You don't belong here," the first man repeated as he stepped closer, close enough to reach her.

"I'm sorry, Desmond," Evie rasped, her throat bone dry. Despite the number of figures all around her, despite the violence that was about to happen, it was still so, so quiet. "I tried . . ."

"Stop!"

A strident voice cut through the silence. A flash of brilliant light blinded her, and Evie raised an arm to shield her eyes. When she lowered it again, she saw that the miners had recoiled from her and seemed stunned into stillness.

Evie gasped and squinted at a blurry figure running toward her.

Holly grabbed Evie's wrist and kept running, her expression defiant. "Come on!" she exclaimed, dragging her toward the mountain pass. "Before they come after us!"

Evie allowed herself to be pulled away, but looked back in confusion at the miners. "But . . . what was that? How did you—?"

"I don't know," Holly said. She seemed more than a little surprised herself. "I just said 'stop' and something happened. This light. I don't know where it came from."

Evie scoffed. "It came from you."

Holly's eyes flicked toward her, but she didn't reply. They ran for a while, checking behind them to make sure the men weren't following. After a while, they slowed to a walk.

Evie shook her head. "I don't understand. You said you were going to stay at the house. What made you change your mind?"

A pained expression crossed Holly's face. "What you said before you left," she admitted. Evie immediately noticed Holly's childlike, singsong voice had faded, leaving behind the voice of a girl not unlike herself. "All those years ago," Holly continued, "Sarah lured me down here because she was lonely and scared. She preyed on my weakness. Made me feel like she was my only friend, the only one who understood me. Isolated me from everyone else, to make the darkness look like a comfort. Just like I did to you. It's the same sad story being told over and over again. But you . . . you broke the cycle. You got away. And now you've come back to this terrible, awful place to save someone you love, and I . . ." Her voice trailed off. "After all this time, I'm still a coward." She hung her head. "I was sitting there in the kitchen after you'd left, and suddenly I just couldn't stand it anymore. You said that you're done being lost . . ." She reached out to squeeze Evie's hand. It was warm. "Well, now I am, too."

Evie's heart squeezed painfully in her chest. But it was a good pain. "Thank you," she said. "I don't think I can do this alone."

"Now you don't have to," Holly replied, a small smile touching her lips.

Evie thought for a moment, and then said, "One thing I still don't understand: Why is Brand doing all this? What does he want? Can you speak freely, now that I'm here with you?"

"I dare not say his name, but I'll try to explain what I know," Holly said. "Since he first came to this place, he's been trying to figure out how to get back to the real world. He was older and dying when he arrived, so his body was weak, but his spirit was just as it was in life. Full of dark ambitions. He soon realized that by pulling Sarah down here with him, he could force her to go back to the surface as a kind of living ghost—a shadow. She was young— she could withstand the strain of the transition. Plus, she was afraid of him, and would do whatever he commanded. Eventually, though, he realized Sarah was limited—too weak to do anything of consequence. That's when he sent her out to get someone new. Me." She swallowed. "Since I was stronger, I could travel farther, but it still wasn't enough. *I* wasn't enough. He realized he needed more. He needed to expand his influence. He put it in my head that I needed a companion my own age. So we waited, and waited. Until you came. A girl living in my house, right where we wanted you, ready to be ensnared. It was perfect—almost like it was meant to be. Through you, I could experience everything I never had the chance to. I could relive those moments, and avenge myself on those who hurt me most. Or, that's what I thought. And it would have worked, but you got away." She shuddered. "He was angry— furious—until he saw that someone had come after you, willingly, right into his domain. A strong, healthy young man. One he could control and send endlessly into the world to do his bidding."

Evie took a shuddering breath as she thought about Desmond. "Does it hurt?" she asked softly. "What he does to you?"

Holly's jaw clenched. "It does if you fight it. I'm ashamed to say that after a while, I just . . . let it happen."

Desmond would have fought, Evie thought. *Fought every single second. He must be in agony.* She was suddenly consumed with guilt. *Why didn't I figure it out more quickly? Why did I wait so long to come here and get him back?* The self-loathing nearly took her breath away.

Holly must have read her expression because the next thing she said was "You did everything you could."

"Not yet I haven't," Evie said, and she started to run the rest of the way up the mountain.

As she ran, she once again recalled the image of the old map from the museum. The road had changed over the course of a century, so it was difficult to know her exact location. Where had she seen the cabin? Had there been any distinguishing features on the map? She thought she remembered it being located after a curve in the road, just before it reached the mine on the other side. So when they crested a hill and the path curved to the right, Evie stopped to scan the area for some sign of life.

"There!" Holly exclaimed, pointing to a hardly noticeable path through the woods.

Her heart leaping into her throat, Evie tore down the leaf-strewn trail, slipping and sliding as she went, but managing to keep her feet under her.

"I see it!" Evie cried as a wood-shingled roof came into view. The cabin was a small, one-room affair, constructed of roughly hewn pine logs and a stone chimney. She made no attempt to approach quietly, running full tilt until she'd made it to the end of the path. "Desmond!" she shouted, crashing through the front door. "Desmond!"

The cabin was empty aside from a few pieces of simple furniture and a filthy rug. She kicked the rug aside, searching for a trapdoor in the floor. Nothing. *He's got to be here*, she thought. *If he isn't here, I don't know what I'm going to do.*

She rushed back outside and made her way toward the back of the house. There was an ax and a pile of chopped wood, but not much else. "Do you see anything?" she called to Holly.

"No, nothing," Holly replied from a distance. "I'll check the road—make sure those miners aren't coming after us."

Evie listened to Holly's footsteps recede. "Come on, come on . . . ," she whispered. She turned in a slow circle, scanning the forest.

Something caught her eye, just below a dip in the land. She could have sworn it was the back of someone's head. It was a deep brown color, the crown cut into a flat-top fade.

Evie's breath caught in her throat. She started to run.

He stood on an outcropping that overlooked the town below. Evie immediately recognized it as the exact same spot where they'd stood together—on a day that seemed like long ago but was actually more than a hundred years in the making.

"Desmond," Evie whispered. She walked up to him and laid a hand on the shoulder of his once-beautiful, champagne-colored suit jacket.

Blast from the Past.

He turned to face her.

How many times had Evie dreamed of this moment? How many nights had she lain awake, thinking of when she'd feel the touch of his skin, and be able to tell him he was coming home?

Still, when Desmond turned and Evie saw his face, it didn't feel like the beginning of a happy ending. He was gray, his eyes black pools, his lips still sewn cruelly shut.

"It's me," Evie said, breathless. "I'm here. I hope I'm not too late."

18

esmond's gaze fixed on her, but his expression didn't change.
"I'm taking you home, okay?" Evie said. She reached for his hand. It was cold.

Desmond stared back at her with bottomless, unblinking eyes. Then, slowly, he turned back to stare out at the town below.

"Come on, Desmond," she said. "We have to go. It's over."

He didn't move.

Evie's gaze locked on the gold pocket watch hanging from his vest, its face cracked down the middle. Up close, she could see that it had stopped at three minutes to midnight. "Brand's watch," Evie murmured. "If we get rid of it, you'll be free—" She reached to rip the watch from Desmond's body, and quick as lightning, his hand shot out and grabbed her by the throat.

The shock of it was so great that it took Evie several seconds to understand what was happening. The blood rushed to her head as Desmond's fingers dug into her flesh. Her vision blurred, and she felt her eyes bulging from their sockets as she struggled to breathe. She choked and scrabbled at his grip, trying to pry it from her neck, but he was far too strong. She pushed at his chest, his face, but his blank expression remained.

Images of Sarah and Brand, lurching across the cellar in their dance of death, flashed through her mind.

It's happening again—

It's still happening—

Over and over and—

No! she thought frantically. *It can't end this way. Strangled to death in some barren place . . .* Suddenly the image of the Hanged Man came into her mind. But the man on the tarot card wasn't actually being hung from his neck—it was from his ankle. The rope wasn't hurting him, it was keeping him from falling.

His act of faith doesn't just bring resolution, it also allows him to see the world from a new perspective.

He's there because he chose to jump.

And he trusts that he'll end up exactly where he's meant to be.

Every bone in Evie's body screamed at her to keep pulling at Desmond's hand, to scratch at his eyes and do everything in her power to stop him. But against every instinct she had, she let go.

Her head felt light as a kind of dizzy euphoria took over, and the world began to fade from view. She fought the desire to go adrift into that abyss, down to the bottom of the swimming pool, and reached for Desmond's other hand.

His hold on her throat slackened for just a moment, and she could have sworn a look of confusion passed across his face. It was just enough time for a blast of oxygen to reach her brain. With her remaining strength, Evie lifted his hand up to her shoulder, holding it there not as if they were locked in a death grip, but instead were getting ready for a dance.

Holding it above your heart will help stop the bleeding.

She filled her mind with thoughts of their first meeting, when she hurt her finger and he wrapped and held her hand in his. When she felt like Cinderella at the ball, wishing that midnight would never come.

Remember me! she thought fiercely. *Remember us!*

She thought of his teasing eyes, of the way he smiled at her when she untangled his sewing machine, of the way he kissed her in the rain when he asked her to homecoming and she said yes.

Her vision began to fade again as the light feeling returned, stronger now, too strong to resist. She felt the void pulling her down into it, like deep water. She begged with her last moment of clarity. *Remember!*

Desmond's eyes widened. And the black cleared from them like storm clouds pierced by sunlight.

The hand on her throat loosened, and in that same instant, she ripped the pocket watch from his vest, dropped it to the ground, and crushed it under her heel.

Evie felt a ripple of air across her face—a sudden, gunpowder-scented breeze.

And then it was gone.

Evie doubled over, retching, hot tears streaming down her face. Her throat was on fire. She gulped air until it burned her lungs, and then, once the horrible tightness in her chest subsided, tried to slow her ragged breathing.

She felt a light touch on her shoulder, and instinctively flinched away before realizing what it meant.

"Desmond?" she croaked, looking up.

He was staring at her, his hands hovering in front of him like weapons he didn't realize he'd been holding. His skin was warm and brown, and his eyes were clear. He tried to speak and remembered that he couldn't—but the malformed sound that rose from his throat still expressed it all perfectly. It was a sound of shock, horror, recognition, and most of all—relief.

Evie stood and nearly collapsed into him. "You're back," she said, sobbing. "Oh my god, you're back."

Desmond brought shaking fingers to his lips, and was about to touch the black thread when she stopped him. "Wait," she said, sniffling. "Don't touch it." She rummaged in her hip pack. When she found what she was looking for, she raised it and cupped the other hand around his jaw. "Just stay still now," she said. "I'm not going to hurt you." With her seam ripper in hand, she carefully cut the threads and gently pulled them from his lips, letting them fall to the forest floor. Desmond winced as they moved through his sensitive flesh, but didn't make a sound. When it was all done, she put the seam ripper away and looked back at him—his soiled clothes, the hollowness of his eyes, the dried blood crusted around his lips. Guilt stung her again like an old wound. "I'm . . . sorry it took me so long," she said, her voice choked with emotion. "I'm sorry for everything. This never would have happened to you if I hadn't . . . if we'd never . . ." She gasped for breath. "Everyone thought you were dead! There was a funeral! Oh god . . ."

He opened his mouth slowly, hesitantly. When he spoke, his

voice was as dry as autumn leaves. "You never gave up on me," he rasped.

Evie shook her head. "How could I?"

He touched her face, her hair, as if to make sure she was real. "Evie," he said, and took her into his arms.

The sound of pounding feet approaching broke their embrace. Holly came bounding toward them, her black dress fluttering behind her like a flag. "Evie, they're coming—" she said, and then stopped short when she caught sight of Desmond. She swallowed. "You found him."

"Brand has no power over him now," Evie said, one hand on his chest. "I smashed the pocket watch."

"Then we don't have time to waste," Holly said, her eyes never leaving Desmond's face. "You have to go home. Your friends eventually found their way out of their nightmares. As soon as they came around, I sent them straight back through the door at my house. They argued, of course, but I promised them you'd be fine. You two can return through the gold mine. It's the only other way. The miners are coming."

"What about you?" Evie asked. "Won't they hurt you?"

Holly scoffed, looking at Evie at last. "We're not so different, those men and me. They won't waste their energy on another shadow. Now go, while you still can."

Evie nodded and was about to pull Desmond along with her when Holly stepped close, laying a hand across his cheek.

"You look," she whispered, "just like him."

Desmond stared back at Holly with confusion. "Who are you?" he breathed.

Holly smiled, a look of pain on her face. "An old friend of your father's," she said simply.

Desmond scoffed. "It can't be . . ."

"Come on," Evie said, pulling Desmond away. She turned to Holly, feeling the bond between them like a physical object, a rope keeping them both from falling into a dark place. It was only then, in that moment, that Evie realized Holly was more than just family. She was a friend. "Thank you," she said softly, wondering if they'd ever meet again.

Holly nodded, her face inscrutable beneath the brim of the black bonnet.

They ran.

Evie saw the dead miners lumbering up the road as they dashed toward the entrance to the gold mine. It looked brand new—not broken down and abandoned as it was in their time. She risked one last look back at Holly as they moved out of view, and Evie could have sworn that instead of being a dark smudge on the earth as the girl had once been, she and her dress seemed to radiate a little—like the sun cresting over the horizon.

They hurtled toward the mine entrance without hesitation, and in seconds they'd passed through the threshold into darkness. Evie screamed as she felt the bottom drop out beneath her, like they'd stepped off the edge of a deep well and were falling through space and time. Her stomach lurched as she felt herself turning head over heels, plummeting into an endless void.

Then, just as suddenly as it had begun, it was over.

Evie found herself face down in the dirt next to Desmond, his fingers still entwined with hers. It was still dark, but the darkness wasn't that thick, impenetrable blackness. It had depth and substance, and smelled like earth. When she lifted her head, she saw two faces hovering like ghostly moons, lit from below by flashlights.

"Holy crap," said Tina, her mouth agape. "You did it."

Evie saw Sai's eyes flick from her to Desmond and back, an expression of relief and sadness passing over his features. "Welcome home," he said softly.

19

"**H**e's alive, h-he's really . . . alive!" Tina stammered, overcome with amazement at Desmond and Evie's sudden appearance.

Evie nodded, still trying to catch her breath.

"Oh my god, is he okay?" Tina said as Desmond leaned against the wall of the mine, his head bowed. The flashlight shone across the ugly wounds around Desmond's mouth and the hollowness of his eyes. "What happened to him?"

"He'll be all right, but he's very weak," Evie replied. "We have to get him to a hospital. How about you? Are you guys okay? The last time I saw you, you were—"

"I don't want to talk about it," Tina said. Even in the dark, Evie could see her expression was haunted by what she'd seen back in the shadow. "Not now, at least."

Sai wouldn't even meet Evie's eyes. He just nodded in agreement.

"We should call an ambulance," Tina went on. "The roads

are covered, but if we get Desmond down the mountain, they'll probably have an easier time getting through." She shook her head. "How the hell are we going to explain this? Any of it?"

Evie shrugged. "We'll say whatever we need to," she said, pulling one of Desmond's arms around her shoulders. "Let's just get out of here and worry about that later."

As Evie tried to get Desmond to walk, he looked up and saw Sai. His eyebrows furrowed in confusion. "Sai?" he muttered. "What are *you* doing here?"

Sai licked his lips. "Erm . . ."

"It's a long story," Evie broke in. "I'll tell you everything when this is all over."

Desmond looked uncertain, his eyes lingering on the other boy.

Sai put both his hands in front of him in a gesture of peace. "I'm just here to help, bruv," he said quietly.

Desmond nodded, putting one filthy, shaking hand up to his mouth and wincing as he touched the wounds there. "Thank you," he said, barely audible.

"It's all right," Sai replied.

Evie glanced back and forth between the two boys, grimacing at the awkward tension in the air. "Come on," she said, and with Tina and Sai leading the way, helped Desmond walk the short distance to the mine entrance and back into the woods. They trudged through the ankle-deep snow back to the mountain pass, where Sai's motorcycle waited by the side of the road. Brushing the bike clean, Sai climbed on and motioned for Desmond to ride behind him.

"I'll drive slow down to Main Street," he said. "You two can follow on foot. Where are we taking him?"

"My house," Desmond said, straddling the bike with difficulty. "It's close by. Just at the bottom of this road, on Blue Stone Court."

"Fine with me," Sai replied grimly, gunning the engine. "Hold on."

As they rolled away, Tina and Evie walked quickly in their wake, following the tracks in the snow back down the mountain. Without stopping, Tina pulled her phone from her bag and dialed 911. As the seconds passed, her expression grew more and more concerned. "I don't understand. No one's picking up," she said. "You try."

Evie pulled her own phone from her hip pack and made the call. It rang ten times before she hung up, a sense of unease growing in her belly. "No answer," she murmured.

Tina was calling her father's cell now, and then her mother's. "No, no, no," Tina said rapidly. "Maybe there's something wrong with the cell phone service. Maybe the snowstorm disrupted the reception and the calls aren't really going through."

"Maybe," Evie said hopefully, though she feared the worst. "Desmond's parents will know what to do." They sped up their pace toward Blue Stone Court.

By the time they got to the house, Desmond was standing on the porch, and the front door of the stately colonial was already wide open. "Mom! Dad!" he shouted into the house. When they approached, he turned toward them, leaning heavily against the door frame, backlit by the light he'd switched on in the foyer. "It doesn't make sense," he said. "The truck and my mom's car are both here. Even the dog isn't around. Where could they be?"

"We can't get in touch with anyone either," Tina said, holding up her phone.

"Not even emergency services," Evie added.

Sai stood nearby, looking uneasy, his dark eyes brooding. "I don't like it," he said. "Something's wrong."

You're too late, my girl. Far too late.

Evie shook her head. No, she'd done what she set out to do. It was supposed to be finished, the spell broken. "We'll take the truck and go to Sai's place," she said. "We can all fit, and it will be better in the snow. If we find Dr. Rockwell, he can help Desmond, and we can figure out what to do from there."

"Right," Sai said, looking relieved to have a plan. "I'll drive." He turned to Desmond. "Keys?"

"Here," Desmond said. He reached into a dish by the door and tossed the keys to Sai. He was about to pull the door shut behind him when he seemed distracted by something inside the house. Evie walked up the two front steps so she could see into the foyer. There, by the spiral staircase, stood the large photograph of Desmond that had been at the church, surrounded by half a dozen flower bouquets and wreaths. "God," Desmond whispered.

Evie threaded her fingers through his. "We'll find your parents," she said, "and then everything will be okay. Everything will go back to the way it was."

Desmond looked at her with haunted, red-rimmed eyes, some of the wounds around his mouth still weeping blood. "No," he said. "Nothing will ever be the same again." He walked past her toward the truck.

Evie took one last look at the face in the photograph—at that bright, shining smile. Then she pulled the door shut and followed, a chill settling into her heart.

The four of them climbed into the blue pickup truck, Sai and Tina in front, Evie and Desmond in the back. Sai turned the key in the ignition and started it up, steering carefully out onto the main road, which was practically invisible beneath several inches of snow. "Guess the plows haven't been out yet," he muttered as he edged the vehicle slowly into town.

Main Street was desolate.

Aside from the Christmas lights that flashed in repeating patterns on some of the storefronts and doorways, nothing moved. Not a soul walked down the sidewalk, nor could Evie see a single person through the windows of any of the buildings. In fact, nearly all the windows were dark. She glanced at the clock. It was 11:11 p.m. Late, certainly, but not so late that everyone in Ravenglass should already be asleep.

"Where is everybody?" Tina asked, giving voice to Evie's dread. She pulled out her phone again and started dialing. The incessant ringing was loud enough that everyone in the cab could hear it. Tina hung up and dialed again. And again. "I thought once we found Desmond, it would all be over," she cried, echoing Evie's earlier thoughts. "What the hell is going on?" A note of hysteria had crept into her voice.

It all felt too familiar to Evie. The emptiness. The silence. The sense of unreality permeating everything. It was just like being in the Shadow Land again—and yet, they'd left all that behind. Hadn't they?

Evie suddenly had the uncontrollable desire to go home.

"Let me out at the corner," she said after they'd turned up the road toward Edgewood. "I have to go to Hobbie House. I'll meet you at Sai's as soon as I'm finished."

Tina and Sai turned to her with the same expression of disbelief. "Are you out of your mind?" Tina asked. "You can't just go off by yourself. We have no idea what's out there!"

"Your priority is to get Desmond medical attention," Evie said, raising a hand to fend off their arguments. "I just . . . I have to check on my family, okay?"

Tina and Sai looked at each other, and then at Desmond, who seemed to be flitting in and out of consciousness. The ordeal at his house seemed have to drained the last of his energy. Evie saw Sai's knuckles go white as he gripped the steering wheel. "Fine," he said through gritted teeth. "But don't be long. If we don't hear from you within half an hour, we're coming to get you."

"Okay," Evie agreed, and hopped out of the truck, slamming the door behind her. The truck rumbled on up the road, its tires making a crisp, crackling sound through the fresh snow. Wrapping her robe more tightly around herself, Evie turned toward the quiet street leading to Hobbie House. Within minutes, she'd reached their mailbox and the bottom of the narrow lane.

She hurried up the drive, cresting the hill until the house came into view. At first, she thought both of the house's two faces were dark, and her chest tightened. But as she got closer, she realized there was a dim light coming from somewhere on the first floor. Not the kitchen or the living room, which was where the family usually stayed, but from the back of the house. *The dining room?* Evie thought, puzzled. That room was a sort of unexplored realm in Hobbie House, a forbidding, wood-paneled space with heavy draperies and a large wooden farm table. Mom hadn't had time to renovate it yet, so she preferred serving meals in the kitchen, where it was warmer and more welcoming. Dining rooms, she liked to say, were obsolete.

So why would anyone be in there?

Evie quietly opened the door and stepped into the dark kitchen. One of Mom's vanilla-scented candles was burning on the table. *She must be home*, Evie thought. *Mom would never leave a lit candle in an empty house . . .* Not only that, but the heat and savory smells emanating from the stove suggested that someone had been cooking.

"Hello?" she called out. "Mom?"

Evie stopped moving and listened, realizing that Christmas music was playing softly in another room. But no voices called back to her.

She swallowed, dread prickling at the back of her neck. Walking down the short hall, she turned left past the stairs toward the dining room and crept up to the doorway. The chandelier hanging above the dining room table was off, and yet the room was aglow with flickering yellow light. *More candles?* Evie wondered. *Maybe Tina's right, maybe there really is something wrong with the electricity.*

"Mom?" Evie repeated as she stepped into the room. "Are you in here?"

The table was laid for a sumptuous meal. Upon a white tablecloth dotted with delicate embroidery stood half a dozen brass candlesticks, each holding a flaming scarlet taper, all of them dripping wax onto the table in messy red blotches. Around them

were large serving plates of food—green beans glistening in butter, roasted potatoes, an apple pie, and a large rack of lamb, the
bones long and white against the deeply charred, tender flesh.

Mom, Dad, and Stan were seated around the table, heads
bowed over their plates as if they were saying grace. Mom was
dressed formally, which wasn't in itself surprising for a nice holiday dinner, except that Evie recognized her black dress as the
same one she'd worn to Desmond's celebration of life. Come to
think of it, Dad and Stan were dressed in the same outfits, too—
black shirts and jeans.

Dressed for a funeral.

The holiday music played.

"Mom . . . Dad . . . ?" Evie managed again. Her throat was dry.

At the sound of her voice, all three of their heads snapped up
like marionettes being pulled by a string. Their eyes fixed on her,
black marbles reflecting the candlelight.

"*Evie,*"

        "*Evie,*"

                "*Evie,*" they chorused, one after
the other, like a song in the round.

"*Welcome home,*"

        "*Welcome,*"

                "*Home.*"

Evie's heart turned to ice. She stopped breathing.

Her mother stood up, jerkily, and leaned to grab a bottle of
wine from the table. "*Come and sit with us,*" she said, pouring
the wine into a glass. It glugged out, bloodred and thick as syrup.

"*Play with us,*" Stan said sweetly.

"*Stay with us,*" Dad added, his voice a deep, wolfish growl.

He smiled at her, and it was too wide, much too wide. It was a Cheshire cat smile. An invitation to madness.

"No," Evie whispered, her voice strangled with terror.

"But you must stay," Mom said. The glass was full, but she kept pouring. Wine flowed over the edges and spilled onto the table, creating a pool of red that grew and grew and grew, spreading to everything through the delicate threads of the tablecloth.

"Yes, you must," Stan said. He was standing now, too, leaning crookedly against his crutch.

Dad was the last to stand, and when he did, Evie couldn't believe he'd ever been that tall. His massive bulk seemed to reach the ceiling—the huge shadow cast by the candlelight on the wall only magnifying his size tenfold.

"This is where you belong," he said, pulling out the last chair.

20

E vie stood rooted to the spot, staring at the empty chair in front of her. She could not make her body move, no matter how much she wanted it to. Adrenaline surged through her veins, heightening all of her senses. The music seemed loud and dissonant—the sour smell of the wine so powerful, it nearly made her swoon.

"The holly and the ivy," a tinny choir sang, "when they are both full grown, of all the trees that are in the wood, the holly bears the crown."

She felt a gentle touch on the back of her neck. A mother's touch.

Evie leaned into it—the instinctual, automatic gesture of a child wanting comfort. Then she felt hot breath near her ear, and words poured in like honeyed poison. *"Sit and eat, Evie,"* her mother whispered, gesturing toward the dinner table, the lamb, the apple pie. *"And we can be a family again. All of us, together for the holidays. Isn't that what you want?"*

Evie thought of the golden apple Holly had offered her that first time down in the Shadow Land, and shuddered. "No," she said, finding her voice.

The fingers tightened on her shoulder, gentle no longer. The pain shook Evie free of her paralysis. She grabbed a steak knife from the table and brandished it. "Get away from me," she said, holding the blade in front of her.

"Oh, but you wouldn't hurt your own mother, would you?" Mom said, her black eyes glittering.

Evie started backing out of the room. "Don't come any closer," she said. She made it out into the stairwell and was about to turn and run when she tripped on the edge of a rug and went tumbling backward, the knife skittering across the wooden floor. By the time she scrambled to her feet again, her parents had moved to block her way.

"You're not playing fair, Evie," Dad growled.

"Not fair at all," Mom said.

Seeing no other escape, Evie tore up the stairs. Halfway up, something grabbed her ankle, and she cried out as her knee hit the hardwood. She turned to see Stan crouched two steps behind her, one pale hand wrapped around her leg. *"Tag,"* he said, his voice twisted and strange. *"You're It."*

Evie kicked him in the chin.

Stan grunted, and she felt his grip slacken.

"Sorry, Stan," she muttered to herself. Yanking her ankle free, she took the rest of the stairs on all fours and dashed into her bedroom, slamming the door and locking it behind her.

She scanned the room. Closet, desk, chair, nightstand, bed.

She tried to imagine having gotten out of that bed just this morning, gone to school, eaten lunch. Never realizing that this would be the day everything fell apart.

A creaking noise jolted her back into the moment. It wasn't until a pink nose emerged from under her bed that she realized it had been a meow. "Schrödinger!" Evie exclaimed. He leaped nimbly onto the nightstand and then onto the windowsill, rubbing his face against the frame. *A way out*, she thought. She undid the lock and slid the window open. It was snowing harder now. She stuck her head outside, peering down to the ground below. It must have been a fifteen- or twenty-foot drop. If only there was something she could use to climb down . . .

The ivy!

The vines had been all over the house when they'd moved in, strangling the front porch and covering nearly every inch of the house. Mom had pulled a lot down—but not all of it. She'd neglected this side of the house, and so it still grew all around Evie's window.

The house, once her enemy, was offering her an escape route.

If the vines could carry my weight long enough for me to get closer to the ground, Evie thought, *I could jump the rest of the way.* The ivy was a thick tangle, and had been clinging to the house for years—but would it hold?

The doorknob rattled. A moment later, the house shuddered as a large body struck Evie's bedroom door. *"Let me in, Evie,"* her father's voice crept in through the keyhole. Then his body struck the door a second time.

Evie wiped the sweat from her forehead with one arm. She

had no idea whether the vines were strong enough to hold her, but she was going to find out. Leaning backward through the window, she was trying to get a good grip on the vines when the door burst open, hitting the wall with a crash. Her father staggered into the room, huge and shrouded in shadow, and lunged for her.

Evie screamed as he grabbed her legs and started dragging her back inside. She held on to the windowsill, trying to kick him off, but he was too strong. She fell onto the hardwood floor, banging her head and knocking the wind from her lungs. She wrenched her body around to face him, still writhing and kicking. "Let go of me!" she screamed.

Schrödinger had backed into a corner of the room, hissing at Evie's father, his orange tail bristling, but Dad didn't seem to notice. "*Come and look in the mirror, Evie,*" he said, extending his hand to her. "*Come and see who you really are.*"

Evie looked at the mirror over her dresser. It was black, reflecting nothing. *Just like the windows in town that night*, Evie thought frantically. *Is that how he's doing it? Is that how it spreads, through reflections?*

"They're nightmares," Holly had said. "But they reflect only darkness."

But he doesn't have Desmond anymore, Evie thought. *The spell should have been broken!*

Maybe Aunt Martha was right. Maybe it was too late.

Her father pulled her to her feet and was shoving her toward the mirror when she turned to face him. "Dad, please," she begged. "I know you're in there somewhere. Please don't do this."

His expression didn't change. He grabbed her by the shoulders and started to turn her around again. The mirror was close now. She almost thought she could feel its dark gravity behind her, dragging her in.

She had to get through to him. Had to find that still-human piece of her father and pull him to the surface. How had she done it with Desmond?

Tell him, a voice inside her said. *Tell him the truth.*

She licked her lips. "You wanted to talk," she said quickly. "You wanted to make things right, remember? Well, now's your chance, Dad. Okay? Now's your chance." Dad didn't let go, but he hesitated. Evie charged on. "The truth is, I felt broken back in New York. After all the doctors and the fighting . . . I was broken, and you just left. I know now you didn't leave because of me, and maybe you really did think that leaving was the best thing for all of us, but . . ." Her breath caught in her throat. "But you never fought for me, Dad," she said, hot tears in her eyes. "You never tried. You just let me go. And I thought—you spend your life making beautiful things, maybe you just couldn't bring yourself to love something so broken."

Dad froze. Something changed in his eyes, and Evie felt a flicker of hope. But he was still holding on to her, still standing between her and the window. Evie could hear Mom and Stan coming up the stairs, Stan limping on his bad ankle as he went. She didn't have much time before they arrived, and she was outnumbered.

"I need you to fight this thing, Dad," she said urgently. "I know it's hard, I know it hurts, but *please*." She touched his hand. "Aren't I worth fighting for?"

A moment passed and he gasped, his face suddenly twisted with agony. He cried out, dropping his hands from her shoulders and putting them over his face. Evie froze, knowing she should run for the window but unable to tear her eyes from her father's pain. As the shadows of Mom and Stan fell through the open door, Dad looked up at her, his eyes clear and blue.

"Go," he said, and he screamed as the inky blackness clouded his eyes once more.

Tears streaming down her face, Evie sprang toward the open window and clambered out, grasping handfuls of vines and pulling herself from the room. As she began her descent, she felt fingertips brushing her hair and the back of her robe, trying to grab hold so they could haul her back into the house.

"Evie!"

"Evie!" the distorted voices cried.

But she had already moved out of their reach. Evie clawed her fingers into the vines, her feet scrabbling for purchase so she could continue her descent. She only had seconds to get to the ground and away before they'd come running into the yard to catch her.

Then the ivy began to fall away from the house.

One second Evie was climbing down, and the next she was falling. Snowflakes whirled around her as she let out a thin wail of terror, her arms pinwheeling in the cold night air. She hit the ground flat on her back, and for a moment she couldn't breathe. She lay there, staring up into the swirling storm, gasping. Luckily, the thick snow banked up next to the house had softened her fall. Unsteady, she scrambled to her feet. Wasting no time, she turned on her heel and started running as fast as she could toward the narrow lane.

Behind her, she heard the front door swing open.

"Come back here!" came her mother's otherworldly cry.

Evie wheezed, still struggling to catch her breath. She was too slow across the deepening snow. They were going to get her.

Suddenly a pickup truck came careering up the driveway toward her, its twin headlights bouncing off the trees. The truck braked hard as it reached the clearing, and the vehicle began to slide across the snow and spin out of control. But the driver turned into the skid and managed to stop it a few feet away from Evie, its nose pointing back the way it had come. Sai ducked his head out the open window. "Get in!" he shouted.

Evie tore at the back door and threw herself inside, barely getting it shut again before Sai hit the gas and sped back down the narrow lane at a dangerously fast clip. Through the back window, Evie saw three dark figures standing in front of the house, watching the truck as it drove away. Turning back around, she found Desmond slumped in the back seat next to her, and Sai and Tina in the front, wild-eyed with panic.

"What's going on?" Evie exclaimed. "Why are you back so quickly? I thought you were taking him to Dr. Rockwell."

Sai glanced up at her in the rearview mirror. She knew from the look in his eyes what had happened before he said a word. "He's gone," Sai managed. "My dad's gone."

Evie sat back in her seat, the reality of their situation descending on her like a physical weight. "Is there anyone left?" she murmured as much to herself as anyone else.

Tina shook her head. "I don't know," she said. "We have to get out of town. We'll take the main road to the highway and drive to Pittsfield. The truck has more than half a tank, so with any luck, we'll make it."

Nodding woodenly, Sai turned toward Main Street. They'd have to drive through town to get to the road out of Ravenglass. The speed limit was only twenty-five, but Sai edged the truck closer to forty. "Once we get there," Tina went on, "we'll find someone to help. We'll make a plan. There has to be a—"

"Watch out!" Evie cried, pointing toward the windshield.

A group of people were standing right in the middle of the road.

Everyone in the truck screamed. Sai slammed on the brakes and swerved to avoid them, and the truck rolled onto the curb and crashed straight into a lamppost.

Evie was thrown forward, her forehead smashing into the seat in front of her. There was a high-pitched whining in her ears as she lay in the back seat, dazed. After a long moment, she pulled herself upright again. "Is everyone okay?" she said, one hand against her aching head.

"We're okay," Tina murmured.

Desmond only moaned.

Sai twisted the key in the ignition. "Come on, come on," he grunted. The truck revved but didn't turn over. The engine hissed and sparked, and finally Sai stopped trying and thumped his fists against the steering wheel. "Damn it!" he shouted.

The four of them got out of the busted truck, Sai supporting Desmond with one arm thrown over his shoulder. Evie trudged through the snow toward Tina, who was standing stock-still, her eyes wide with terror. "What's that sound?" Tina whispered.

It was singing. A haunting melody made by many voices.

"In the bleak midwinter, frosty wind made moan,
Earth stood hard as iron, water like a stone."

The people stood in the street facing them, all wearing matching red scarves. Evie recognized the mayor, Colin Flanagan, and Kimber among them.

"What are they doing?" Sai whispered.

Evie just shook her head. They sang on.

"What can I give him? Poor as I am?
If I were a shepherd, I would give a lamb . . ."

"Kimber! Colin!" Tina shouted at them. "Listen to me!"

"If I were a wise man, I would do my part
But what can I give him?"

Desmond was trying to say something. "What?" Evie asked, placing her ear near his lips.

Each word seemed to cause him pain. "It's . . . a distraction . . ."

Evie straightened as if electrified and spun to look around them. As they'd stood watching the carolers, other people had crept out of the darkened shops, out of parked cars and alleyways.

Mr. and Mrs. King. Birdie and her mother. Lorraine and some of the cast members from the play, still wearing their costumes. Even Ms. Jackson, her normally warm, sparkling eyes glistening with malevolence.

They encircled Evie and the others, moving with inhuman grace, blocking any avenue of escape.

"Give him my heart," the carolers sang. "Give him my heart . . ."

21

"We're trapped," Tina muttered, her back against Evie's. The shadow people moved closer, slowly tightening the circle around them. They should all have been freezing, but none of them seemed to notice the cold. Now that the carolers' song had ended, the only sound was the rustle of a hundred whispers carried on the wind. Evie couldn't discern distinct words, but she could have sworn many of those whispers were speaking her name.

"Evie—"

"Evie—"

"Evie—"

"Evie—"

"Evie—"

"Don't look at them!" Evie cried, averting her eyes. "They're carrying Brand's darkness. We can't let it get into us . . . we can't—"

"We're . . . ," Desmond began, taking wheezing breaths, "the only ones . . . left. That's why he left me . . . back in the other place. He didn't . . . need me anymore. He got. Them. All." Desmond's head dropped forward, his body becoming limp.

"Hey! Hey!" Sai said through gritted teeth as he held Desmond upright. "Stay with us, Des! You gotta stay awake!"

Desmond's eyes fluttered open again, and he licked his dry lips. "I'm awake," he said.

The whispers grew louder.

Evie saw Tina's gaze being pulled to the crowd. "Kitty?" Tina whimpered.

Evie grabbed her by the shoulders and turned her friend's body toward her. "Don't look at her, Tina," she said, her voice shaking. "That's not Kitty. Not anymore."

Tina's red-rimmed eyes flicked from Evie's face to something behind her.

"Look at me, Tina!" Evie shouted.

"All right, Mr. Footballer," Sai said, panting. "How do we penetrate their defense?"

Desmond looked sidelong at him. "You're joking."

"Dead serious, bruv," Sai said.

"We're going to die, aren't we?" Tina said softly.

Desmond was scanning the crowd as it slowly converged on them. "There," he said, pointing to a gathering near the opposite sidewalk. "Crowd's thinner there, nobody behind them. Easier to bust through." A faraway expression passed across his face, and he scoffed. "If ever there was a time for the Flying V . . ."

"Flying V?" Sai asked.

"Offensive formation—banned in football now, though."

"Good job this isn't football, then," Sai replied. The shadows were closing in. "What do we do?"

"You're the strongest, you're in front," Desmond murmured. "I'm . . . hurt, so I'll be right behind you. Evie and Tina will flank me. Our best chance is to find another car we can use to get out of town."

"My aunt Martha's hatchback," Evie broke in. "It's not far from here, and she keeps the keys in the sun visor."

"Fine," Sai said.

Evie nodded, moving Tina into position. "You can do this," she said to her.

"No," Tina gasped. Tears streamed down her cheeks. "No-nono . . ."

"You've got no choice," Evie said roughly. She recognized the look of abject terror on her friend's face—she'd seen it reflected in her own so many times before, starting with that first day in the attic of Hobbie House, in Holly's old mirror. It seemed so long ago now. The girl she had been seemed like a stranger.

Nothing will ever be the same again.

"On my count," Sai said. "One . . ."

Tina began muttering the words of a prayer under her breath. "Padre nuestro, que estás en el un o, santificado sea un ombre . . ."

Someone stumbled out from an alley nearby. Evie instinctively looked over at him for an instant—it was a tall man with a stubbly beard. A large DSLR camera hung like an albatross from a strap around his neck, and his white button-down shirt was spattered with blood. Bile rose in Evie's throat and she looked away.

"Two . . ."

"Just one picture, Miss Archer," the man said in a hollow voice.

Evie took a deep, ragged breath, crouched into a runner's stance, and kept her eyes trained on the back of Sai's head.

"Venga a nosotros tu reino, hágase tu voluntad, aqui en la tierra como en el cielo . . ."

"Look here and smile."

"Three!"

Evie and the others took off as one organism, blasting toward the weak section of the crowd. Desmond struggled to move, so Tina and Evie hooked their arms around him, carrying him along with them as they ran. Sai roared as he hit the first body, his shoulder slamming into a man in a suit and tie, who stumbled back into two other people standing behind him. Evie, Tina, and Desmond bolted through the hole Sai had made and kept running, shouldering past other bodies, making their way down the street toward Aunt Martha's apartment.

Evie could sense the crowd coming after them, their footsteps softened by the fallen snow. "Don't look back!" Evie shouted. "Just keep going!" Desmond's weight grew heavier and heavier as they went.

"Just . . . leave me . . . ," Desmond groaned.

"No way," Tina said.

"A few more blocks and we'll be there," Evie panted.

Just as they were crossing an intersection, a car came speeding from the left and slid to a stop right in front of them. Not just any car—a police cruiser.

Tina skidded to a halt. "Dad!" she cried.

"Tina, don't stop!" Evie told her.

Chief Sànchez climbed out of the driver's seat, wearing dark sunglasses despite the late hour. "Dad, you're okay!" Tina said, turning toward him. "Thank goodness you're here—"

Evie felt Tina moving away from them and screamed for her to stop. *"Tina!"* She tried to hold on to Tina's coat, but the girl pulled away. *"No! Don't!"*

Tina ran to her father. "Dad," she sobbed. "You have to help us. Where's Mom? Are Tito and Tati okay?"

Evie felt her heart lurch. The darkness traveled in reflections. Windows, mirrors.

Sunglasses.

Tina had gone quiet. She stood very still with her arms at her side, facing her father.

"Tina!" Evie screamed again.

Chief Sànchez stepped up to Tina and took her hand. His sunglasses didn't reflect the streetlights. Tina turned around. She was smiling.

"Sorry, Evie," Tina said, black eyes flashing. *"But Daddy needs me. He needs all of us."*

"No . . . ," Evie sobbed, reaching toward her friend.

"Leave her!" Sai said, taking Tina's place under Desmond's arm. "We have to go!"

With Desmond between them, Evie and Sai skirted around the police car. Snow spattered their faces as they ran, and they could see people coming down the street in pursuit. Tina and Chief Sànchez joined them. They didn't hurry. They walked as if they had all the time in the world.

Aunt Martha's neon sign burned like a beacon from her

second-story window. "There's the car," Evie managed between breaths, pointing to the rickety old hatchback parked in front of the building.

Sai opened the driver's-side door and rummaged around inside. "There's no keys!" he exclaimed.

Evie shook her head. "She must have taken them upstairs. We'll go to her apartment and find them."

"But—" Sai began.

"There's no other way!"

Sai's jaw tightened and he nodded. Evie led them up the narrow stairwell to Aunt Martha's door. "We might have to break it down if it's locked," Evie said. But the knob turned easily in Sai's hand, and the door swung open with a high, thin whine. She exchanged an uneasy glance with Sai and peered through the open doorway. The apartment was dark, save for the yellow glow emanating from the neon sign. A chill wind wound its way out from within, raising the hairs along the back of Evie's neck. *Why is it so cold in there?* Suddenly, the last thing she wanted to do was go inside. *You have to*, she told herself. *You have no choice.*

She took a deep breath and went in. The reading room was a mess. Broken pieces of things crunched under her shoes, and the floor was damp with melted snow. Books had been torn from the shelves and lay scattered in messy, wet piles. As she moved, something stuck to the bottom of her shoe, and Evie bent to pull it free. It was a tarot card. Three women, dancing in a circle, wearing dresses of white and gold, raising their goblets to the sky.

The Three of Cups.

Evie set the card on the table. "Come on," she called to the others. "We've got to find the car keys. They're either in here or her apartment . . ."

Sai walked inside, squinting in the dim light, and immediately began searching the shelves and floor. Desmond lurched inside after him and locked and bolted the door. Then he went to one of the armchairs in the middle of the room and collapsed into it.

"I'm sorry," he said softly. "I can't . . . I can't . . ."

"Desmond, it's okay," Evie said as she scanned the room. "You're in shock, you're severely dehydrated, and god knows what else—you don't need to apologize for anything."

"I'm slowing you down," Desmond went on. "If you two just went on—"

"No!" Evie barked, slamming one fist into the wall. Sai stopped what he was doing and looked at her. Their eyes flashing white in the dark, both Sai and Desmond regarded her with wariness. Evie swallowed. Her hands were shaking. She was trying to think, but her brain was full of cotton. Her thoughts kept creeping to her family, to Tina, and she had to drag them back to the present. Madness lay in those thoughts. She couldn't afford to lose herself now, not while they were still in such terrible danger. She had to focus.

"Keys, keys," she muttered, resuming the search. "Where would she have kept them?" Minutes passed. Evie checked the apartment next door, but with no success.

"What if she has them with her?" Sai asked. "They could be in her pocket or something."

"If the car is here, the keys should be here, too," Evie said stubbornly. She refused to admit that this was a fool's errand. They needed a way out. Any minute now, those shadow people would come walking up the stairs and pound on the door. It was only a matter of time.

"I'm all used up, Evie," Desmond said, his words slurred. "No good anymore."

"Stop saying that," Evie said. She looked through a drawer for the second time and slammed it shut in frustration. Sai was pacing back and forth, running his fingers through his sodden black hair.

"He got what he needed from me, and now he's got them all," Desmond went on.

Evie turned to him. "What's he going to do with them?" she asked. "Do you know?"

Desmond let out a shuddering breath. "He's too old to leave that place on his own. Too weak. Not like Holly could. Not like I could. He needs . . . *bodies*. Living flesh. So that he can use them to make a new one for himself. So he can be . . . more than just a shadow again."

"But why so many?" she said. "Wouldn't one be enough?"

Desmond's eyes were bright with remembered terror. "He was in my head, you know?" He tapped at his temple with one finger. "I could *feel* him in there, every second, all the time." He sniffed, and his eyes met Evie's. "That *hunger*."

At that moment, a heavy wind buffeted the room, throwing one of the picture windows open and sending the curtains flying into the air, furling and unfurling. Evie raised an arm against the flying snow and squinted into the storm, edging forward to try to close the window again. But as she got closer, she saw the deep shadows behind the curtains shift and change. She blinked, wiping snowflakes from her eyes, and looked again. Someone was there. The deep purple fabric was turning and twisting in the wind, and within them Evie saw a mass of silver hair, thin white hands, and a pale sunken face.

"It's time, my girl," Aunt Martha said, the curtains and her long purple shawl intermingling as one. "It's almost midnight." She took a step toward Evie and smiled, holding out a hand, the skin hanging dry from her bones.

22

Aunt Martha reached out to Evie, the curtains still whirling about her body in rippling waves. The silver chains she wore around her neck moved with the wind, making a sound like a hundred tiny bells that were somehow audible over the gale. Behind her, the windows darkened, one by one, until Evie could no longer see the streetlights below. It was as if the outside world were a theater, and the house lights were going to black.

The show was about to begin.

Evie forced herself not to look at them or Aunt Martha. She looked at the floor, strewn with sodden tarot cards—a mess of swords and cups, angels and devils. The sight of them filled her with a sudden intense regret, for although she had been warned that this whole nightmare might come to pass, she'd been powerless to stop it.

It's not over yet, she told herself, but the words rang hollow.

"Evie, we need to run!" Sai shouted over the din.

She turned to see him. He was soaked through, his leather

jacket shiny with snow, his hair plastered in curls to his face. "We can't leave Desmond!" she shouted back, and ran to the armchair where Desmond was lying, half conscious, his face as pale as death. She tugged on his arm, but Desmond wouldn't budge. His eyes cracked open, and he gazed up at her.

"Go," he croaked.

"No, I won't," Evie said, stubbornly holding on to him. "I can't. Not after everything—"

"You still have a chance to stop him," Desmond said. "But not if you stay here."

"*Come on, Evie!*" Sai shouted.

Evie could see Aunt Martha moving toward them out of the corner of her eye.

"No, no, not again," Evie moaned. With effort, Desmond pulled his arm out of her grasp, and Sai immediately swept her up and ran out the door.

It wasn't until they were downstairs and out in the alleyway between Aunt Martha's apartment building and the one next door that Sai stopped. He slid his back down the brick wall and sat panting on the snow-covered ground, Evie lying across his lap. She was barely aware of her own body, her own voice, as she repeated *no no no*, and beat Sai's chest with her fists. He let her do it at first, and then he gently took her by the wrists and held her shaking body tightly against his own.

"I'm sorry," he whispered. "I'm so sorry . . ."

She didn't know how much time passed before she was able to slow her breathing, before her awareness returned. She blinked away the blur of tears, wiped her nose with the back of her hand,

and glanced reluctantly up at Sai. He returned her gaze, his expression soft. She laid one palm flat against his chest, making no move to stand up or remove herself from his embrace. "Did I . . . did I hurt you?" she asked.

Sai shook his head. "Takes more than that, luv."

Evie sighed, the adrenaline crash and cold exposure making her suddenly feel sleepy. *We could just stay here, curled up like this, and wait for the end to come.* The idea sounded comforting. She wouldn't have to do anything else. Wouldn't have to lose anything else. It would be so easy.

"Thank you," Sai said, his voice shivery with cold.

Evie scoffed. "For what?"

"When I was down there, in that shadow place," Sai said, "and I saw my mum—I knew it wasn't her. Not at first, but after a bit, I realized that my real mum would never have blamed me for what happened. But it took seeing her like that, saying those awful things right to my face, to get me to realize it. I never would have found that out if it weren't for you. And I never would have gotten out of that nightmare if I hadn't promised you I'd come back. Whatever happens, I know now that Mum would have wanted me not only to survive—but to *live*. To grow up, have a life, just like I've done up to now."

Evie shook her head, the pain in her heart nearly overwhelming. "It can't end like this," she said.

"You're right," Sai agreed. "If I become one of them shadow blokes, who'll give Bonnie her tune-ups when she needs them?"

Evie shook her head. "Dummy," she muttered, but she couldn't suppress a small smile. "Speaking of those shadow blokes," she said suddenly. "Why haven't they found us by now?" They both went still and listened for movement. But the whole town had fallen silent as a tomb.

Weak-kneed and lightheaded, Evie struggled to her feet. Sai followed, brushing snow from his jacket and jeans. Together, they crept to the edge of the alley and peered around the corner to Main Street.

There wasn't a soul in sight.

Warily, Evie stepped out onto the sidewalk, scanning for signs of life. Nothing moved except the falling snow.

"Where did they all go?" Sai murmured.

Just then, the church bells began to ring.

Evie and Sai looked at each other in confusion. The bells never rang at night—they usually sounded just three times during the day. Sai pulled out his phone and turned it on. His nostrils flared as the glowing screen lit up his face. "Midnight," he murmured.

Evie swallowed. "Something's about to happen," she said.

As soon as the reverberation of the bells ceased, the silence was filled with another sound. A soft rustling, like something large being dragged across the snow. Then, a figure turned the corner and began coming up the street toward them. Evie blinked rapidly, unable to focus, her eyes trying and failing to make sense out of what they were seeing.

It was as if the figure had pulled the very darkness from the sky and wore it like a shroud. A creature of colossal size, at least twenty feet tall, featureless except for having the vague shape of a man wearing a hooded robe, the ends of it dragging across the earth in tatters made of smoke.

She'd seen something just like it in a dream once. Twice,

maybe. She'd sketched a picture of it in Ms. Jackson's class, thinking it would be just the thing for the Christmas show. An image of a harbinger of death, of a Future Yet to Come.

But she'd been mistaken. It hadn't been a dream about that at all. It had been a premonition about this very moment. The moment Wallace Brand would escape the shadow and arrive on her doorstep on the longest night of the year.

A Future Yet to Come, yes. But not Ebenezer Scrooge's.

Hers.

23

The dark goliath advanced, unhurried, down the silent, picturesque street. The wind and snow had ebbed, and everything save the creature was absolutely still. Evie stood rooted to the spot, her eyes fixed on the spectacle before her, hardly remembering to breathe.

"What is that . . . thing?" Sai whispered next to her.

"It's him," she said. "It's Brand."

Sai threaded his fingers into hers. "Don't look at it, Evie," he said. "Remember? We have to keep running."

But Evie couldn't look away. She could feel herself being drawn into the creature's gravity, like a moth to a flame. Whatever limitations Brand once had on his power were gone. He needed no herald, no reflection, no trickery to capture her in his thrall. She felt calm, somehow, knowing it was over. No more fighting. No more fear. It would be so peaceful there, in the darkness. Quiet. Like floating at the bottom of a pool. "It's too late," she said softly. "Much too late."

"No," Sai blurted. "No, I won't let it get you, I won't—" He tried to pull her away, but Evie wouldn't move.

Then, the creature spoke.

"Come to me, child," it said. And the sound was at once the voice of the man from their vision in the cellar, but also a hundred other voices besides—all of them saying each word in unison, like a Greek chorus in a play that was always going to end in tragedy.

From the dark shroud an arm materialized, a skeletal hand at its end, one bony finger pointing straight at Evie.

She took a step toward it.

"No!" Sai shouted, and before Evie realized what was happening, he'd moved in front of her, blocking it from view. He wrapped his arms around her, one hand on the back of her head, his lips at her ear. "You can't give up, Evie, all right? I'm sorry, but you can't. You've always been at the center of this. Whatever it is you've got to do, you need to do it now. All right, luv? Do it now."

Evie felt herself being pulled back into consciousness, and with it came pain. She was so cold, so scared, and so, so tired. She desperately wanted to fall back into the welcoming darkness and forget about all this. "Why?" she gasped, her head lolling back into his hand. "Why does it have to be me?"

Sai smiled bitterly. "Why anything?" he said with a shrug. "Because. Because you moved into that house. Because you chose to listen. Because you believed when no one else did." He pressed his forehead against hers, the holly crown still pinned to her head catching in his curls. "We can't change what we are. The more we push it away, the more it hurts."

The words cut straight to her heart, because they were hers.

"Come here, boy," the multitudinous voice boomed.

Suddenly, Sai's eyes widened, his mouth opening into a perfect O. His body arched and was wrenched backward, away from her embrace.

"Sai!" Evie screamed. She tried to hold on to him, her fingers gripping the sleeve of his leather jacket, but the pull was unstoppable. She would only have been dragged along with him toward the beast. She fell to her knees in the snow, speechless with horror as she watched Sai stumble closer and closer to the dark shroud. As he reached it, the shadow seemed to part like a curtain, exposing a nightmare within.

There, beyond the veil of shadow, she saw faces. Faces that seemed to flit in and out of sight, all of them twisted and grotesque, all of them screaming. She saw hands as well, pressed against some unseen barrier that was keeping them inside. There were small hands, too. Children's hands.

Every soul in Ravenglass.

That teeming mass of life was somehow trapped inside the creature, which despite its immense size seemed far too small to hold so much.

When Sai reached that barrier, the hands found him. Their fingers wrapped around his wrists, his legs—tore at his clothes, and tangled themselves up in his sodden black curls. But all the while that they pulled him inside, to join them in their suffering, Sai's eyes never left hers. He looked at her until his eyes turned to black, until he disappeared behind the curtain and was gone.

Evie gasped, her despair total. She'd been working on the assumption that everyone who had been taken could be brought back—like Desmond had been. But seeing them all inside that impossible monstrosity—what was left of them—she suddenly wondered if she'd been wrong.

Terribly, fatally wrong.

"*You're alone, Miss Archer,*" the thing that was Wallace Brand said. "*Now come. I have waited several lifetimes for this night.*"

"You're a murderer," Evie whispered.

"*I am a god!*" Brand shouted with hundreds of voices. "*When I fell into that hole, I thought I fell straight into the depths of hell. But I was wrong. Within that holy shadow, there is unending power. Power that, over time, I harnessed and nurtured into greatness. It was my weak body that held me back from returning here, to this place, to take what is rightfully mine. Now I have no need of my own flesh, for I have the flesh of many.*"

"You . . . you k-killed my family, my friends . . . ," Evie stammered, feeling numb.

"*Killed? No. They live still, within me. Their hearts will beat forever in the shadow, where the sun's harsh gaze cannot reach, and the finger of death cannot touch. I have not killed them. I have given them eternal life.*"

Something changed in Evie upon hearing those words. If they weren't dead, then they could still be saved.

"*Come, child,*" Brand repeated. "*I am a generous god. Join my flock, and you'll live forever, too.*"

"You're mistaken," Evie said softly.

"*Mistaken? About what?*" the creature replied.

"I'm not alone."

Evie turned on her heel and ran in the opposite direction down

Main Street, taking to the alleyways, crisscrossing streets, going as fast as her feet would take her.

"*Evie!*" Brand boomed after her, his voice legion. "*There is nowhere to run!*"

She wouldn't be able to evade him for long, but she needed time. Time to find the only other person who could help her stop him.

She came out of an alleyway and found herself directly across the street from Ravenglass Congregational. The little church, all covered in snow and Christmas garland, looked like something out of a storybook. Evie stopped and looked back down the street. She could see the enormous creature coming her way, as relentless as an oncoming storm. Then, out of the silence, came a sweet, familiar sound.

"Whip-poor-will?"

It was coming from the church. Without hesitation, Evie took off toward it. As she got closer, she heard it again.

"Whip-poor-will?"

Following the sound, she found herself back in the old cemetery, among the graves. A little brown bird perched on a branch of a maple tree, its feathers fluffed against the cold. Under the maple's boughs, beside the empty, forgotten grave of a little girl, stood Holly Hobbie.

"*You called me?*" Holly said, her hands clasped in front of her.

"You came," Evie said.

Holly gave a little shrug. "*He doesn't much care about me anymore,*" she said. "*Now that he has what he wants.*"

"He took them all," Evie said, leaning heavily against one of the gravestones. "He's here and he's become this—this *thing*. He won't stop until he's gotten me, too."

Holly nodded. *"I know. I'm sorry."*

"But what happens after that?" she cried, speaking very quickly. "What if he just moves on to the next town, and the next? What if he never stops? He's going to keep hurting people, just like he hurt you and Sarah." She gulped a breath of frigid air and kept going. "He's right behind me, Holly. You have to help me, *please*. You're all I have left."

Holly shook her head. *"There's nothing I can do, Evie. I did my best to help you, but I guess it wasn't enough."*

"No, that's not true," Evie said roughly. "There is something you can do. I don't know what Brand told you and Sarah all those years while you were trapped down there, but the man is a professional liar—in life *and* in death. The power he's taken from the Shadow Land, you have it, too! Don't you see? What happened down there with the miners, that light that drove them away—that was no accident. That was *you*! Why can't you use that power to fight back?"

Holly looked confused. *"But he . . . he was always different from us. He could do things we couldn't."*

"That's what he *wanted* you to think!" Evie shot back. "But who was it that moved freely between the shadow and the light? Who was it that had the strength to enter dreams, to shape reality? You and Sarah did. He was too weak to do anything alone, so he convinced you two that you were the weak ones, that you deserved to be under his command and do his bidding. But it was all a con, Holly. Just like the gold. *It was all a lie.*"

Holly gasped.

The wind shifted, and Evie caught the scent of something bitter in the air. Gunpowder.

Whirling, Evie stared up at the monstrous figure of Brand looming before them, his shadow nearly blocking out the moon.

"Disobedient whelp!" Brand thundered, seeing Holly standing in the graveyard. *"Didn't I tell you to stay in the shadow?"* He paused, the faceless hood shaking slowly back and forth. *"Now I have no choice but to teach you a lesson."* He raised his arm, opened his bony hand toward Holly in an offering gesture, and then snapped it shut.

Holly screamed in agony and fell to her knees.

Evie dashed to where she kneeled on Sarah's grave, her head in her hands. "Holly," Evie said. "Holly, are you all right? What did he do to you?"

Holly was still for a moment. Then she lowered her hands.

Her beautiful face had been ripped away.

There was no blood, no mess of muscle and sinew. Only a clean, perfect skull, as white as snow, peering out from underneath the black bonnet.

Evie backed away from her, shaking her head in disbelief. "You monster . . ."

With jerky, trembling movements, Holly got back to her feet and stood silently, her shoulders slumped.

"Little girls," Brand mused, his disdain mirrored by a hundred voices. *"Who knew they could be so much trouble?"* He turned to Evie. *"Now, enough running. Your time is up."* And just like before, the bottom of his shroud parted, revealing the

writhing mass of souls within. Evie felt it tug at her, and saw the darkness begin to collect at the corners of her eyes.

"Holly!" she shouted, turning to face her cousin. "Please! You have to fight! He has no power over you!"

Holly's hollow eyes stared back at her, two depthless black holes. Could she even hear what Evie was saying? Did she understand?

The force of Brand's will dragged Evie backward across the graveyard. She fell to the ground, trying and failing to hold on to the headstones as she went. "This has always been about us, Holly," she cried. "You and me and Sarah! We have to stop running! We have to take a stand!"

The darkness was closing in.

Show's over.

"Holly . . ." Her voice was getting weaker.

Curtain call.

24

Time seemed to slow as Evie was dragged backward by the force of Brand's power. She resisted the urge to turn around and face the darkness, to let herself fall into the embrace of all those trapped within it. Instead, she kept her gaze trained on Holly.

Maybe it was over, maybe she'd lost, but she'd never give Brand the satisfaction of seeing her give up.

It was ironic, in a way, that the Lost Girl of Ravenglass would be the last soul in town now—that she alone would be left to mourn them. Evie tried to call out to her again but could only move her lips to form the word. Her voice had already begun to join the legion within.

She blinked, and between that moment and the next, it looked as if someone else stood next to Holly at the grave. Evie's breath caught in her throat, and she blinked again. Was she seeing double? No. There was someone else there. Someone small.

"*Holly,*" said the little girl, her face a tiny, delicate skull. She had no lips to speak, and yet Evie could still hear her. *"Are you hurt, Holly?"*

Sarah! Evie thought. She felt the pull on her body subside slightly, as if Sarah's appearance had interrupted Brand's concentration.

Holly turned to face the girl in the patchwork dress. *"What are you doing here?"* she asked. *"You should have stayed home, where it's safe."*

"I got scared," Sarah complained. *"I don't like being alone. And I could feel that someone had hurt you. I don't like it when you get hurt, Holly. You're my best friend."* She reached out with a tiny, skeletal hand and slipped it into Holly's.

Holly's head drooped. *"You're my best friend, too."*

"What happened to your face?" Sarah asked, her bonneted head cocked. *"That other girl made you pretty again, but now it's all gone."* Then she seemed to notice the rest of the tableau before her. The graveyard, Evie on the ground, and the dark goliath towering over everything. *"Mr. Brand . . . ,"* she whispered, her childlike voice suddenly full of terror. She clung to Holly's skirts, pressing her face against the bigger girl's stomach. *"Don't let him hurt me anymore, Holly,"* she cried. *"I didn't mean to be bad! I just didn't want to be alone!"*

There was a moment of stillness, and then Holly placed one hand, still flesh, gently on the back of Sarah's head. Her shoulders straightened. *"I won't let anyone hurt you,"* she said, her voice suddenly stronger. *"Ever again."* When she looked up, her hollow eyes bore directly at Evie. *"Tell me what to do,"* she said.

Evie's mind whirled. She only had seconds left before she was consumed.

The Three of Cups, hand in hand, dancing with goblets raised.

A sisterhood, bound together by unseen connections.

Without speaking, Evie sent the words to the other girls on the wind of her thoughts. *He may think he is many, but he is alone. We have one another.*

"But even if we have the power of the shadow," Holly replied, *"we have no body as he has. We can't affect this world without a body."*

Evie took a deep breath and reached out toward them. *Then take mine.*

Holly and Sarah turned to each other, and each nodded in agreement. Hand in hand, they flitted out of the world and appeared once more standing directly in front of Evie. They bent, Holly taking one of Evie's hands and Sarah taking the other.

Suddenly free of Brand's unseen grip, Evie rose to her feet once more. The three girls stood in a circle, facing one another. An eerie calm fell over them.

"What are you doing?" Brand thundered. The chorus of voices lagged this time, creating a strange echo that sounded uncertain. *"You will all be punished for this impudence!"*

Holly ignored him. *"Are you sure about this?"* she asked, her head turned toward Evie.

I'm sure, Evie replied.

Holly nodded. *"Come on, Sarah,"* she said. *"Let's slide down . . ."*

Evie swallowed and closed her eyes just as a wave of force slammed into her body, once, and then twice. She wanted to cry out in pain but had no voice to do so. She felt like her skin had been stretched too taut over her bones, like there was suddenly too much inside her and she would split at the seams. Thoughts, memories, feelings—none of them her own—flooded her mind. The overwhelming sensation seemed to last for hours, but it could only have been seconds before the maelstrom within her settled and went still.

With great effort, Evie threw back her shoulders and stood tall. She felt larger somehow, and saw the world as if through the lens of a kaleidoscope, through six eyes instead of two.

"What have you done?" Brand said. The other voices had quieted, leaving his to speak alone.

The world was hushed. Waiting.

"We are three," Evie said, and Holly said, and Sarah said. *"And we are one. We are past, present, and future. We are your reckoning, and your time on this earth has come to an end."*

The creature seemed to shrink from the sound of their voices. *"Impossible . . . ,"* he said. *"I'll kill you,"* he growled, suddenly sounding more human than demon. *"I'll rip you apart until there's nothing left but pain . . ."*

Evie felt a sudden wind lift her hair beneath the holly crown, throwing it into a wild halo around her head. Warmth filled her frozen body, as if generated from within.

Of all the trees that are in the wood,
Holly wears the crown.

"You are darkness," the three girls chanted. *"You are nothing. You are void."*

Brand raised a skeletal arm against them. *"Stop!"* he commanded.

Evie felt everything within her, all the fear, all the despair, all the pain, fall away to perfect stillness. She was exactly where she was meant to be. And she only had three more words to say before it was done.

"*We are light.*"

A bolt of light brighter than the sun burst from Evie's body. She screamed in three voices, blinded by the sudden radiance, as power burst out from her eyes, her mouth, from the top of her head.

That radiance struck the great shadow with such explosive force that for a moment, night turned to day. Brand's enraged scream joined theirs as his back arched, face turned skyward. The scream grew in volume, louder and louder, as his shroud of darkness burned away, holes appearing all over its massive bulk like paper burning in a bonfire. It recoiled and twisted in on itself, filling the air with acrid, foul-smelling smoke.

At the same time, the invisible barrier within the shroud seemed to give way and release the souls imprisoned within. Bodies surged out in a torrent of arms and legs and faces, gasping like they'd just emerged from the bottom of the sea. They tumbled over and over each other in an unending flow of living flesh, crying out in confusion and pain. Even when Evie thought no more could possibly come out, bodies continued to appear.

Finally only the head of the creature remained in a pile of hissing, smoking shadow. "*This isn't over,*" Brand rasped through ragged breaths.

Evie felt herself walking over to what was left of him, past hundreds of people lying still in the street. They breathed as one, as if all were still trapped in some terrible dream. "*Oh, it is,*" the three girls said. "*Slide down, Wallace Brand. Death has been waiting to play with you. And it's been waiting for a long, long time.*"

"*No!*" Brand shrieked as the last of the black hood withered away. For a moment, there was a ghost of an image left behind, something vaguely like a skull—and then it blew away into the night.

When the light ran out, Evie fell to her knees. She was exhausted. Whatever strength she'd used to contain two other souls was completely spent. Her skin felt as if it were ripping in half. *I can't . . . hold you . . . anymore . . .* she thought. She felt movement all around her, bodies shifting and rising, but she was in so much pain, she was only dimly aware of it.

Maybe this was the end. People weren't meant to hold more than one soul inside of them. Even so, she could die knowing that her final act had been worthwhile, that she'd done what she'd set out to do. She thought of Desmond and Sai, and hoped that they'd forgive her.

But just as consciousness was slipping away, she felt a great weight lift from her body, shrugging itself out of her like someone stepping out of a coat. First one, and then another. She squeezed her eyes shut from the hot, white agony, gritting her teeth as they went, nearly tearing her apart along the way.

Then, it was done. She was alone in her body once more.

Evie gasped, feeling so light that she wondered if she might float away on the wind, like the snow. Instead, she collapsed onto the cold, soft earth.

The snow embraced her. She tried to move but found that she couldn't. Still, the pain had gone, and she was blissfully numb. She could sleep now, knowing that it was all finished.

She lay staring at the deserted graveyard, and saw Holly and Sarah materialize out of the shadows. A surge of joy passed through her as she saw that their faces were flesh once more, their hair bright and tumbling out from beneath their bonnets, their bodies luminous in the moonlight. Tears fell from Evie's eyes, intermingling with the snow pressed against her cheek. She'd contained them both like a Russian nesting doll, one smaller and another smaller still, and now they'd left her and were whole again. She was empty, and yet the shape of the other two girls remained etched in her soul, and in that moment she knew they always would be.

"She'll be all right, won't she?" Sarah asked, her head cocked, gazing at Evie where she lay.

"Yes, with time," Holly replied, her hand curling around the younger girl's shoulder.

"What do we do, now that he's gone?" Sarah said, gazing toward her own grave.

"We go home," Holly replied.

"To the shadow?"

Holly bent to look into Sarah's eyes. *"It doesn't have to be the shadow anymore,"* she said. *"Now it's our game. We make the rules."*

Sarah grinned. *"Maybe we can plant a garden. Or build a little house for the birds!"* A worried expression crossed her face. *"You won't be lonely down there with just me to keep you company?"*

"I have a feeling we'll have plenty of new friends to play with when we get back," Holly replied. Evie wondered if Holly was thinking of the dozens of young men who were probably waking up at that very moment in the Shadow Land with clean, fresh bodies, wondering what in the world had happened to them. *"Besides,"* Holly continued, *"we'll have to keep a close eye on Evie*

and the rest of our friends in Ravenglass, too. It's our job to make sure this never happens again."

Sarah nodded and stood up a little straighter. Purpose was a gift she'd never received before.

"Come along now," Holly said. "The night is nearly over, and we're needed back home. Everyone is about to wake up."

The two girls turned around and began to walk away, past the wrought-iron gate surrounding the old graveyard, past the church and the woods, and into the dawning. At the same time, Evie sensed movement all around her. Shadows fell upon her in a silent parade as a crowd of people drifted through the streets, their dreams slowly burying this nightmare under a cover of unbroken snow.

In some distant corner of her mind, Evie knew that she should get up. Knew that the snow's embrace was very cold, and very dangerous. But she was so tired. All she wanted to do was sleep. So she ignored that warning voice, closed her eyes, and let the darkness take her.

25

*B*eep.
　Beep.
　Beep.

The rhythmic noise drew Evie back to consciousness, like a lighthouse flashing across a dark sea. She drew herself toward it, toward the feeling of warmth and softness, until finally she opened her eyes.

She was in a hospital bed, weighed down with blankets, her hands and feet swathed in bandages. An IV drip stood sentinel next to the bed, along with a squadron of beeping machines. Evie shifted her arm and felt the needle taped there.

Everything was so bright.

She turned her head and saw Dad sitting at her bedside, squashed into a narrow plastic chair that strained to contain him. His broad back was bent, his head in his hands.

Evie licked her lips. Her mouth was dry. "Dad?" she croaked.

Her father sat up at the sound, and he looked at her with red-rimmed eyes.

Clear, normal, tired eyes.

"Evie," he said, his voice nearly as hoarse as hers. He put one hand on her forehead, smoothing the hair away from her face. "You're awake." He sighed and squeezed his eyes shut, dropping his head against the bed pillow. "Thank god."

He's okay, Evie thought as a wave of relief crashed over her, too. *And if he's okay, maybe everyone else is, too.*

She was suddenly struck with a thousand questions. "What happened?" she asked. "How did I get here? What's going on?" She tried to sit up, but Dad shook his head and pressed his palms gently against her shoulders.

"Evie, stop. You have severe frostbite on your hands and feet. You have to try to stay still for now, okay? The pastor found you unconscious in the church cemetery very early this morning and called an ambulance. We came as soon as we heard. Your mom and Stan are getting some hot chocolate in the cafeteria—they'll be back soon."

Evie's head felt like it was in a fog. She tried to think, tried to make sense of what her dad was telling her. "But . . . ," she began, unsure of how to phrase the question. "Did anything . . . else happen?"

Dad blew out his cheeks and leaned back in his chair. "Craziest thing," he said. "Bunch of people from town ended up in the ER last night, too. Woke up with bumps and bruises they can't explain—even your brother's got a bit of a shiner this morning! Can't imagine how he got it. They're saying this strange illness that's been sweeping through Ravenglass over the past few weeks might have had some psychological effects. Making people sleepwalk, suffer from short-term memory loss, stuff like that. They think you must have come down with it, too. Some people remember seeing you at the play, but it gets pretty hazy after that—busy night and all. Do you remember anything?"

Evie shook her head. *All those memories, buried under the snow*, she thought in disbelief. Evie longed to do the same. To forget. But she knew that was impossible. The burden of memory was hers to bear.

"Huh," her father said, nonplussed. "Seems to have passed over, though. Everyone in town has been accounted for."

"And you," Evie said carefully. "You don't remember anything . . . different about last night?"

An odd expression crossed Dad's face. "Now that you mention it," he said, "your mom and I both felt pretty out of it this morning, so maybe we had a touch of it, too. And I had the strangest dream. More of a nightmare, really." He wiped his mouth with the back of his hand. "Come to think of it, it might have been about you. But to wake up to your mother calling me to say you were in the hospital, now, that was a real nightmare." His voice broke, and he pressed his lips into a line, pausing for a few moments before surging on. "Look, I know I should have said this before, probably a long time ago. But I can't wait any longer, not after last night. Not after I almost lost you." He took a deep breath. "I guess I haven't always been the greatest father, Evie. What you said to me yesterday in the kitchen—I deserved that. But I want you to know—I always tried to do what was best for you. Everything I did, I did it because I thought that was what you needed. And I know sometimes it turned out to be stupid and wrong and selfish, and I was too wrapped up in my own life to realize it. But I want that to change. Okay? Just because your mom and I aren't together anymore, it doesn't mean we can't be a family." He put a hand on her arm. "So can we start again? I want to be a part of your life, Evie. I want to fight for you."

A lump rose in Evie's throat. Did some part of him remember? That moment in her bedroom when he'd kept the monsters at bay? Everything that had happened under Brand's thrall seemed to have been erased from his mind. But perhaps something, some shadow of a memory, still remained.

"Okay, Dad," Evie replied. "Let's start again."

Dad nodded, frowning with emotion. He wrapped his burly arms around her and kissed her forehead, the scruff of his beard comforting on her skin. "Good," he said. "Good. Now, as soon as they give you the all-clear, we can get you home."

Evie smiled and lay back on her pillow, feeling relaxed for the first time in ages. She sighed, and something clicked in her mind. "Wait," she said, sitting up again. "You said *everyone* is accounted for? No one from town is missing?"

Dad's brows furrowed. "Yeah, why?"

She was almost afraid to ask. "What about Desmond?"

A strange expression passed over his face as he regarded her. "Evie . . . ," he said slowly. "How could you possibly know about Desmond?"

It took all of Evie's willpower not to jump out of the hospital bed. "Is he alive, Dad? Tell me he's alive."

Dad shook his head in wonder. "Yes, he's alive. But how did you know? You were unconscious all night, you were here when they found him."

"I just . . . ," Evie struggled to complete that sentence. "I just . . . had a feeling." She looked at her hands, swaddled in white. "I promise I'll tell you more later, but right now, just tell me about Desmond."

The answer didn't seem to fully satisfy him, but it was enough. "Well, all I know is that his mother found him at home this morning, asleep in his bed. Just like that. Like nothing had ever happened. He's not in the best shape, and they're still trying to get some kind of explanation out of him about where he's been all this time, but the boy's all right. He's upstairs, actually, in a room with his folks." He blew out his cheeks. "Talk about a Christmas miracle, huh?"

Evie was already moving, trying to get up.

"Hey, whoa, whoa, what do you think you're doing?" Dad exclaimed.

"I have to see him, Dad," Evie begged.

"The nurses won't like it. They said you shouldn't move a muscle. And your mother—"

"Please," Evie broke in.

Dad met her eyes, and after a moment, he squared his shoulders. "Well then. Let's find you some wheels, chickadee . . ."

After leaving a note—DON'T WORRY, BE BACK SOON—behind on the hospital bed, Dad lifted Evie into a wheelchair and snuck her out of the room and up to the third floor. "What if we get caught?" she whispered as they peered around a corner of the hallway.

"Listen. I've got a mean left hook," Dad whispered back. "Those doctors won't know what hit them. Besides, if they get their noses broken, they're already here, so—"

Evie snorted.

"Shh!" Dad glared at her, trying not to laugh.

Moving like some kind of action hero, Dad pushed her down the hallway with exaggerated stealth, coming to a stop in front of room 309. The door was cracked open, and they could hear voices inside.

"Should we knock?" Dad asked.

"Wait a minute," Evie murmured, and strained to listen.

"—and we understand that you've been through a lot, honey," a woman's voice was saying. Evie recognized it right away as Mrs. King. "We just want to know something, anything, about what happened. The police want answers. Where were you all this time? Why didn't you come home?"

"Can't we talk about something else?" That was Desmond. His voice was flat and breathy with exhaustion.

There was a pause. Then Mr. King's voice came abruptly, seeming to cut his wife's words off before they were spoken. "Of course we can," he said with finality. "All those questions can wait for another day. We're just so happy to have you home. Aren't we, dear?"

"Yes," Mrs. King replied, her voice suddenly weak with emotion. "Of course. My god. My beautiful boy . . ."

"Mom, Dad," Desmond said after a moment. "I have to talk to you about something."

"What is it?" Mr. King asked.

There was a pause. "This whole experience has made me realize that I have to be honest with you. I thought I had time to figure out exactly how to tell you, but after everything that's happened . . . I feel like I've been given a second chance, and I don't want to waste another minute of it pretending to be something I'm not."

"What are you trying to say?" Mrs. King asked warily.

"I'm trying to say . . . ," Desmond went on, "that I don't want to carry on the family business. I don't want to run the quarry. I know it's what you've always wanted for me, and for a while, I thought it was what I wanted, too. But it isn't. I want to go to nursing school. I don't want to stay in Ravenglass forever. It will always be my home, but it can't be my life. I'm sorry."

"Honey," Mrs. King replied after a moment. "You've just been through a terrible trauma. Let's not make any rash decisions—"

"It's not rash," Desmond broke in. "I've thought about it. A lot."

Silence descended on the room. All Evie could hear was the faint beeping of machines as they counted each of Desmond's heartbeats.

The tension was so intense in that room that Evie could feel it radiating through the door. *Well*, she thought, *a little more can't hurt*. She knocked on the door.

"Come in," Mrs. King said, barely audible.

Dad pushed the door open, revealing the Kings standing at Desmond's bedside, looking haggard. When Desmond saw Evie in her wheelchair, his shoulders sagged with relief. "Evie," he said in amazement. "You're all right."

"And you," Evie replied softly.

Mr. King smiled, a polite mask to cover the chaos of emotion beneath. For her part, Mrs. King didn't immediately throw her out. She just stared at Evie, too exhausted to summon up a reaction to her presence.

Dad cleared his throat, sensing the awkwardness in the room. "Hi there," he said warmly. "Sorry to barge in like this. But Evie here was about to crawl on her hands and knees to visit your son, so I thought I'd just roll her up here instead. She's, um, eager to see that he's all right."

"Of course," Mr. King said, nodding. "That's very kind. We can step out and give them a few minutes, can't we, dear?" He looked meaningfully at his wife.

Mrs. King glanced at Desmond, at the way his eyes hadn't left Evie's face since she'd come through the door. "For a few minutes, yes," she said, her expression just as bittersweet as her husband's. As she walked past them into the hallway, her fingers brushed across Evie's shoulder, light as a feather. Evie could easily have missed the touch altogether, but she didn't.

Maybe she was mistaken, but it felt a little like forgiveness.

Mr. King followed. After they'd gone, Dad pushed her into the room and bent to whisper in Evie's ear. "Let me know when you're finished," he said. "Just don't take too long. If they put me in hospital jail, it will be your fault." With that, he left, closing the door behind him.

Evie looked at Desmond, feeling strangely shy. He was sitting up in his hospital bed, dressed in the same kind of blue gown as she was. The wounds on his lips had been cleaned, and his skin had returned to a healthy, deep brown color. He looked nearly identical to the boy she'd danced with on homecoming night, but something in his eyes had changed. There was a darkness within them that hadn't been there before.

Desperate to break the silence, Evie said, "How are you feeling?"

Desmond gave a little smile. "Hungry." He tilted his head toward the empty cafeteria tray on the table next to him. "That's my second lunch, and I'm ready for a third. I have half a mind to call Birdie and get some delivery. I'd destroy at least four of her gamja hot dogs—"

"Or one of those cinnamon doughnuts she makes?" Evie broke in.

"Oh yeah," Desmond said, wistful. "I'd eat a dozen of those things. Easy."

Evie nodded and bit her lip. The elephant in the room sat between them, huge and waiting to be addressed.

"It all feels like a dream, you know?" Desmond murmured. "I *want* it to be a dream. But I know it wasn't. And that knowing . . ." He frowned. "That knowing is killing me inside. I don't know what to do with it. I can't talk to anyone, because no one remembers—"

"I remember," Evie said. "You can talk to me. Tina might remember, too—she was with us until the end. And . . . Sai."

Desmond's mouth quirked at the mention of Sai. "How is he?" Desmond asked. "Is he all right?"

Evie shook her head, suddenly feeling guilty for not asking her father about him. "God, I don't know. I hope so. I came as soon as I woke up and found out you were here. Dad said everyone was accounted for, so I assume he and Tina are both okay. Whenever I get my hands on a phone, I have to call and check on them."

Desmond nodded. "So how, um," he began, "how did you do it? How did you stop him? How is it that we're all here, and not still trapped inside that . . ." His voice trailed off, and she could see him reliving the nightmare inside his mind.

Hesitant, she reached out and put her bandaged hand over his. At her touch, the darkness faded slightly from his eyes, and he refocused on her face. "To be honest, I almost didn't stop him. But I had help." She spent the next few minutes telling him what had happened after they left Aunt Martha's apartment, and how the shadows of Sarah Flower and Holly Hobbie joined Evie to defeat Brand.

When she was finished, Desmond scoffed and leaned back onto the hospital bed. "If I hadn't been through it myself—" he said.

"You wouldn't believe it, I know," Evie finished. "You were right, though. About the town. You told me at the dance that there had been darkness here long before the Hobbies ever moved in. That was Brand. He was here, lurking in the shadows, for all those years. But now, I think it's finally finished."

"And what about us?" Desmond said softly, not meeting her eyes.

Evie sat up, startled by the abrupt change of subject. "What about us?"

"Are we finished, too?"

Evie flushed. "What? No. Why would you say that?"

"Because I've changed. You've changed. Everything has changed. I just—" He stopped, rubbing his face with his hands. "I just don't know what's real anymore and what isn't. And I don't want you to feel like you have to—"

"Desmond," Evie said, leaning close to him. "For weeks, every single day I thought of nothing but you. How to bring you home. Now that you're finally here, how could I want anything more than to be together?"

Desmond cupped her cheek with his hand. She leaned her head into his palm, warm and smooth. "Maybe we just need some time," he said. "A little taste of normal before we figure out what this is."

Evie chuckled. "Normal . . . what's that?" she said. And, after a moment, "I thought you said that this whole experience taught you that there's no time to waste."

"I'll make time for you," Desmond said, the rich, buttery quality of his voice returning.

Warmth bloomed in her belly. Next to her on a table, she saw a plastic bag containing Desmond's champagne-colored homecoming suit, so filthy it was nearly unrecognizable. Seeing it filled her with shame. "You shouldn't have come after me that night," she said. "If you had just stayed at the dance, none of this would have ever happened."

Desmond pulled her close and placed a feathery, gentle kiss on her forehead. "I promised you wouldn't have to be alone in the dark anymore," he murmured. "I keep my promises."

There was a knock at the door. Evie jerked back from Desmond's touch just in time before Dad walked in, looking sheepish. "We really need to get back downstairs," he said. "Pretty sure they've noticed our great escape by now . . ."

Evie nodded. "Okay," she said. She suddenly felt drained.

"Thank you for bringing her to see me, Mr. Archer," Desmond said.

"Sure thing, Desmond," Dad replied. "Glad that you're back in the land of the living!"

Evie nearly choked. He had no idea how close he'd come to the truth. "You'll text me?" she asked Desmond. "When they let you go home?"

"I promise," Desmond said. Dad had just started to wheel her out of the room when he called out. "Hey, Evie!"

"Yeah?"

He smiled—the same old crooked grin. "You still owe me that last dance."

Evie put a hand to her cheek where the ghost of Desmond's hand still touched her, and smiled to herself as they left the room.

26

The rest of the day was a blur of visitors—first Mom and Stan, who returned from the cafeteria none the wiser about her and Dad's little jaunt to Desmond's room. After a flurry of hugs and tears of relief over Evie's recovery, Mom noticed the change in energy between Evie and her father. "Did something happen between you two?" she asked.

Evie shrugged. "We talked," she said, and then added, "He really is trying, Mom."

Mom let out a small, exasperated sigh. "I know. And I'm trying to let him. It's the most any of us can do."

Aunt Martha dropped by with a carafe of specially brewed tea—"for warming the spirit." She complained about an awful mess in her apartment—one of the windows had blown open—and a sore wrist. She must have taken a fall at some point during her experience with the mysterious illness everyone had, but had no memory of it. Evie—knowing what her aunt had been through over the past twenty-four hours—urged her to get an X-ray while she was still at the hospital.

"Is this your psychic intuition talking?" Aunt Martha asked.

"Something like that," Evie replied.

"Got it working again, haven't you?" Aunt Martha said with a knowing look. "I heard that Desmond is back. It's incredible news. Did you . . . have anything to do with that?"

"I'll tell you if I can cash in my rain check on that gingersnap."

Aunt Martha's eyes sparkled. "Deal."

Even Lorraine and Ms. Jackson came to wish Evie well and tell her that her performance would be missed at the second showing of *A Christmas Carol* that night. Evie rummaged inside her plastic bag of belongings to find the green robe she'd been wearing. The costume was rumpled, damp, and torn in a couple of places, but otherwise intact. She handed it to Ms. Jackson, apologizing for its condition.

"Don't worry, Evie," Ms. Jackson replied, draping it neatly over her arm. "I'll get it dry-cleaned today and it will be as good as new."

"Do you still have the holly crown?" Lorraine asked.

Evie reached inside the bag and pulled it out. The deep green leaves and red berries shone, still wet with melted snow. She laid it on top of the blanket covering her legs. "Actually," she said, "would you mind if I kept it?"

Lorraine shrugged. "Sure thing. We have enough materials to make another one. It's yours!"

Evie touched the prickly leaves with affection. "Thanks."

Tina arrived sometime later in the evening, after Mom had

taken Stan home to bed. Dad was out buying dinner from Birdie's when she showed up wearing what appeared to be an ugly Christmas sweater with the words I'M HERE FOR LOS PASTELES stitched into the design.

They spent ten minutes catching each other up on what had happened the previous night, and Tina recalled how she'd woken up in her bed at home that morning, feeling unusually tired and wondering if it had all been a long, strange dream.

"No such luck," Evie replied. "But no one seems to remember anything about what happened except for us. They just remember feeling off for a while leading up to yesterday, and then last night is a big blank. It's probably better that way, honestly. Can you imagine trying to explain all of this to the rest of the world?" She quirked an eyebrow at Tina's garish red and green sweater. "What are you wearing, anyway? I mean, it does match your hair, but I'm a little surprised. Normally you wouldn't be caught dead in that sort of thing."

Tina peered down at the sweater and shrugged. "Tati gave it to me," she said. "The first thing I did this morning after I woke up was go and have a long talk with her. What I saw, down in the shadow—I know it wasn't real, but it made me so scared. Scared of losing her." She glanced up at Evie with worried eyes. "What if we hadn't made it back? What if the last words between me and Tati had been spoken in anger? So I went down to the kitchen— she was already cooking, of course—and told her everything. How I felt like she didn't understand me, or didn't love me the same way she loves my brothers. And that I didn't want it to be that way anymore."

Boy, Evie thought. *A lot of tough conversations happening today.* "What did she say?"

Tina grinned. "She just sat and listened the whole time. Didn't say a word. And when I was done, she hugged me really hard and said of course she and Tito love me as much as my brothers. She said maybe they don't understand me that well, but they want to. And she said"—Tina scrunched up her face to look stern, like her grandmother's—"'I'll learn all about your computers and green hair, mija, but *you* have to learn how to make a decent sofrito!'"

Evie laughed. "That's great, Tina," she said. "I'm so happy for you."

"Me too," Tina said. "Anyway, she gave me this sweater as an early Christmas present. I know it's a little cringe, but . . ." She hugged herself. "I kind of like it."

They kept her overnight for observation before sending her home. By the time they'd put together the bandages and ointment Evie needed and signed the discharge papers—her father insisted on being the one to handle it all—it was already early afternoon. One of the nurses pushed her wheelchair out to the parking lot where Dad's black SUV was idling, the front seat already warm. Dad helped her into the car, and they were soon on the road back to Ravenglass. Dad hummed under his breath as he drove, some strange amalgamation of "White Christmas" and "The Christmas Song" all rolled into one.

Evie stared out the window at the snow-covered valley spread out below them, thoughtful. Only one person hadn't come to visit during her hospital stay.

He'd sent her a text that morning, all lowercase, no punctuation.

no regrets

Evie wrote back immediately, asking where he was—but she didn't get a response right away. The three little dots would appear onscreen for a moment, then vanish, as if he was going to respond, and then reconsidered. Finally, she texted him again.

sai, please, why won't you talk to me?

In the car, Evie stared at the two words in their single bubble. Reading them made her chest ache. They sounded far too much like goodbye.

When they finally turned onto the narrow lane, the sun was already beginning to set. Hobbie House nestled atop the frosted hill, its flaws hidden beneath strings of garland and twinkling white lights. Through the front window, Evie could see Mom and Dr. Rockwell in the living room. She was standing in front of the Christmas tree, arranging gifts underneath it, while he stood watching, mug in hand. Evie snuck a sidelong glance at her father to see his reaction, but if he'd noticed, he didn't seem bothered.

"Hard to believe it's Christmas Eve already," Dad said.

"Wow, I completely forgot," Evie said, putting one hand to her head. With everything going on, she'd lost track of what day it was. Dad put the car in park, but left the engine on. "Wait, aren't you staying?" Evie asked.

Dad sucked his teeth. "I'll definitely come see you before I head back to New York," he said, "but I think it's best to give your mother a little space to celebrate her new life here. It seems like it's going to be a good one." He glanced over at the window, where Mom and Dr. Rockwell were chatting. "But don't worry," he went on, patting Evie on the knee. "I'll be back before you know it. Maybe in the spring for your birthday?"

Evie chuckled to herself. *So he* does *remember when it is . . .*

"And I was thinking," he continued, "maybe you can plan a trip back to the city sometime before then? There are some fashion industry folks I'd like to introduce you to. You know . . ." He cleared his throat. "If you want."

A huge smile spread across Evie's face. "Yeah, that sounds amazing," she said. "You'd really do that?"

Dad shrugged. "You've got talent, Evie. I can see it, and pretty soon, other people will see it, too." He was about to get out of the car to help Evie when his eyebrows jumped. "Oh!" he exclaimed. "I almost forgot. I have a little Christmas present for you." He reached into the back seat and pulled out a small cardboard box. "Sorry, I didn't have time to wrap it."

"Should I open it now?" Evie asked, hefting the box in her hand. It was surprisingly heavy.

"If you'd like."

Evie pried the tape off the flaps and pulled a wad of newspaper out of the box. Beneath it lay a blue glass heart, about the size of her palm. She picked it up and turned it over in her hand. Initials were etched on the back: RA.

"I, um . . . I saved some of the broken glass from our old dining room table," Dad explained. "It sat in a box in my studio for months and months, but I came across it a little while ago and decided to melt it down to make this."

Evie held the heart up to the fading light. Tiny bubbles were stilled inside the watery blue glass, like a piece of the ocean frozen in time.

"See?" Dad said, gazing at it with affection. "Things don't have to stay broken forever."

Evie bit her lip and squeezed the gift in her hand. "Thanks, Dad," she said softly.

Dad smiled. "Merry Christmas, chickadee."

Everyone made a lot of fuss when Evie came through the kitchen door. Mom was pouring her a cup of tea before she'd even taken off her coat, and Dr. Rockwell came to help Dad with her things and shake his hand. Aunt Martha was over, too, wearing a wrist brace, watching over a pot of chicken soup on the stove. She and Mom both attacked Evie with simultaneous hugs before starting to bicker over whether Evie should use Aunt Martha's homemade calendula salve on her hands and feet. Stan eventually hobbled in, still leaning on his crutch. Evie winced at the sight of the purple bruise on his cheek—shaped not unlike the heel of her shoe.

"What's up, nerd?" he said as he pushed past Evie to get at the bowl of Chex mix on the counter.

"Hello to you, too, loser," Evie replied.

Stan popped a mini pretzel in his mouth. "Nice job not ruining Christmas by getting frozen to death."

"Yeah, you're welcome."

Stan smirked, and bumped his shoulder against her before scooping some Chex mix into a bowl and hobbling into the living room, calling out—with heavy irony—"Evie's home, fam! God bless us, every one!"

"So glad to see you're all right, Evie," Dr. Rockwell said after things had settled down a bit. He set down a copy of the *Pittsfield Post* that sported a glaring headline: TOWN OF NIGHTMARES: PITTSFIELD PHOTOGRAPHER TELLS ALL AFTER RETURN FROM MASS NARCOLEPTIC EVENT IN RAVENGLASS. "Awfully strange thing, wasn't it? I'd say I want to study the phenomenon and try to tease out what happened, but frankly, I wouldn't even know where to start."

"I'm just glad it's over," Mom said, stirring honey into Evie's tea. "Maybe we can all finally have a bit of peace around here."

While Mom and Dr. Rockwell set the table for dinner, Aunt Martha helped Evie take her things upstairs. Schrödinger was waiting in her bedroom, curled up on her patchwork quilt, fast asleep. Setting her bag down on the floor, Evie listened to the sound of Mom and Dr. Rockwell laughing downstairs. The formality between them was clearly a thing of the past. "Do you think Mom and Dr. Rockwell are going to . . . like . . . get together?" Evie asked hesitantly.

Aunt Martha chuckled. "You never know. But honestly, your mother doesn't need another man right now. She needs a friend. And I think the doctor needs one, too. Maybe that's enough for them both."

"Maybe," Evie said with a smirk. Just then, she heard the familiar rumble of an engine coming down the lane. She ran to the window just in time to see a black motorcycle and rider come rolling to a stop in front of the house.

"Sai," Evie whispered, and shouldered past her very confused aunt back down the stairs, flying through the kitchen door before anyone could stop her.

She watched as he killed the engine and dismounted, pulling his helmet off and tucking it under his arm. He gave her a small, strained smile, and tucked a loose lock of black hair behind his ear.

He looked fine. Unharmed. More than that, he looked so very *alive*. Seeing him, feeling that vibrance rolling off him in waves, Evie felt her own aches and pains melt away.

"So," Evie said, nodding toward him. "You wear a helmet now?"

Sai shrugged. "What? You think I've got a death wish or something?"

Evie snorted and shook her head. "Unbelievable." Silence fell between them. Evie drew a circle in the snow with the toe of her shoe. "Why didn't you come see me?" she finally asked. "Or text me back? Or call?" She hadn't realized how hurt she felt until she heard it in her own voice. "Maybe you just want to forget everything that happened, but I—"

Sai closed his eyes and tilted his head up to the sky. "No, no, that's not it at all," he said. "Look, you came to me in the first place because you wanted to save *him*. Right? Well, we did. He's alive, he's waiting for you. That was the whole point, wasn't it? You don't need me anymore. So, I just thought . . . I thought it would be less confusing for you if I wasn't around." He licked his lips. "For me, too."

Evie's mouth dropped open. "Don't *need* you anymore? Did you think I only—?"

"Anyway," Sai interrupted, "I didn't want to leave without seeing you."

"Leave?" Evie said, her confusion growing with every passing second. "What are you talking about? Your dad is inside, I thought you came to join us."

Sai grimaced. "I'm taking Bonnie down south for a bit. At least until the end of winter break, but maybe a little more than that. I'll see. I've already spoken to my dad about it." He chuckled humorlessly. "He knows better than to try to talk me out of it. And, actually, I think he gets it. He's finally sort of . . . happy. And I'm getting there, too."

"But why do you have to leave?" Evie asked.

"Why?" Sai echoed. "Why?" He moved close, his face so near to hers that she could feel the cloud of his breath on her lips. "Because if I stay . . ." Their eyes met, and she saw his pupils dilate and the pulse in his throat quicken. The moment seemed to stretch out, until finally he took a step back and let out a shuddering breath.

"Sai, please don't leave on my account," Evie said. "I'm sorry if I've made you feel this way, but we've gone through so much together. You don't need to run away—"

"I'm not running away," Sai broke in. "I know—I know it looks like that, but I'm not. I *am* leaving because of what happened, but not just in the way you think."

Evie blinked. "I don't understand."

Sai took a deep breath and let it out, slowly. "I have been stuck in time, Evie. For years. I haven't really moved forward since Mum died in that car accident. But everything feels . . . different now. Remember that breathless, insane freedom I told you about? The way I feel when I'm on the bike? I felt that the moment I woke up in my bed yesterday morning—*alive*. I just want to keep feeling it, for as long as I can. Does that make any sense at all?"

Evie's heart squeezed in her chest. "Yes," she murmured. "It makes perfect sense." There were so many things she wanted to say. That she still felt a connection with him that she couldn't put into words. That maybe she didn't need him anymore, but she still wanted him in her life. But just as he didn't want to cause her pain with his feelings, she didn't want to hurt him with hers.

So instead of all those things, she just said, "I'll miss you."

A bittersweet smile crossed Sai's face. "I'll miss you, too." She opened her arms, and he stepped into them, wrapping her up in a tight hug that smelled of kerosene and leather. When they parted, he hefted the helmet back into his hand and glanced over at the house. Everyone was in the kitchen, working on ladling out bowls of chicken soup and passing out dinner rolls fresh from the oven. "Take care of my dad while I'm gone, would you? You wouldn't know it, but he's a bit helpless on his own."

"I think my mom has got that covered," Evie said with a wry grin.

"Home sweet home, eh?" Sai said.

Evie wrapped her arms around herself. Hobbie House twinkled cozily in the dying light, a beacon in a sea of twilight darkness. "Yeah," she said. "It is."

27

It was the best Christmas morning Evie had had in years.

Mom had bought her the professional dress form she'd always wanted. It was pretty easy to guess what it was when she rolled it into the room, given that it looked like a headless woman mummified in wrapping paper. "I thought being a dressmaker was only for women stuck in towers," Evie said after she opened it.

Mom looked sheepish. "People can change," she said, right before Evie grinned and gathered her into a hug.

Stan got a new video game and an army-green hoodie that he actually liked—so much so that he immediately abandoned his black one. "Quick, throw it in the fire," Evie muttered. Mom laughed. Stan glared at them both, snatched his black hoodie off the floor, and sat on it.

Mom loved the blouse Evie had made for her out of some of the vintage fabric and buttons from the attic, and was delighted at the box of authentic English teas that Dr. Rockwell had gifted her.

Dad had left a card, and Evie watched her mother's face as she read it by the morning light. At first, Evie thought she was going to cry, but she just slipped the card back into its envelope and sighed.

"Is everything okay?" Evie asked.

Mom glanced over at her and nodded. "Yes, honey. Everything is finally okay."

The following week passed quietly. With everyone on winter break, Evie divided her time between home and Birdie's, where she met up with Tina for strawberry milk and kimchi fries almost every day.

Later that week, Desmond had recovered enough to meet up with her for a walk outside. Evie was surprised to see his dog prancing next to him, sporting a brand-new blue collar and leash.

"Hey, Rocky," Evie crooned, giving the dog a rub behind the ears.

Desmond chuckled. "He and my mom haven't left me alone since I got home," he said. "I can't decide who's clingier."

"You sure she didn't send him along as a chaperone?" Evie asked.

"Nah," Desmond replied. Then he cocked his head. "Maybe."

Main Street was teeming with visitors who'd driven in to shop and enjoy the sights. Evie could hardly believe it was the same place where such horrible things had happened just days before. Evie gave Desmond a sidelong glance. "What?" he asked.

"Just wondering what you're thinking," Evie said.

Desmond sighed and shoved his hands into the pockets of his letterman jacket. "I'm thinking how weird it is that everything looks just the same, even though nothing is." He kicked a rock across the pavement. "My parents are finally coming around to the idea of nursing school—they actually seem kind of proud. Like they respect the fact that I want to stand on my own two feet, even though they'll have to find someone else to run the quarry. Who knows—Kimber Sullivan might end up gunning for the job. If she can't have me, at least she could have the family fortune." He laughed. "But even though things have been pretty good, I've been . . . having trouble sleeping. Wouldn't be great for my teammates to find out their MVP is afraid of the dark, would it?"

Evie shrugged. "We're all afraid of the dark," she said. "I think as we grow up, we just get better at hiding it."

Desmond moved a little closer to her, so that their shoulders touched. They walked the rest of Main Street in comfortable silence until they reached the church.

"Hey, do you mind if we stop here for a second?" Evie asked.

Desmond shrugged. "Sure, why?"

"There's just something I've been meaning to do."

They made their way to the little cemetery in the back. Evie threaded through the graves until she found the one she was looking for and brushed the snow off the headstone. Kneeling, she opened her backpack and pulled out a parcel from inside. "Thank you for everything you did, Sarah," she whispered, laying the holly crown on the grave. "For standing up to him, you know? For being brave. Your father would have been proud."

It was New Year's Eve, and Evie was sitting at the front desk of the Blue River Inn, listening to the sound of a band playing in the dining room and nearly two hundred people enjoying the biggest party of the year.

Although many of Ravenglass's holiday tourists ended up having expensive steak dinners at All That Glitters or sharing pitchers of beer at one of the pubs, most of the locals enjoyed New Year's at the inn. Fiona usually got a DJ and decorated the room for the occasion, but Mom was having none of that. Together, they had planned out a party to end all parties, complete with a four-piece band, catered food, and a "black-tie" dress requirement for all guests. There was so much to do that Mom had asked Evie to keep watch at the front desk while she and Fiona managed the event. "I know it won't be much fun," Mom said, apologetic, "but Fiona will make it worth your while, and it would be a huge help. I doubt anyone is going to need a room that night, anyway."

Evie had agreed—Stan would be sleeping over at a friend's house, and she was actually looking forward to seeing everyone in town dressed up for the evening. For her own outfit, Evie wore the emerald-green cocktail dress with the black rhinestones she'd been working on, which fit her like a glove. Stuffed with hors d'oeuvres and cake that she'd salvaged from the buffet, and having spent the past few hours sitting in the uncomfortable wooden chair, Evie felt heavy and sleepy. She glanced at the old grandfather clock beside the door to the inn. 11:55 p.m.

Her phone pinged, and she picked it up to look at the screen.

It was a text from Sai, with a picture attached. It was a selfie of him in front of his bike, with a vista of ocean and fireworks lighting up the world behind him.

> Happy new year. Saw these masses of explosions and chaos and thought of you.

Evie snorted and texted him back with a laughing emoji.

> 😄 Happy new year to you too, dummy!

Evie sat back and sighed, wondering what the next year had in store for her. She found herself wishing she could talk to Holly about it. Maybe she'd see her cousin again someday. Maybe she'd visit in Evie's dreams.

In the dining room, a dance song ended and Fiona's voice came on the microphone. "Hello, Ravenglass!" she announced. "I hope you're having a good time!"

The crowd cheered.

"We're going to start our countdown in just a few minutes, so everyone grab some champagne and your sweetheart, and get those lips ready for a New Year's kiss!"

A few people hooted and laughed.

Just then, the door to the inn opened, and a gust of wind blew into the lobby, fluttering papers across the desk. Evie looked up, surprised to see someone coming in so late.

"Desmond?"

He was wearing a tailored black suit and a deep green tie that was almost perfectly matched to her dress. The wounds on his lips had completely healed, and he looked radiant. "Sorry I'm late," he said, breathless.

"Y-you're not," Evie stammered, surprised to see him. "I thought you were at the house party at Colin Flanagan's tonight."

"I was," Desmond said. "But I had somewhere else to be at midnight." He looked pointedly up at the mistletoe hanging from the ceiling above the threshold.

Evie scoffed, smiling, and walked around the desk toward him. "Des," she said, thinking of Sai and the complicated feelings surrounding all three of them. "I don't know."

Desmond took her hand and looked into her eyes, as if he knew exactly what she was thinking. "Look," he said. "I know you need time to process what happened. So do I. And honestly, I have no idea what tomorrow will bring. But tonight, I want to forget the past. And I don't want to worry about the future."

"It's time, everyone!" Fiona shouted from the other room. "Ten, nine, eight, seven . . ."

"I just want to be here with you," Desmond continued, his other hand reaching for her face. "In this moment. Right now. Can we do that?"

"Six, five, four . . ."

Evie thought about everything that had led to her standing there with Desmond that night. About how many thousands of decisions and accidents of fate and little tragedies had altered the course of time to lead her to be there with him, alive and hopeful. She thought about the sad story of the three little girls that had kept repeating over and over again, until she finally wrote them a happy ending.

Or was it the beginning of something new?

"Three, two, one . . ."

"Yes," Evie whispered, putting her arms around Desmond's neck. "Yes, we can."

The clock struck midnight.

"Happy New Year!" everyone shouted, and as the band played, the crowd began to sing.

Desmond bent to kiss her, his lips warm and whole. And when it was over, he lifted her hand high, and they danced to the sound of many voices.

"Should old acquaintance be forgot,
And never brought to mind?
Should old acquaintance be forgot,
And auld lang syne?"

THE END

ACKNOWLEDGMENTS

The Ten of Cups. If I had to choose a card that perfectly exemplifies my feelings right now, signing off on the last pass of this book, that would be it. It shows a couple and their two dancing children, reaching up to acknowledge the rainbow stretching over them. I'm so glad my editor reminded me to write *these* acknowledgments, because it's so easy for me in my busy life to forget to pause, to remember, to *acknowledge* all that has happened to lead me to this moment. To look up instead of ahead and see what is shining right above me. There are so many people to thank for their hand in creating this series, but I'll start with the person who made it all possible. To my agent, Allison Hellegers, who took my fledging career in her hands and has been nurturing it with patience and love, year after year. This is all possible because of you. To my editor, Gaby Taboas Zayas, who is a bright star and a fierce advocate—your passion for this series and your editorial talent made working on these books such a joy. To Benj Dawe and Hsiao-Pin Lin, thank you for the gift of another truly exquisite design, and to CloudCo, thank you again for entrusting Holly Hobbie into my guardianship. To my beta readers—Heather Allen (#TeamSai), Brittany Kozlewski (#TeamDesmond), and my wonderful mom, Mania Jabès, thank you for all your notes and support for everything Holly. To Nathan Allen, thank you for teaching me about motorcycles—hopefully I got it right! To my daughters, who have been there with me every step of the way, thank you for understanding when Mommy needs to go away to her tower to write, and for being there to give me tea and a hug when I'm done for the day. And finally, to my husband, Adam, who has read every word, cheered every success, and gave me strength when I had none left, I'm so grateful to be standing under this rainbow with you. And if you're here reading these words, thank you for going on this journey with me. I truly hope we meet again.